Praise For Walter Jon Williams

"Williams tells [the] story with a propulsive yet elegant prose...."
— *Fantasy Review*

"Williams understands that science fiction can breathe life into language.... [His] writing is always lean, lively and engaging."
— *The New York Times Book Review*

"The story moves with the speed of a hovercraft, the climax has all the action and excitement of *Star Wars* and the ending has a delightful twist."
— *Providence Journal*

"Williams' use of language is as explosive and as techno-tinged as the world he describes. "
— *The Rockland Courier-Gazette*

"Despite his manifest cyberpunk leanings, Williams has an imagination all his own—along with a supple, subtle technique and a polished, lucid prose style."
— *Kirkus Reviews*

"Fans of high-tech SF will enjoy Williams's sizzling prose..."
— *Library Journal*

"...amplified, rock-'n'-roll prose."
— *Publishers Weekly*

"Possessed of a venomous, mechanical grace... notorious for a reason."
— Elizabeth Bear, author of *Hammered, Scardown* and *Worldwired*

D1475672

VOICE OF THE WHIRLWIND

Other books by Walter Jon Williams

Novels:
Ambassador of Progress
Knight Moves
Hardwired
The Crown Jewels
House of Shards
Angel Station
Elegy for Angels And Dogs
Days of Atonement
Aristoi
Metropolitan
Rock of Ages
City on Fire
The Rift
Destiny's Way
The Praxis
The Sundering
Conventions of War

Collections:
Facets
Frankensteins and Foreign Devils

VOICE OF THE WHIRLWIND

WALTER JON WILLIAMS

NIGHT SHADE BOOKS
SAN FRANCISCO

First Edition

ISBN 978-1-59780-087-7

Printed in Canada

Night Shade Books
Please visit us on the web at
http://www.nightshadebooks.com

FOR KATHY HEDGES

CHAPTER ONE

Steward hung suspended beneath a sky the color of wet slate. Below him the ground was dark, indistinct. There was the sensation of movement, of gliding flight. Sometimes Steward's stomach fluttered as he dipped closer to the dark opacity beneath him. He could feel his nerves dancing, his own readiness building. The sky tipped and spun.

On the horizon there was flame. A ripple of deep, pulsing red, throbbing like an artery laid bare by shrapnel, shrouded in a drifting black cloak. Not the sun, Steward realized; something burning....

He was never afraid or surprised when he came awake from the dream. He woke refreshed, his limbs ready to move, dance, fight.

He knew that whatever it was he was drifting toward in that cold gray sky, it was something he wanted.

Dr. Ashraf had a corner office high in the hospital complex, invaded on two sides by bright Arizona sky. Etienne Njagi Steward could sit on a padded couch and gaze through glass walls across Flagstaff to the mountains: three peaks cut into fragments by rows of mirror-glass condecologies that reflected the rising land, the sky, the hospital, the shimmering line of bright alloy highway that cut through the towers. The mirrored buildings reflected reality, distorted it, multiplied it. Made it interesting.

The room was perfectly soundproofed. Even the bullet railway below the hospital failed to do more than create a minor vibration in the room's glass wall. Steward could watch the world in the mirrors, but he was insulated from it, heard only Ashraf's emotionless voice, the whisper of the air conditioning, the distant vibration of the bullet train. He wondered who Ashraf wanted him to be.

Ashraf sat behind Steward at a desk. There were readouts on Ashraf's side of the desk, Steward knew, connected to monitors in the couch, voice stress analyzers, pulse and respiration indicators, maybe even sensors for analyzing perspiration and muscle tension. He hadn't seen them, but sometimes when he

1

turned to face Ashraf he saw the reflection of red LEDs in the doctor's eyes.

Steward had been taught how to defeat such machines. He remembered long hours spent under deep hypnosis, drugs, biofeedback mechanisms. He couldn't think of any real reason to use his skills, so for the most part he didn't. He used them only when he talked about Natalie. This, he told himself, was more to keep himself calm than to fool Ashraf.

Once he told Ashraf about his dream. "Maybe it's a memory of Sheol," he said. "A parafoil assault or something."

"You know that's impossible," said Dr. Ashraf.

Sometimes it seemed to Steward that he had as many personalities as there were reflections of the world in the condecos, that he was trying on personalities like masks in a store, one after the other, just to see if any of them fit. It was clear that the person who dreamed was unacceptable to Dr. Ashraf.

Steward never mentioned the dream again.

The walls of the hospital were striped with narrow bright colors that matched the identifying colors on the bracelets of the patients. If a patient was lost in the bustling, scrubbed corridors, he had only to follow the minute arrows on the wall stripes. They would lead him to his own ward, where the walls were painted in his own color, where he was welcomed by the familiar antiseptic smell, and the familiar nurses. The nurses' uniforms were pin-striped in the colors of the wards. Yellow was for Burns, red for Intensive Care, soothing blue for Maternity. Steward's bracelet was a pleasant light green and signified his home in the Psychology ward.

He wasn't physically ill, so they let him wear regular clothes. When he took his strolls through the other parts of the hospital, he always wore long sleeves so that he could push the green bracelet far up his arm, under the cuff.

He didn't want people thinking he was crazy.

"There was a war in Marseilles between the teen gangs," Steward said. "They broke out from time to time. I was a member of Canards Chronique, had been since I was twelve. We dealt in information, mainly. Software, proscribed wetware. Drugs, too. The whole range of what Americans call juvecrime. We were bright kids." He remembered sitting with a blond-haired girl on a wrought-iron balcony, drinking whiskey and watching the Mediterranean for the last time. Heartbreakingly beautiful, the sea, bluer and deeper than the blond girl's eyes, bluer than the reflected skies he saw from Ashraf's window. He remembered the way distant automatic-weapons fire sounded, echoing off the stucco fronts of the houses, the low concrete gutters. He remembered as well his own weariness, the feeling that he didn't want to do this anymore. He could play the game too well. He was tired of manipulating people.

The girl cocked her head, listened. "Sounds like the Femmes Sauvages on turf defense," she said. "Who's attacking?"

Etienne had been shopping that information around in the last twelve hours. "Skin Samurai," he said.

The girl shrugged. There was a touch of sunburn on her cheeks, her nose. She looked at him. "Want to go inside?" she asked.

Etienne Njagi Steward lit a cigarette. "D'accord," he said. He didn't plan on seeing her again.

"I was only sixteen," said Steward, "but I knew there were better things in life than dying for a couple square blocks in the Old Quarter."

Dr. Ashraf's oiled hair hung to his shoulders. His fleshy, immobile face betrayed little interest. "Is that when you decided to enlist?" he asked.

"D'accord," said Steward.

Steward was weak when he came awake for the first time. There was a machine that breathed for him and a tube down his throat. He missed things: the implants, the socket he'd had at the base of his skull to take the cyber interface. His mind held memories of reflexes that he couldn't match, strength that had somehow ebbed away while he wasn't looking. He spent hours each day brutalizing himself beneath weights, running on the hospital's treadmills, stretching the tender muscles in his legs, arms, shoulders. He practiced the martial arts, too, in a lonely corner of the physical therapy area, throwing punches, kicks, and combinations over and over again in cold, purposeful, sweaty repetition. Men and women recovering from surgery, or old people taking their first few trembling steps in new young bodies, turned their eyes away from him, from the grim savagery with which he was assaulting the air, his memories, himself.

The exercises filled the long hours, built muscle, honed reflex. They kept his mind occupied with immediate sensation, which was what he wanted. He had too much idle time. He didn't want to dwell on memories.

Over and over again, in his corner, he went through the motions of crushing bone, gouging eyes, snapping spines.

As yet, he didn't know whose.

In the room next to Steward's was a man named Corso, who lived with a crazed secondhand load of guilt and paranoia, having come awake and discovered that all his worst fears had come true, that his Alpha personality's whole world had come apart like a broken mirror, and that he'd tortured himself for months with the shards before he finally threw himself off a bridge. And, now that he was back, it wasn't over; all he could see in front of him was the yawning horror, the nightmare going on and on....

The doctors were trying to soften Corso's world with medication, turn it warm and pleasant again until his therapy began to make a difference, but Corso still woke Steward every night with his moans, his screams. They rang out from the darkness as Steward lay in his bed staring into the soft-edged curtains of gauzy darkness, seeing in his mind's eye the fading afterimage of the burning horizon, the sky that was a deeper darkness than that surrounding his bed.

In the room on the other side was a married couple, the Thornbergs. They'd made a lot of money in their lives and had invested in a couple of young bodies. They spent most of their nights making love. They seemed nice, but their conversation was all about investments, windows of opportunity, sports like squash and golf. Steward knew jack about investments, and the only sports he cared about were the ones he could bet on—racing, jai alai, the Australian firefight football that, back in a former life, he could pick up, about two in the morning, from the pirate satellites. The Thornbergs lived in some kind of Presbyterian condecology in California that forbade things like pirate satellite receptors, betting sports, news programs from the wrong side of the world, pornography. Their bodies were young, their minds elderly. Steward simply had nothing to say to these people.

A lot of the people in the Psychology wing were like the Thornbergs. It didn't seem to Steward that this was one of the personalities he would ever succeed in adopting. He wondered if Ashraf wanted him to try it on.

"Have you ever wondered why they chose you?" Dr. Ashraf asked.

"I fit their profile," said Steward.

"But do you know what Coherent Light was after?" Ashraf persisted. "There were a lot of people trying to get in. Out of all those, they picked you. Educated you, fed you, housed you, trained you. You and the other Icehawks cost them a lot more than their normal run of employee. Didn't you ever wonder why?"

"They wanted me. That was good enough."

"You didn't feel any loyalty to the Canards," Ashraf said. "Not to their purposes or their territory."

"That wasn't the Canard ethic. The Canards were conscious anarchists, deliberately amoral. Their game was selling stuff. They didn't care to whom."

"You knew you didn't want to do that."

"No. I was tired of it. After a while it didn't...offer anything."

"I've seen Coherent Light's profiles," Ashraf said. "They're declassified now. They're pretty standard for most of the Outward Policorps." Ashraf had a habit of steepling his fingertips in front of his mouth, and Steward knew without looking, from the muted quality in his voice, that he was doing it again.

"They desired people who needed to give themselves to something," Ashraf said, "who felt something missing from themselves, who lacked purpose. They didn't want to buy anyone. They wanted people—smart people, talented people—who would give themselves heart and soul to whatever Coherent Light stood for. They wanted the Icehawks to substitute CL's purposes for whatever they felt was missing in them. They wanted complete loyalty, horizontally within the group, vertically to Coherent Light. So they looked for people who desired something to be loyal to. Who were searching for a personal savior, a savior named Coherent Light." Ashraf paused. Steward stared at mountains cut by reflective ice. "What do you think of that?" Ashraf asked.

"I think they got who they were looking for," said Steward.

Dr. Ashraf didn't think it would be a good idea for Steward to look up Sheol just yet. Steward, curious, didn't know whether he should follow Ashraf's advice in this matter or not. In the end he compromised by calling up the library and asked for information on the Powers.

"Powers" was a translation of the aliens' name for themselves. They were four-legged, two-armed, about the size of ponies—in the vids that Steward watched they moved fast, making odd, quick body movements, bobbing and jerking, their language a combination of clicks and snorts and organ-pipe whines that sounded like something akin to music. Their heads had no bone in them and kept twisting and collapsing, like balloons inflating and deflating.

Steward watched, wondering. This was, according to his data, what the war had been fought over.

Steward reran the vids a last time, then exited the file. He knew that this was not what Sheol was about, not really.

"What happened to him?" Steward asked. He was sitting in the padded chair today, facing Ashraf's desk, the glass wall behind him.

"He died. On the Ricot habitat."

"I know that. How?"

"Does it matter to you?"

It mattered, Steward thought. But he wasn't sure he wanted Dr. Ashraf to know just how much it mattered. So he shrugged. Felt the power in himself to suppress what he was feeling. Used it.

"I might run into people who knew him. It would be convenient to know something about what happened to him."

Ashraf thought about it for a moment. Red LEDs gleamed in his eyes. "He was murdered, Mr. Steward."

Steward felt electricity humming in his nerves. Not surprise—somehow he wasn't surprised—but something else. He couldn't be too eager here.

"How?" Trying to be casual.

"That doesn't matter."

"Who killed him?"

"Person or persons unknown."

Now he *was* surprised. "And he died on Ricot?"

"Yes."

"That's odd. Ricot has a small, controlled population. Very tight security. It shouldn't be hard to find a killer there."

"Apparently they didn't. He was working in security. Maybe he got killed trying to stop a criminal."

Maybe they know, Steward thought. Maybe they know and the information was suppressed.

He decided not to ask any more questions. Ashraf obviously didn't want him to.

"You fell for their program." Steward felt surprise at the apparent feeling in Dr. Ashraf's voice. It was hard to remember Ashraf ever being emotional about anything.

"Coherent Light taught you martial arts and Zen," Ashraf said. "Zen of a certain kind."

"Mind like water," Steward quoted. "The unmeaning of action. Union of arrow and target. The perfection of action, detached from anything except the spirit."

"They were programming you," Ashraf said, "with things that were useful to them. They taught you to divorce action from consequence, from context. They were turning you into a moral imbecile. A robot programmed for corporate espionage and sabotage. Theft, bomb throwing, blackmail."

Steward was surprised by the harshness in Ashraf's voice. He turned from the window and looked at him. The doctor's fingers were steepled in front of his mouth, but Steward saw the anger in his eyes. "Let's not forget murder," Steward said.

"No," Ashraf said. "Let's not."

"I've never pretended to be anything but what I was," Steward said. "I've always been honest about what I've been."

"What's honesty got to do with my point?" Steward felt himself tense at the attack on Coherent Light, at the things that still provoked his loyalty. He forced himself to relax. Coherent Light was dead, dead in the long past. Mind like water, he told himself.

"You've been programmed to divorce corporate morality from personal morality," Ashraf said. "You're a zombie."

Steward frowned at him. "Perhaps," he said, "morality is simply latent within me. You're awfully combative for an analyst, you know."

"I'm not here to analyze you. I'm here to give you a crash course in reality and then kick you out into the world." Ashraf carefully flattened his hands on his desk. He looked up at Steward.

Mind like water, Steward told himself. Trying to stay calm.

It didn't work.

"My wife's still alive, correct?"

"She lives in orbit. She doesn't want to see you."

Steward frowned at the gray ceiling. "Why not?"

"We've been over this."

"I know you have the information. I need to know this. She must have given a reason."

There was the short pause that meant Ashraf was wondering which tack would be best in getting his patient to understand and accept the situation, what Ashraf referred to as "reality." Whether it was best to lay a ghost to rest, or pretend it didn't exist.

"She says," Ashraf said deliberately, "that she was used. Badly. And doesn't want to be used again."

Steward felt his nerves go warm. He felt, obscurely, the touch of something important. "Used? How?"

"I don't have that information."

"Is that what the second wife said? What's her name, Wandis?"

Another little pause. "Yes. She said that he only manipulated her, that she doesn't want to see you."

"It wasn't me."

"You must form your own attachments, Mr. Steward. The past is closed to you. And Wandis, to you, is only a name. She shouldn't mean anything at all."

Steward felt a little claw tugging at his mind, pointing at something significant, if only he could understand what it was.

"It wasn't me," he said again.

"I met someone," Steward said. "Someone from before." Inside him he felt a phantom desire for a cigarette. He had given up smoking during his internship with Coherent Light. They'd thought it would be good for him.

"Where?" asked Dr. Ashraf. "When?"

"It was an accident. I was walking in the zoo two days ago and saw her. She recognized me. She was there with her—I think she said niece."

"Who?" asked Ashraf.

"Her name was—is Ardala. Her parents were our neighbors in the CL complex in Kingston, that time Natalie and I were both training there. She was thirteen or fourteen then, I think."

Steward was seeing Natalie's face, the broad white forehead that wouldn't take a tan no matter how she tried, the dark hair that framed her strong jaw, wide cheekbones, green eyes, thick, generous lower lip.

"We met for a drink that night, after she'd returned her niece to—to whoever. Talked about things. She works in a career placement office."

"You didn't tell her?"

Natalie sitting on a balcony twined with wrought iron, her face obscured by cigarette smoke. While gunfire echoed from the pink stucco walls.

"I told her I was divorced. She said it made me younger." Steward could almost taste the tobacco.

"You should have told her, Mr. Steward," Ashraf said.

"She asked me if I wanted to come home with her." She'd had Natalie's eyes. "I said yes." The rest of her had become Natalie, in the smoke, the dark, the fire.

"Mr. Steward"—Ashraf was displeased—"this is your first attachment outside the hospital." Attachment? Steward thought.

"You cannot allow a relationship to begin with such a fundamental deception," Ashraf said. "Furthermore, I don't think it's healthy that your first such relationship is based on a past that, for everyone except you, does not exist. Better to have involved yourself with a complete stranger than to have tied yourself more thoroughly to a delusion."

"No one's deluded," Steward said. "No one's unhappy."

Ashraf's voice was brutal. "We can't have this woman think," he said, "that you're the original, can we?"

CHAPTER TWO

Molten city towers cut a darkening sky, reflected a burnished Arizona sunset that was itself invisible from where Steward walked down among the groundlings. He had his green bracelet pushed up high under a light blue cotton sleeve as he stepped across an air-conditioned pedestrian plaza whose translucent roof crawled with mutating art forms and whose floor was flecked with the droppings of pigeons. Green-eyed Ardala, her light brown hair swinging, waved from across a sea of bobbing heads. The makeup rimming her eyes was extravagant, like butterfly wings, a new fashion that had originated somewhere beyond the orbit of Mars.

She and Steward kissed hello. There was a slight shock in the realization that this woman was a stranger. Steward wondered how he'd ever managed to see Natalie in those eyes, in that smile.

They walked into the bar where they'd agreed to meet. Dark, plush seats, white plastic tabletops, waitresses in corsets and short skirts, styles from thirty years before that were supposed to seem quaint. Standing in a corner was an ornate piano/synthesizer, all gleaming black plastic with chrome trim. Steward didn't like the place. It seemed like the sort of bar where people went to smoke hash and discuss their investments. Steward didn't want to think about investments. In a sense, an investment is what he was.

He ordered a trailing willow, paid for it with the allowance the insurance company would provide him for the next ten months. Little anxieties seemed to leap like sparks of static on the surface of his skin. Ardala called for a glass of wine. "I should tell you something," he said.

She cocked her head, bright. "I'm listening."

He told her, and she shook her head and grinned. "I'll be damned," she said. "No wonder you look so young. You *are* young."

"I'm three months old," he said.

"And you only have his memories from fifteen years ago? Before the war and everything?"

Steward nodded. "They call him the Alpha body, his memories the Alpha memories," he said. "That's how they're teaching me to think of him. I'm

Beta."

"What a bitch." Ardala's eyes narrowed. "I thought for a minute he was killed in the war, you know, with all the others. But he couldn't have been, right? Otherwise you'd be older."

"He was killed about eight months ago, in the Ricot habitat. Murdered. I don't know how. He never had the memory store updated. I really wonder what happened to him."

She reached out a slim brown hand and took his fingers. He could see comprehension in her look. "It didn't have anything to do with you."

"I feel that it does. Somehow."

"So all you remember," she said, "is what he knew just before he left. Still married to Natalie and everything."

Steward took a breath. "I keep thinking…maybe he just didn't want me to know about the war. What he went through. Maybe he just wanted to spare me the pain."

It was more likely, Steward knew, that the Alpha just didn't care anymore, or had forgotten that, before everything he cared about was destroyed, he'd recorded his memories on thread and deposited a bit of flesh in a cryogenic vault, the both to be awakened if he died on Sheol. So that Natalie wouldn't be a widow, wouldn't go without the comforts that went with being married to an Icehawk.

The drinks came. Ardala pulled a credit spike from her bracelet and gave it to the waitress. Steward sipped his Chinese willow. Fire burned deep in his throat.

"What are you going to do now?" she asked.

"Look for a job."

"What sort?"

"I don't know. Coherent Light gave me some very specific skills. I imagine they'd be unsuitable in today's job market."

"Security work?"

"That's what…the other one did. The Alpha. It didn't work out for him."

Ardala gnawed her generous lower lip. "Let me think about it. I'll bet I can place you somewhere."

Steward looked uneasily left and right. "I don't like this place," Steward said. "Any second now somebody's going to start playing old favorites on that piano, and they're going to be favorites from ten years ago and I won't remember them. Can we finish our drinks and go somewhere else?"

A smile tugged at her lips. "My apartment?"

He felt, deep in the pit of his stomach, an anxiety dissolve.

"D'accord," he said.

She looked up at him, touched her tongue to her teeth. "Before last night, I never made it with a clone."

The willow trailed fire down his throat. "Fortunately," he said, "that's a skill that's still in memory."

When he returned to the hospital in the morning, the police were waiting for him.

The walls in the interrogation room were pink, trimmed with chestnut brown and marred with graffiti that no one had bothered to wash away. Steward remembered somebody telling him once that pink walls subliminally soothed the violent. There was a portable recorder/computer, an institutional bunk bed, a pair of detectives. Lemercier was a short young man, aggressive, who made many sudden, angry gestures. When he gestured, he often bared his teeth. Hikita was older, gray-haired, with a little toothbrush mustache and a weary air. They had tried to run a Mutt and Jeff on him earlier, but neither of them seemed to have his heart in it, not after he told them where he'd spent the night.

Hikita was drinking coffee out of a foam cup. "Your alibi checks," he said.

"Thank you," Steward said. "We agree on that."

"You seemed an obvious suspect. Being a trained killer. Not being where you were supposed to be."

Steward shrugged. He didn't like cops, whether they agreed with him or not. Call it an old reflex. Lemercier looked at him and sucked in his lips, his mouth becoming a thin, angry line.

"You have no idea who would want to kill Dr. Ashraf?" he asked. "Just for the record?"

"I only saw the man between five and ten hours per week, and even then I did all the talking. I don't know who else he knew. Check his records."

"He didn't die in a nice way, Mr. Steward." Lemercier was showing his teeth again. "He was tied into his office chair and tortured. First with something very sharp, like a scalpel. Then with pliers. Then they garroted him. Almost took his head off. Would you like to see the pictures?"

Steward looked at him. "No."

Lemercier leaned closer. Steward was thinking about the soundproofing in Ashraf's office and how no one could have heard anything. The doctor's screams wouldn't even have been as loud as the bullet train. Someone knew that.

"Field interrogation," Lemercier said. "That's what they called it, right? When they taught you about how to do things like that. You learn anything about the use of pliers?"

Steward gazed into Lemercier's eyes. "Yes," he said. "I remember the lecture on pliers. They made us take notes." His eyes moved from one detective to another, then back. "You still trying to make this case, or what? My alibi checks, remember?"

Hikita and Lemercier exchanged featureless glances. Hikita turned to Steward. "We can't check Ashraf's records," he said, mumbling into his coffee cup. "Somebody broke into the hospital main computer and wiped them. We only have his appointment book."

"Did they teach you to wipe computers in the Icehawks, Mr. Steward?" Lemercier, of course.

"I imagine anything I know is out of date," Steward said.

He looked at the graffiti on the pink walls, LOUNGE LIZARDS RULE. MANX MAN WAS HERE. Dates. ÉCRASEZ L'INFÂME.

The last was his own, drawn two hours ago while he was being observed through the two-way glass set in the wall. It had been the motto of the Canards. He said, "Did he have an appointment scheduled for last night?"

"No."

"Not much help, huh?"

"Écrasez l'infâme," Hikita said mildly. "I looked it up. What infamous thing do you wish to eradicate?"

"What infamous thing do you have?"

Hikita put down his cup of coffee. "You can go," he said.

Steward eased himself out of the bunk, opened the soundproofed door, and stepped into a corridor. It was yellow and smelled of fresh paint.

Outside, the view of the mountains was cut into strips by glass towers. Steward chose one of the long reflective canyons that had a mountain view and walked along it, toward the green on the horizon.

He decided it was time to find out about Sheol.

At the hospital they told him it would be several days before he would be assigned his new doctor. They gave him a chit for the pharmacy in case he felt anxious in the meantime. He cashed the chit, put the capsules in his pocket, and forgot about them. He went to the library and looked up the Artifact War.

There wasn't much that filtered through the Outward Policorps' security. There hadn't been many survivors, and after the breakup of the policorps responsible, those remaining in authority preferred to discourage interest. A mistake, swept under the rug in an atmosphere of universal embarrassment.

Steward had the sense that things had been worse than anyone had ever imagined. The war had been triggered by the near simultaneous discovery of three planetary systems, each crammed with ruins and artifacts built by an unknown starfaring alien race that had vanished or been wiped out a thousand years before. The Powers, though no one knew it yet. The Outward Policorps, with their monopoly on star travel, had leaped madly into unregulated space in order to exploit the new technologies and techniques resulting from the investigation and understanding of the alien culture.

Out in the far reaches things had fallen apart very quickly, particularly on a planet called Sheol, which orbited around an obscure star called Wolf 294. There were sixteen separate armed forces, each maneuvering for sole domination, each months away from home in terms of communication time. What had begun as exploration and investigation degenerated into a mass plundering of the alien ruins. Commanders in the field made and broke temporary alliances independently of their superiors, who were creating their own temporary alliances and enmities back in the Sol system. Every latent, aberrant military technology in the ancient inventories was brought out and used: biologic weapons; extermination drones; tactical atomics; terraforming techniques stripped of their benign aspect and used to blacken tens of thousands of square kilometers of forest, plain, herbage; asteroids captured and used as weapons, creating craters on the surface of the planets where suspected enemy positions had been, and used as well to destroy the enemy's alien loot so as to make one's own more valuable. The ultimate aberration of a war out of control: the demolition of everything they had been sent to capture.

At the end, there were still a few survivors who fought on, isolated from the superiors in the Sol system who had proved unable to support such a war at such a distance. Amid an escalating round of Sol system bankruptcies and "retrenchment," the Powers, having finished whatever mysterious business had drawn them away, returned to their devastated homes: The war was over.

The Icehawks had been brought back from Sheol by Power craft, delivered like a package at Earth's door. Coherent Light had long before written them off, had sold them in a complicated deal with Far Jewel. Had assumed they were dead, or hadn't cared if they were alive.

Steward thought for a moment about the faces he remembered. Colonel de Prey. Wright. Freeman. Little Sereng, solemnly drawing blood from his finger every time he sharpened his kukri. Dragut. A hundred others. How many had survived? A handful, the reports said, and no names were given.

Years ago. The other survivors would have had time to forget, build new lives, start again.

All except Steward, whose loyalties still drew him to a company that no longer existed, comrades that were dead or scattered, a child he had never seen born to a woman whom he had loved but from whom, in the fifteen years that he did not remember, he had been divorced.

Who was lost in time, adrift as in a glider under a featureless sky, nothing but blackness below, with nothing to guide him but the sight of distant fire.

The next day, after lunch in the hospital cafeteria, he went to his room. There was a package on his bed, a plain brown-paper envelope with his name written on it. No stamps, so it hadn't come with the mail. He tore it open and found a black metal video cartridge, the size of a cigarette lighter. He looked in the envelope. Nothing else.

He turned on his vid and put the cartridge in the slot. The screen, gray, hissed at him for a moment, then the hissing stopped and a voice began. A coldness settled in Steward's spine.

"Hi," it said. "There are some things you should know."

The video portion was nothing but interference pattern. Steward tried to adjust it but couldn't find a picture.

"If you get this," the voice said, "it means I've been killed. I've given this to a friend of mine who can be trusted so far as to give this to you. Don't try to find him. He won't be able to help in any other way."

Steward looked up at the screen, seeing his own pale reflection in the glass, a ghost of himself: bushy dark brows, hair cut short, eyes like darting shadows.

"I'm on Ricot right now. I'm working for Consolidated Systems, and I'm involved in something very complicated..." The voice seemed to fade away for a second, as if the man had taken his mouth from the mic. Maybe he was just trying to make up his mind how much to tell, or how to tell it. Then the voice was back, louder than before. Steward almost took a step back.

"The thing is"—gratingly—"that when you become important in certain ways, there's no one you can trust. That's the lesson the Icehawks learned, that everything on Sheol taught us. Because we were trained and set up and then sold by our own side.

"So when you can't trust anyone else, you learn to trust yourself. That's what I've had to do. And when the official rules that they give you, all their morality, all turns out to be a fabric of, of ..." The voice faded again. When it came back, it was almost a scream, each word forced out with such intensity that Steward's throat ached to hear it. He was glad he couldn't see the man's face, the taut throat muscles, the way the eyes must be glaring into the blank face of another video set. "When it's *all lies*, when you can't *turn around for the lies*...well, you have to find the truth yourself. Find morality in your own mind. Do what you have to do. Like I'm going to try and do."

Steward heard a clatter very close to the mic, the sound of glass on glass. The man was pouring himself a drink, none too steadily. Steward looked down at his own hands. They were perfectly calm.

"I'm doing a job for a guy named Curzon. He's my chief here. I'm going to get into the Brighter Suns complex on Vesta, and do something…that doesn't entirely feel right. It looks as if I'll get in and out okay. Listen up now."

At the sound of the command, Steward's eyes snapped to the screen again. He laughed at his nervous reflex.

"The reason I'm going is that Colonel de Prey is there. He's the one who's responsible for what happened on Sheol. It was all his idea. Now he's back in business for Brighter Suns."

No, Steward thought. The Colonel wouldn't…He felt his fists clenching by his sides, the nails digging into the palms.

The Colonel *had*. He'd trained the Icehawks and then sold them. The… other…wouldn't lie about something like that.

Steward's eyes were burning. He felt a pain in his throat. The betrayal had a name.

"But to get to the Colonel I'm going to have to do some things…that I'm not comfortable with…that I'm not going to talk about in a recording. I may end up dead because of that, but I don't think so. It looks as if Curzon has things planned pretty well.

"But remember what I said. What I'm going to do is important to Curzon, and that means I can't trust what he's telling me. And there are people higher up the ladder who might be lying to him." There was a pause. Steward heard a glass being put down on a table, close to the mic. The warming vid smelled faintly of hot plastic.

"What I'm trying to say is that I want de Prey, and Curzon wants something else, and we both know it. So after I get de Prey, Curzon won't have a hold on me anymore, and that might mean I won't be of any more use to him. He may decide to put the ice on me. So if I end up dead, it's most likely my own side that did it."

The glass made a metallic slipping noise near the microphone, as if he'd tried to pick it up but only pushed it farther away. Then there was a space of silence just long enough for him to pick up the glass more carefully and take one long swallow. When the voice came back, it was tired, the pauses between each word long.

"I don't know why I'm sending you this. Except to say I'm sorry. For the years gone. It's just…for the record, I guess."

Another silence. Another drink. "One last thing."

Three beats of Steward's racing heart.

"Sorry I took so long."

A silence, a click that echoed a distant, months-old termination. Then nothing but a long, endless hiss.

He played the video several more times that afternoon. The rest of the time he lay on his bed, watching the reflections of sunlight from mirrored windows stretch slow-moving fingers across the precise pale white of the ceiling.

Several times the telephone rang. He let it alone.

Late in the afternoon he changed into sweats and went down into the therapy room. Before he left, he taped the cartridge to the back of a sliding door in his bathroom cabinet, then tore the envelope across twice and put it in a wastebasket in the hospital lobby.

The therapists had gone home for the day. The place smelled of chlorine from the whirlpool and echoed to the slap of his sandals. Steward did his warm-ups and stretches, then stepped to the treadmill and turned it on. He pushed up the speed till he was sprinting, the sound of his breath louder than the whine of the machine, the thunder of his footsteps. It seemed to him, in some unclear fashion, as if he were running toward something. His breath became a pain in his lungs. He stumbled against the cool chrome railing, caught himself, ran on until the machine's automatic counter turned it off. His hand hovered over the switch for a moment, then he stepped to the floor.

He stood still for a moment, catching his breath, waiting for the room to tell him what to do. He walked to the mats. He began running martial-arts exercises, first kata to find a rhythm, then short, violent patterns, imagining there were hands behind him that wanted to touch him, seize him, hold him back. He spun, parried, drove elbows into bone, fingers into eye sockets. The patterns grew longer, stronger. He felt a furnace of anger burning somewhere in his belly, driving each punch, each thrusting kick. He spun, his leg cocking, then lashing out. He tottered for a moment on the edge of balance, recovered…his vision was blurring, the dark empty room fading. Air poured like liquid down his throat. The patterns were driving him now, holding him up, moving him like a purposeful tide. He kicked out again, seeing a face, or something like a face, on the distant edge of his blackening vision, bushy brows, intense eyes, a background of stars…. He felt he could brush the face with his fingertips, break it with the torque of his instep, but he lost it, the face or whatever it was, and fell, the mat slamming hard against his shoulder, the side of his head.

Galaxies created themselves in vast blooms of light, all in the small universe behind his eyes. He rolled onto his back and sucked in air. His eyes blinked at the sweat flooding his vision. He put out a hand to touch whatever had been there, but it was gone. *Soon*, he thought.

Sight came back slowly, the room leaching into him like a slow dawn. He sat up, stood, bounced on the balls of his feet while he cooled down, until his breath was no longer a shriek in his throat.

He went to his room, threw off the soaked sweats, showered. As the warm mists rose around him, he felt the tingle of anticipation. He'd look behind the medicine cabinet door after drying off, not before. As if he didn't care.

When he looked, the cartridge was still there. Satisfaction danced from his fingertips as he peeled the tape away. He drew on slacks and a T-shirt and put the cartridge in his back pocket. As he stepped out of the room and locked the door, he heard the telephone begin to ring.

Outside he chose a mirrored canyon and began walking, heading toward the dim shadow of the mountains beyond. It was early evening. Cars slid dimly through gridded streets. People were pouring out of apartments and restaurants, moving along the concrete. The interface between the condecos was lively, full of people looking for fun, for something new, hustling each other. At a fast-food store Steward bought a plastic bottle of beer, and vatshrimp in a red chili sauce. He ate dinner as he walked.

The buildings diminished in size. This was the old part of town now, winding streets cut by bits of rugged terrain left in its natural state, like parks. The people were different, livelier, probably without as much money. They played instruments, passed bottles. Steward went into a liquor store and bought a bottle of old genever wrapped in foam insulation that would keep it cold for days. He drank as he walked, rekindling the fire inside him, feeling it spread warmly to his toes, his fingertips. The mountains were fully visible now, three peaks clothed in twilight gray. He kept walking.

Cars hissed by on the dark street, trailing wisps of music. His leg muscles were driving him steadily uphill. The moon rose, a narrow sickle cutting through the fixed stars of satellites, power stations, orbital habitats. Shining on the metal cylinder where Natalie lived, alone with her postwar child. Cool breezes touched Steward's face, his arms. The air smelled of pine.

In another hour he was in the foothills, still moving. He sipped the genever whenever he felt his fires threatening to burn low. He was surrounded by a darkness that seemed tangible, friendly, like the inside of a tented blanket. Through the pines he glimpsed occasional glimmers, distant houses stuck to the rising slope like limpets. He walked toward the moon.

When he came to a place where he couldn't see any more lights above him, he stopped. He took a couple of slow swallows of genever and turned, looking at the jeweled spiderweb of the city below, the flashing red lights on the upper corners of the glass towers. Coleopter turbines moaned somewhere in the distance. He sat down, crossing his legs in front of him, and wondered if a telephone, somewhere, was ringing for him. Carefully, Steward imagined the sound.

I'm getting there, he thought. I'm getting near the center. The cartridge, in his back pocket, dug into his flesh. He ignored it and took another drink. Lights guttered through a haze of rising air. Wind moved high in the pines but failed to stir the hair on his scalp. The wind sounded like a million people cheering, all seated around him in some dark and vast stadium. Cheering what he was becoming.

In the morning, unshaven, unbathed, reeking of juniper gin, he had some difficulty hitching a ride back into town. He'd slept on needles, under a blanket of boughs, and there was pine sap in his hair, staining his clothes. He filled his empty bottle with spring water and sipped it as he walked most of the way to the hospital.

He could hear Dr. Ashraf's voice murmuring in the sound of his room's air conditioning. Protesting. Telling him he had to forget what he thought he knew, what he thought he cared about. Telling him to make his own life without reference to a deformed, crippled past.

"Fuck that, Doc," he said out loud. "They cut you into chunks with a knife and I bet they never even told you why."

If you wish to find the unclouded truth, he told himself, do not concern yourself with right or wrong. Conflicts with right and wrong are a sickness of the mind.

The oldest Zen poem. He liked the sound of it.

He called Ardala at work and told her he was checking out of the hospital.

"What happened to you yesterday? I was calling. Police again?"

"Can I stay with you till I get some work?"

She laughed. "Why not? Stop by for the key."

"Thanks. I'll see you in a few minutes."

Steward showered, changed, and packed. His possessions filled one small athletic bag. He put the bag on the bed, took a last look around the room. His gaze lit on the vid, and hesitated. His hand moved involuntarily to his back pocket, feeling the outline of the vid cartridge through crisp denim.

Kill the Buddha, he thought.

He put the cartridge in the vid set and pressed the ERASE button. He thought of the variable-lattice alloy threads that filled the cartridge, the video coded on their molecular structure, and then he imagined them all changing, the message disappearing, becoming void. As he looked into the blank face of the set, it seemed to him as if his reflection was sharing a secret with him.

The clerk was surprised when Steward told him he was leaving the hospital. "Your course of treatment isn't over," he said.

"I'm not sick. I've adjusted." Steward crossed his heart. "Honest."

"But it's already paid for."

"Maybe I'll come back later. If I fuck up."

He signed a form that made him responsible for himself and added his thumbprint. Before he left the lobby, he reached for the bracelet on his left wrist, hooked it with two fingers, pulled. It stretched like mint licorice, then snapped. He put it in an ashtray and then stepped out onto the street.

Sounds boiled up around him. Noonday heat. Realities reflected in bright mirror glass.

Steward felt right at home.

CHAPTER THREE

Steward went through the heavy security in front of the condeco's door and registered as a guest, a process that included thumbprinting an agreement to comply with the rules of the condecology's constitution. As usual, this was based on the concept of "self-limiting options," which so far as Steward could tell meant the inhabitants agreed not to think about mutually agreed aspects of reality that might prove troubling. The rules here were fairly liberal, Steward saw, and forbade him to possess or distribute weapons, certain recreational drugs, named types of religious or political literature, proscribed software, and the more extreme forms of vidporn. Public nudity was forbidden, cohabitation was all right. Watching vid or headvid on channels not licensed by the condeco was grounds for expulsion. Steward was given a six weeks' temporary pass, took the elevator to Ardala's apartment. Once there, he walked among the small rooms, just orienting himself.

The apartment had all the signs of the upwardly mobile: tasteful furniture, small alloy-and-crystal tables, a bookshelf filled with uniform black cartridges with little white labels, a flat liquid-crystal video display hung on the wall. Abstract wall paintings, all desert tones, that were careful not to make any kind of statement.

The intention of the decor—the careful abstraction of all hint of personality—was carelessly sabotaged by the artifacts of habitation: Ardala's laundry scattered over the furniture, a few of her niece's bright plastic toys sitting where her niece had left them, by the jumble of filled ashtrays and cigarette lighters, the wineglasses misted with fingerprints, the cream blur of scansheet printouts, half-worked crosswords, and dogeared issues of magazines called *Gals* and *Guys*, which turned out to be weekly publications in which the unemployed advertised their talents. A turtle-shaped floor-cleaning robot wandered hopelessly among the ruins. The only place that was spotless was the kitchen, which she apparently never used. He looked in the refrigerator and found only wine and a few vegetables.

Steward remembered furnishing the apartment in Kingston he'd shared with Natalie—how they went to fifteen stores before they could agree on a kitchen table, a rectangular transparency supported by a single twisting column of orbital alloy, seeming too thin to support the weight of the glass.... It had been the first piece of furniture Steward had ever bought new.

Steward and Natalie had always kept their series of apartments spotless, the glass table shining. It had seemed a sort of military virtue to care for their equipment.

He hadn't really noticed the litter the first time he'd come here. The lights had been off when they came in and never really got turned on. The second time, he'd been bothered. He was still thinking like an Icehawk.

Now he didn't mind at all. He was something else now.

He paced across the carpet. Fabric scratched his bare feet. His mind hummed, a blur of ideas that hadn't yet taken shape, flickering, assembling, dissolving without his conscious thought, moving against a background of stars.

His mind elsewhere, he stepped out for supplies. He bought the makings for salmon en croûte and, just because he felt like celebrating, two bottles of champagne. There weren't any glasses, so he washed the dishes.

Ardala came home with perspiration smearing her butterfly-wing makeup and dark sweat stains under her arms. Steward poured her a glass of champagne while she cursed her boss, the heat wave that Steward hadn't noticed, the crowds after work, the awfulness of the boring people she met in the elevator. She threw her clothes into the bedroom, drew a cool bath, and drank the champagne. Steward, carrying the bottle, followed her into the bathroom. It smelled of the scented oil she'd added to the bath. He watched Ardala as he poured champagne for her, the small tanned breasts with their nipples that bobbed in and out of the water, the knees rising like islets, the dark submerged pubic moss. He put the bottle down and began to pull off his shirt.

He remembered waves slapping at his shoulders as he lay atop Natalie on the shelving sand of Port Royal, partly hidden from view by pink and turquoise Jamaican boats bobbing in the warm bay.... About a hundred yards away a congregation of local Pentecostals was singing songs about rapture and redemption and the Glory of the Coming of the Lord, their high-pitched keening cries of praise echoing Natalie's salt moans. Across the bay the Coherent Light ziggurat glowed in black self-contained hubris. Fish struck painlessly at their legs and thighs. The night had seemed full of certainty and love. Under them was the Port Royal of Henry Morgan, built on buccaneer pride and booty, which a backhand swipe of history had slid right into the warm welcoming sea, just as the whirlwind that was Sheol would sweep away Steward, Natalie, the certainty that was Coherent Light, the certainty and pride that had come from humanity's sole possession of the vast universe....

"Hey," Ardala said. "This hurts my back."

"Okay," Steward said. "Let's switch places."

From his position Steward admired the arch of Ardala's throat as she threw her head back, eyes closed, intent on her pleasure. Her sun-browned skin outlined the hollows of her clavicles, the bony points of her shoulders. When she came, she pushed her arm under his head and bent over him, her back arching, to make her choked whimpers right into his ear.... He put his arms around her, holding her close. The sensation of her breath on his ear, the sounds she was making, brought him to a sudden, unexpected climax. He heard, for a moment, the voice of the whirlwind.

They finished the bottle of champagne lying in the bath, Ardala half-lying on him, her arm still under his head. Little threads of sperm floated densely in the water amid rainbow dots of bath oil. Ardala stirred the sperm with a finger. "Might as well give the homunculi a ride," she said. "One last thrill before they go down the drain."

"The salmon should be ready," he said. "Are you hungry?"

"You should have saved your money," Ardala said. "I know you don't have much. From now on, have dinner on me."

"I wanted to."

"What am I going to do with all that wheat flour you bought? I never bake."

She rose, water sliding in rainbow sheets down her flanks, and Steward kissed her, crawled out of the bath, and reached for a towel. He went to the kitchen, put their dinner on plates, and opened the other bottle of champagne. He brought the bottle back into the bathroom. Ardala had wrapped herself in one towel and was rubbing her hair with another. He poured champagne for her. She dropped the towel and took her glass. She drank, combed her hair, followed him to where he'd set dinner.

"I'm going to try to get a job in one of the policorps," Steward said after they'd eaten.

Ardala looked up at him and crossed one leg over the other. Behind where she sat on a white plastic chair, a self-polarizing window resisted the sun, darkening the view of a bright aluminum-alloy expressway headed south to Phoenix.

"You don't have the money to buy in, right?" she asked. "You could do okay on their exam, but your knowledge is fifteen years out of date and you won't be in the two percent they take for free. What's left is terran indentureship, and that takes years."

"An Outward Policorps. Starbright seems like a good one. Into transportation. I think I'd like to travel."

Ardala frowned and reached across the table for a Xanadu, a blend of marijuana and mentholated tobacco. She flicked on a lighter. "You haven't been listening."

"Yeah, I have. But I just want to get into space. I'll figure out a way."

She drew on her cigarette and looked moodily out the window, where the brilliant serpent writhed its way to the Valley of the Sun. With her thumb, she rubbed an invisible smudge between her eyebrows. "Is space all that great?" she asked. She held out her cigarette.

"It's where things are." Where, he thought, the answers are.

She looked at him. "Where Natalie is?"

Steward didn't answer. He took the cigarette and drew on it deeply, welcoming the invasion of THC and carcinogens. Xanadus were one of the worst things in the world to smoke, since holding the marijuana smoke in gave the tobacco time to wreck lung tissue. The Canards, being what they were, had loved Xanadus for just that reason.

Ardala sighed. "Okay," she said, "I've got some material in my office. It'll help you study for the tests. Maybe you'll get lucky and qualify for waste disposal tech on Ricot."

The name of the artificial planetoid sent a cool thrill through Steward's nerves.

"Ricot's all right," he said. There were answers there.

The next morning, after Ardala left, Steward worked the weights in the condeco's health club, showered, dressed, decided he didn't want to breakfast alone. He didn't like the look of the coffee shops in the condeco: too much stained wood, soundproofing, tasteful music, conservatively dressed professionals reading the type of scansheets that weren't forbidden by the constitution. He headed north into the old city and found a coffee shop with a broken holographic sign that read FRIENDL ES REST RANT IN TOW . The booths were upholstered in bright orange Jovian plastic, and the waitress was an overweight woman who greeted him with a scowl.

After eating, he smoked a Xanadu with his coffee and watched the scowling waitress cope with a Chinese visitor who thought her chicken fried steak was supposed to have something to do with chicken. The Chinese woman thought she was being cheated, but her English wasn't up to expressing her outrage.

Steward leaned back in his booth and grinned. He'd made the same mistake the first time he'd visited the United States.

The problem resolved itself with the appearance of the manager, and Steward finished his coffee. He strolled around the old town, watching the battered old storefronts, the people, old men selling lottery tickets and scansheets, young hustlers wearing T-shirts with liquid-crystal displays that advertised their product: software, literature you couldn't get in condecos, drugs. Steward remembered scenes from Marseilles, the way the street had seemed more intense there, the dealing more critical—even the colors had seemed brighter.

He sensed that these people were just going through the motions—it didn't matter to them. America hadn't had a war in 100 years. These people hadn't been on the edge of starvation for months at a time; they hadn't had to deal to survive. They hadn't been through Petit Galop.

America was getting old, he thought. Like the rest of Earth. Absorbing fashions brought down from space, ways of life—condecologies, ideologies—that were imitations of the way people lived in a vacuum. Steward's olive skin was fashionable because olive skin had a more interesting texture to those who lived in cultures that never saw sunlight, and heavy makeup was fashionable for the same reason. Earth had shot its bolt. Space was where things mattered now, like it or not.

He bought a scansheet and walked into one of the wilderness parks that cut the city and sat on a grassy slope. In the bright cloudless sky he could see a pattern of fixed stars, orbital factories, and habitats. One of them, he knew, was the orbital complex where Natalie lived now. He wondered which star was hers, what she looked like now, after fifteen years had passed, years that he hadn't known. He felt the brightening pain in his throat and nose, and lowered his eyes to the street. Sadness fell on him like rain.

"So how did you end up in Canard Chronique?" Ardala asked later.

"Canards Chronique," he corrected. They were stretched out in bed, Ardala on her stomach, propped up on her elbows while reading this week's copy of *Guys* and taking notes. He was reading some of the study material she'd brought with her. "It has a double meaning, either Chronic Ducks or Chronic Hoaxes. Which had a lot to do with their ethic."

"You didn't answer my question."

"How I got in? It's all the fault of my African grandmother."

"Don't keep me in suspense, Steward," Ardala said.

He put a marker in the book and put it down. "Okay. My African grandmother got educated in Canada and fell in love with cold climates, so she became an arctic geologist. Then she fell in love with this Scotsman she met in Novaya Zemlya, who was also in love with the arctic, et cetera. Their second son hated snow and permafrost, which was all he ever saw when he was a kid, so he moved to the Mediterranean, where he married my mother, who was from Marseilles. He had himself a good job in Nice, working as an indentured economist for Far Jewel while my mother was going to school." Steward frowned at the opposite wall. He was trying to decide what attitude to take, which personality to use for this. "He got killed during Petit Galop," he said.

"I've heard of that."

Heard of it, Steward thought. Europe's collapse into anarchy following a failed attempt to remodel its sociology along the lines suggested by a space-dwelling policorp. Earth had larger populations than the policorps and less fragile ecological systems; sometimes the policorps ran programs down the gravity well to see if they'd work, before going to the trouble of restructuring themselves along similar patterns. The possibilities inherent in such tampering were one of the reasons the policorps bothered with Earth at all.

But the thing had gone wrong, Europe being more fragile than anyone knew, and people—policorp people, and citizens, and a lot of presumable innocents—all had paid the penalty.

How, Steward wondered, to tell Ardala about it? A Canard would just shrug. Everybody in Marseilles had it bad; everybody had a father or mother who was dead, or a sister or brother or at least an uncle or aunt. That attitude might seem callous to an American, though. Stewart decided just to tell it straight out. "It was bad, particularly down south. Some of the rioters were up on the tall policorp ecodromes, dropping big plate-glass windows on the people below. They explode like grenades, you know? That's how my father died, he and a couple thousand others, all in one afternoon. Not that it's likely he would have survived anyway—he had biological implants, a hand modified for microcircuitry work and head sockets to take a DNA-computer interface. He hadn't had his skull capacity increased or the extra brain tissue, but he'd had the superchargers put into his neck for an expanded brain. Anyone with that kind of hardware wouldn't get past the gangs' metal detectors and would end up in front of a firing squad."

"Jesus. People here have been taking implants for a hundred years. What was so bad about it?"

This time Steward couldn't keep himself from shrugging. "It was part of Far Jewel's program, so it was evil. The modified people were the only ones the mob could find...the decision-makers were living in the asteroid belt and out of reach. Far Jewel's facilities in France were gutted, so suddenly there wasn't employment for all their people or for their survivors. Far Jewel washed its hands of the whole experiment once things went bad. The French government got chased to Portugal, so there wasn't any help for people like my mother and me. We ended up moving to Marseilles, to live with my aunt. And even then we almost starved." Steward looked at her. "You got any Xanadus left?"

"In my shirt pocket. I heard some people ate each other. That true?"

Steward frowned. "I'd believe it," he said. "None of that was going down where I was living, though. The gangs kept things going."

"The Canards came to the rescue?"

"Yes." Steward stood, moved toward the chair where Ardala had thrown her shirt. He found the last Xanadu and began looking for the ashtray. "The teen gangs were running the city, more or less," he said. "The Old Quarter, anyway.

Keeping power and water running for people who weren't living in ecodromes. But most of them had all sorts of funny French ideas about honor and turf and ideology—Jesus, half the gang fights weren't even fights, just a bunch of kids screaming political slogans at one another. Issuing manifestos over the public datanets. Proclaiming their loyalty to the Société Bijoux or the New Rejuve Movement or Genetic Behaviorism. The Canards weren't asking for that kind of loyalty. They just wanted to survive and get rich and have a few laughs at the expense of the kids who were taking it all so seriously."

He found the ashtray and brought it back to bed with him. He lit the cigarette and leaned back against the pillows.

"Did you get rich?" Ardala asked.

He put the lighter on the bedside table. "I was a good boy and gave it all to my mother. She bought her way into an ecodrome about the time I enlisted in CL."

"Sort of rich, then."

Steward inhaled, closed his eyes. "The Canards wanted to be middlemen. They figured that's where the money was. Tried to know who was putting moves in certain directions, what the policorps were up to, where to find certain commodities. Acted as brokers, collected a percentage. Never allied with any of the other gangs. And we'd sabotage the others, too, just for fun. Issue funny absurdist manifestos over other gangs' signatures, that kind of thing."

"What happened to them?"

"Mostly they got killed. The gangs had a war. Being in the middle, the Canards were right in the crossfire. They'd never made any friends, so they were nothing but stationary targets. I took what I'd made and split for Coherent Light." He grinned. "The other Canards would have approved, I think. They always tried to do the smart thing."

"And CL actually let you in."

"I fit the profile."

"A profile for an extinct policorp. Great." She closed the issue of *Guys* and threw the magazine off the bed. "I can't imagine you being in a gang. When you lived next door to me you were such a good soldier. Such a"—she shrugged her shoulders—"such a straight arrow. You know. Everything was always tidy and in its place. You were always full of Coherent Light's programs for this and that. Making the galaxy a safer, brighter place."

"After what I saw in Nice and Marseilles, Coherent Light made a lot of sense. Seemed to, anyway. Besides," he added, "there's not so much between a good soldier and a good gang member. A matter of style, mostly."

"Huh." She reached out for the cigarette and took it from his fingers. "What were you like, back then?"

"Skinny. Intense."

"You're still skinny and intense. If it weren't for the muscles, you'd be just a wisp."

"Intense maybe. But this body's been fed. My former body was on the edge of starvation for a lot of years. I was fond of big shades and raw silk jackets and high-topped sneakers with little red balls on the sides. I had a nice home comp with all the latest in stolen software. I chain-smoked Xanadus and traveled on a matte-black fuel-cell scooter. The usual hustler stuff."

Odd to think of that as being over twenty years ago. In memory it wasn't so long. A past that hadn't even got fuzzy.

"Hell. Motherfucker." The Xanadu had burned her fingers. She squashed it in the ashtray, too fast, spilling ashes on the bed. Then she was cursing on her hands and knees, bent over, brushing the ashes off the bed onto the floor. Steward watched the way her spine flexed along her supple back, how her haunches moved as she shifted her weight, the muscles in each thigh tautening alternately, a play of shadow and motion.

He remembered Natalie, the way she moved, sure of herself, graceful, remembering how she used to slide between the covers as if they were a lover's arms.... Hell, he thought, if I was as smart as I think I am, I wouldn't have lost her. Stupidity's something you learn to live with, just like everything else.

Morning, next day. Steward sat in the FRIENDL ES REST RANT, working on his second cup of coffee. It seemed to Steward that he could feel the caffeine moving through his body, switching on first one system, then another. Little bits of his consciousness reawakening, blinking on like a row of little green lights giving a GO signal. A half-eaten sweet roll sat on a plate in front of him. Around him the midmorning coffee-shop crowd lazed over scansheet printouts, read the news, yawned, stretched.

Steward raised his head to signal the waitress for another cup of coffee, saw a profile moving along the distant aisle between the waitress's station and his window booth, and suddenly the little row of GO lights in his mind was flashing on and off in hot synchrony, green, yellow, red. His nerves burned. He turned in his seat to watch the man as he walked down the aisle and sat in a corner booth, followed by the waitress with a coffeepot. Steward craned his neck for a view of the man's face. The waitress was standing in the way, pouring coffee. Steward began to feel foolish. A stranger in an out-of-the-way coffee shop, a chance resemblance, and he was beginning to see ghosts.

The waitress moved out of the way. Steward looked at the man's face and felt his mouth go dry. He turned, finished his coffee in a gulp, and stood. He swayed. His balance seemed a little off. He walked down the long aisle, seeing the man's face foreshortening toward him. Nerves leaped in Steward's hands, his legs.

The man looked up as he raised his coffee cup. He was a dark-skinned European with medium-length hair, dressed tidily in a dark short-sleeved suit over a collarless light blue shirt. His arms were gaunt, wiry. His skin was parchment stretched over bone, tied in place with the blue ropes of veins. He wore a graying mustache that was unfamiliar. Steward felt a touch of uncertainty. His memory was of another man, younger, well-muscled, smiling. Then he saw a white splash on a biceps where a tattoo had been removed, and uncertainty was over.

He felt himself teetering on the edge of something, as if the ground under him was about to spill away, dropping him into a new place, somewhere uncertain, where the rules were different and he would have to learn them as he moved.

"Griffith," Steward said.

The coffee cup stopped halfway to the man's mouth. His wet eyes glistened, surrounded by dark lines. New eyes. Ghost eyes.

"Steward," he muttered, apparently to himself. He put the cup down without moving his glance. His voice was harsh, grating. Steward remembered him singing, a baritone voice that rang from the metal walls of Steward's apartment in the Coherent Light Mars Orbital Complex. Half the songs were in Welsh and sounded like hymns, the other half were filthy rugby songs. The voice was different now.

"Jesus," Griffith said. A grin began moving across his face, moving in an odd way, not all at once but jerkily, invading Griffith's face zone by zone. "You caught me by surprise. You look good, Captain. Sit down."

Captain? Steward thought.

Griffith's smile faded. His face clouded over at the cold touch of memory. "I haven't seen you since the Icehawks," he said. "Not since we came back from Sheol."

CHAPTER FOUR

Griffith didn't so much eat breakfast as tear it apart, nervously shredding eggs and ham, ripping up his toast, now and then eating a bite, otherwise just pushing the food around his plate. Steward understood how he'd grown so thin. While watching Griffith mutilate his breakfast, Steward explained that he was a clone, that he had his Alpha's training but not his memories of Sheol or anything since.

Griffith looked at him. "He didn't update the memories at all? Didn't give you anything?" Steward shook his head. Griffith leaned back in his booth with surprise on his face. "Why?" Griffith asked.

"He didn't say."

"Shit." He rubbed his mustache. Then his puzzlement turned to wary concern.

"He's dead then, right? You wouldn't be here otherwise."

"That's right."

Griffith was silent for a moment. His watery eyes seemed turned inward, watching a memory landscape printed inside his mind. "How'd it happen?" he asked. "Did they tell you?"

"He was killed on Ricot, or maybe Vesta. Hunting Colonel de Prey."

Griffith was silent again for a long moment. "Yeah," he said. The voice wasn't disapproving, or approving either. "That sounds like the Captain." And then he went back to ripping up his food, slowly, not even looking at what his hands were doing. Steward watched him, not wanting to break into Griffith's reverie, his mourning for someone he hadn't known he'd lost.

The Captain. That was the Alpha personality's name, now. It symbolized a rank, an authority, that Steward did not remember possessing. He hadn't even been an officer. The Captain had come into being on Sheol.

Griffith put down his knife and fork and took a breath. He seemed suddenly pale. He excused himself and went to the men's room. When he returned, his color was back. He lit a cigarette and inhaled.

"I've got some kind of stomach thing," he said. "It's been following me for days."

"What are you doing in Arizona?"

"I'm staying in a condo suite my company keeps here. I'm working as kind of a salesman," he said. "For an outfit called Lightsource, Limited. We provide various kinds of communication services for businesses. Software aimed at solving particular problems, communication equipment built to specific configurations, that kind of thing. Are you working?"

"Not at the moment. I've got some things lined up. I'm going to try to get into Starbright."

Griffith's face grew wistful. "Getting back into space, huh?" he asked. "Wish I was."

"I want to travel. I think I'd be restless if I stayed in one place."

Griffith nodded, puffed smoke. "I'd like to see the Powers again. Live with them in a real Power environment. That's what I miss most about space. The Powers turned out to be the only thing up there worth the trip."

"You think so?"

Griffith gave him a glance. "The Captain was that way, too. Wasn't impressed by them. Kind of a blindness in him." He shook his head. "But when you meet them, you realize how centered they are. How *real* they are. And you see by comparison how humans are almost...transparent. As if we're not really there. And you know how far we have to go." He looked down at his plate, his mutilated food. Frowned. "I think I know someone in Starbright," he said. "A drive jockey. Let me think a minute. Maybe she can help you get in on an apprentice program." He shook his head. "I'll have to make some calls."

"Thank you. I appreciate it."

Griffith waved a hand. "Don't thank me yet. I don't know if I can do anything."

"Griffith." Steward felt an adrenaline touch on his nerves. Griffith looked up at his tone.

"I want to know what happened on Sheol."

Griffith looked down at his hands. He shook his head. "It wouldn't mean anything to you, buck." His voice was low, his voice absorbed by the table, his crossed arms. "It's something you'd have had to live through. I'm sorry, but—"

"It's important."

Griffith wiped his forehead with the back of an arm. "Sorry," he said. "It's not...possible."

Steward felt his breath going out of him. "That's all right, man," he said. Knowing it wasn't. "If you can't, you can't."

Griffith shook his head again. "Sorry," he said. He looked at his watch. "I've got a sales meeting coming up. It's gonna run all day."

"Want to get together tonight? Have some drinks?"

"Can't. I'm going to have to dine with a client tonight. Probably have to get him laid, too, the asshole." He looked up, took a drag from his cigarette, and stubbed it out. There was an uncertainty in his watery eyes, and Steward found it odd—it was as if Griffith was about to say something against his will. He wondered if Griffith, too, was a clone, if the Alpha Griffith had died on Sheol and the Beta refused to talk about the war because he hadn't been there.

"Breakfast tomorrow?" Griffith asked.

"Yeah. Sure."

"Here? Nine o'clock?"

"Good."

Griffith slid out of the booth and gave a wave that looked almost like a salute. "See you tomorrow," he said, and walked away. Steward glanced after him, looking carefully at the back of Griffith's receding head.

At the base of Griffith's skull Steward could see the implant socket under the short hair, and he felt satisfaction at the certainty that this was the original Griffith, not a clone. The implant socket was an Icehawk thing, enabling a soldier to interface with his weapons, transport, and environment suit. A lot of people carried them, but a salesman for a software company wouldn't need one: He'd be able to demonstrate his wares with a headset, not needing the extra fraction of a second the socket would provide. So Griffith still had the interface socket, that and the implant threads that jacked his reflexes and programmed them with martial arts and small-unit tactics.

Steward watched Griffith as the man left. He could feel a high, his nerves stirring, connections being made in his head. Griffith was a pathway to something else, something he wanted.

Griffith was going to lead him to his Alpha.

However long he thought about it, things kept coming back to the Powers. They'd inhabited the planets where the Artifact War was fought; their return had ended the war. In the pictures Steward had seen, they hadn't seemed at all attractive. Yet Griffith loved them; perhaps there was a reason for it. Steward accessed the library and read everything he could find. Though there was more than there had been in the hospital library, there still wasn't much that wasn't speculation. It was as if people who had met them preferred not to say anything concrete.

"Powers" was a translation of the aliens' name for themselves. Their own language was a combination of clicks and singsong mutterings that often dipped into the subsonic range: No human had ever come close to translating it in anything approaching its full idiom.

The Powers had inhabited Sheol and a number of other planets that humanity had discovered, then abandoned them. After a thousand years the

Powers came back and found humanity warring in their ruins. They had not yet explained why they had left, why they had come back. They'd merely announced that a vast area of the sky, an eighty-six-degree cone expanding from its entering point at Ross 986, was now off-limits to human exploration. Presumably that was where the Powers lived, or where they wished humanity to think they lived. Humanity, eager for trade and knowledge, fearful of the consequences of being thought unfriendly, was happy to oblige.

The Powers were vaguely centauroid, four-legged, two-armed. Their lower bodies were about the size of a small pony, their upper bodies slightly smaller than the human. The proportions of their bodies did not in any other way resemble ponies or humans: Their legs were too short, too powerful, with spreading, clawed ostrich toes, while their upper arms were too stalklike to be reminiscent of anything on Earth. Their heads were a flat, boneless muscular protrusion, with a large single nostril on top and a pair of eyes, armored like a lizard's, that could be twisted so as to cover the entire horizon, or focused forward or back for binocular vision. Their brains were in their chests, with a secondary brain in the middle of the back. There was a combination mouth/voicebox/nostril between the forelegs and a complex organ for synthesizing aerosol hormones in the rear. Along the back, placed on either side of the spine, were light-colored spots, like a salamander's third eye, that acted as primitive eyes, ears, scent detectors. Apparently much of their communication was by scent, from airborne hormones created in their hormone synthesizer and then communicated to special sensory organs in the upper nostril. By this means they could impart moods, emotions, perhaps other things peculiar to the Powers alone. They could communicate many things at once—emotional text via hormones, main text through the deep vocal cords in the lower voice box, and subtext through whining, singsong overtones made by forcing air through the upper nostril.

In color they were a deep violet, individuals ranging from a deep purple to an almost-black. Their skin was smooth except for the stiff hairs sprouting from the top of the head and along the spine. The hairs were packed with nerves—apparently the hairs had some sensory function as well.

The Powers were omnivorous and warm-blooded. Each individual was bisexual and oviparous and at least some were very long-lived—evidence suggested that some of the leaders were thousands of years old. They seemed to spend most of their time sexually inactive, and sexual contact seemed to be an act devoid of emotional context. Eggs were raised in collective crèches: Emotional allegiance belonged to the group, not to biological parents. Some sociologists saw this as a great advantage. Others found it troubling.

The Powers' social organization was confusing and highly ritualized. It was autocratic in the extreme. Personal interaction was marked by a great deal of body and hormonal language that defined the status and role of each individual. So far as anyone could tell, loyalty was universal, responsibility and reward running from the few individuals humanity had met all the way to some big boss Power in the vast field of stars the Powers called home. If there were dissent and dissatisfaction among the Powers, none had ever been displayed before humans.

The following terms did not translate into the Powers' language: government, dissent, individual, rights, justice, religion, progress, law, freedom. Sociologists were unanimous in asking humanity not to be judgmental about this. Other species, other mores.

Some humans had been bold enough to suggest that the Powers were in their racial decadence, that their ritualized and autocratic social structure was indicative of a race that had lost the adaptability necessary to a starfaring, expanding culture. Others offered the possibility that humanity, following the evolution of the policorps, was headed in the same direction. Still others, by way of rebuttal, simply pointed to that great off-limits cone of space. If the Powers were in a decadence, you couldn't prove it from that.

Coterminous with the arrival of the Powers was the collapse of the Outward Policorps following the military and economic disasters of the Artifact War. The remaining policorps, picking up the pieces, had ended the Outward Policorps' monopoly on faster-than-light travel and had created two new trading policorps from scratch, Consolidated Systems, operating from the manmade planetoid called the Ricot Habitat, a Coherent Light project that had survived its builder, and Brighter Suns, headquartered on Vesta. These two systems were partly owned by the policorps that had created them and existed for the sole purpose of trading with the Powers. Apparently the Powers also had a financial interest in their existence, since they refused any other offers of trade, even those made at favorable terms by Earth governments.

There were no longer any Powers on Earth. They had lived on Earth for some months, then left abruptly. There was a rumor, which Consolidated Systems and Brighter Suns did not deny, that they had proven susceptible to Earth bacteria. They now lived in hermetic isolation in the two space colonies, behind seals that guaranteed sterile isolation. They communicated almost entirely by electronic means, rarely face-to-face. They sold pharmaceuticals, bacteria, terraforming techniques, and knowledge, cutting deals with intelligent rapacity in order to purchase electronics, pharmaceuticals, bacteria, terraforming techniques, knowledge. They remained enigmatic.

Steward watched vids taken of the Powers after their first appearance on Earth. They were faster than they looked. Movement was accompanied by fast shuffles, bobbing, and arm waving that defined status and zones of influence. The muscular head changed shape like a balloon caught between cold fronts.

It was repulsive and fascinating.

Griffith loved them. Steward couldn't see why. But he felt it was important, and he watched the vids over and over. He found no answer.

The next morning he saw Griffith waiting for him outside the coffee shop, smoking a cigarette. He seemed energetic, nervous almost. He was dressed in boots, an open-collared, short-sleeved shirt, and black jeans.

A robot car went by silently, wreathed in a hologram halo announcing Darwin Days.

"Hi," Griffith said. "I couldn't get a hold of my friend. She's not on the planet."

"That's okay. Thanks for trying."

"I'll keep after her. She's coming back next week."

Griffith jerked his head up the street. "Want to go for a walk? I have an idea."

"Sure."

They walked up the street, ignoring the lottery sellers. It was too early for the hustlers to be out of bed. Griffith turned and led them to one of the town's rugged parks. He looked Steward up and down as they walked.

"You look in good shape. Been working out?"

"Yeah. Every day."

"I've let it slide." Griffith reached in his pocket for a handkerchief and mopped his brow. A compressed-gas inhaler fell out of his pocket and clattered on the sidewalk. It was the sort used by asthma sufferers and people who shot drugs up their noses. Griffith picked it up without comment and put it in his pocket. He looked at Steward again and narrowed his eyes. "You don't have the hyped nerves anymore, right?"

"No. If I wanted threads, I'd have to pay."

"Well"—Griffith was silent for a moment—"you probably won't need them."

Steward looked at him, but Griffith turned and began to climb a steep grassy slope. Steward fought down his annoyance and followed. Griffith was breathing hard by the time they got to the top. From the ridge they could see bright banners on a sward, temporary tents, models of ships and tooled DNA. Distant amplified voices muddied one another in the air. The NeoImagists were having their Darwin Days celebrations.

Steward decided he was tired of the game Griffith was playing. "What is it I won't need the nerves for, Griffith?"

Griffith held up a hand for patience and lit a new cigarette from the old. "Okay," he said. "Salesman isn't all I do. I have a...another kind of job on the side." He looked at Steward and smiled a jittery smile. "Maybe I can help you earn some money toward getting into Starbright."

A feeling of nervous familiarity settled on Steward. He remembered sitting on his fuel-cell scooter back in Marseilles, hiding behind his shades and his big white jacket, talking to a boy and a girl who were dealing in suspect wetware, the sort that a lot of the Marseilles factions felt was ideologically incorrect. They were offering him a deal on it, but Steward wasn't sure whether it was anything he wanted to handle.

Steward remembered the way the girl's jewelry flashed in the sun, the boy's stance, hands in pockets, feet in cowboy boots covered with silver wire and microcircuitry, and most of all Steward remembered the strange taste on his tongue. A taste of something he wanted, and something he was afraid of. The taste of a proposition that he wasn't sure he was able to handle.

He looked at Griffith now and wondered what had really happened on Sheol. Whether anything he knew about the young Griffith had any relevance now. If Griffith had a grudge that went back to the war, and had planned to set Steward up for some long fall.

"NeoImagery," an amplified voice said. "More than stepped-up evolution. More than a vision of life outside human parameters. More than anything you've ever dreamed."

"What sort of moonlighting have you been up to?" Steward asked.

Griffith looked at him with a nervous smile. "I had a lot of medical bills," he said. "Sheol wasn't good to healthy young bodies."

"You come back with a habit?"

Griffith seemed surprised. He shook his head. "Nothing like that. I breathed in some nerve toxins, some nasty bugs. Liver damage, kidney damage, pancreatitis. A scarred lung. That's what the inhaler's for." He laughed. "A habit. Jesus. I can see where you might get that impression." He puffed tobacco smoke. "No, I play thirdman. It's a small operation, just between friends."

"What sorts of things do you move?"

"Depends." Griffith shrugged. "It's pretty irregular. My friends and I ask around and see what's wanted, what's available. Take a cut. It's all amateur league." He squinted up at the sun and began moving across the park. Steward followed.

"What I have now," he said, "is a package that I've got to deliver to LA. I was going to call someone else to deliver it, but since you're here, I thought I'd throw the job your way if you want it."

"What does this involve?"

"Flying to Los Angeles. Looking up some guy. Giving him the package, collecting the fee. Your cut is two percent, which should come to about two thousand dollars in Starbright scrip. That should help you to get into Starbright, if that's what you want."

Steward laughed. This situation was striking him as more familiar every minute. He could feel Canard reflexes coming back, fitting him like an old jacket. "Two percent is two thousand Starbright?" he asked. "That doesn't strike me as amateur league."

Griffith seemed annoyed. "Give me some credit, man. I *run* this operation, and *my* fee's five percent. There's a lot of competition here. For hell's sake, it's even legal. There's no law against possessing what's in the package, or trading in it. The cops might want to know where you got it, but you'd be within your rights to tell them to fuck off. I'd deliver the damn stuff myself if I weren't tied up here all week."

"Yeah. Okay. I see your point." Steward looked up into the sky, narrowing his eyes against the brightness. A contrail from a suborbital shuttle was scarring the blue, marking a path between fixed orbital stars. "Why are you working as a traveling salesman if you can pick up this kind of money just flying to LA?"

Griffith scowled. "Because of who I'd have to fucking deal with, that's why. If I keep it small, no one's interested in taking over my action. But the big leagues play by different rules. If I did this full-time, I'd have every hotshot juvecrime scumbag in the world after my ass. And, shit, they're faster than I am. These days."

"I want to know what's in the package."

Griffith looked at him sidelong, then nodded. "You have the right. It's Thunder."

Steward shook his head. "I remember reading something about it. But I've been out of touch for a while."

Griffith began to walk across the grass. He flipped cigarette ash onto the deep green. "Okay," he said. "It's a neurohormone developed by Pink Blossom a couple years ago. The trademark name is Genesios Three, and it's also called vitamin B-44. On the streets it's called Thunder, or Black Thunder. It stimulates the nerves to repair damage—it can grow a severed spine together, man. The cripples are skipping in the streets."

"So why's there an underground trade in it?"

"Because it gets you high. A nice buzz. Also raises your IQ by twenty points if you take it long enough. But after that, Thunder begins to repress vasopressin and oxytocin levels in the brain, which suppresses brain function, so you need more of the vitamin to restore it, which suppresses brain function even more, so . . ."

"Negative feedback loop. Addiction."

"Join the great adventure." An amplified voice, from the carnival.

"Yeah," Griffith replied. "What I said. Not physically addicting, not in the classical sense, but bad enough. Anyway, Pink Blossom's being cagey about making the stuff and distributing it. And the stuff's so complicated and expensive to make that the underground hasn't been able to produce it in quantity at a price people can afford. But I have a friend who works on the Orlando shuttle. And he's got a system."

"And you get a packet every so often."

Griffith nodded. "That's the idea. You want the job?"

"It sounds inviting. Who am I supposed to give this to?"

Griffith wiped his forehead with his handkerchief again. "A faceback named Spassky. Little guy, about fifteen. Runs an unaffiliated mob and wears Urban Surgery." He looked at Steward. "You seen those?"

"On vid." The new style, bizarre facial surgery mixed with elaborate, abstract tattooing. A cool style. Deliberately repulsive.

"You can't tell those little pricks apart," Griffith said. "That's why they do it to themselves. It's city camouflage."

"Whatever works."

"Shit. I can't look at it. On Sheol I saw what real mutilation was like."

Steward hesitated for a moment, feeling a wave of coolness moving through his nerves. He looked at the carnival, the flags. The colors and the sky seemed different, as if a cloud had passed across the sun. There was a sense of motion inside himself, a movement like a thrown switch, that suddenly he was on a different side of things, as if he'd crossed a bridge without knowing it.

"I'll carry your package," he said.

Griffith dropped his cigarette, stepped on it. "Good," he said.

"I want something else, Griffith."

The other man didn't look at him. Just stood with his hands in his jeans, watching the glass urban horizon, the mirrors that reflected the scarred sky. He was making Steward say it.

"Sheol. I want Sheol."

A shudder moved through Griffith at Steward's words. As if they hurt him, somehow.

"Yeah," Griffith said. "I knew you'd say that."

Steward's mouth was suddenly dry. He tried to summon saliva, failed, spoke thickly. "What's your answer?"

Griffith was still looking away. "Tomorrow," he said. "When I give you the package."

Relief flooded Steward's limbs. He could feel himself getting closer.

"I need to know," he said. "I'm sorry."

Griffith looked down at the grass beneath his feet. "No you're not," he said.

Steward reached in his shirt pocket for a Xanadu. He wanted this high to last awhile.

"You're right," he said. "I'm not sorry in the least."

Steward was on the roof of Ardala's condeco. It was late at night. Grass-colored carpet, stretched over concrete, scraped against his feet. The open deck was lit by the fluttering blue-and-gold radiance of the swimming pool and by colored spots planted behind metal tubs that held scentless bushes.

Sweat dripped on the carpet. Steward punched forward, repeating the movements over and over, trying to achieve a perfection in his balance, the slick flow of his muscles, the rhythm of heart and breath, his concentration perfect on the invisible target before him, the phantom objective toward which he directed his controlled violence.

He came here often, usually at night, for the long solitary workouts. In the daytime there were too many people, too many distractions, too many disturbed looks. At night there was just the darkness, the nuclear blue glow of the pool, the cold distant hum of the city.

Steward began alternating his punches with kicks. He was full of adrenaline, but he'd been drinking earlier with Ardala and was on the edge of a sugar crash. The result was a strange, disturbing high in which he felt perpetually on the edge of losing control, adrenaline battling insulin for command of his body. The feeling was unsettling but exhilarating, a perpetual fight for possession of his own actions, something like he'd felt when he'd been peddling wetware from his moped and didn't know whether his customer would pay him with a hot credit spike or a knife, when his arms and legs were trembling with the urge to run but he'd just given the boy a smile from behind the comfort of his shades and asked him if he'd had any money down on the jai alai....

Colors began to flicker at the edge of his vision. The sugar crash was coming in like the shock wave off the ablative nose of a commercial shuttle. Steward decided to face it, ride the shock wave to a last attempt at Zen, at perfection. He set himself, balanced forward, leaning toward the target. His knee cocked up, his foot thrust out, his balance going forward as the kick delivered, as one arm punched forward, withdrew as the other arm drove his power through the target, the target that seemed, for a fractional hallucinatory moment, to bleed like a torn artery at the dark edges of the swaying earth, and then the crash moved through him and the glider swung out of control, spiraling down into the darkness of the dream. As it spun, Steward laughed.

He was there. At the center.

CHAPTER FIVE

LA. Night. Steward looked down from the window of his descending aircraft and saw a web of Earthbound stars that marched from the mountains right into the rising ocean, stars that blurred with heat shimmer and promise.

The plane began to buffet as its plastic and alloy skin changed configuration, braking from supersonic to landing-approach speed. Below, Steward could feel Los Angeles reaching up for him with mirrored fingers.

He smiled. At home, though he'd never been here before.

Steward put the package in his pocket. He was to deliver it to Spassky in LA tomorrow evening.

"Beer in the refrigerator," Griffith said. "Make yourself at home."

Lightsource's apartment in Flagstaff was furnished in a utilitarian way, very like a hotel room: bed, sturdy chairs, video, refrigerator, cooking range—just like a hundred other apartments in the same building, most owned by corporations. Steward sat on one of the chairs. He felt scratchy brown fabric against the backs of his arms.

Griffith stubbed out his cigarette and disappeared into the bathroom. Steward watched a silent vodka ad on the vid. The vodka was photographed so that it looked like liquid chrome. Griffith reappeared after running the sink for a while. The Welshman took a Negra Modelo longneck from the kitchenette refrigerator and twisted off the foil top. "Want some?" he asked.

Steward shook his head. He watched as Griffith walked to a cloth-covered chair placed next to the vid. He sat down, sipping at his dark Mexican beer.

Steward took a breath. "Tell me about Sheol," he said.

Griffith looked at him for a long moment. "I don't like to talk about it," he said. "You know that."

"You said you would." Steward felt a kind of pressure on his neck, like a brush of wind from distant exploding stars. "I need to know what it did to—to the Captain. What I became, out there."

Griffith looked away. "I know. I wasn't trying to weasel out. I was just telling you this was going to be hard."

"Okay. Sorry."

Griffith's voice was low. The words came slowly. "I don't think you can know. Even if I tell you. It was just…not a thing you can understand secondhand."

Steward just watched him. On the vid, a small child was choking on a piece of food at a birthday party. Adults moved in silent, screaming panic; other children were crying. Colors from the silent drama bled over Griffith's face. Without looking up, Griffith flung an arm up and snapped off the picture. He looked up. He was pale. "Okay," he said. "I'll tell you what I know."

Steward waited. Saying nothing.

"First thing to realize," Griffith said, "is that the psychological dimension isn't all there is. It's not just a matter of forgetting, or learning to adjust. I got married when I came home. She was a nice lady. Had herself, her life the way she wanted it. Knew where she was going. We tried to have kids, and each time it was a miscarriage…and that turned out to be lucky, because they were all monsters. My genes are all screwed up. From what happened out there. There were biological and chemical weapons that fucked with chromosomes. A lot of the medicines we took with us were experimental Coherent Light Pharmaceuticals, and the manuals that gave the dosages were just guessing. Some didn't work, some had side effects. Some broke chromosomes. Coherent Light didn't care. The Icehawks were an experiment, too, and even if we failed, we'd generate some interesting data."

Griffith put a hand on his chest. "I'm marked, wherever I go, by what happened on Sheol. Not just in my mind, but on the microscopic level, in the little bits of DNA that made me. Poisoned. I could die of some new kind of cancer, and that would be Sheol. Or some kind of chemical I'd breathed in years ago could strip the myelin sheathing from my nerves, and I'd be crippled. That would be Sheol, too. It's happened to other survivors. Like we're all carrying little time bombs inside us." Griffith was sweating. He wiped his brow with the back of his hand. "That's something I can't forget, that I'm carrying those little bombs. And the bombs keep reminding me of everything else." He looked up at Steward. "You're lucky, you know? You don't have that stuff in your body."

"Can't you get a new one?"

"I didn't buy the clone insurance, the way you did. I didn't have family. I just took my hazardous duty bonus and had a big party the week before we took off. And now I can't afford a new body." Griffith looked at him. "You knew that," he said.

Steward pointed a finger at his temple. "Not this memory. These are old recordings."

Griffith breathed out, a harsh sigh. "Yeah. I keep forgetting. That you're so much younger than I am. Even if you were born before me."

Ardala leaned back on pillows. She was wearing a white T-shirt, smoking a Xanadu. *Guys* was open, lying unread on her stomach. "Two thousand Starbright," she said. "Not bad for a day's work."

"Not bad," Steward agreed. He had one of her cram books open in front of him, but he hadn't looked at it in a while.

Ardala drew up a leg, scratched a bare calf. "I assume this is against the law."

"It isn't. I used your comp and checked the library."

"If it isn't illegal, then it's dangerous."

Steward frowned. "Maybe so. Griffith says not."

Ardala handed Steward the Xanadu. He inhaled. "How well do you know Griffith?" she asked.

"At one time, very well."

She sat up, leaned toward him, propping her elbows on her knees. "He's changed a lot. You said so."

"Yes."

"So it's dangerous."

Steward shrugged and handed the cigarette back to Ardala. She looked at it in her hand and ignored it. "What was the company he worked for?"

"Lightsource, Limited."

She shook her head. "I don't know it, but I'll check my files. I should be able to find out something about it."

Steward shrugged again. Ardala's green eyes narrowed. "You act," she said, "as if you don't care whether or not your old friend is going to fuck you over."

"He's giving me something else I want."

She put the cigarette to her lips, inhaled, made a face at the discovery that it had gone out. She dropped it in an ashtray. "He's giving you a chance to get into space, right? Money? Lotta good it'll do if you're dead."

He looked at her. "Sheol," he said.

The word seemed to hang in the air for a long moment, like honey dropping from a spoon. Ardala shook her head and fell back to the pillows. "It's like you want to give Sheol a second chance to kill you. As if it wasn't bad enough the first time."

He reached out, put a hand on her knee. "I can't do anything about whether the job's dangerous or not. All I can do is be ready. I'm ready."

She turned her head away. He could see her throat working. "Dead man," she said. "A fucking dead man."

Steward took his hand back, gazed down at the book. "I'll be back in a day or so," he said.

Ardala was still looking away. "So you say."

"At the beginning it was easy. Sheol was pioneered by Far Ranger, but Coherent Light got the Icehawks into the Wolf 294 system before anyone else. Mobilized, declared hostilities Outward, and went. Only the male Icehawks were sent Outward; the women's battalions were kept in-system to guard against sabotage and maybe try some themselves. The women weren't happy about it—what were they trained for, anyway?—and a lot of the men were pissed off because they got separated from their girlfriends.

"Far Ranger only had a few pioneers down in the northern hemisphere, and a small base on the big moon. We captured all their personnel and got all their artifacts and data. Fortified the moon base, put some ships in orbit, put our people down. We had the Icehawks plus two brigades of corporation grunts that had been recruited and shipped up from Earth at the last minute. Plus support personnel and a couple hundred archaeologists, xenobiologists, scientist types."

Griffith let his head fall forward. He passed his forearm across his eyes, wiping away invisible sweat. His voice changed, lost in a grating reverie. "Sheol was...lovely," he said. "It was summer in the northern hemisphere when we landed. The planet had been tamed by the Powers over thousands of years...they'd arranged it like a garden, landscaped the mountains and rivers. It had overgrown and changed, but the intent was still there. The...harmony of the way they'd set things."

He raised his head. "The Powers—they're not like us." Griffith's watery eyes seemed to shine. "They're older," he said. "Better. They...they know how to live with each other. What we found on Sheol and its moon reflected that. They built well, but after all the years they'd been away, there wasn't much intact above ground. But they live in tunnels as well as on the surface, and there was a regular underworld there, hundreds of thousands of tunnels and rooms, some wrecked or collapsed but most intact, filled with stuff that had been packed carefully for storage... and there were tunnels on the moon as well, still pressurized with air we could breathe. The Powers knew they were coming back, even if we hadn't twigged to that. It was...beautiful. A wonderland." He shook his head. "And we fought our filthy little war in there. In all that magnificence, amid all the beauty...."

Steward sat quietly in his plump chair, feeling the scratchy fabric against his forearms. There was a tingle in his limbs, a lightness, as if he'd just warmed and stretched and was ready to move, waiting for the signal that would take him into whatever was waiting.... It felt right. He tried to picture in his mind the waiting planet, green and blue against the black and patterned stars, the surprised Far Ranger personnel, the waiting tunnels where the Icehawks, taller than the Powers, would have had to crouch as they moved....

Griffith was fumbling for a cigarette. "I remember that at the beginning, you—the Captain—said we were dispersing too much, trying to hold too much ground. There were just stacks of artifacts everywhere we looked—there was no point in dispersal, he said. We could concentrate and still have more loot than we'd know what to do with. But Colonel de Prey said he didn't have any choice. That the plans were based on maps of Sheol that our agents had got out of Far Ranger, they'd been set in advance, back in the Sol system. And then the Colonel left, returned to headquarters with the data we'd captured. He said he'd be back, with reinforcements, once he made his report. He left Major Singh in charge." Griffith shook his head. "The Captain was right. When the next wave came, it was from Far Ranger, and they hurt us bad."

As Griffith spoke of what happened next, Steward tried to picture the Far Ranger ships leaping across the blackness, the sudden blossoms of light in the sky that marked the battle in space where the Coherent Light ships were blown apart. The atmosphere cutters coming down, swooping on the Coherent Light positions out of a sky cut by the trails of defensive rockets, rising slow-motion tracer, straight-line bolts of lightning that were particle beams... the arc of the bombs and rockets as they fell, the way the flames leapt boiling from the perfect green landscape. Troopships landing, disgorging soldiers in Far Ranger colors. Fire snapping from ruins, from tunnels. Soldiers groping for one another amid the dense green. Urgent cries on microwave channels.

And then a repeat as the whole thing happened all over again—first the silent flares in the sky, then the shriek of the cutters, these from Policorp Derrotero, which had come to seize their share of Sheol. More flares in the sky as Derrotero and Far Ranger ships, united in a brief alliance, drove off an assault from Gorky. Then treachery on the part of Far Ranger, a preemptive strike on Derrotero once Policorp Gorky was driven off, a strike that weakened Derrotero but didn't knock them out. A counterstrike, and Derrotero ships held the sky. The Coherent Light troops, barely holding on, went on the offensive, in an alliance Singh had arranged with Derrotero against Far Ranger. Then a new flood of invaders, Policorps Magnus and OutVentures in alliance, blasting away the Derrotero presence from the system, landing fresh, well-trained troops in vast numbers.

A flare on the face of the largest moon. "We'd put a tactical atomic under the moon base, just in case we lost it. De Lopez was hidden in one of the moon tunnels with the detonator. Killed a lot of people that way. Took out ships that were in for maintenance." Griffith swallowed. "Maybe that wasn't good, to be the first to use atomics. Maybe that meant they weren't inclined to be civilized with us anymore."

Then, the winter.

Griffith was drinking his second beer. "The grunts died like flies. They were tough and smart, but they hadn't trained together long enough, didn't know how to work with each other, and their bad deployment at the start just made them targets, isolated them so their units couldn't support one another. Only the Icehawks stood a chance against the numbers, the weapons they were using. We had the training, the morale. The capability. We could fight a sustained guerrilla war with a limited base, but once the grunts lost their cushy foam bunkers, their fuel-cell heaters and vid sets, they just fell apart." He shook his head. "Christ. They had no winter training at all." The parchment skin of his face was pale. His eyes were black and empty, staring blindly into the landscape of his memories. Smoke drifted up from the cigarette in his hand, but he'd forgotten it was there.

"Winter is bad, there on Sheol. That's why the Powers built so many tunnels—to hide in the wintertime. It's a flat planet, mostly, with a lot of ocean…. The winds just build up to hurricane velocity, pushed by Coriolis force and Christ knows what, and there's nothing to stop them. They just come howling out of the prairie like perdition on a picnic. Storms could go on for days, weeks sometimes. The Far Ranger people, the first pioneers—they had landed in the winter. They knew what they were talking about when they called the place Sheol." Cigarette ash fell on his trousers. He looked down in an abstracted way, brushed it off. Stubbed the cigarette out with a savage gesture.

"We were getting messages from home every now and then. A ship coming in-system, firing off messages, then running. Sometimes a supply ship would get in past the blockade. But eventually they stopped trying to supply us. We didn't know that CL was devoting all its energies to supporting Far Jewel's fight in another system. That two battalions of women Icehawks and a new wave of grunts had been sent out there, instead of to help us. We had to live off what we captured, that or what we found in the tunnels. Or could grow ourselves in the vats.

"We were still hitting them, though. From the tunnels. Flying in on isolated posts under cover of the storms. Sometimes we'd attack just to steal their food. We'd have to kill any that surrendered. We had no place to put them, no food to give them. If enemy reinforcements came after us, we'd hide in the tunnels."

Griffith was shaking now. His hands were trembling, the beer splashing up the sides of the bottle. "They couldn't get us out of our holes. It would cost too much to dig us out. That's when they started using gas on us. Extermination drones. And biologicals." Tears were running down Griffith's face. He swallowed hard. "That's when things broke down. That's when we all knew… we'd been sacrificed. That Coherent Light wouldn't be coming back for us."

The warm night seemed full of sound and light. Todo music throbbed from the small shops crowding the wide alloy street that mirrored the bodies of those who walked on it, the crystal windows and bright holograph displays that soared soundlessly above the walkways. Steward wore a charcoal-colored jacket over a black T-shirt that featured a liquid-crystal display on the front, one that ran the text of Jack Totem's poem "551" in three-inch rainbow letters across Steward's chest….

"Our tongues are electrons, tasting the silicon heart of America." Magic. An incantation. Invoking the local demons, calling them to Steward's aid.

He was spiraling inward to the meet, trying to get a feel for this town, for the connections that existed here and for the rhythm of its life. He couldn't match any of the locals for knowledge, but maybe he could taste a little of this city's silicon heart, enough to give him a purchase on the way things worked here. He walked on tennis shoes with red balls on the sides, shoes he'd been unable to resist buying in his last hour in Arizona. A reminder of where he'd been, why he was here.

He felt the weight of the package in his pocket and wondered whether or not to carry it to the meet. Griffith said it was safe. Not to appear trusting might cost Griffith something with the people he worked with.

He moved down the bright reflective street, weighing things in his mind.

Griffith was lying on his bed. Smoking, staring at the ceiling. Breathing easier now. The trembling fit had passed. "A message came through. From Colonel de Prey. He ordered Singh into an alliance with Far Ranger and Gorky against Magnus and OutVentures. Ordered us to take the offensive. They didn't even know, back home, that Gorky had never landed.

"We were living behind biologic seals, down in the tunnels. The food vats had been poisoned. Whenever we went out, we had to wear our environment suits, live in them every minute. People were getting sick, wasting away. There were only a thousand of the grunts left, and they'd lost all their heavy equipment…. They were just guerrillas now, like the Icehawks, only not as well trained. Far Ranger was worse off than we were. Singh decided to obey his instructions. You— the Captain—you argued against it. Told him that Coherent Light was months out of touch, couldn't possibly know the situation. But Singh trusted the Colonel, said that CL must have based their decision on factors we didn't know, that there was probably help on the way, or alliances that we didn't know that would work for us."

He turned toward Steward. Steward saw the recognition in his eyes, sensed that he wasn't talking to himself anymore, or to Steward, but to a dead man. To the Captain.

"I heard you and Singh shouting at each other. But I saw you after the meeting, and you were calm. I remember you quoted Corman at me. Our old martial-arts teacher. Remember when Corman was talking Zen? She said that the world, that reality, was like a whirlwind. That the Zen warrior did not fight the whirlwind, that she gave the whirlwind nothing to strive against, that the whirlwind passed through her and left her unaffected, unmoved."

You, Steward thought. He called me "you," talking about the Captain. I'm enough like him, then. A feeling, cold and then hot, passed through his bones.

"You were a little sick, like we all were. Feverish. Either the enemy's biological weapons, or our own preventive vaccines, always had us sick. You'd lost weight, you hadn't slept in days, kept going with speed. You looked like a fucking phantom, man. We all did. And what you said was, that it wasn't enough to be unmoved, to let the whirlwind pass. You said that the only way we'd survive was to *become* the whirlwind."

It seemed to Steward that he could see right into Griffith's head, that his eyes were black holes leading into an emptiness, a place where invisible snow beat against the confines of his skull and the voice of the whirlwind shrieked in his ears.

"I've been through combat," Griffith said. "I've been shot at and gassed and lost in a snowstorm. But I've never been as scared as I was when I heard you say that. Because I knew you were the only one who understood what kind of war we were in. And that you accepted it, and that you could still act. You were crazy, I think, out of your mind on combat and speed. But I knew that if I wanted to get out of this, I'd follow you. I wasn't alone. People were trying to get out of other units, to join the Captain. Trying to find reasons to be with him. People were starting to figure that if anyone was gonna live, it would be him." His voice dropped, and he spoke with calm authority.

"*You* were the whirlwind, Captain," he said. "The rest of us just followed along. But you were the whirlwind. You were Sheol."

No cabs. Steward noticed that right away. Lots of private cars and cycles, but no cabs.

There were a lot of little neighborhoods here, condecologies on a small scale. Self-contained, easily defined. The buildings were old, sometimes centuries old. On the ground floor only, the facades were recent—clubs, shops, boutiques, all striving for something new.

Turf, Steward thought. Where the kids who ran the real LA did their business. There weren't many people over twenty-five here. Not at night.

Most of the little neighborhoods were full of people in brocade and paint, butterfly-wing eye makeup, hair done in extravagant little braids, with jewelry implanted in their wrists, cheeks, the backs of their hands. Their music was loud, insistent, full of revolution and defiant joy. But another style was creeping in. Cooler, quieter. The music was based on complicated rhythms mixed in complex ways, the stance ambiguous, calculated.

Steward saw his first Urban Surgery here. Metal tooth implants of sharpened alloy, ears removed and replaced with flat black boxes, audio scanners. Sunglasses with crystal videos on the reverse sides, so that their wearers could see everything as if it were on vid, or, if reality wasn't interesting enough, could switch to a video program. Eyes replaced, not with natural-seeming implants but with obvious ones: metal scanners, clear plastic eyes that you could see through, liquid-crystal eye whites that created shimmering, abstract patterns shifting like quicksilver in the eye sockets. Flattening the nose seemed popular, an alteration that made the entire face a canvas for the tattoo artist. Entire heads were covered with monochrome circuit diagrams, mathematical statements, urban skyscapes.

Steward felt his nerves tingle. Something in him wanted to get out of this. He resisted the impulse to speed up. These people were unsettling.

A short-lived phenomenon, Steward decided. This extravagant style of self-mutilation wouldn't appeal to enough people to last. But while it lasted it was going to be powerful.

He felt again the weight of the Thunder in his pocket and came to a decision. He wasn't going to go into a club full of these people with anything worth a hundred K of Starbright scrip. He began looking for an all-night safety deposit company.

They were all over the place. It looked as if there was a lot of business for them.

Griffith's eyes were closed. He lay like a dead man on his bed, his arms and legs splayed. His voice was soft now. Steward had to strain to hear it.

"Our offensive collapsed in two days," Griffith said. "Far Ranger was worse off than we were and couldn't give us proper support. The counterattack creamed us. We lost almost two thousand people. The last of our heavy weapons. The Captain's command was the only one that survived more or less intact. He disobeyed orders to do it. We hit our preliminary objectives, then took off in captured aircraft before the counterattack developed. We stole some biologic weapons and rode into one of their command centers using some false codes we'd captured, dumped the germs into every ventilator we could find, then flew off again. Hit-and-run stuff. It was all we could do, really. It was weeks before we got back to where Singh had set up his command center. Sometimes I wonder if the Captain ever intended to go back, because Singh had kept the offensive going as long as he could, and the Captain just wasn't following orders. Maybe Singh was hoping Gorky would come back and help us.

"But new instructions came in from Colonel de Prey. Coherent Light had concluded that Magnus was ready to stab OutVentures in the back. We were ordered to join Derrotero and Magnus in a new offensive. Even with our united commands we had only about eight hundred men left. The Captain had fifty who'd been with him. The grunts, support people, and scientists had either joined us or died. The winter was supposed to be coming to an end, but there wasn't any sign of it."

Griffith shook his head. "There was another face-off with Singh. He wouldn't give in. He had faith, he said. CL knew what they were doing. This time the Captain wouldn't give in, either. He assumed command. Just took over. Major Singh didn't have anyone left who'd follow him."

"Just like that," Steward said. His own voice sounded loud in the still apartment. Inappropriate. He thought about Singh. Intelligent. Hard. Not an easy man to know, but a fighter. Tenacious. Steward couldn't picture Singh giving up that way.

"No, not just like that." Griffith's eyes opened. He was staring at the ceiling. Steward couldn't read his expression.

"I was there," Griffith said. "I was right behind the Captain when he took out his pistol and shot Major Singh in the head. Then I held my gun on the staff while they were disarmed and then split up and sent to other units. I didn't—I didn't see any other way. The whirlwind had us by then, and Singh was trying to stand against it. He didn't understand that everything had changed. That was when the Captain gave himself a promotion. After that, he was the only officer we had. The only one we needed. He got us through."

"NeoImagery," said a recorded voice. "More than a philosophy. More than a way of life."

A NeoImagist street carnival burbled in one of the streets. Sullen girls in brocade handed out literature. They belonged to an affiliated gang, Steward assumed. Displays, live and on holo, showed orbital second-stage habitats, smiling people, sleek zero-g humans modified for space, models of the DNA helix that you could alter yourself to new configurations.

The Pink Blossom logo rotated over the street. Major contributors to the cause.

"We are reconstructing the human race," the voice said. It was female, friendly but authoritative. A software construct, designed to attract attention and inspire trust.

Darwin Days. Steward thought about people on top of glass towers hurling windows into the void, unconscious agents of evolution. Reconstructing the human race in their own irreverent fashion—*that* was as close to messing with the gene pool as Steward ever wanted to get.

"The Captain knew that Magnus was going to hit Outward Ventures pretty soon, allied with Derrotero. So he let Magnus know he was joining them, and as he made plans with Magnus, he established covert relations with OutVentures and let them know exactly what Magnus was up to. Magnus noticed OV making their preparations and accelerated their own schedule. Then we just stood back while they preempted each other. They blew each other apart while we hid in the tunnels. We weren't a part of it. We were on the move all the time, nibbling at the enemy, stealing their equipment so we could live. When they'd come after us in the tunnels, we'd ambush them, then come up again somewhere else. The Captain called it eating the dead."

There was a hologram running over the counter, OUR BUSINESS IS RUN ON TRUST, it said. WE TRUST YOU WILL PAY IN ADVANCE.

There was an advanced scanner in the doorframe that would detect any weapons that weren't actually implanted in the body and precision lasers hanging from the ceiling.

The sign on the outside said LOANS, SPORTING GOODS. The interior said pawn shop.

Trust, Steward thought. Right.

A thin woman with bad skin, about thirty, stood behind the counter, her arms folded across her chest.

"Monowire," Steward said, pointing. "The Officier Suisse."

She looked up at his French pronunciation, then reached behind the counter and took out the weapon. It was about the size and shape of a switchblade knife. "Hold on a second," she said. "Gotta hit the deadman. Stay inside the tape."

"D'accord," he said.

She stepped behind a clear plastic shield and pressed a button on the floor with her foot. If the pressure was removed, the house lasers would cut him up in a fraction of a second.

Steward made certain he was inside a ten-foot square marked with duct tape on the floor, then pressed the On button on the end of the wire, then pressed the thumb toggle. The stabilized monofilament line, with a little lead weight on the end, extruded from the handle to about two and a half feet. Steward whipped the sword through the air.

It made no sound at all.

Steward rocked the thumb toggle back, and the monofilament lost its rigidity, hanging from the handle by its weight.

"I don't take any responsibility for what happens next, jack," the woman said. "You cut off your own head, it's nothing to do with me."

Steward began to move the whip, gently at first until he got his reflexes back. Icehawk reflexes. He'd never had the nerve to try these when he was a Canard. The possibility of damaging himself with the unpredictable weapon was too high.

He began to move faster, whirling the line through long arcs, changing from whip to sword to whip again. The woman watched, expressionless.

He turned off the monowire and put it back on the counter. He stepped away. The woman disarmed the deadman.

"How's it go through detectors?" Steward asked.

The woman shrugged. "Depends on the detector. Don't try wearing it through *my* door."

Steward glanced at the lasers above his head. "Okay," he said. He put a credit spike on the countertop next to the monowhip, then stepped off to look at something beneath the glass top of one of the other counters. Nautical flares, the kind that burned even underwater. "I'll take the flares, too," he said. He'd been thinking of making a trip to the oceanfront for just this item.

In a boutique next door he bought a tote bag to carry them in. It was made in Malaysia of white linen, with an abstract black pattern on one side and the words FINE WHITE APPRECIATION SET OF WHEELS on the other. The first three words were in black, the others in red. Steward had no idea what it meant.

He hitched the tote bag over his shoulder. His T-shirt talked to the metal streets.

He began to spiral inward, toward the club that was his destination. Picking up vibrations, the Zen of the city, as he went.

"Gorky came back, allied with Far Ranger. It was their last shot. Their landing force got beat off, so they just took the moon and held it. Captured asteroids with their mass drivers and started dropping them on the planet, wherever they saw life. Magnus and OutVentures tried to throw atomics back at them, and some got through. There was no real spring on the planet. Too much shit in the atmosphere. All we had was a kind of half-winter, sleet storms instead of ice storms. With dead people in tunnels, piled in the drifts."

Steward put the tote bag in the slot outside the club entrance. The machine accepted the bag and gave him a chit, a piece of paper with magnetic code written on it. He put the chit in his pocket and walked in.

He'd concluded that it would be embarrassing to walk into the club and have every alarm in the place go off. It was the sort of thing guaranteed to start him off at a disadvantage. He decided to check the monowhip at the door instead.

The holo outside said CLUB BAG in letters that looked like molten bronze, and he could see through the open doorway that the interior featured concrete floors and walls of sprayfoam, both painted black. Tables were clear plastic on chrome stands that doubled as computer terminals. About half the people inside wore Urban Surgery or at least made a bow in that direction.

People at tables looked at him as he walked through the doors. Tattoos, drinks in strange colors, heads nodding to music. Steward looked back at the crowd for a moment and then walked to the bar. The bartender was a middle-aged man with a massive chest, vast arms, and the hoarse voice of an old prizefighter. "Star beast," Steward told him.

Trebles shrilled off the walls. The bass was lost somewhere in the void. People were dancing to recorded music in front of an empty stage. None of them looked very interested.

The night was young. Things really hadn't started yet.

"I wonder why we never surrendered. It would have made so much sense." Griffith rubbed his mustache. "Because our loyalties were so strong, I guess. The Icehawks had esprit. We couldn't disappoint each other by surrendering. And after a while, there was no one to surrender to. We were all living in the tunnels like savages. Fighting over food. We couldn't accept surrender because there was no food for the prisoners, and we couldn't surrender because we'd be killed for the same reason. So we'd kill everyone, there being no choice. A lot of them were just corporation grunts, cannon fodder. Little girls from Korea, street kids from Rio. Just there to get swept away." He shook his head. "We would have eaten one another, eventually."

Steward sipped his beast and watched the crowd. More people had come in. The level of conversation had risen, sometimes drowning out the music.

He thought he knew which one was Spassky—a small, active kid dressed in blue jeans, half boots, a bright yellow short-sleeved jacket with lots of zips and straps. His hair was done in black cornrows that turned into jagged vertical tattoos that marched down his face. He had pointed metal teeth, sharpened and staggered to fit into sockets in the gums so that he wouldn't bite himself every time he closed his mouth. He wore glasses with video screens set into the backs.

There were a girl and two boys at the same table. The girl hung onto the small boy's arm, ignoring the fact that he paid her no attention. Her forehead was tattooed and there was a bandage across the middle of her face. Steward figured she'd just had her nose altered.

The boys were big, six and a half feet tall at least. Heavy boots. Shaved heads with tattoos. One was fat, one was thin. The fat one wore video shades, the thin one had transparent eye implants that let you see the circuitry inside. Steward wondered if they had combat thread woven into their brains and concluded that they probably did.

Steward could see their heads turn slightly every time the door scanners flashed the green light for someone to come in. They never looked at the door directly. It would have made them seem anxious. But they were clearly waiting for something.

The music stopped abruptly. The people who were dancing stopped, hesitated, and returned to their chairs, looking lost.

A pale boy, about fifteen, walked onto the stage. He had a spotty, sunken chest and wasn't wearing any clothes. He carried a pouch in one hand. There was scattered applause. A microphone lowered itself from the ceiling. Colored floods turned the boy's skin pastel green. He shouted into the mic, "The deathworm coils in their hearts!" His voice broke on the last word. The boy took a six-inch alloy needle from his pouch. Holding the needle in his right hand, he put it through the middle of his left palm. Blood gleamed on the alloy. The applause became general.

Steward felt the tang of metal in his mouth. This was interesting.

"In the hearts of the dog pack that eases through the tear-streaked streets," the boy said. He bent and picked up another needle. His skin was pastel pink.

There were cheers. Steward watched carefully to see how it was done. It was possible, with the pastel lights, that there was a trick here. The boy put the needle through the loose skin under his arm, chanting his poetry. More needles went in. Steward decided it was real. After that he lost interest.

Instead of being a technician with an interesting trick, the boy had become another fool who couldn't think of a way to be famous other than to hurt himself in public.

Darwin Days, he thought. Natural selection, right here on stage.

Steward ordered another star beast and waited for the bartender to bring it. He pointed at the table with the people who looked like they were waiting for someone. "Is that Spassky?" he asked.

The bartender gave him a wary look. "That depends on who you are," he said.

Steward took his drink. "Thanks," he said, and walked to Spassky's table. Video shades turned toward him.

"I'm from Griffith."

"Sit down." Spassky's voice was alto, so young that Steward was surprised. He chided himself. The reflexes hadn't come back yet. When he was a Canard, when he was Spassky's age, this was the sort of thing he dealt with every day.

Steward gazed at the boy as he sat down. He saw that the glasses had two tiny cameras set above the nose bridge, and mind-interface pickups in the bows so that Spassky could change channels by thinking about it, without having to go through the bother of pressing buttons. Mind and video grown together.

Steward tasted his beast. Fire touched his palate, made him wary.

On the stage, the boy was bending over to put a needle through his foot. His fingers were growing slippery with blood and he was having a hard time. His head was down, away from the mic, and his voice had faded away, but he was still talking.

The girl on Spassky's arm was watching the show with interest. Steward saw bruises around her eyes, revenants of recent surgery.

He looked at Spassky. "You have my Starbright?"

Spassky nodded. He moved his chair back. "Let's go to my place. I have it there."

Steward shook his head. "We do this in a public place. That's the agreement."

Spassky gazed at him in an odd way, as if he was dialing new settings on his spectacles, looking at Steward in as many ways as possible.

"I don't have the money on me."

"Maybe I don't have the package, either," Steward said.

The boy on stage was beginning to breathe hard. The pain grew raw in his voice.

"You and Griffith," said Spassky, "are both too old to be in this business."

"Do you have the money or don't you?" Steward asked.

"Come to my place and I'll give it to you."

"Fuck you," Steward said. He pushed his chair back. So did the two big boys. Steward stood up, gazed into their flat tattooed faces.

Spassky was still looking at him in his strange way, as if Steward were a vid show he didn't quite understand.

"It's my city, buck," he said.

Steward turned and walked away. Lightning danced through his nerves. A surge of adrenaline hit him, and his hand trembled as he reached for his chit, walked through the detectors, and then put it in the machine.

No cabs in this town. No time to call one. He looked behind, through the open door.

The fat boy and the skinny boy were following, taking their time. It was their town after all. He could see chits in their hands, ready to reclaim whatever was being held at the door.

Behind them the pastel blue boy was sobbing onstage as he tried to put a needle through his foreskin.

The machine coughed up Steward's tote. He took it and ran.

Griffith was pale. He seemed drained of blood, emotion, feeling. "The Powers came then, and it was all over. A whole lot of them on the move. Hundreds of ships, big ones. The Gorky ships in-system didn't dare to try anything against them, just pulled out and ran. Left us on the ground." His hands were trembling again. He reached for a tissue, blew his nose, then stood up and walked into the bathroom. Steward heard water running. When Griffith came back, he seemed better; his color was back. He sat in the chair by the silent video and took a few long breaths.

"That was when the Captain and the Icehawks had their showdown. The Captain didn't want to come in, didn't want to admit it was over. We told him this was the end, that we weren't going to fight against a whole alien species. He was like a crazy man, fighting to keep the war going. He had become the whirlwind and he didn't want the whirlwind to stop. I thought it would be Major Singh all over again, that we'd fight it out then and there. But then I figured out how to bring him over, to make him see reason. I told him that if we went on fighting, he'd never see Natalie again." Griffith took a breath, let it out slowly. "That brought him over," he said.

Griffith hung his head. "He put down his pistol and walked away, back into his little command center. I could see he was crying. A few minutes later he came back out, told us to destroy our codes and break our weapons. We took our transport to where the Powers were waiting." He gave a short laugh. "De Lopez was there. The guy with the atom bomb on the moon. He'd just sat in his tunnel for months and listened to the war on the radio. He was fat, healthy, laughing.... He looked at us like we were some other species.

"I don't know why the Powers didn't just wipe us out like a bunch of bugs, especially after what we'd done to their planet. The place was a mess—cratered, looted, poisoned. But they took care of us. Fed us some of their own food, distributed whatever Earth medicines and clothing were left. They even asked us how to dispose of the dead. It was important to them to do it right. I was scared of them at first. The way they look, the way they move, the sounds they make—it's like discordant organ music. We didn't really have a way of communicating yet. But I realized, eventually, that they were better than we were. By the end of the first month, I didn't want to be anywhere else. A lot of us had that reaction.

"When we came back, there wasn't any Coherent Light. The people responsible for its policy were in prison. No one had responsibility for us, no company hospitals, no benefits. We were on the streets. And we found out how we'd been sold.

"CL didn't plan to win. The Icehawks were like a bargaining chip that CL was using to get leverage out of other companies. Coherent Light decided Far Jewel had the best chance of winning control over one of the other systems, so they put all their logistical effort into supporting Far Jewel's efforts in return for a share of the loot. All the attacks we were ordered to make—they were designed to tie up Far Jewel's enemies in the Sheol system, so they couldn't fight Far Jewel elsewhere. When I found that out—well, I'd just had it with humanity. When we came back to Earth, I went to work for the Powers, like a lot of the others. I was rated a translator, but I didn't really have the skills for it. Then the Powers moved offplanet, and I was out of work. In a way, losing the Powers was worse than Sheol. I don't know how to explain it. I was sick in bed for a week. Literally sick."

Down a side street, through an alley. Heading for someone else's turf, but zigzagging, trying to keep out of their line of sight. Steward reached into his tote, pulled out the monowire, and jammed it into a jacket pocket. He turned off the crystal display on his shirt by way of changing his profile. He looked behind him.

The big boys were moving faster now, eating up the street with their long stride and heavy boots. They hadn't missed his evasions, which argued for good scanners in their eyewear. They'd stopped to put chits into the weapons detector at the club entrance, and Steward didn't want to know what they'd come out with. Maybe even guns.

Steward was riding the adrenaline boost now, the first shock over. Moving easy. A liquid feel in his limbs. Ready for Zen.

Another alley. This one was of old concrete, T-shaped, with a turn at right angles. There were no lights at all. Steward began to run, putting distance between himself and his pursuers before they turned the corner. The warm summer air burned his throat as he ran. He neared the T-intersection, skidded, and ducked behind a dumpster. A damp brick wall slammed against his back, jarred breath from his lungs. He put the monowhip next to him on the concrete, then reached into his tote for the nautical flares. Their surface was cool against his palms. He held one in each hand and waited.

Heavy footsteps, coming fast, then slowing. Good eyewear, then. They'd seen body heat and warm breath radiating from behind the dumpster and knew to expect him. He gathered his legs under him, ready to spring. The cautious footsteps were coming closer. Ten meters? Eight? Five?

Steward felt sweat gathering at his nape.

He scratched the fuzes against the old concrete, saw them strike, and tossed them into the alleyway, toward his pursuers, just as the fire and smoke began to boil out. He heard a pair of cries as IR scanners were overloaded by sudden thermite heat.

Steward clawed for the monowhip and sprang. Orange smoke gushed into the alley. The big boys were moving fast, already striking out blindly, knowing he was there. One of them had a neural sword; the other, some kind of short hand weapon. Reflexes hardwired in, a union of implant thread and boosted nerve, speed Steward couldn't match.

He struck for the face of the nearest, wrapped the wire around his head, pulled. There was a shriek, blood spurting into the smoke. The other had disappeared into the billowing orange haze. The neural sword hummed near his head and he ducked. He lashed out with the whip again, felt it wrap around something, hit the toggle. The line should have straightened into a sword, cutting right through whatever it was wrapped around, but there was resistance. Maybe the line had gone around a pipe, something too strong to cut through.

Cries were echoing from the brick walls. Tears filled Steward's eyes. He toggled again, but the wire was yanked from his hand, and he fell backward in pure reflex as the neurosword swung through the place where he'd been. Steward kept moving backward, found a wall with his hand, followed it to a turning, ducked around it. He was out of the smoke and he could breathe. He drew in the hot summer air, jogged slowly so he wouldn't trip over something, and wiped his streaming eyes. There wasn't enough air in all of Los Angeles to fill his aching lungs. Screams pursued him as he ran.

He reached into the tote and dropped another lit flare behind him. He was beginning to see again. Brightness flickered at him from the end of the alley.

Steward burst into the street. Lights dazzled his eyes. The Pink Blossom logo reeled overhead.

Darwin Days, he thought. Whirlwind days.

There was a cab right in front of him. It was the only one he'd seen in the entire town. He dove for the door, shouted the address of his hotel.

Behind him, the skinny boy came out of the alley. The monowire was still wrapped around the armored sleeve of his jacket. He wiped his nose on the back of his hand, stared at the bright lights of the carnival.

The taxi was already out of range.

"I never saw the Captain again. He had Natalie to go back to, and I didn't have anything like that. Eventually I got a job, got married, tried to have those kids. Having broken chromosomes bothered me a lot more than it did my wife. She just kind of shrugged and said, okay, no kids. But I wanted to start something new, something that wasn't poisoned. I kept falling apart, my wife kept putting me back together. Eventually she quit trying. I can't blame her. She gave me much more than I ever gave her."

Griffith fell silent. He had his arms folded over his eyes. Steward rose slowly from his chair, feeling blood pouring into his awakening limbs. His head spun, then righted. "Thank you," he said.

"If it was anyone but you, Captain," Griffith said, "I would've told 'em to fuck off. But…I owed you, I guess." His voice was drained of color, of emotion. He shook his head, blindly. "What time is it?" he asked.

"Two o'clock."

"Shit. I had a sales meeting at one-thirty." He sat upright, reached for the phone.

"Sorry."

"My own fucking fault. Goddammit."

Steward, feeling the package against his ribs, let himself out while Griffith was on the phone, walked to Ardala's condeco, let himself in. He wanted to be alone for a while.

He sat cross-legged on the bed and thought about Sheol, the wind whipping across the long prairies, scattering snow across the entrances to the old, narrow tunnels…people moving across the white in reflective camo suits that chilled their exteriors to outside temperatures so as to fool infrared detectors, walking hunched over and carrying weapons, their faces masked against gas and bacteria…a storm rising far away on the flat horizon, conjuring a wall of white, advancing like a cloud. The whirlwind that Sheol had summoned, that Steward had become.

Steward took a breath and wondered if he could summon the wind here, ride it outside the gravity well to the source of himself, to the origin of the voice he'd heard on the blurred video, the grating phantom voice that was his own, his Alpha. Who had gone through his own process of becoming, of finding the heart of himself on the skin of the frozen prairies and in the cold tunnels that led into Sheol's secret womb, in these places and in the howling Coriolis madness that had become his mind.

CHAPTER SIX

It was dark in the hotel room save for the soundless rain of color from the vid. Steward lay on his bed, staring at the ceiling, his hair and body still damp from the shower. A wisp of smoke from his Xanadu twisted into his field of vision, gaining tint, faint green and faint flesh, from the wall video. Steward was coming down now, feeling the adrenaline draining from him, pouring away like rain down a gutter.

The telephone receiver adhered warmly to his mastoid, plastered over his short wet hair. The receiver signal went straight to the audio centers of his brain, bypassing the imperfect human ear. Griffith's voice echoed in his head in perfect audio clarity. "Jesus, man. Spassky did *that?*"

"I fucked somebody up bad, Griffith. That monowire might have taken his head right off."

"Jesus." Steward heard, very loud in his skull, Griffith's hacking smoker's cough. He winced. The cough went on and on. Then Steward heard the hiss of Griffith's inhaler. When the man's voice returned, his tone had changed. It was faster. Hyped. Angry.

"That fucking fastbuck punk. I've still got friends. He'll regret the fucking day."

"It seems to me you don't quite know who your friends are," Steward said. Tinted smoke curled in his vision. "It seemed to me that Spassky had perfect confidence in his ability to take me off and retain your friendship. If your friendship meant anything to him."

There was a moment of silence. "Look. You're okay, right?"

"No damage." The Xanadu marijuana tendrils were creeping through his muscles, replacing the fading adrenaline, turning the ebbing high into a buzz of another kind.

"And you've still got the Thunder."

"I put it in a deposit box before I went to the meet. I didn't like the neighborhood."

"Look. Don't even bother to get the stuff. It'll be safe where it is."

"That suits me."

"I'll give you your fee. Then you give me the key, and I'll have someone else pick it up."

"Sure," Steward said. "Let's just do it in a public place, okay?"

"Shit, buck. Whatever you say. I'm sorry this thing happened."

The Xanadu was relaxing the muscles in the back of Steward's neck. He pushed his head back into his pillow, making an arch of his neck. Vertebrae crackled, the sound more intimate even than Griffith's hoarse voice. He relaxed, felt his body awareness dissolving, sleep creeping closer.

"I'll call you tomorrow," Steward said.

"Yeah. Listen. I had no idea that little punk was gonna—"

"Tomorrow," Steward said. His hand went to the phone and broke the connection, then reached for the receiver on his mastoid. The adhesive tried to take some of his hair along with it, and he peeled it away carefully.

He took the Xanadu from his mouth and dropped it into the hotel ashtray. Video colors prowled along the ceiling.

Steward shut his eyes. Lights moved on the roof of his closed lids, video of his own devising. He willed the lights to coalesce, become a mirror image of himself, lying on a bed, spread-eagled, eyes closed. At the center, in the air.

Griffith looked as if he had the flu. His eyes were red, his nose was running. He was shaking. Every time he tried to puff on his cigarette he began to cough uncontrollably. He hadn't even bothered to order breakfast, just coffee. The surly waitress looked as if she wanted to tear the bones from his back.

"Here." Griffith pushed a credit spike across the table. "Two thousand Starbright, plus five hundred. Call it hazardous duty pay, okay?"

"Thanks." Steward took the spike and went to the public telephone by the men's room. He put in a coin, jacked in the spike, and transferred the dollars to an account he created for himself at the Canyon State Insured. He called again a minute later to make certain the money was there and hadn't disappeared and that his password was working. Canyon State's banking software should have made such an event impossible, but all manner of things had been known to happen.

Griffith's money was good, Steward concluded, even if his knowledge of his business associates was a little shaky.

He returned to the table. Griffith was coughing again.

"Maybe you better invest in a new body," Steward said.

Griffith scowled. "It's expensive."

"It looks like you have outside sources of income."

"It all passes through my hands, buck. I've got overhead, payoffs…shit. I don't want to talk about it anyway."

Steward reached into his pocket and took a spike from his spike ring. "Here you go. The place is called SourceBank, it's on Winnetka, and the code is MALAFIDES."

Griffith patted his pockets for a pen. "Better write that down," he said. He wrote it on his plastic reusable napkin and pocketed it. Across the room, the waitress glared.

"I'm gonna spend the rest of the day in bed," he said. "And I'm leaving tomorrow. But I'll still try to call my friend in Starbright."

"I'd appreciate that. Thank you."

Steward sipped his coffee, feeling the lights in his body going green in long, slow rows, and hoped Griffith's person in Starbright was a better friend than the people he knew in LA.

Steward lay shirtless on the floor of Ardala's apartment, his arms thrown up above his head. He'd just come in from a walk outside and this seemed the best way of dealing with the heat. Faint, cool patterns of air stirred on his chest. *Alien Inquisitor* babbled at him from the vid.

One of Ardala's cleaning robots moved toward him on the floor, sensed his presence, turned away. Ran into a pair of Ardala's discarded jeans, thought for a moment, turned again, moved back the way it came. Steward guessed it ought to be used to these situations by now.

The door swept open and Ardala came in. She dumped her briefcase in the hallway and stood over Steward. She bent to work at the fasteners to her high-heeled shoes. He gazed up at her frowning face.

"Lightsource is a funny company," she said. "It doesn't recruit. I didn't have any literature on it."

"So it's small," Steward said.

She kicked off one shoe, began working on the other with her toes. "It's privately owned anyway. I found that much out. And it's based in Los Angeles."

She kicked the other shoe off. It landed in front of the cleaning robot, which thought for a moment, then moved in another direction.

"They *do* consult on communications problems," she said. "I called a friend of mine who works for Macrodata and asked."

"Thanks," Steward said.

"So why did your friend send you to his own home base with a package? He could have delivered it himself."

"Maybe he was in a hurry. Maybe he wanted to do me a favor."

"Some favor."

Steward sat up, flexed his shoulders and neck. Cervical vertebrae crackled, the snaps and pops echoing inside his skull. He wondered what it would be like never to work out as heavily as he did, never to have to feel his bones crack every time he changed position.

"It's over now," he said. "Whatever it all meant, I don't have anything to do with it anymore."

"You got Sheol. And that's what you wanted. Right?"

Steward rolled to his feet. The Alien Inquisitor was doing something to a captive girl's toenails. "I'm surprised your condeco management lets that program in here," he said.

"*Alien Inquisitor* comes from Network Noir, which is a wholly owned subsidiary of the Destinarian Party. Our condeco management rents time on the artificial intelligence of the Marketplex in order to run our investment program, and Marketplex has adopted official Destinarian ideology. Network Noir was part of the deal. We make it available and we get a break on use of the AI."

Steward stared at the screen. The feet were small, plump, photographed with care as pink objects of love. Thin streams of blood ran in artistic patterns. "Pulling toenails serves the Destinarian philosophy?" he asked.

Ardala shrugged. "Demonstrates the fragility of flesh as opposed to hardware. I'm going to take a bath."

Steward turned the video off and watched as the liquid-crystal display turned into a random mutating kaleidoscope pattern. The sound of pouring water began to echo from the bathroom. Steward padded into the kitchen and poured himself a glass of wine. The cleaning robot had preceded him and seemed to have trapped itself in a dead end formed by the cabinets and refrigerator. Steward nudged the white plastic bubble around with his foot, and the machine moved happily back toward the living room. Steward followed it. From the bathroom he heard the tap cut off, then the sound of Ardala lowering herself into the tub. He watched the fluffed carpet that marked the robot's passage, seeing its twisted pattern on the floor as it encountered bodies, litter, furniture.

Moving like a rat in its maze. Programmed. Performing a function that it was not capable of understanding, on behalf of people whose entire existence was outside its knowledge, detected only as feet occasionally planted in its way.

Steward looked out of the polarized terrace window, seeing the pyramids and blocks of the condecologies, each serving the purposes of its builders, performing its tasks of reinforcement, providing shelter from disturbing patterns, offering ideological or religious programming as necessary. Each as self-contained as technology could provide, invulnerable as possible to leakage of realities from the outside.

Steward felt a sudden intuition, bordering on certainty, that his money had just vanished, had become unreal. He went to the telephone and called Canyon State Insured.

The money rested in its account, having gained an insignificant amount of interest since that afternoon.

He broke the connection and walked to the bathroom. Ardala was submerged to her chin, her extravagant eye makeup providing a surprising contrast to her tanned body. Steward sat down on the edge of the tub and offered her his glass of wine. She thanked him and took a sip.

"I've got money now," he said. "I've increased my personal wealth by a factor of ten in the last twenty-four hours."

"It's still not enough to get into Starbright."

"It's enough so that I could pay you what I owe you."

Ardala closed her eyes and leaned back against a foam neck cushion. She raised her knee and rested her calf on the side of the tub, pressing her wet foot against Steward's leg. "You don't owe me anything," she said.

"Two weeks' rent, at least."

"Put your money into the funds here in the condeco," she said. "You'll get a much higher rate of return. Our AI is one of the best."

"If I put them there, I can't get to them if I need them."

Ardala opened her green eyes and looked at him. She nudged him with the foot. Dampness was spreading on his trouser leg. "So where are you going, ex-Canard, that you're gonna need access to this money anytime soon?" she asked.

"Space," he said.

"You're dreaming."

"That's where the answers are."

"So you say."

Steward gazed back at her, saw the strands of fair hair plastered to the side of her neck by the bathwater. "I think I owe you some money, Ardala."

She held his gaze for a moment, then leaned back against the foam pillow and closed her eyes. "Whatever you think is fair," she said.

Steward took a drink of his wine. "It's Darwin Days all over the universe," he said. "Whole cultures are being selected out. The Outward Policorps all disappeared, and so did their monopoly, and that means every institution, every ideology or philosophy that hopes to have a future, is pushing into interstellar space. So there's always a chance for another Artifact War out there, with even more groups involved, even more uncontrolled than the last one. With the Powers around to pick up the pieces.

"Paranoia is becoming a way of life. We've got hundreds of little communities in space, all tens of thousands of klicks apart, and the isolation is making them funny. They're tightly wrapped and conscious of trade secrets and security, and they're scared of all these other communities they don't know anything about. The NeoImagists are breeding their own populations in artificial wombs rather than import people and ideas from outside. People are looked on as contamination. And what are Earth condecologies but ways of imitating that way of thinking?

"We've got machines that are smarter than we are, and people have put them in charge. We're being pushed around for reasons that we can't even fathom. It's not just people that are evolving, it's their machines. Their institutions. The whole situation is scary. People are looking for cover."

He stood up, feeling his spine crackle. He put his hands on the edge of the sink and leaned forward, watching himself in the mirror. Dark skin, dark eyes, thick black brows. Words coming out reasoned and slow. "Most people cluster in anthills for security, like this condeco. Base their lives on investment strategies or religion or a return to obsolete modes of life like feudalism. Neo-Imagists are trying to evolve themselves ahead of any trouble. Destinarians plug themselves into machines that'll live longer than they will and hope that artificial intelligence can span the gap between themselves and what they don't understand. They think they're safer because they can process data faster than the competition. But data's just numbers that represent a way of looking at things. Destinarians confuse it with reality, and it isn't. It's just their preconceptions in an ordered form."

Steward heard the bright splash of water as Ardala adjusted herself in the bath. "So what's the correct strategy, O Mighty One?" she asked. Her voice took on a singsong tone, emphasizing each syllable of a downward-tending scale. "Ex-Ca-nard. Ex-Ice-hawk. Ex-men-tal pa-tient."

He looked at himself. "Stay at the center. Look for such of the truth as seems to matter. Watch the winds of change."

Or maybe become a change wind. The voice seemed to come from the mirror, from a darker image of himself. Steward fell silent for a moment, wondering if the voice was his own, if Ardala had heard it.

Ardala's tone was flat. "This truth of yours is in space, I take it?"

Steward frowned at himself and turned away from the mirror. "It looks that way."

"None of this nonsense about the secure life for you. You want to be right out there all by yourself in the middle of the hurricane."

"Security is a delusion. If I've learned anything, it's that." He leaned his back against the sink and drank his wine. "Tomorrow morning your condeco's investment AI could find itself outsmarted by someone else's AI and lose every penny of the investment bank. Then your condeco could get taken over by the Krishna Firm and you find yourself with a choice of living by ashram rules or losing everything you've worked for. What do you do then?"

"Learn to contemplate my navel. At a guess."

Steward smiled into his wineglass. Ardala turned over in the bath, lying on her side facing away. Steward saw the bare wet shoulder, hair pinned up on top of her head.

"I'm going to take a nap, philosopher," she said. "Then, since you're so bent on paying me back, you can take me to dinner. Maybe some dancing, like up at the South Rim. Ever dance on a glass floor above a canyon a mile deep?"

"Not yet."

"Maybe it'll teach you something about security. And dinner there is *really* expensive. It should make you feel a lot better about paying me back."

He grinned again and finished his wine. "D'accord," he said.

Griffith's voice was energetic, all hint of illness gone. Steward turned down the audio portion of Ardala's cram recording. "Hey, man," Griffith said. "I've got some news about Spassky."

"Nothing good, I hope."

The mastoid receiver seemed to be having problems adhering to Steward's skin. Steward held it on with his thumb.

"Somebody walked up behind him on a street with a .66 caliber gauss express. Blew his spine clean out through his chest, right through his armored coat."

"Sounds like a neat job."

"Up to Icehawk standards, man. The little fucker's gonna need all the Thunder he can get to grow his spine back together. And I'm not planning on selling it to him."

"Well. Thanks for making my day a little brighter." Steward settled onto Ardala's couch.

"And I talked to my friend in Starbright. It's her turn to nominate someone to the apprenticeship program, and she wants to meet you."

Steward leaned forward. He could feel his heart speeding up. "Where is she?"

"Her shuttle landed at the Gran Sabana port yesterday morning. She's got two weeks' leave coming, and right now she's in Willemstad, Curaçao. Spindrift Hotel. Her name's Reese. Give her a call."

"I'll do that. I could get there tomorrow if I use the suborbital from Vandenberg to Havana."

"Steward. By the way"—for the first time Steward heard a hesitation in Griffith's voice—"it's customary to, ah, offer a little present in these cases. A thousand Starbright should do it."

"I'll keep that in mind. Thanks a lot, man."

"What the hell. It doesn't cost me anything to do my friends favors."

"I'm surprised you're not taking advantage of this yourself. Considering how badly you want to get offplanet."

"I couldn't pass the physical. Too many latent Sheol bugs."

There was a moment of silence. "Oh. I'm sorry, buck."

"Not your fault." Griffith's voice had lost a bit of its brightness. He made an effort to put more energy in his words. "Hey," he said. "Call me in a few days and let me know how you and Reese got along. Here's a number where I can be reached."

Steward reached for the pen he'd been using to underline his study material and made a note of the number.

"Thanks, friend," Steward said.

"No problem, buck," Griffith said, and broke the connection.

Steward took his thumb off the mastoid receiver and felt it fall off onto his shoulder, then down his chest. He anticipated this and caught the device in his hand, reflex unsullied by conscious thought. Steward returned it to the phone rack.

He looked out the window past the terrace that was already baking in the morning sun, and peered up past the rows of condecos to the sky darkened by the window's polarization. He looked for the bright fixed stars of orbital habitats and failed to find them. No matter, he thought.

With luck he'd be there soon enough.

Steward had never been to Willemstad before, but from the hydrofoil that brought him from the floating airport, the skyline looked familiar, its blue bay surrounded by blocks of reflective ice, resort condecos for those who couldn't stand the idea of not living among a thousand strangers. The hydrofoil slowed, settling into the waters with a distant thump, and moved into a canal whose banks echoed the whine of the foil's turbines. Locals and tourists watched dully from the banks. Music scattered from nearby buildings. The canal led to the Schottegat, a lake chilled and darkened by the shadows of the towers that surrounded it.

The customs building was in shadow, a temporary foam structure on a pier surrounded by flags, both the Curaçao national ensign and the Freconomicist flag. Another small nation, Steward thought, adopting an ideology from space, probably by way of protecting itself from its neighbors. Curaçao was a negligible power, but the Freconomicists were not.

From the customs house Steward took a cab to the Spindrift Hotel. It was some distance out of town, removed from the clusters of condecos on the bay. In spite of the nearness and presence of the sea, the island seemed arid, filled with scrub and cactus. The air was bright and crisp, the sky a vivid blue. Steward paid his cab driver in his new Starbright dollars and walked between divi-divi trees to the hotel. It was an old stone building with a new reflective, polarizable alloy roof and a series of jagged antennas that cut the sky. The trade wind hummed through the aerials. Steward felt it plucking at his shirt.

The desk clerk was a heavyset black man with phosphorescent bacteria beads woven into his cornrows and a T-shirt proclaiming his allegiance to the Sint Kruis Conch Club. His eyes were distant. There was a receiver pasted to his mastoid, and Steward could hear faint music coming from it. Steward put his little traveling bag on the desk, took off his shades, put them in his shirt pocket. "I'm Steward," he said. "I called."

The desk clerk smiled. His eyes stayed a hundred miles away. "Welcome, Mr. Steward. I have put you in room number seven. There is a message on your phone from Miss Reese."

"Thanks."

"The dining room will be open from seventeen-thirty to twenty-thirty." The clerk gave him orbital time, presumably because he thought that Steward, being a friend of Reese's, had just shuttled down.

Steward took his key spike, and as he moved to pick up his traveling bag, he saw something under the clear desk top. He hesitated, then frowned. "Is that stuff what it says it is?"

"Bolivian cocaine, sir. Eight dollars per gram Lesser Antilles, or two dollars Starbright."

"It's real? Not synthetic? Not a substitute?"

"Direct from the mountains, sir. Two grams?"

Steward stared at the packets in their small green envelopes, sitting under glass beside compressed-air inhalers and chewing gum. "I didn't think anyone made it anymore. Isn't it supposed to be addictive or something?"

"I wouldn't know, sir. Personally I do not cloud my perceptions with chemicals."

Steward looked up at the clerk's distant eyes. "Good idea," he said. He took his bag from the counter.

"God is love, sir."

Steward concluded, on his way to his room, that he had Curaçao figured out.

The room was smaller than Steward had anticipated, the walls whitewashed to make it seem larger. There was a water bed, a bureau of battered Jovian plastic, woven straw mats on the floor. A gecko splayed motionless on one wall. A crystal video was set into the ceiling in a position to be watched from the bed, with a camera pickup in case it was yourself you wanted to watch. The phone winked at him in slow red calypso tempo. He picked it up.

Reese's voice, a deep American Midwest alto. "Hi. This is Reese. I'm going to be diving all day, but if you're open for dinner, I'll meet you in the dining room at six."

Steward looked at his watch. Three hours. He looked up at the gecko on the wall, scented the breeze that gusted through the window. He remembered

Port Royal, the touch of warm water, singers crying their hymns to the trades, the ziggurat across the bay sitting black above the glowing city.... He'd been doing seize and hold training then, spending weeks marching along endless alloy corridors, hot city streets, learning what was important in an urban combat zone.

Seize and hold, he thought. He thought he'd had the drill down, but somehow the things that had mattered had all slipped years away, and now he was a million miles from where he wanted to be, standing in a whitewashed room watching a gecko and hoping it might eventually move and provide some entertainment. All he was doing was picking up another man's wreckage, hoping there might be enough of it to put together and call a life.

Reese was a means to an end, he thought, as others had been: Ashraf, Ardala, Griffith. Rungs on a ladder that would take him up out of the gravity well, beyond the reach of the Caribbean trades to where other winds were blowing, where there were people that mattered. Natalie, de Prey. And Curzon, as yet only a name. People in whom he could see a reflection of himself, and of the Alpha.

The gecko was still motionless. Steward dropped his bag on the bed and turned to the window, gazing out at the divi-divi trees, the ocean beyond. The beach looked as if it were all sand, rocks, and lizards. He decided to visit it anyway.

Steward had seen a video Ardala had about presenting yourself for a job interview. The vid advised what to wear, how to act, how to sit, how to smile, and featured two men in conservative dark jackets without lapels—one younger, one older. The older one wore puttees, a fashion that had come and gone during the postwar adjustment. Steward remembered that the item that clinched the younger man's job was that he shared an interest with the interviewer in indoor tennis. The recording called this achieving rapport with the subject. To the best of Steward's recollection the recording didn't seem to offer any useful advice concerning how to meet the drive rigger of an in-system freighter on the terrace of a hotel/bar on a Caribbean island so as to offer a bribe for a job appointment.

Just as well, Steward thought. Bribery was a skill best learned on the job.

When Reese arrived, Steward was dressed in tropical white, sitting on the dining-room terrace with his third piña colada. Reese seemed to be in her mid-thirties, about an inch taller than Steward, wiry and small-breasted, with a long-legged stride that was all confidence. Her hair was short, a dark bronze that the sun was turning to copper. She wore white cotton drawstring trousers, sandals, and a sleeveless bright tropical shirt. Steward could see dark floss beneath her arms, silver ear cuffs dropping bangles that gleamed against her neck, fading imprints on her cheeks where the mask and gill unit had pressed into her flesh. She was carrying a tall iced drink of a mellow golden color.

"Try the grilled flying fish," she said. "The conch salad isn't bad, either."

"I'll have one of each," Steward said. "I haven't eaten since morning." He stood up to shake hands. Muscle moved catlike in her upper arms as she clasped his hand.

"Are we alone in this place?" Steward asked.

Reese looked around at the rows of blank linen tablecloths. "It's the off season," she said. "And it's early."

They settled into their chairs. The sun on the terrace was bright and Steward was wearing his shades. Reese looked at him without squinting. Steward concluded the dark gray eyes were artificial implants.

"You're pretty young to be such a good friend of Griffith's," Reese said.

"It's a new body. I'm a clone."

"Griffith ought to get a new body soon," Reese said. "He looks worse every time I see him."

"How did you come to know each other?"

Reese smiled. "We were dumped on the street together. After the Artifact War."

Steward sensed himself stiffening. "You were on Sheol?"

"No. I was on Archangel. Ross 47, with Far Jewel. It wasn't as bad there."

Steward sipped his drink and settled back into his seat. "Griffith and I were in the same unit," he said.

"That's what I heard." She put her drink on the tablecloth and frowned at it for a short minute, then looked up at him. "You've done vac training?"

"Yes."

"Rad suit?"

"Yes."

"How long ago?"

"About eight or nine months ago, in terms of my memory. Years ago, real time."

Reese seemed startled. "Your former...personality...he didn't update your memories?"

Steward was mildly surprised she had realized this so quickly. "I lost about fifteen years."

"My god." She looked at him. "I don't suppose he told you why?"

"Afraid not."

She shook her head. "I hope you're not as forgetful as he was."

"He didn't forget. I think there were just some things he didn't want me to know."

"Yeah. Well." Reese shifted uncomfortably in her seat. "I guess we all have memories like that." She took a sip of her golden drink. "I don't suppose you're familiar with the specifications of a Fiat-Starbright FSVII inertial drive? Because that's what you'd be working with on the *Max Born*."

Relief trickled into Steward. "As a matter of fact, I know the FSVII," he said. "Some of Coherent Light's ships used them." The specifications he knew were mainly for purposes of sabotage, but at least they gave him a good idea of how the engines were put together.

Reese grinned. "So. That makes things easier."

"I was afraid you'd have some fancy new system I'd never heard about."

"A lot of ships do. But the *Born*'s a venerable beast. Sixty years old, but they keep rebuilding it." She sipped her drink. "I should tell you something, by the way. *Born* isn't owned by Starbright—it's a tramp ship, owned by a company called Taler. But the drive system is owned by Starbright and on perpetual lease to the owner of the ship. So the drive riggers are Starbright employees, and the rest of the crew are Taler people. At least *Born* owns its own computer and telemetry systems. Otherwise there'd be another group of techs on board."

The news didn't particularly surprise Steward. Expensive equipment on the order of large complex drive systems was often leased rather than bought, particularly by smaller freight companies operating on the margin.

"I imagine that gives the riggers a certain amount of autonomy," Steward said.

Reese nodded. "Something like that."

Steward rubbed the bridge of his nose where his shades were chafing him. "There's this other thing I want to mention," he said. "I have this investment opportunity you might be interested in."

Reese seemed amused. She put one of her feet up on an empty chair. "What sort?"

"It's this special account where they start you off with a thousand Starbright dollars. And then you do whatever you want with it."

Reese laughed. "Okay." Her silver ear cuffs flashed in the sun. "The last guy offered me thirteen hundred Pink Blossom, but I'd have to train him. It might be worth three hundred not to have to bother. Hey." She was waving at someone over Steward's shoulders, presumably the waitress. She looked at Steward. "I'm starved. Do you mind?"

The waitress was about sixteen, black, with severe acne and a jacket that flashed scenes of beaches, palm trees, and Heineken greenies. Steward watched the pictures' reflection track across Reese's face as they ordered. The waitress smiled, then padded back into the interior of the hotel.

Reese finished her drink and leaned forward across the linen tablecloth. "The major thing about this job is that it takes someone who can be comfortable with himself, all alone, for long periods. You're gonna be spending months in a bottle with only four other people. If you're the kind who needs other people around him all the time, you're going to drive everyone crazy."

Steward shrugged. "I can be as solitary as the next person."

"Griffith said that about you, but sometimes I don't know what to think about Griffith's friends."

Steward smiled. "I know what you mean."

She was frowning at him. "You got religion?"

"I'm sort of a Zen agnostic."

"People who babble about God all the time make a trip a lot longer than it has to be. How about ideology?"

"I thought Starbright has no official ideology."

"No, it doesn't. Do you?"

"No."

"Do you smoke?"

"Yes."

Reese's look turned cold. "You'll quit. That's a condition of employment. I'm allergic, and I'm not going to live with it."

"I've quit before."

"I'm talking permanently. No sneaking smokes, either, when I'm not around. I'd rather have a pork junkie on board than a nicotine junkie. At least when you stick things in your veins, it doesn't pollute the air."

"I can quit."

Reese seemed dubious. "Okay. As far as benefits and votes are concerned, you spend the first three years as an apprentice. The pay's shit, but you get room, board, and your health is taken care of. After that, you get citizenship and one vote. There are stock options and such built in, so every ten years you get another three votes. If you buy more stock, you get more votes, but on the basic fifty-year plan you'll be able to contribute sixteen votes to the political health of our plutocratic democracy. Of course that's balanced by the tens of thousands of votes that the chairman, board members, and major stockholders can command, but that's politics. Things are more liberal in Starbright than elsewhere."

"How does the pay advance?"

"It stays shit. You don't get into drive rigging if you want to make money. It's just for those with a yen to travel." She smiled. "I think that falls under the category of tradeoffs."

"Clone insurance?"

"Available, but expensive. You put yourself into hock for thirty years if you want it." Reese leaned closer. "There are some options available on most ships, though, under the heading of private enterprise. If there's space in the cargo hold, you can ship a limited number of personal goods. These are known as ventures. You pay the shipowners by the ventures' weight. But if you want to get into making money on the side, you can get enough to retire on in thirty or forty years."

The girl with the photojacket arrived with Steward's conch salad and Reese's second drink. Reese ignored her.

"Something else I should mention," she said. "I don't fuck other people in the crew. Neither does anyone else on the ship. That's a rule. If you think you're irresistible, or if you have to prove something to yourself by jumping every woman you meet, this job isn't for you. And if you can't keep your hormones under control, we have plenty of drugs aboard that will do it for you."

Steward glanced up at the waitress to see if she was enjoying this. She glanced at him, expressionless. "Another drink?"

"Not just yet. Thanks."

She took Reese's empty glass and left. Steward turned to Reese. "I can live with that," he said. "I have in the past. I had transit time as an Icehawk."

"A lot of people can't deal with it. And once the crew starts snuggling up to each other, they start playing favorites on the job, and that's bad."

"I see your point." Steward began working on his salad.

"Just want to make sure it's made."

"This is pretty good salad. Thanks for the recommendation."

Reese narrowed her eyes, said nothing. Then she relaxed, took her drink, and settled back into her chair. She shook her head. "You're not what I expected. I'm not sure how to read you at all."

"If I get the job," Steward said, "you'll have months to figure me out."

"I guess so." She looked over her shoulder, toward the beach. "What do you think of Curaçao so far?" she asked.

"Lots of rocks and lizards. I haven't seen much else."

"Parts of the island are lovely."

Steward glanced up at her. "Care to show me a few later?" he asked.

Reese laughed. "Hey," she said. "If I give you the appointment, we'll have months in which to get sick of each other. Why start now? I want to preserve my mystery for the moment."

"As you like."

Steward watched Reese sip her golden cocktail and concluded that he could get along with her. She insisted on being in charge, which was okay, but she hadn't made a fetish of it, which was better. It argued for her confidence, that she wasn't interested in scoring points off him, and that would make someone he could live alongside for a long time without it getting wearisome.

He also decided he'd liked the way she'd accepted her bribe. Like it was part of business, an accepted thing. Not as if she were royalty. She'd even laughed.

Steward, like Reese, had standards for the people he had to live with.

Bright color reflected on Reese's face told Steward that the waitress was bringing their dinners. The girl set plates on the table and asked if there was anything else she could bring.

"Coffee," Steward said, and she smiled and nodded.

When she brought the coffee later, he thanked her.

"God bless," she said.

The next morning, before breakfast, Steward worked out on the beach. The sand provided elusive traction that tired his calves early but proved interesting in terms of balance and coordination. Accordingly, he practiced spin kicks, which were harder on the inner ear anyway: whirling, cocking, looking over his shoulder, stabbing the air with his thrusting foot.

Rhythm built. Heart, lungs, body, mind, all working in synchrony. Balance became second nature, even on the treacherous ground. The sea was white noise in his mind, background noise for an empty universe, a null filled by his motion.

He spun, cocked, glanced, and saw Reese rounding a headland. He lashed out with the foot, retracted, planted on the sand.

She was wearing a dark green one-piece swimsuit and running barefoot on the sand.

Steward whirled, spun, cocked, fired. Into the rhythm.

She was running wind sprints, Steward concluded.

He spun again, kicked again. Sand flew in a wave from his lashing foot.

She passed him without speaking, without acknowledging his presence, absorbed by her own rhythm. Sun gleamed on the coppery hair on her arms and legs.

Steward kicked again, then again. Sand adhered to the sweat on his body.

He decided he had the job.

Griffith met him as he got off the coleopter that had taken him from Vandenberg to the Los Angeles airport. He was dressed in a dark silk shirt over a pair of tan slacks. He seemed healthy, even exuberant. "Congratulations on your new job," he said, as he offered his hand.

"It was all your doing. Thanks."

Griffith smiled. "I had ulterior motives."

Steward looked at him. "Please don't tell me that you want me to deliver a package to some friend on Titan."

"No. I don't. I want you to pick up some packages." He saw the warning look in Steward's eyes. "No," he said quickly. "It's not what you think."

"Tell me how it's different."

"Come with me to the coffee shop, and I will. But first. Do you play chess?"

"I know the moves. Not much else."

"At least you have some idea. Good." The coffee shop was a small dim place, almost deserted at one in the morning. Half the place was roped off. The hum of scrub bots came from the closed section.

Griffith bought two cups of coffee and paid. He led Steward to a small table in a corner and lit a cigarette. "Okay. Here's the deal."

"You're going to tell me that this isn't even illegal, aren't you?"

Griffith seemed surprised. "It's not. Would you rather it was?"

Steward didn't answer. A craving for tobacco was stirring in him. He ignored it and sipped his coffee.

"See, my friends and I, we usually move information. Moving goods, like last week, is kind of a sideline."

Steward looked at him. "How big is this group anyway?"

"Counting part-timers, a couple hundred. Mostly veterans of the Artifact War. I don't deal with very many, not personally."

"If there are a couple hundred, people know about them. There are files. Probably lots of files in lots of places."

Griffith shrugged. "So maybe there are. Who cares? We don't break any laws."

"Being on file somewhere can be bad for one's career," Steward said.

"Being a drive rigger," said Griffith, "is not a career. It is a dead-end job that people take because they want to get into space and can't find real work."

"Exchanging information. That sounds like espionage, right?"

"Hey. You'd be a mailman. Mailmen don't know what's in the letters they carry. They don't end up in jail for carrying mail."

Steward looked at his coffee cup. The smell of tobacco was making his mouth water. "Tell me how it works," he said.

Griffith laughed. "Okay, buck. It's actually very simple. You know chess people, they have bulletin boards on computers in a lot of locations, right?"

"It wouldn't surprise me."

"Well, a lot of these people put chess problems up on the bulletin boards for other people to solve, okay? Or they play chess against one another on computers, or whatever."

"I follow."

Griffith smiled, sucked in tobacco smoke, exhaled. "Okay. So here's how it works. You go into the station, find a terminal or a telephone, get onto their chess bulletin board, and look for a particular chess problem. You take a memory spike with you and plug it into the terminal. You punch in a certain incorrect answer that we'll give you, then a password. The computer will feed your memory threads some data. You unjack and go back to your ship, you get some time on the ship's transmitter, you aim the antenna, and you shoot the data to a certain address in Antarctica that I'll give you. After that the information is put on the market and you get a cut, ten percent, wired to an account of your choice anywhere between here and Neptune."

"Why can't the guy who steals the data in the first place send it off?"

"Because he wouldn't have unrestricted access to transmission equipment. A lot of these corporate habitats are worried about signal intelligence, and they monitor transmissions very carefully. They can't do that with a ship halfway between Jupiter and the asteroid belt." Griffith grinned. "Pretty good, huh?"

Steward frowned, tried to think of a problem with it. "I don't even have to see the guy I'm dealing with?" he asked. "Not at either end?"

Griffith shook his head. "That's the beauty of it. And if you access the chess problem over public lines from the station, and not through any commo hookup from your ship, they don't know who's doing it even if the whole system is compromised."

"I'll have to think about it."

A smile creased Griffith's face. "Let me know before you go up the well. I'll give you the problem and the password, and we'll set up your mode of payment. And some way I can contact you. The chess problem and password change from time to time."

"I'll think about it." Steward watched Griffith stub out his cigarette and knew that his delay, his insisting on thinking about it, was just a method of retaining a certain amount of his self-respect, that in the end he would agree to Griffith's plan. He couldn't find anything wrong with it. He wouldn't have to meet any more of Griffith's friends, not unless he wanted to go looking. And he'd make some money.

But more important, it would keep him in touch with the way things moved in the real world. Keep some of his reflexes honed, keep him looking over his shoulder at least part of the time. So that when he wanted to do some things, up there in the vacuum, he wouldn't have to worry about being entirely out of practice.

He could look on it, he thought, as free training.

The night flight from LA arrived at six in the morning. Steward took a cab from the airport, trying to sleep in the back, but caffeine was still trickling across his nerves, keeping him awake.

When Steward opened the door to Ardala's apartment, he saw her across the living room, dressed for work, watching the silent video while holding the mastoid audio receiver to her skull. She looked up at him quickly and raised a finger to her lips. Steward moved into the room and saw Ardala's niece, age five, lying on the couch under one of Ardala's discarded jackets. Ardala put down the mastoid receiver and stood, walking into the hallway where they could talk.

"Lisa's picking her up before I leave for work," she said. "She wanted a night out."

"I got the job," Steward said.

Her eyes narrowed. "Congratulations. It's what you wanted, right?"

"I still have to pass the corporate exam. But with an apprenticeship appointment all I have to do is pass, not get into the top two percent. I can do that easy enough."

"Space. Freedom. Destiny. Adventure. Vacuum." Ardala waved her arms. "How can a place be free if you can't even go out of doors and breathe?"

"I've got a week before I have to take the test," Steward said. Ardala looked at him. He gazed at the elaborate eye makeup, saw tension twitching the pale eyelids.

"It could be a nice week," Steward said.

There was a moment of silence. Ardala looked away, back in the direction of the living room. "Yeah," she said. "It could be."

He reached out, touched her arms. A grudging smile crossed her face. "Fine," she said. "D'accord."

"D'accord," he said. His mind already somewhere else, a shuttered place traveling across an endless darkness, a movement, a velocity, there in the center of a perfect emptiness.

CHAPTER SEVEN

Charter Station. Formerly the spindle-shaped Mitsubishi Permanent Orbital Complex at Lagrange Four, its silhouette was now enlarged and complicated by a century's worth of technological barnacles—new habitats, dockyards, laboratories, solar collectors, floodlit ships awaiting docking, a giant second-stage habitat free of gravity. In an airless space of black velvet sown with diamonds, Charter hung surrounded by a gray floodlight glow, reflecting on its silver skin the blue and white of Earth, the gray of Earth's moon.

Charter existed as a complicated legal entity, its ownership and registration not so much obscure as complex beyond understanding. Parts of the station and its equipment were rented or leased for long periods to policorps or individuals; others were operated by the Charter company itself for its own inadvertently obscure purposes. For the most part, it was a way station, a place where people came on their way to someplace else. A place where business was done.

There was a sense of discipline in the place, of purpose, and it belied the chaotic tangle of owners, leaseholders, inhabitants. There were serious people here, doing serious work; the sense of irrelevance that possessed affairs on Earth was absent. Steward remembered being caught up in such a life once, as a part of Coherent Light; having direction, discipline, a place…. There had been a satisfaction in that, in seeing himself as a part of an intricate mechanism whose purpose was the expansion of human possibilities, an evolution to the next step of existence. He stood outside it now, watched the bustle, heard the hum of business going on here, the complex network of transactions, movements, cooperation, competition… the web that was life outside Earth.

Things that were affectation on Earth were part of business outside the gravity well. The artifacts of Urban Surgery, the implants, the sensors, the tools grafted onto flesh—here they weren't merely fashion but had purpose, were a way of getting things done. There was style in the way they were flaunted, the way they were used, but it was a style with a basis in practicality. Other styles that were not often seen on Earth were part of the background here. There were surgically evolved individuals with skulls greatly enlarged to encompass increased brain tissue, their presence always signified by the whine of the superchargers fitted around their necks to keep their brains supplied with oxygen. Computer interfaces—sometimes entire computers—were grafted onto skulls, living in complex interaction with the brain. Other individuals boasted extra arms or fingers, either implanted or the result of altered DNA, and there was an entire colony of second-stage humans, genetically altered to live entirely outside gravity, an extra pair of arms grafted to the shoulders and another where the feet should be, people who looked like boneless insects, stretching like frogs as they swam across the vacuum.

The *Max Born* was not connected to the station and lay some distance away, undergoing routine maintenance of its seals by the station work gang. It was an elderly boat, its control panels and equipment a strange mix of old and new, from stuff installed before Steward was born to state-of-the-art rigs jacked in during the last refit. *Born* never carried passengers and had no reason to keep itself pretty for the benefit of outsiders; it didn't bother to hide its age. Bundles of fiber-optic cable laced the riggers' control spaces. The ancient quilted padding that covered most of the hard surfaces was held together with duct tape, and Steward's cabin featured several layers of pornographic photos and holos left behind by the previous occupant.

While seal maintenance was under way, the living quarters were subject to occasional decompression, so Steward and Reese were barracked in inexpensive station accommodations, coffin-quarters, hexagonal in cross section and stacked eighteen high, surrounded by catwalks and scaffolding and each containing a rack, folding desk, toilet, video, and computer access. There was one other member of the *Born*'s crew onstation, a woman named Cairo, who was the chief engineer. Steward had been introduced on his arrival but hadn't seen her since.

Even off the ship, he had little in the way of leisure. He had passed the tests necessary to get into Starbright, but he had yet to learn the details of the engines he would be maintaining. He had given Reese the impression he knew more than he did and he didn't want to disappoint her. He spent most of his time in the bed, tanked up on drugs that aided his long-term memory in absorbing the details about the *Born*, its systems, its way of doing things. Starbright was a nonideological policorp, almost solely into transportation and drive systems, its organization as streamlined and purposeful as one of its atmosphere cutters. Survival was its business, and it survived by producing state-of-the-art systems, ships, and personnel.

Even when Steward had free time he didn't venture out much. The drugs never seemed to entirely wear off, and they affected his perceptions in odd, unpleasant ways: He found himself remembering small things that otherwise he would have forgotten, and the insignificant memories were somehow disturbing—the way Reese's tongue moved behind her glistening smile; his own reflection, distorted in a piece of curved alloy; a disturbing harmonic in the whine of a nearby brain supercharger; the profile of a dark-haired woman he had been admiring in the hi-grav gym, and who turned suddenly to regard him from eyes that were surrounded by yellowing bruises and filled with inexplicable hatred....

So he worked hard, fifteen hours at least, out of every twenty-four, and passed his tests in record time. The drugs made sleep uneasy, parts of his mind churning the entire time, and he slept little—he spent the rest of his time learning chess, filing away past games in his mind, wondering about the game's structure, the closed nature of its system, the way it seemed invulnerable to entropy and the breakdown of order. Each piece, in its place, *meant* something, was a packet of specific potentialities existing in a unique relationship with the other pieces, a relationship that altered when the piece moved. Contemplating the game, he began to feel himself in his own hexagonal space, the hotel room, locked in a transforming relationship with the others around him, and he seemed strangely close to his Alpha, who was a piece in another, perhaps a similar, game....

The drugs finally wore off, and he slept for two days. He woke with information locked in his mind, but the sensation of himself amid a complex of relationships was gone, replaced only by the hum of the station, of business, all so complex and baffling as to amount to little more than white noise, the hiss of meaningless background information. His sense of the meaning of it all, its relationship to him, had gone; it was as if he'd lost his ability to discriminate between signal and noise.

He wandered around the station for a while, trying to regain a sense of what he'd lost. The place seemed strange to him, the personnel bizarre. Communication seemed impossible; words had become noise. He stopped in a bar and ordered coffee, chicken mole, corn tortillas, and he was surprised that the bartender understood what he was saying. He spilled half the coffee carrying it to his table. He tried to catch it on his food plate, but the liquid spilled off to the side—he wasn't yet used to living in a centrifuge. As he ate, he watched himself in a chromium-alloy wall, unable to watch anything else. The green lights in his mind started to wink on again, slowly. He began to feel himself moving toward a sense of normality, a slow interface with the rest of reality; the noise was fading into the background. He had more coffee, managed to avoid spilling any of it. He began to feel more at ease. Maybe he'd take a shower, then go exploring. He went back to his berth and found Reese waiting for him, sitting on his rack. She wore a battered gray coverall and grip boots.

"Don't you ever read your fucking messages, Steward?" she demanded. "We're docking the *Born* in forty minutes."

He looked for a long moment at the blinking LED on his commo unit. "Sorry," he said.

Reese stood, crouching beneath the low ceiling. "We're taking our taxi from Dock Sixty-one," she said. "You are *not* making a good first impression."

During *Born*'s docking Steward tried hard to stop himself from yawning and never succeeded. Sitting in the rigger's area in the central part of the ship, he wore a headset that fed an analog of the power system readouts into the visual centers of his brain, and which monitored the internal power system as he brought it up and readied it for the maneuver. It was an undemanding task and one without surprises. The main generators and engines were not needed, and only enough of the fuel cells to support the radars, maneuvering computer, and life-support systems. Reese, strapped in behind him and wearing another headset, monitored the maneuvering engines and verniers, a task that scarcely required any more attention. They were only present, Steward suspected, because Starbright's contract required their presence any time the *Born* did anything that might endanger the precious engines.

"Grapplers engaged," reported Cairo, the chief engineer. In the absence of the captain, who was still on leave, she was handling the ship during docking. "Airlock pressurizing. Prepare for low station gravity. Airlock pressurized. Docking cone removed. Station power coupling engaged." There was a moment of silence. Gravity was tugging at Steward's inner ear. The room swayed slightly, then settled.

"Everything's green," Cairo said. "Let's shut the bitch down."

"Leave four-A and seven up," Reese said.

"Four-A and seven up," Steward repeated, just like in the manual. He knew perfectly well which of the cells were used for backup power on the life-support system. Lights in his mind and on the board in front of him began flickering from green to amber standby. "Shifting to station power." The room lights brightened slightly.

"Shutdown complete. Four-A and seven on backup status," Steward reported. He plucked at his safety harness, let it fall free. Looked above his head at a bundle of fiber-optic cable that had come loose from its rubber clamp and pushed the cable back into place.

"I'm clearing the docking cockpit," Cairo said. "Cargo loading begins in thirty minutes. Before then I'd like to see Steward in the lounge."

Cairo was a small woman who had been born in space and was proud of the fact that she'd never set foot on anything bigger than a planetoid. She was rail-thin and sharp-faced, and her dark hair, worn short in the style of most people who worked in space, was shot with gray. Martian diamonds had been implanted in the flesh of her cheekbones, and impact rubies studded sunburst patterns on the backs of her hands—people who lived in free-fall often had implants and thought jewelry dangerous because it could snag on something. When Steward entered, Cairo was sitting on the tape-scarred surface of one of the lounge chairs, drinking coffee from a bulb. Steward bobbed in the low gravity, checked his momentum, moved into a slow, controlled fall into another chair.

"You wanted to see me?" he said.

Cairo looked at him with dark, intent eyes. "Steward," she asked, "are you troubled in spirit?"

Surprise trickled slowly beneath Steward's skin. For a moment he wondered if the background noise here had grown significantly, if there was some context to this question that he'd missed. "No," he said.

"Taler made me morale officer here," Cairo said. "That translates to political commissar. I'm responsible for ideological indoctrination and self-criticism sessions."

"I'm a Starbright employee, not Taler," Steward said. "Our contract says I don't have to listen to your lectures."

Annoyance flickered in Cairo's eyes. "I can read contracts," she said.

"Just thought I should point it out."

"I wasn't asking you to show up for the sessions. But I *am* required to point out they exist. Just in case you're troubled in spirit and need guidance and understanding."

"Right," Steward said. "Thanks."

Cairo pointed at a document pouch near Steward's head. It was filled with papers restrained by Velcro straps. "That's Freconomicist literature," she said. "It's available. No one says you have to read it, but it's there if you want."

"I assume I have a choice of recordings from the video library as well."

She looked at him without expression. "I won't be bringing up this subject again. But now I can sign the chit that says I did and get some good-conduct points in my dossier at Taler."

"If you want, I'll sign an affidavit that you did a great job."

Her face hardened. "Your contract also says you don't have to be present during cargo loading. So that means I'll be pulling a sixteen-hour shift. See you in two days."

"Maybe I'll move my gear to the ship," Steward said. He was trying hard not to yawn again. "I'm getting tired of my hotel."

Cairo shrugged. "If you like. But you'll get a lot sicker of your ship quarters in the forty-three days before we dock at Vesta."

A cold rush of current poured through Steward's body as neural floodgates slammed open. Any urge to yawn vanished. "Vesta?" he said.

"Priority cargo of gravity-free crystals. General cargo, too, since there'll be room. Ventures, if you want them. The orders came down in the last twenty-four hours. We're changing our route out-system, and the company's making a lot of money." She laughed. "You really *didn't* read your messages, did you, Steward?"

"I got carried away testing on the power system."

She shook her head. "Usually people take a little longer. I don't know what the hell you're gonna do to occupy your time on the way to Vesta. Maybe you'll have to read some of my literature."

"There's always drugs."

Cairo stood, carefully adjusting her balance in the low gravity. "If I were you," she said, "I'd throw myself a party before I leave."

"Maybe I will," Steward said, but Cairo was maneuvering out of the lounge, aft toward the cargo door, and gave no sign that she had heard.

Steward's party turned out to be a fourth-trimester college student named Torner, stuck on Charter on a forty-eight-hour layover before heading to the Seven Moons mining school on Luna. She'd seen what sights existed on Charter during her first twenty-four hours onstation, and for the remaining time she wanted company.

She had braided dark hair, olive skin, a diamond stud in one nostril, a tattoo of a manticore coiling around one ankle. Steward met her just after leaving the *Born*, in a bar called the Mi Minor, where he'd gone for some combination of caffeine and alcohol. When he arrived, Torner was playing the slots in the front, dressed in dark corduroy pants, a blue pin-striped shirt, collarless jacket. As Steward ordered, he noticed her bouncing up and down to some internal rhythm as the machine spun and lights flickered on her profile. There was a clang and the machine delivered something to her. "Damn," she said, in a disgusted tone. She had an accent that came down hard on the *d*. She looked around, saw Steward watching, held up a packet of Players.

"The machine pays off in merchandise," she said. "You smoke?"

"I'm trying to give it up."

"Piss. What a cheap way to run a slot." She stuffed the cigarette pack in her pocket, glanced at his drink. "What are you having?"

"Irish coffee."

"I've been drinking growling tigers all afternoon. Maybe I'll try an Irish coffee for a change."

She sat on the stool next to him and tapped a credit spike on the bar to attract the bartender's attention. She and Steward drank slowly and exchanged life stories. She was from a former Mennonite habitat in the belt that had gone bust during the financial readjustment that followed the Artifact War and that had then voted to join Seven Moons. She'd never left home before college.

Steward concluded that she was trying to do a lot of catching up.

"Look," she said. "You're from Earth. I want to know something. When I ask someone else, I just get laughed at."

"Tell me," Steward said.

She frowned, concentrating. "I want to know about wind. I've never been in a place that had it. On Earth, do you have wind *all the time?*"

"Just about. Sometimes the air is still, but usually not for long."

"What does it feel like? I mean, is it like what you feel standing in front of a ventilator?"

"Sort of." He'd never considered this before. "Except the velocity of wind is changing all the time. With a ventilator, you have the compressor at the same speed."

"Mmm." She cocked her head and looked at him. "Does it—I don't know—smell different, or anything? Or does the wind blow away smells so they never get to you?"

"Wind smells of whatever there is to smell. Trees or flowers or soil or garbage or ocean."

"Organic stuff." She wrinkled her nose.

"Whatever's there."

"Wow. Do you miss it?"

He thought about this for a moment. "Yes. I do. Now that you mention it."

She finished her drink, wiped cream off her upper lip. Looked at him again. "Want to go dancing?"

Steward didn't have to think about this at all. "Why not?" he said.

They went to another place, a low-gravity club on the end of the original Mitsubishi spindle. Torner paid for the drinks, took off her grip slippers, and danced in bare feet to todo music, the tattoo flashing as her trouser cuffs bounced free. Later in the afternoon they moved to Steward's room, carrying skewers of beef with hot peanut butter sauce. Torner fell asleep on Steward's rack, her bare feet hanging off the end, her jacket wrapped around her, slippers sticking out of the pockets.

The caffeine kept Steward from drowsing. He sat in his desk chair and contemplated Torner as she slept, then saw the winking message light reflected red in her diamond and decided it was about time he listened to his mail.

There were two messages from Reese, both about the priority cargo run to Vesta and the docking he'd done his best to miss. There was an automated voice from the hotel that informed him about his checkout time, and another note that wasn't on audio. He punched it up on his terminal and saw that it was his chess problem and code word, along with a note from Griffith wishing him good luck.

The problem was called Tsiolkovsky's Demon.

The solution Griffith provided, even to Steward's inexperienced eyes, was clearly flawed. The password was "Marshal Stalin." Whatever that meant. He wondered if "Marshal" was a title or an imperative.

Steward asked his console for Charter's directory index, looked up the chess bulletin board, and paged through the messages. There were a lot of chess problems.

One of them was Tsiolkovsky's Demon. Steward's mouth went dry.

He fumbled in his bag for a data spike and slotted it, then tapped in the erroneous solution. The computer told him he was wrong. He tapped in "Marshal Stalin."

The computer hesitated, then an LED next to the needle lit up, signifying it was being fed data. Steward watched numbly.

Why on Charter? he wondered. Charter was an open free port: There was no need for espionage here; nothing was classified. Maybe, he thought, someone had been passing through on a ship and dropped off classified data while in transit. Maybe that person's own communication was monitored and he couldn't use his ship transmitter.

But why couldn't whoever sent the message use Charter's antennas? There were dozens of them, many of them available to the public. Maybe whoever had the data didn't have the Antarctica address. But if he didn't, why didn't he?

But however the data got there, Steward's spike was receiving it, and once received, it was worth something to him. The LED winked off, and the computer thanked him and asked if he wanted to try to solve the problem again. Steward told it no and logged off.

He took out the spike and held it in his hand, feeling it balance in his palm. Wealth bound in variable-lattice thread, a potential for future profit. But to use the data would connect the spike, and Steward, to things he didn't understand—connect him to Griffith's schemes, to a whole network of people engaged in data theft and the movement of black market items, people outside of Steward's purpose…and he didn't know, if he should decide to, whether it would be entirely possible to sever the connection once he'd made it.

Torner muttered in her sleep, rolled over on her back. Steward closed his hand on the spike, held it by his side. Torner passed the back of her hand over her forehead. She opened her dark eyes, blinked, focused on Steward. Smiled. "Hi. Guess I fell asleep." She sat up, shook her head. Did up a button on her shirt. "I don't suppose there's room service in this place, is there?"

Steward smiled. "It's not that kind of hotel."

"I thought we could get a bottle. Maybe some food." She looked at the monitor screen. "You working or something?"

"Chess problems." He shook his head. "I've had too much alcohol to work them properly." He bent and dropped the spike in his bag, then switched off the monitor. Torner was reaching over her head, adjusting the flow of the air vent.

"There," she said. She looked at him. Hair riffled across her forehead. "Wind. Sort of."

Steward left his chair and lay next to Torner on the narrow bed. A strong breeze spilled across his face. Torner's dark eyes were very near. "We can pretend we're on a beach, huh," she said. "Back on Earth. You figure we can do that?"

"I don't see why not," he said. She leaned forward and kissed him. She didn't close her eyes. Neither did Steward. She wasn't at all like Natalie, and Steward didn't know whether or not to be grateful. But memories came anyway, like butterfly kisses…sand, ocean, breeze, Earth, a pair of green eyes very close to his own. He closed his eyes and let the memories take him.

For a brief while, Steward became the wind.

In the end, he hadn't been able to think of a good reason not to.

The address in Marie Byrd Land was not presently visible to the *Born*'s antenna, so Steward decided to bounce the signal off a Pink Blossom satellite in GEO over the South Atlantic. He put the spike into slot one, aimed the antenna, pressed the TRANSMIT button. His eyes rose to a picture of Everest's summit bulking above curling wisps of cloud, a photo the absent commo officer had stuck on the wall.

Before Steward's finger had entirely retracted from the button, the transmission was completed.

Connections that had existed in potential were now coming into being. Whatever they were. Whatever they meant.

A folding door screen slammed open behind him. "What are you doing with my equipment?" demanded a voice. Steward looked over his shoulder and suppressed a reflex to snatch his needle from the slot.

Blue eyes gazed at him out of a sunburned face. A green tropical shirt seemed to fill half the *Born*'s radio room.

"I'm sending my mail," Steward said.

"That's what I thought." A large hand appeared. It was covered with freckles. Steward shook it. "I'm Fischer. Commo." There was a light Middle European accent.

"Steward. Assistant rigger."

"I figured." Fischer bent over the console and looked at the readouts. Steward could see an interface implant on the base of his skull. Fischer could probably talk to his radios in his head.

"I used antenna two," Steward said.

"It's all right, then. Mind you do it in the future." He bared his teeth at the console, a wolf's warning grin. "We might miss a transmission from our bosses," Fischer growled. "An important command to study the next *Freconomicist Weekly* for the changing line. Is Seven Moons' placing a tariff on variable-lattice alloy ideologically defensible, or a sign of creeping deviationism? Galaxy-shattering news, buck, if you know what I mean."

Steward pulled the spike and put it in his pocket. Fischer was gazing at the readings and appeared not to notice. Steward looked at Fischer's peeling forehead. "Been at the beach?"

Fischer shook his head. "Alaska. Climbing glaciers. You know someone in Asunción?"

"Antarctica."

"Ah." He tapped his head. "Got confused about transmission prefixes, there." Fischer gave Steward a glance. "Who's in Antarctica, then?"

"It's just a forwarding box. I've got a friend who travels. Like us."

Fischer's eyes flickered slightly, looking at the length-of-transmission counter. "Forty-four nanoseconds. That's a long transmission for a letter."

A cool warning signal, quiet but clear, was spreading through Steward's mind. He was going to destroy whatever was on the spike as soon as he got back to his cabin. "I'm sending my friend a copy of a video I got off the station net."

"Hope it's ideologically correct, whatever it is. Pink Blossom is a NeoImagist concern. They don't like freaky stuff bouncing off their satellites."

"I find NeoImagery pretty freaky all by itself."

Fischer grinned. "You know it, buck."

He jabbed at the console over Steward's shoulders, bringing the antenna back into its sheath. "SuTopo's on board. You might go knock on his cabin door in a little while. Give him a chance to unpack first."

"I'll do that." The warning signal still vibrating low and clear.

The Captain's cabin was filled with the mingled fragrances of the five bonsai trees that stood on shelves against the far wall, their ceramic bases secured against changes in gravity. Gro-lamps clung to the ceiling on suction cups.

The *Born*'s Captain was a short, middle-aged Javan, his body knotted with muscle. Complex dark tattoos wound about his wrists. He wore a formal round-collared jacket of some dark material and a black pitji hat with his badge of rank pinned to it, a constellation of three four-sided stars on the red Taler triangle. The middle fingernail of his left hand had been replaced with a liquid-crystal computer readout. Presumably his eyes had been altered so as to magnify the minuscule type. Steward wondered where the keyboard was: In SuTopo's head, threaded into his brain? In someone else's head, so SuTopo could receive messages from elsewhere? Steward decided he was becoming more paranoid than strictly necessary. No need to put a receiver in a fingernail when it could be spliced right to the auditory nerve.

"Welcome aboard," SuTopo said.

"Thank you. Happy to be here."

SuTopo stood flat-footed, his hands cocked at his sides. His eyes were half closed, his tone mild. "Cairo says you've been working hard."

"It's something I'm used to."

SuTopo frowned. "Useful. But the best ability, on a ship like this, is to be able comfortably to do nothing."

That, Steward concluded, is where the bonsai came in. "I can do nothing, too," he said. "It'll be a relief, really."

The Captain's eyes opened slightly. "You have military skills." A flat declarative. "Specialized skills of a high order." Steward couldn't tell how SuTopo felt about this, if indeed he felt anything at all, if this was something other than an awkward conversation.

"Yes," Steward said. "But I don't want to do that anymore."

"Ah," SuTopo said. "You are taking a new path entirely."

"Yes." He wondered if SuTopo was trying to recruit him for something.

SuTopo nodded, as if confirming something to himself. "Good," he said. He turned slightly and reached above his head to adjust one of the gro-lights. It was as if he wanted it to be clear he was speaking only in the abstract, without direct reference to anyone in the room. "It has been known for one policorp to plant agents in other policorps. Transportation companies like Starbright and Taler are particular favorites—they grant agents mobility. It would be a great shame were the *Max Born* to be involved in any difficulty over one of its personnel going on board a station and doing something he shouldn't."

"It won't happen," said Steward.

"I am pleased to hear it." He turned to look at his wall of bonsai. "Do you know bonsai?" he asked. "It is a passion with me."

"I don't know any details," Steward said. "I admire the results."

SuTopo stepped close to one of the pots, bent to look at the tree it contained. "This is graybark elm," he said. "It was planted by my grandfather. It is almost a century old. The style is called chokkan. The straight, dignified trunk is intended to inspire restfulness."

"It's quite lovely. Restful, as you say."

SuTopo turned to another bonsai. His eyes softened. "Arizona cypress," he said. "A gift from my wife. She lives on the Apollo habitat in the Moskva Complex. Every time I see her, I bring her a tree. We exchange them, so that we can look at the trees and think of each other."

Steward looked at the little trees, the simple pots with their glazed exteriors. "Do you have any other family?" he asked.

"Two daughters. They grew up in Taler habitats, have good positions with the company now. A son, who died on Archangel." SuTopo fell silent for a moment.

"I'm sorry, sir. I didn't know Taler was involved."

"It wasn't." The voice was gentle. "My son went his own way." He reached out a hand, as if to touch another of his dwarfs, but the hand stopped a centimeter short. "I keep this Yeddo spruce in his memory," he said. "Something will live in his name."

SuTopo, Steward thought, was another casualty of the war, and he hadn't even been involved. Living on a memory, like Steward, of something he hadn't been a part of. "That's a lovely thought," Steward said. SuTopo glanced over his shoulder at Steward, and his eyes were hard. Resentful, perhaps, of what might have sounded like Steward's judgment of his memorial.

The Captain turned to him, all business again, his hands brushing the front of his jacket, smoothing it into place. "You will excuse me, I hope. I must take a look at Cairo's reports. And examine the stowage in the cargo holds."

"Certainly. Pleased to meet you, sir," Steward said.

He wondered, as he bounded down the corridor toward his own quarters, about the existence of certain files, and how widespread they were. Griffith's friends probably had hundreds of dossiers between them, scattered throughout the security bureaus of every policorp in space, and quite probably the chess problem code was not as much a secret as Griffith thought. Was there a little warning indicator in Steward's file, a code that meant, *Known associate of Griffith, possible courier?*

And then, in a single frozen instant, Steward realized how stupid he'd been. He'd accessed the chess problem through a terminal in a hotel room registered in Starbright's name. If someone had been monitoring, Steward's name, as one of the few Starbright personnel onstation, would have flashed in bright red letters on the security desk.

But Charter didn't do things like that, so far as Steward knew. The place was a sieve—Charter security had been a joke for years, even when Steward had been in the Icehawks. Taler was another matter—they might run Starbright employees through their own security checks in order to make sure the Starbright people working on Taler ships weren't going to do anything to embarrass them, but they probably wouldn't bother to monitor suspect chess problems on the off chance that someone they knew would access them. Taler, Steward thought, was safe. And SuTopo probably gave his little speech to every new buck from Starbright.

Steward began to breathe easier. His misstep had probably gone unnoticed, but on a solid policorp habitat like Vesta it could have been fatal. Starbright wouldn't be at all happy with an employee who got himself barred from a major policorp, might even send him back to Earth with a nowhere job—recruiting maybe—and black marks all over his file.

Damn Griffith, Steward thought. He could have got me popped.

No. Steward corrected himself immediately. *I could have got myself popped.*

He reached his cabin, put the spike into his terminal, and randomized it. If somebody's security was looking at his possessions, he'd be clean.

He looked up at the walls. Vulvas larger than life winked at him, the porno he hadn't yet got around to tearing away from his walls. Somehow his relief and anxiety had got mixed up with a craving for tobacco, and his mouth was salivating for it. He clamped down on the desire, tried to concentrate on the vision of himself at liberty inside the insulating blanket of the vacuum. In another fourteen hours he'd be helping to boost the *Born* toward the Belt, and then no one was going to catch up with him.

Flames burned in Steward's mind. *Born* was accelerating at a steady one point five g as it slammed around Luna, using the moon's weak gravitational field in a game of snap-the-whip that would send *Born* cracking beyond Mars, toward the Belt. The engines would continue to burn for another three days, accelerating steadily the entire time.

If anything were to go wrong, it would most likely be under the stress of the first few hours of a high-g acceleration. For the first critical twelve hours Steward and Reese were both linked to each other and into the engines, the combustion chambers, high-pressure coolant pumps, control surfaces, fuel feeder monitors, backups...graphic analogs of entire systems hung in their minds, flamed in their brains' sensory centers. Fuel coursed across their tongues, electrons screamed across their vision, the white null sound of fusion roared in their ears.

Reese took the first four-hour shift with Steward observing, watching the way she gave her precise orders to the vast Starbright engines. Then Steward took the next four hours, Reese standing back, ready to flick the override with a push of her mind and take command if Steward couldn't handle a situation or acted the wrong way.

Steward tried to relax in his webbing, to flow with the Zen of the burning analog in his head. Decisions came automatically, easily—his long-term memory seemed to hold the necessary information, and the decisions themselves were simple. Shut off a vernier engine that had jammed full on, compensate for the increasing pitch of the ship by a precise firing of another vernier, inform the attitude computers about the change, monitor the other vernier engines so that the same problem didn't crop up again...basic stuff that he could almost have performed without any of the training. The Icehawks had given him some time in atmosphere-descent assault-craft simulators, and most of what he'd learned applied here—was simplified, in fact, by the lack of atmosphere and by Luna's weak gravity. There was a leak in a hydrazine line seal and he shifted hydrazine flow to a backup line. One of the fuel-feeder pumps was running warm and he monitored its temperature frequently.

Simple as it was, he was relieved when his shift ended. He could feel his jaw muscles unclench and only realized how hard he'd been gripping his webbing only when he began to feel the raw abraded flesh of his palms. He lay back, divorced from the action, watching Reese's checklist flicker through his mind, happy to let her make the decisions and decide priorities.

"I'm going to bed," he was told at the end of Reese's second shift. It seemed strange to actually hear anything important through his ears and not the headset. "If anything major comes up, go straight into a shutdown. We can afford any time lost to correct a problem. That feeder pump's cooled down, but keep an eye on it."

Steward raised a hand in the heavy gravity and gave a wave to show he had heard. Reese nodded and moved to a heavily padded elevator chair that moved upward through the bulkhead seal, taking Reese and the gravity monkey on her back to her living quarters. Ladders were too dangerous in high-g—ankles could snap like twigs in the event of a fall.

In Steward's mind the flames burned on. He could feel himself tensing again, battling the one and a half g as he clicked through his checklist, waiting for some disaster. He noticed an overloading energy pump on some communication lasers and switched to the backup, then watched for two hours as the checklist produced nothing but green lights, a perfectly stabilized burn leaving Earth and its dozens of shining metal moons well behind.... He began to feel his muscles relaxing, giving way before the heavy g, before his own reduced tensions.

And then something seemed wrong. He sensed it before he found it on his displays, a fluctuation in the pattern that made him uneasy, a power transient somewhere that lasted only a fraction of a second, but that affected other systems in a pattern like a wave, spreading out as the systems absorbed the transient and acted to automatically stabilize the energy flow.... Steward began to look seriously at the systems affected, trying to see where they were hooked together, what relationship they had with one another. The image of another problem came to his mind, and suddenly the two problems merged. He began to isolate systems, patterns forming and dissolving in his mind, and then he realized the problem.

The fuel-feeder pump was still overheating, white-hot by now, ready to slag itself and splash lithium slurry over the engine compartment. Somehow the sensor that monitored its temperature had been disabled—melted out by the rising heat, possibly, or most likely defective from the start—and none of the automated systems that were supposed to shut the pump down had been triggered. The melting sensor was sending out spikes through the system, but they hadn't been large enough to trigger an automated response.

Steward activated a backup pump and shut the hot one down. That was all it took, a simple command, and the situation created by the two malfunctioning pieces of equipment was over. Someone would later have to don a vac suit and go out into the airless engine spaces to replace the sensor and remove the pump for repairs, but that could wait for the end of the burn, and it was minor compared to the results of the fusion reaction running out of control due to irregularities in its fuel supply.

For the rest of his watch he didn't succeed in relaxing at all.

"I'd say you earned your pay," Reese said when she returned for her next shift.

"Thanks."

"That kind of intuitional leap is what we're here for," Reese mumbled as she webbed herself in. An interface stud was already jacked into her head socket; she had taken command of the engines. "The AIs that Starbright can afford to put into a small boat like this one can't handle that kind of thinking."

"Thanks," Steward said. Even though he'd removed his headset, garish displays were still blazing in his optical centers. "Can I go to bed now?"

Reese grinned at him. "Sweet dreams, buck."

"Enjoy."

After the first three-day burn and a short correction burn partway through the flight, there was little to keep the Starbright personnel busy during the long drift to the Belt save repairing the things that had gone wrong during the long acceleration.

Once the burn was over, the ship's centrifuge was started and eighty percent Earth-normal gravity prevailed for a few days, a relief from the heavy g of the burn, and then gravity was increased to one hundred percent Earth normal.

A few days into the trip there was a coded message for Steward from his bank in Ulan Bator: 1,500 Seven Moons dollars had been deposited to his account. And there was another two-word message from Griffith, sent in the clear. It read, *Lucky beginner.*

Steward watched the vid, learned to cook Chinese in the *Born*'s well-supplied kitchen, and exercised a lot, running through martial-arts drills and building muscle on the compact weight machine. He and Reese often worked out together, sparring in the *Born*'s small gym, Steward honing his reflexes fighting an opponent who was more than a shadow.... Reese was better than he, faster, making full use of the variable-lattice threads that had been woven through her nerves and brain to give her combat reflex and boosted nerve response. Steward was forced to become subtler in his attacks and learned to make multistrike combinations to draw Reese out of her guard, and even then he usually had to take some punishment before getting through.

The others worked out, too: Keeping fit was of prime use in surviving high-g burns. But Fischer was more interested in aerobic and muscle-building exercise that would help him in his hobby of mountaineering, Cairo preferred various kinds of gymnastics, and SuTopo ran endless tedious miles on a treadmill, his face expressionless, his motion unvarying. Daily, from ten hundred to eleven hundred, then sometimes again in the evening. It was the only time Steward ever saw him without his pitji. Steward could set his watch by the Captain's appearance in the gym.

Fischer was friendly and inquisitive, always wanting to compare Steward's life on Earth with his own youth in orbit. He wore loud clothes and always opened his mouth wide when he laughed, showing square yellow teeth. His pale Nordic complexion was unsuitable for space; he took carotene supplements to give his face some texture. Cairo was vaguely distant, always preoccupied, always with a squeeze bulb of coffee. SuTopo was less a person than a presence, a calm source of authority, like a reigning monarch.

Aside from sparring in the gym and the times they were involved on the same job, Steward hardly ever saw Reese, but when he did, the sparring seemed to extend to the rest of their relationship; their speech was always strewn with verbal booby traps, barbs, insinuation.... Despite the fact they worked together, Steward knew very little about her. He knew about SuTopo's bonsai, Fischer's interest in mountains, but whatever Reese did when she was by herself was unknown. She was often in her cabin, and when she was, the door was closed. Steward was never invited in. But in spite of the wariness of the relationship, in spite of the fact that he knew very little about her, Steward felt closest to Reese. However cautious they were, however little they knew each other, there was a friendship there, a mutual respect. Steward was careful not to presume on it, to tread on Reese's privacy. That, he concluded, was what friends did.

Steward was surprised by how many layers of pornography were on his walls—there seemed to be six or eight—and the process of removing them and repainting the plastic surface was a long one.

After two weeks in space, he began to regret that he'd taken all the pictures off. Porn would at least have given him something halfway pleasant to think about.

After four weeks he was happy to have scraped the stuff off. The same pictures day after day would have grown both tedious and frustrating. He began to understand why the previous occupant had kept pasting up new photos.

Steward thought about SuTopo's bonsai, Fischer's picture of Everest. The bonsai trees were representative of what SuTopo wanted, what he longed for—his family, his past, his memories.... Everest, to Fischer, was also an object of desire. Steward wondered what object would serve best in his own quarters, would serve to define his own longings.

He had no photo of Natalie, no reminders of his previous life. Ashraf had discouraged anything of the sort. He wished he had a picture of her, reminding him of what he'd lost, what he wanted to regain.

But there was another image that persisted, a video screen, flickering with interference pattern, and behind it, a face, a voice that was his own, a knowledge that was beyond him but that was approaching, coming closer with every second the *Born* continued its approach to the Belt... the face that was clarifying as Vesta approached, the hollow asteroid where the Alpha had gone in search of Colonel de Prey.

He called up the computer for its maps and history of Vesta. The amount of data surprised him—there were detailed maps, with recent updates that included such information as major power, water, air, and communications mains, location of environmental seals and security zones, details of security procedures, and local laws. It was far more reminiscent of an Icehawks briefing than a travel brochure, and Steward's respect for Taler's intelligence service increased.

Vesta had been pioneered by Far Ranger, who had first burrowed into the place as part of its mining operation and then turned it into a major Belt habitat. At one time, eighty thousand individuals lived in its interior. That number had been reduced by about a third after the Artifact War, when Brighter Suns was created in the wake of the collapse of the Outward Policorps, and the population was evicted from half the habitat while the Powers were brought in behind a wall of security and biologic shields.

The center of the sprawling hollowed-out section was given to docking bays and ship maintenance, power generation, and various forms of industry, primarily production and refining of metal and crystal. Much of the work, particularly the power production and smelting, had been moved to the surface of the asteroid. There was a large colony of 6,000 second-stage colonists, living free from gravity except for the small amount created by Vesta itself, all involved in industrial production of gravity-free items. The standard human population was concentrated in one area of the colony, living in three vast centrifuges that provided Earthlike gravity.

Mining was still going on—Vesta was a big asteroid, with a diameter of more than 300 kilometers, and only a small part was occupied. But mining had become secondary to import-export: With half the trade with the

Powers funneling through Vesta, the place had become the busiest trading station in the Belt.

Of the Powers, little was known or said. Access to their areas was strictly controlled through three airlocks: two for personnel, one for goods. Security was tight all over Vesta, every public area under the supervision of security AIs, and with the wealth that trade with the Powers was providing, Brighter Suns could afford the best in police personnel. Brighter Suns policorporate warriors were the equal of any in human space, and their duties were clear: Everything was secondary to the security and well-being of the Powers and the trade they represented. All internal communications were monitored, and access to outside communication was strictly controlled. There were several layers in the security bureaucracy, but the highest was called the Renseignement General, which meant simply General Information and which made Steward smile, remembering the spy romances of his childhood. The business arm of the RG was the Pulsar Division, an elite counterintelligence unit. The *Born*'s computer actually had a flow chart of the Pulsar unit's organization.

There was another, more shadowy group that handled outside intelligence and industrial espionage. They were called Group Seven. The comp had no organizational charts, no information on them save that of their existence.

Brighter Suns was a policorp created by other policorps for the express purpose of carrying on commerce with the Powers, controlling access to the aliens so that no new trade war could result. Brighter Suns held sovereignty over no territory other than Vesta—its charter forbade it—but it was one of the wealthiest policorps in existence and had one of the largest trading fleets. There were more Brighter Suns employees off Vesta than on it, occupying trading stations and docking ports throughout the rest of human space.

Colonel de Prey had lived here, Steward knew, in the employ of Brighter Suns. The Alpha had found him and probably killed him, and then had been killed here or later by Curzon. This was a piece of Vesta's history that had not been picked up by Taler's computers.

Steward thought about it all and tried to plan a course of action, then gave up on it. Even with all the information here, there wasn't enough available about the things he needed to know. He was going to have to begin searching data files on Vesta before he could make any further decisions.

And Griffith's scheme? With communications being monitored, it was riskier here than elsewhere. He wasn't going to start accessing chess programs until the end of the stay here, when it would no longer matter if he were brought under suspicion.

He didn't want to be greedy.

Then came the deceleration burn, lasting another three days, marked by the four-hour shifts split between Reese and Steward that left them both exhausted and floating limp in their webbing, grateful for the return to weightlessness. Steward had been planning to charge off the ship as soon as he could, but he found he didn't have the strength for it, and floated up to his cabin to go to sleep. Reese followed him, heading for her own quarters. They found SuTopo waiting for them, hanging upside down outside Steward's cabin door, his pitji still firmly on his head.

"If you'll give me your passports," SuTopo said, "I'll clear us all through customs."

"Thanks."

"You'll also need to report to Cairo to give a blood sample. They're fanatical about contamination here, and they need samples from all of us before they'll let anyone onstation."

"You'd think they'd just keep my records on file from last time," Reese muttered.

Steward's Starbright passport was a black plastic wafer with the policorporate sigil on it, contained a permanent-lattice thread with his official identification, finger and retinal prints, and any unique medical history that emergency doctors might need to know. Apparently it didn't have whatever information Brighter Suns needed from his blood. Steward took the passport from his cabin and gave it to SuTopo.

"Have a good leave," Steward said.

"You'll leave the ship before I will, I think," SuTopo said as he put Steward's passport in his pocket and closed the Velcro flap over it. "I'm supervising the unloading."

"Sorry," Steward said, trying hard to raise some genuine sympathy. He swam to the sick bay with Reese, where Cairo stuck a needle in his arm and efficiently removed some blood, then he floated back to his rack and raised the harness webbing.

He closed his eyes. Engine analogs pulsed on the back of his lids. Sleep came in less than a hundred breaths.

He slept about seven hours, showered, pulled on his Jack Totem T-shirt, cords, and jeans jacket, and, before he left, checked his messages—he wasn't going to make that mistake again. There was a garbled message from Fischer, obscured by a lot of clatter and laughter in the background, about a good party at a place called the Time Zero, and nothing else. He floated forward to the personnel tube that led to the Vesta airlock.

His passport had already presumably cleared him through customs, so he pressed his thumb to the plate with the Brighter Suns logo on it and the airlock opened. He stepped in, pressed the button that let the lock mechanism know he was inside, and watched the door behind him hiss shut. Lights ran green above the inner door, it opened, and he floated into a noisy concourse sheathed in dark alloy, where cargo was being moved in vast weightless packets to the sound of blatting warning horns and the muted hiss of control jets.

Steward glanced at the holos that pointed him in the direction of human-occupied Vesta, then pushed off from the airlock door toward a tunnel entrance a hundred meters distant.

As he drifted slowly across, Steward heard a hissing behind and to one side, and saw two men floating toward him. They each wore roomy, dark quilted jackets buttoned up to the throat, and each carried a small hand-held gas jet to help him maneuver in the weightless cavern. One had a hand stuffed in his jacket pocket. They were watching him with mild, uninterested eyes.

They were moving on a collision course, but Steward wasn't worried—the others could control their movements, and he knew they saw him. But as they drifted closer, he saw that the bulky jackets, though in a civilian style, were the kind worn by military and security people, with interior pockets that could be filled with alloy and ceramic inserts to deflect bullets.

Adrenaline gates surged open and he could feel a shift in his perceptions, in his body, as nerves and mind slammed into overdrive. These people were after him. He could waste time trying to think of a reason, but thinking was pointless in view of the fact that they were already here.

He looked around, scanning the vast room. There was no one near him, and the two men were growing ever closer. He could flail about in hopes of altering his trajectory, but the two jacketed men could alter their course at will, and had the advantage as long as they were in a weightless environment. Steward was going to have to survive the first impact and then get his back against a bulkhead. Then he might stand a chance.

Steward looked back at the two men. They were within ten meters now, and he could tell from their expressions that they knew he was aware of them. Their eyes flickered, calculating trajectories, angles. Steward cocked his arms and legs, waiting. They drifted closer in silent slow motion, unhurried.

He tried to kick the first one, hoping to connect and push them apart, but the man was ready and Steward kicked only air. The other seized his cuff, and then took his hidden hand out of his pocket. His fist was encased in a black zap glove, and Steward could feel panic begin to rise deep inside him. He kicked his foot again and managed to get his cuff free, but he could see the triumphant, tight-lipped smile as the man drifted closer, as he raised his fist and punched out against Steward's knee.

Laser light burned in Steward's brain as his every neuron misfired, as he stiffened from the electric shock and air burst from his lungs in a single shrieking exhalation. Tears stung his eyes. He tried to shout, to move, but his body had gone limp as his nerves wailed in shock, and nothing in him would respond save his own rising fear. The two men had seized him now, were drifting with him toward the tunnel.

One of them had a hypo in his hand. He looked at Steward and grinned. "Bye-bye, asshole," he said. Steward felt the pain of the needle driving through his corduroy jeans into his thigh, and the burn as the drug was injected.

He wanted to ask them why, at the end, but decided not to. He concluded he'd just as soon not know.

CHAPTER EIGHT

Steward panted through a mouth that was swollen and dry. He tried to lick his lips, but there was no moisture there at all. It seemed to him that he could feel his tongue splitting as he moved it. There was a ferocious pain behind his eyes. The nape of his neck felt moist. Cautiously he cracked his eyelids open.

This was, in fact, worse than he anticipated. He was in a metal cube about three meters square, the walls dull silver alloy with dark mottling. One wall featured a door with a slot for food, heavily screened ventilators, and a pair of bright floodlights, also behind screens, that were incapable of being controlled from Steward's side of the door. He was stretched on a too-short foam mattress encased in a dark plastic cover and lying on the floor. Two blankets were thrown over him. There was no furniture except for a combination sink/toilet. He was naked.

He felt very heavy. This was a high-g room, about one point three, designed to wear him down.

He was probably being monitored. The dryness in his mouth was painful. He juggled the two ideas for a while, wondering whether he cared if they knew he was awake, then decided there was no point in being quiet. He stood carefully, his spine and knees popping. There was a wet area on the plastic mattress cover where he'd sweated out the drug. He saw two round burn marks on the flesh above one knee where the zap glove's electrodes had hit him. Breathing seemed to take a lot of effort. Maybe the oxygen content of the air had been lowered, again to wear him down. Steward moved to the sink to rinse his mouth.

He was very thirsty. He held his mouth to the tap and drank for a long time. The water was flat and tasteless, fresh from the recycler.

Water dripped on his chest as he straightened. He wiped it off with his hand. G dragged at his legs, his spine, his kidneys. Steward moved back to his mattress and began to stretch out, getting the kinks out of his spine, his body. Tried to compose his mind, build his mental armor.

He finished his stretches without interruption. He was feeling better, the headache ebbing.

What the hell, he thought. He pushed the mattress and blankets aside and began to do calisthenics. He could think of little else to do.

About the sixtieth high-g push-up he began to reconsider, but it was too late and he wasn't going to give his watchers the satisfaction of seeing him give up. So he pumped out another forty, trying hard to keep his form perfect, and then stood up for a few rounds of squat jumps.

"Prisoner Steward." A toneless male voice that came from behind one of the screens on his door. "Get on your knees, facing away from the door. Put your hands behind your back."

"In a minute," Steward said, and continued with his current set.

"Get on your knees." The voice was as expressionless as before. "Face away from the door. Put your hands behind your back."

"Nine. Ten." Steward wondered how many times they'd repeat the instructions before sending in people with zap gloves, decided that this wasn't the best time to find out. He obeyed instructions and knelt with his hands behind him.

The door opened. From the sound of their boots on the metal floor he sensed at least two guards, maybe three. Hands seized his forearms. He felt a garment being pushed roughly up his arms, dropping onto his back and calves, and then handcuffs closed around his wrists. He tried the handcuffs, found that they were the kind with a solid bar between them instead of a flexible chain.

"Stand up." The voice was odd, filtered somehow, as if heard over a telephone.

As he stood he looked at the guards, two men and a woman. The woman stood behind the other two with a zap glove on each hand, gazing at him with butterfly-wing eyes. Each was taller than he was, muscular, stone-faced, dressed in a gray uniform complete with big armored jacket. They were wearing black plastic helmets with face shields lowered. If Steward tried to hit them, all he could do was break his own knuckles. The odd quality of the voice was due to its coming from a speaker on a guard's belt and originating from a mic inside the helmet.

Before cuffing him they'd pushed a thin cotton robe onto him from behind. One of the men stepped to Steward's front and drew the robe around him, fastening it with Velcro tabs. Steward looked down at the robe. It was faded blue and had a number and Steward's name stenciled on it in bright new black letters.

The guard dropped a pair of heelless plastic slippers in front of Steward. Steward stepped into them.

"Turn around," the guard said.

"I don't suppose it would help to ask why I'm being held." Which, Steward knew, would have got him a backhand across the face in two-thirds of the jails in the human sphere. He wanted to find out what their orders were.

"Turn around." Without a blink. Maybe they'd been told to exercise special care.

Steward turned, felt the guard seize the bar that kept his handcuffs apart. He was going to try to remember every detail of what he saw next.

"Follow."

The corridor was bare alloy and was lit by fluorescents set into slots in the ceiling. The guards marched Steward past the featureless doors of six other cells—Steward counted each one—and then through an armored security door. Here was a desk with another guard, his helmet off, holding papers that one of Steward's escort had to sign. Presumably they released Steward into his custody. Beyond him was an elevator door. In order to work it one of the guards had to feed his plastic ID into a slot next to the buttons. The elevator rose four floors. Steward felt lighter as he rose in the massive centrifuge. His knee joints crackled.

The corridor was busier, filled with guards and businesslike, incurious people in civilian clothes. The ceiling and floor were alloy, the walls plastered and painted beige. There were closed doors, each numbered, with electric keyboard combination locks. Signs on the walls warned about security, safety, and procedural matters, and there was a bulletin board with notices pinned to it, the board next to a vidscreen on which notices—possibly the same notices—scrolled continuously.

The escort moved Steward into a large room full of desks and people. Steward noticed a durable carpet on the floor, soundproofing on the ceiling, clutter on the desks. There were murmured conversations and the tapping of console keys. Coffee and soft-drink dispensers were built into the walls. "Stop," said the man behind Steward, tugging on the crossbar of his handcuffs. Steward came to a halt.

The guard in the lead left the group, moved to a nearby, empty desk. He raised the faceplate of his helmet to talk to a woman at the next desk, who nodded and indicated a man who was standing against the near wall, pushing buttons on a coffee dispenser. The guard moved toward him. When the man turned at the guard's approach, Steward saw he was of middle height, age about forty, a little puffy around the middle. He was dressed in dark trousers, bulky quilted jacket, light blue shirt. He was going bald on top and his dark hair was cut short. The guard stopped near him and addressed him respectfully. The man sipped his coffee from a foam cup, made a face, and then looked across the room to Steward.

A warning moved up Steward's spine. The man's eyes were angry, intelligent, almost savage, cold as the solar wind. *I'm going to break you like a twig.* That was the message Steward read. It was like looking into the void.

The man nodded again, then moved back to his desk. He picked up a key spike from a box filled with papers that sat on his desk and put it in his pocket. He punched a number on his phone and spoke briefly, then picked up a file folder from his desk and moved toward where Steward waited. "Number twelve," he said to the guards, and brushed past Steward without looking at him. He had an accent that Steward couldn't place.

"Turn around," said the guard behind. Steward shuffled around till he was facing the other way, then let himself be marched down the corridor in the other direction.

He could smell the balding man's coffee. It made his mouth water.

The balding man took the spike out of his pocket and pushed it into one of the locks on the door. He pressed a code into the keyboard, and electronic bolts shot back. He stepped back from the door, putting the spike back in his pocket.

"Put him in the chair," he said. Steward's guard moved him through the door and ordered him to sit.

The chair was black gas-planet plastic, backless, and bolted to the floor. The bar on Steward's handcuffs was fastened to a metal projection that thrust from the back of the chair.

There was a small desk in front of Steward. The balding man sat behind it. Steward could see LEDs reflected in his eyes, monitoring Steward's condition through the cuffs and through stress indicators in his voice.

Monitored. Steward tried to bring moisture into his mouth, failed.

He possessed nothing, he knew, but himself. Nothing else could help him. He had no armor, no weapons. He had to build them, somehow.

I have no tactics, he thought. I make existence and the void my tactics. A Zen chant.

I have no castle. The immutable spirit is my castle.

I have no sword. From the state which is above and beyond, from thought, I make my sword.

The universe was hostile; he would therefore, he decided, make his own. He decided to build constellations in his head, remember the stars and the way they were arranged. One by one, until he had heaven in his mind. Scorpius first. He tried to remember how many stars it had, how they were arranged. Antares, M4, M7, just so. All learned in his night navigation classes.

"Leave us," the balding man said. "I'll let you know when we're done."

The guards left. The alloy door closed behind them. Steward thought of stars as the balding man stared at him in cold silence and sipped his coffee. Steward breathed deliberately, flexed his muscles in the cuffs, testing the limits of his posture. Tried to keep his mind elsewhere, away from the stare he felt on him, away from the metal box that was holding him. Tried not to react when, after a long time filled only with the whispering of the vent, the man finally spoke.

"I'm Colonel Angel," he said. "I work for the Pulsar Division. And you're my meat."

Achernar, thought Steward. At the end of Eridanus.

Wolf 294, he thought. Sheol.

Angel was trying to hold his eyes with his stare. Aldebaran, thought Steward. In Orion. Wrong. In Taurus.

"Firstly," Angel said, "the Procureur has declared your case a matter covered by the Internal Security Code. That means you will be held as long as we feel like holding you, and any records will be under permanent seal. You won't be talking to anyone, not an attorney, no one. No habeas corpus, no bond. You've just disappeared into a pit, and I'm the only man who has the ladder that can get you out."

Steward looked up at him. From the universe in his head Angel seemed a long way. "I don't suppose the code authorizes you to tell me exactly what I've supposed to have done."

There was a vein pulsing in Angel's temple. "Multiple murder, for a start."

More than one? Steward thought.

"Sabotage. Espionage. Attacks on accredited members of the Power Trade Legation. Minor things like theft and customs avoidance."

"When am I supposed to have done this, exactly?"

"Nineteen February. This year."

Steward forced himself to smile. "Got you there. I was someplace else."

Angel seemed unimpressed. "I suppose you can prove it. Witnesses and everything, right? You never left Ricot."

"I've never been on Ricot. Last February I was in a cryogenic vault in Flag-staff, Arizona, USA." Angel didn't react.

"That's on Earth, spacebuck," Steward said.

"New bodies happen all the time. I can see you're younger than you're supposed to be."

"I don't have memories of anything that happened after the age of twenty-two. So you're throwing me in a pit for something I have no memory of committing." Steward grinned again. "I guess you'll look pretty silly to the Procureur."

"Consolidated would be stupid not to give you a new identity after what you did."

"Consolidated didn't. That's my point. My Alpha—that's the buck you're after—he died on Ricot in March. Consolidated Systems isn't interested in me. They didn't give me a new identity. If I were still working for them, do you think they wouldn't give me a new name and prints, at least?"

Angel's expression didn't change. "Delaying tactics won't work, Steward," he said. "Your only hope of getting out of here is to cooperate."

"Look it up. Get my records out of the hospital."

"Records can be altered."

Steward shrugged as far as the handcuffs would let him. The door behind Angel opened and another man came in. Ghostly fingers brushed Steward's belly at the sight of him, a fear that mutated rapidly to anger. The man was big, bullet-headed, narrow-eyed. Steward recognized him as the one who had hit him with the zap glove when he was arrested. The second man leaned against the back wall without saying anything. He had his hand stuffed in his coat pocket, as if he still had a zap glove on.

I'd like a minute with you, Steward thought. A minute without your glove or jets or whatever technology you've got threaded into your nerves. I don't care if you've got twenty kilos on me.

LEDs winked red in Angel's eyes.

Steward took a breath. M44, he thought. In Cancer.

Interrogation technique, he thought. The primary rule was always to isolate the individual: That was the first thing. Make him feel alone in the world. Put him naked in a metal box. Shine spotlights on him all the time so he doesn't know if it's night or day, so that one of the first things to go is his sense of time. March him through the security station so that he will feel even more alone, an individual caught in a vast machine. Then put him in a small room, tell him the only way he'll ever get out of the machine is to do as he's told, and provide just that extra burst of fear by putting him in with a very large man who, very recently, has just caused him vast pain….

By contrast with the other, Angel would become the good guy. Steward would become dependent on him to keep the other away. Would wish to please him, confide in him. Give him everything he wanted.

Steward knew all the moves, exactly what Angel was doing. But that didn't mean Angel's techniques wouldn't work. The only way not to crack was to keep himself intact, integral, away from this. Inside the universe of stars that he was building in his head.

There was more than one interrogation here, Steward thought, and he was the only one who was aware of it. Angel and his partner knew what had happened here on Vesta, and were trying to find the answers to what they didn't know. Steward knew less than they, couldn't give them anything new. But the very questions they asked might tell Steward something, and he had to keep them asking. He had protested his innocence because it would have seemed odd if he hadn't. But really he wanted the interrogation to continue, wanted Angel and the other to talk about what they thought Steward already knew. And in order to do that, he had to interest them, had to convince them somehow that he had the answers they wanted. He had to act as if he knew things they didn't.

Angel crushed his foam coffee cup, dropped it onto the desk. He held up the file folder, opened it, glanced through it. Steward saw the name on it: FILESECUR: STEWARD.1 "What were you going to do, Steward?" he asked. "Were you going to a meet? Visit someone you knew? Or were you just going to check the extent of what you did last time?"

"I was going," Steward said, "to a place called Time Zero."

"To meet somebody?"

"To meet Fischer. He's communications officer on the *Born*. He called me and told me there was a good party." He looked up at Angel and grinned. "I'm sure you were recording communications on and off the ship. Listen to it. Maybe it'll satisfy the Procureur that you know what you're doing."

Angel's partner took his hand out of his pocket. He was wearing a zap glove. He held an inhaler in his gloved hand. He put the inhaler to his mouth and pressed the trigger.

Great, Steward thought. An asthmatic goon.

Angel's voice filled the silence. "Who do you know on Vesta, Steward?"

Steward turned his eyes to Angel and tried to put as much venom into the look as possible. "You tell me. You're the fucking expert."

"Who did you see in February?"

Steward only looked at him.

"On whose orders were you here?"

Mira. In Cetus. Angel's partner was taking off his jacket.

"Did the order come from high up? Or was it Curzon?" Steward felt something inside him leap at the mention of the name. Seen on Angel's readouts, no doubt, which might make him think he had something.

Angel's partner, carrying his jacket, was slowly moving around the desk, toward Steward.

Procyon, Steward thought. In the Little Dog.

"Was Curzon working on his own? Did the Board know? The Chairman?"

Angel's partner was standing behind Steward now. The hair on the back of Steward's neck prickled at his closeness. Suddenly the man threw his jacket over Steward's head, held it close around him. Steward smelled sweat, plastic, his own sour breath. He felt panic rising, tried to bite it down. Angel's voice went on, toneless.

"Did the Prime know? Was it the Prime's idea?"

Steward's pulse crashed in his ears. He felt the touch of the zap glove against his shoulder, two hard electrodes pressing through his flimsy robe. He fought against the fabric that was trying to smother him and tried to remember what constellation Fomalhaut was in.

Spit into the void, he thought.

"Fuck off, Angel."

The lights went out for a while.

After several interrogations Steward couldn't sleep on his back because of the scorch marks from the zap glove. His right hand was going numb and he wondered about neurological damage from the repeated jolts of electricity.

Angel kept coming back to the same questions. Who on Vesta had he worked with? Who had sent him to Vesta, and with whose knowledge? Was the Prime involved? Angel never tried any tricks, never used rhetoric, just came back to the same questions. Monotonously. With his partner there to administer the zap when Angel got bored with the questions he was asking.

Steward couldn't answer the questions if he wanted to. And he wasn't getting asked anything new.

Steward wondered why they weren't using drugs. He had gone under drugs and deep hypnosis as an Icehawk, part of techniques designed to help him resist interrogation. But that kind of conditioning could be broken, given enough patience. And though interrogation under drugs was suspect—the subject might not only babble what he knew, he might cheerfully invent information or tell the interrogator what he thought he wanted to hear—the drugs would certainly work better than anything Angel had tried so far, and careful interrogation could winnow out truth from hallucination.

Maybe Angel was just addicted to classical methods. Maybe he thought the use of drugs would be like cheating.

Maybe he just liked the smell of scorched flesh.

And then it occurred to Steward: Maybe they tried drugs, when he first arrived, while he was still out. And they hadn't worked.

The Prime, Steward thought. That was all he'd got out of this, the only thing that was new. He wondered if the Prime was someone in Consolidated Systems' security apparatus.

He looked around his cell, flexed his shoulders, and winced at the protest of scorched flesh. This was one of the few times when he hadn't awakened to the voice of guards ordering him to kneel facing away from the door, hands behind his back.

A small gesture of defiance might be in order. He rolled off his mattress and started to do push-ups. On his fists. Yelling on each upthrust. At the end, gasping for breath, he tossed a finger in the direction of the monitors concealed behind the screens on the front wall and muttered, "Take that, Angel."

He drank water from the sink and started shadowboxing. The two bright floodlights gave him two shadows to dance with. They both reeled drunkenly. Something had happened to his balance.

The electric bolt on the door slammed back. It opened. Steward spun, felt a wave of vertigo at the too-sudden move. He stood, his fists still up, and saw one of his guards, the woman he saw the first day, standing in the doorway. Her helmet was off, her armored jacket was open to reveal the uniform blouse underneath. She was blond and square-faced, her eyes distant beneath the butterfly-wing makeup. She was holding his clothes folded neatly in one hand.

She tossed them onto the mattress. "Put them on," she said. "You're being released."

He lowered his guard slightly, not believing this. "Why?"

She shrugged. "I don't know. I don't know why they were holding you in the first place. Not my job." She stepped back behind the door. "Check your pockets, make sure everything's there. You'll have to sign for it. Knock when you're ready." The door closed again.

Steward stood breathing hard, his mind swimming, his eyes dazzled by the floods. He thought for a moment, then slowly put on his underwear and socks, drew on his cords, then his boots. He checked his pockets, looked at the shirt and jacket and thought, If I get my chance. He put the T-shirt and jacket over one arm and knocked.

The door opened again, and Steward realized that it hadn't been bolted. The woman looked him up and down. "You going to put your shirt on?"

"I like the way I look, with zap marks all over my back."

The guard frowned at him. "Up to you, I guess."

He followed her to the desk down the hall, then signed for his belongings. She took him into the elevator, then down the long beige corridor, past Room Twelve to the big room where people were tapping their console keys and talking into their telephones.

Steward stopped and looked at them and wondered how many of them knew the sorts of things that happened in Room Twelve. Maybe they all did. Maybe that was just part of the working day to these people, taking in a torture session before the afternoon coffee break.

"This way." His escort had stopped and turned to face him. Steward looked slowly over the room. Angel and his partner were not to be seen. Maybe it wasn't their shift.

"I want some coffee," he said, and turned.

"Hey," the guard said.

"Brighter Suns owes me *coffee*, for shit's sake!" Steward snapped, his voice very loud. People looked up at him; saw the burn marks; looked down. No one seemed particularly troubled. He passed by Angel's desk and looked down at it as he passed. What he wanted was there, just where he remembered it had been on the first day, that first interrogation. Sitting on a pile of papers, on a bunch of file folders with classified stamps.

Steward was swaying slightly as he walked. His balance was still wrong. He exaggerated the motion slightly, found himself overdoing and almost fell, caught himself in time. Okay, he thought. Slow and easy.

He punched coffee with extra cream and turned to glare at the room. People were looking down, suddenly fascinated with their display terminals. Steward laughed. He took his coffee and affected a swagger as he moved back up the aisle. Only his escort was watching; he would have to be careful to conceal the movement from her.

He raised the coffee to his lips and walked into Angel's desk, bumping his knee and falling forward, the coffee spilling over the file folders. "Shit," he said, and tossed his jacket and shirt down on the spill, as if to mop it up. He swabbed the desk until he felt what he wanted under his hand, clutched it, then pulled his arm violently back, as if he'd realized what he was doing.

"Fuck it," he said, loudly. "A wet desk is the least thing I can give him."

His escort was hurrying toward him. She looked from Steward to the desk and back. "Finished now?" she asked.

"Spilled my coffee."

"You want to go or what?"

He crumpled the foam cup and tossed it in a waste container. "Okay," he said. "Let's go."

And, as he followed his escort out, he tried very hard to keep from smiling.

In the waiting room just inside the detention station Steward saw the crew of the *Born* waiting for him. They were all in uniform, Reese in the light blue of Starbright, the others in dark gray Taler jackets. There was another man in Starbright uniform that Steward didn't recognize, with violet collar tabs of a kind that Steward hadn't ever seen. They rose as he entered.

Reese came forward, reached out to touch Steward, brushing his shoulder with the backs of her knuckles. There was shock in her eyes, followed rapidly by anger. "You have a bad time?"

He tried to be offhand. "Depends on your feelings about torture, I guess." He looked at them each in turn. "How long was I in there?"

"Six days."

"It seemed longer."

She cut her eyes to the stranger in the Starbright uniform. "This is Mr. Lal," she said. "He's the Starbright consul."

Lal's handshake was brisk. His uniform fit him well. "Glad I was able to get you out," he said.

"I don't think you had much to do with it," Steward said. "I think they just finally decided to believe my records."

There was hesitation in Lal's eyes.

"I want you to get pictures of my back," Steward said. "They tortured me in there."

"We can't get involved with matters of internal Brighter Suns procedure," Lal said.

"So that they can't object next time Starbright decides to torture some Brighter Suns citizen, right?" Steward said. "Fuck this. I'll file the complaint myself. And I'll publicize it." He looked at the others. "Let's get out of here."

Steward brushed past Lal and moved out the door. He could see Reese's grin out of the corner of his eye. The others followed.

The door was blastproof, covered with monitors, and had some kind of exploding star on it, burning in the middle of a spiral galaxy. The Pulsar Division. Outside, the street was cold dark alloy with a bright ceiling that reflected the people below.

A few people were drifting up and down the street. Vesta was between shifts.

"Lal was worthless, you know," Reese said. "I had to stand over him the whole time. Once he found out it had gone to the Pulsar Division he said it was hopeless."

"I'm not surprised," Steward said.

"You should have seen the Captain, though." Reese looked at SuTopo. "I've never seen him madder. Beating his fist on the cops' desk and roaring about them wrecking his schedule."

Steward turned to him. "Thanks."

SuTopo only smiled. "My job," he said.

"Not yours. Lal's."

"What was it your Alpha did that made them all so mad?" Reese asked.

"Killed some people. They said."

"I guess that might make them cross."

Reese had fallen in step with him, to one side and slightly behind. Steward looked to the other side and saw Fischer, grinning under a new blond mustache, unbuttoning his uniform coat to reveal a green and red tropical shirt. SuTopo was striding behind him and to one side, his face solemn under his pitji hat. Cairo was on the other side of Reese.

A wedge, Steward thought, marching in lockstep along the third level of the Vesta mainline centrifuge, Steward at the ardis, cleaving apart the Brighter Suns citizens. There was a feeling of belonging here, a glow of comradeship, one that Steward knew wouldn't last—his purposes weren't theirs, nor theirs his—but still it was good to know that there were people here who would go to trouble on his behalf, who would fight for him, at least in some things.

And there was another reason for Steward's glow. His hand was still clutching Colonel Angel's spike, the key he used to get access to secured places, to Room Twelve, to his sealed computer files. Security, Steward had been told, was only as good as the people who enforced it. Angel had been careless with his key, and Steward was going to open as many doors with it as he could.

CHAPTER NINE

"**G**ive myself some painkiller first," Steward said. "Then sleep." Cairo pressed the silent button of a camera behind him, coding the burn marks on his back into the molecular structure of its variable-geometry threads. She shifted to another position and took another picture.

"Yeah," Reese said. "Take care of yourself first."

"I'll file the complaint when I get up," Steward said. "Then maybe broadcast the pictures to some news agencies on Earth. Some of them might be able to evade Brighter Suns' pressure."

"You want a doctor to look at you?" Cairo asked.

Steward flexed his right hand, still feeling the numbness there. "Maybe," he said. "I'll see how I feel when I wake up."

Cairo straightened, then looked into the viewer of her camera, clicking backward through the recorded photographs. "I've taken six," she said. "That should be enough, don't you think?"

Steward nodded. "I suppose." He rubbed the bridge of his nose and yawned. "Sick bay," he said. "Then bed."

"Let me dress those burns," Reese said, standing up.

"That many dressings would just get in my way," Steward said. "I'll just wash them in the shower before I go to bed."

"Ouch," said Cairo.

Reese looked at him. "You sure?"

He nodded and yawned again. "Just some sleep," he said. "That's all I want."

She nodded slowly. "Okay. But if you need anything…"

"I won't. Go out onstation and give yourself a party. Celebrate. Drink a few for me."

Steward walked down the corridor to the sick bay. He collected some disinfectant and bandages for later, then put some painkiller in a pneumatic hypo, pressed it to his arm, and pulled the trigger. Then he went to another cabinet and shook some speed into his hand.

He'd have to stay awake for a while.

He dry-swallowed the pills and headed for his quarters. Once there, he showered, shaved off his six days' growth of beard, leaving himself a dark mustache, and collected a dozen empty data spikes. He put on a pair of dark trousers that gathered at the ankle with a drawstring. He drew on a high-collared shirt, wincing at the pain, then put on slippers and a dark collarless jacket that looked vaguely like someone's uniform, without the insignia. Looking at himself in the mirror, he concluded that he could pass for a young Brighter Suns exec. He turned on his terminal and printer and punched up the map of Vesta that was in the ship's computer. He made copies of some of the maps that interested him, then turned off his terminal. The data spikes went into an anonymous leather pouch, along with Angel's spike, then Steward stepped to his door, opened it slightly, and listened.

The old ship whispered from its vents. He heard no other sound.

Steward slipped out of his door and closed it carefully behind him. Speed was beginning to hum in his nerves, his spine. He grinned and moved to the downship access, opened it, stepped into the gravity-free machine space. He pushed off from the access, floated up to the main outside airlock, and looked through the rack for his vac suit. Once Steward found it, he took it and drifted aft to a smaller personnel airlock. Sometimes Cairo had occasion to use the main airlock to perform routine maintenance outside, and he didn't want to run into her there. In the aft lock he put his air bottles into the ready compressor and put the levers on CHARGE just to assure himself the old bottles would have plenty of air.

He cycled himself through the airlock and hovered outside, letting his eyes adjust to the darkness. Vesta was a dim glow beneath him. Floodlights spotted the surface, reflected by the shining skin of dozens of transport ships plugged like oxygen bottles into the rugged flesh of the asteroid. His breathing echoed in his ears. Speed twitched at his muscles. He drifted slowly downward, caught in the asteroid's slight gravity.

Orienting himself carefully, he fired his directional jets and winced as a shoulder seal rubbed against his burns. He weaved between huge, glittering transports, then out of the dock area and above the bare rock surface of the asteroid. Networks of red and white lights strobed across the skin of the rock, each pulsing out a pattern that identified a particular manufacturing dome, radar station, airlock. He oriented himself mentally, then jetted toward the white flashing light that marked an airlock, landed on the Velcro strip surrounding the door, his boots adhering to the strip as his knees absorbed the shock. The airlock door was labeled in black Roman letters: LEV L, S 33, ACCESS 7. This would bring him into a main transport tunnel, South 33, rather than a secure industrial complex that might require him to log his identity on entry. He lowered himself to the lock controls, hearing in the small world of his suit the strange scrunch of Velcro ripping free, and requested the airlock door to open. It accepted his request without comment.

He stepped through the lock into a large anteroom, armored against radiation, that was supposed to be used in case of decompression in S 33. Two emergency vac suits hung on racks. He put his own suit next to the Brighter Suns suits, straightened his jacket, and opened the heavy plated door. People soared by, tugging themselves along by ceiling loops or kicking themselves from one Velcro strip to another. Steward moved into traffic and flew along the ceiling loops until he came to an intersecting tunnel on which Brighter Suns inhabitants were hitching rides on a moving belt that took them to one of the giant habitation centrifuges. The speed welled up his spine. He pulled himself along the belt from one loop to the next, happy for the activity. Steward moved through a vast door into the central mainline centrifuge.

Once there, he moved downward to point eight g, a comfortable level of gravity. This level was composed mainly of offices belonging to one or another of the policorporate bureaucracies. It was second shift and there weren't many people in the area. The speed made Steward want to dance down the corridor. He could feel a grin tugging at his face and he tried hard to look serious.

He entered a place that rented computer hardware and plugged a credit spike into a unit. He called up the Brighter Suns news bureau and began to look for scansheets dating from the nineteenth of February, the day that Angel told him Colonel de Prey died. There were no notices of violent deaths, no obituaries, no mention of someone named Steward.

What Steward found were urgent headlines and public announcements concerning a contamination alert in the Power Trade Legation. No details were given, but the Power section of Vesta was sealed, biologic decontamination teams were mobilized, and all trade had ground to a halt. Something approaching martial law had been declared, then rescinded five days later. Scansheets were more heavily censored than usual, but sheets available on file from other policorps, which had themselves been censored during the emergency but put on file later, hinted heavily that some Earth bacteria had got across the seals into the Power section and made the Powers ill. Steward remembered the rumor that the reason the Powers left Earth in the first place was because they'd proved susceptible to Earth diseases.

No permanent damage had been done, according to the sheets. The Head of Legation, a Power known as Samuel, had expressed his thanks to the Brighter Suns administration for their prompt and effective action during the emergency. The seals were opened on the twenty-fourth and normal trade recommenced.

So, Steward thought. The Alpha had probably been sent by Curzon to spread some kind of contamination in the Power zone. But whatever contamination it was, it hadn't lasted long—normal trade had resumed within days. Of course, considering the completely restricted access to the Power zone, it could have been a raging plague that killed hundreds of the aliens, and the news might simply have been censored.

Someone knocked a stack of printout onto the floor behind Steward, and he almost jumped out of his chair. The speed was making him nervous. He broadcast a self-conscious grin over his shoulder and went back to his machine.

Steward then realized that the trade might not have resumed at its former levels, that the announcement of normal trade may have been exaggerated. He went from the news sections of the scansheets to the section on ship arrivals and departures. The numbers of ships departing took a dramatic dip during the contamination alert, as might be expected, and then leaped upward after the alert had been ended. He flipped downtime and counted the number of ships leaving each day, finding an average of thirty-five to forty, then did the same count uptime from the twenty-fourth.

There *was* a perceptible dip, four or five fewer departures per day less than average, even a week after the alert had been ended.

Steward wondered if the drop in commerce running through Vesta was sufficient to motivate Consolidated Systems to make their attack. The loss to Brighter Suns was probably colossal, but even at the new, less efficient rate there was still an implausible amount of money flowing in, and the decrease was sure to be short-lived as soon as the Powers could send in more personnel. And of course such a blatant attack was certain to invite retaliation. Steward wondered if Consolidated Systems' biological defenses were more elaborate than Brighter Suns', if they were confident in fending off a Brighter Suns strike.

Perhaps there was a greater dimension to all of this, Steward thought. Perhaps the purpose was to make the aliens doubt Brighter Suns' ability to protect them against biological hazard. Perhaps the Powers would be convinced to do most of their business with Consolidated from now on.

Steward logged out, took his credit spike out of the machine, and stepped out onto the silent second-shift street. His next bit of business would require a place more private.

He walked along the dark alloy, looking at the names and corporate emblems that blazoned the long street. Deciding that Satellite Office Four of the NovaDiv Communications Subsidiary seemed most promising, he walked briskly into the building, nodding at the elderly uniformed security guard as he passed. The security guard nodded back.

Inside, Satellite Office Four seemed to consist chiefly of small cubicles, each with a comp terminal and desk. Most of them were empty. Steward chose one at random, closed the door behind him, and activated the terminal.

The first thing he did was jack Angel's data spike into the terminal, then request a readout on what it contained. There was a complex identification number and a series of twelve telephone listings through which Angel could access various Pulsar Division offices or files. PERSONFILE was one of them, number six, and sounded promising. Steward told the computer to dial him number six. Speed was accelerating through his nerves and he kept missing the number on the keyboard. He saw an interface wire on an adhesive disk and stuck the disk behind his ear. Mental commands would be quicker anyway.

The NovaDiv computer finished its dialing and the video monitor cleared to proclaim, WELCOME TO THE FAR RANGER C-71. The busy light above the needle jack went on briefly, then the screen read, IDENTITY CONFIRMED. PLEASE CHOOSE OPTION AND ENTER CORRECT PASSWORD. There was no list of options. Anyone requesting the wrong data base was asking for an operator to come on line and inquire what he was doing here.

The Far Ranger systems, Steward knew, were based on an assembly language called C-Matrix. Steward didn't know C-Matrix except for a few commands drilled into him during his data-penetration training, but he hoped they would get him where he wanted to go.

Steward told the machine to DIVE, a standard command used by C-Matrix programmers to get into the core language itself. The busy light above his spike glowed again briefly, and then suddenly he was in. Apparently Angel had the security clearance to look at the C-Matrix programming.

Steward breathed a sigh of relief. He suspected he was as far as the spike would get him, but the Far Ranger C-71 was an old model, dating back to the Outward Policorps' occupation of Vesta. His Icehawk training would cover getting into a machine that old.

He gave the machine an LDC command to get access to the directory of commands. He moved through the long file for a moment—the long column of commands and programs scrolled onward in his mind, projected onto the optical centers by the interface wire. The video screen was irrelevant now. There seemed to be a list of files with special prefixes that read, PULSAR. One of them was PULSAR*FILESECUR.

Bingo.

Steward was suddenly aware of his fingers drumming a long tattoo on his thighs, his feet dancing on the carpet. The goddamn speed was twitching his body like a puppet. He ignored the effect and told the computer he wanted to edit the C-Matrix program that surrounded FILESECUR.

The extent of security programs is always a question of balance. The voice of one of his old instructors echoed in his head. *Any file can be made safer by adding more and more levels of security, but soon the security will begin to take up more and more space in the system, and will begin to interfere with normal access by working personnel. At some point, security always becomes counterpro-*

ductive. Balancing security and access is an art. For an outsider trying to gain access, an understanding of that balance is crucial.

Pulsar was an outfit that by its nature maintained a high degree of institutional paranoia, so FILESECUR was probably studded with booby traps, sudden-death programs that would either terminate his inquiry or silently inform someone in the Pulsar hierarchy that their data files were being meddled with, thereby allowing Steward to be traced. But the traps couldn't be too elaborate, or Angel would have difficulty getting to the files himself.

Balance, Steward thought. Security versus convenience. How well was FILESECUR guarded?

Carefully Steward slid through the C-Matrix programming. Blocks of symbols formed in his brain. Many of them were apparent gibberish. He mapped the program as carefully as he could, tracing every line of programming that led into or out of PULSAR* . He was trained to recognize some of what he was looking at, the if/then statements that constituted a trap. Each time he came across such a statement, he modified it so as to accept his own password ANGEL, which, when his intrusion was discovered, he hoped might get the Colonel in some trouble.

His various trapdoors wouldn't last for long. A group like Pulsar would have a backup of its C-Matrix core security program on file somewhere, and every so often—every few days or maybe every shift—it would be compared with the working program to see if there were any discrepancies. Steward's modifications would be wiped and someone would be alerted.

He worked deliberately, in a trance of concentration. When he came to himself, he realized he had spent two hours in the matrix, that he'd been pacing up and down the cubicle at the limit of the interface wire. The place smelled of sweat. His calves were aching. He flexed his legs, took off his jacket, and draped it on the back of his chair. He sat down again, jacking one of his empty data spikes into the terminal.

He wiped sweat from his forehead and went out of C-Matrix and back to the login routine. He gave his password ANGEL and asked for access to FILESECUR: STEWARD.1. When the C-71 gave him the file, he laughed out loud. He didn't bother to look at it, just dumped it into the data spike. He asked for a directory list of FILESECUR and found the files DEPREY.1 , CURZON,AC.1 , and CURZON,CD.1 , which he also moved into the cube. There was no listing on PRIME . He found ANGEL.1 and took it.

Steward moved through the directory list again, FILESECUR: PERSONNEL.1 , -.2 , and -.3 seemed interesting, so he took them. Lists of spies, maybe, or security classifications. His spike signaled him that the variable-lattice thread had been coded to its limits. He slipped it out and put in another.

There were hundreds of files. He began copying them at random, filling up his spikes and moving on. He figured he could sell the stuff to Griffith and let him sort it all out.

When he'd filled the last spike, he sat and stared at the shimmering monitor for another few minutes. He wondered if he wanted to leave his trapdoors in place, then decided against it. Even though it would be fun to envision the panic that would strike Pulsar, and particularly Angel, when the extent of Steward's depredations were known, any data stolen would be more valuable if Brighter Suns didn't know it was gone. He slipped through the C-Matrix programming again and restored it to its original state. Then he sat back in his chair and peeled the interface wire from his skull.

Reality began to fuse slowly with his mind. His bladder was aching. The speed had largely worn off except for a nervous jitter and a sensation of skin crawling. Phlegm coated his throat. It hurt to breathe. His right arm and shoulder were entirely numb, and he wondered again about neural damage. He put the spikes in his jacket pocket and closed the Velcro seals, then he threw his jacket over his arm and went in search of a lavatory.

The place was almost deserted, and the lighting was subdued. It must have turned third shift. He found a toilet and walked in to stare at himself in the mirror.

His eyes had sunken into red-purple caverns. The circular imprint of the interface wire and its adhesive disk was outlined clearly behind his ear. There were blooms of sweat in his armpits and on his chest. He washed his face, ran his fingers through his hair, and took another pill to get him through the trip back to the *Born*. He put his jacket on, careful of his burns, and walked out toward the lobby, trying hard to bounce as if he were enjoying the light gravity.

The old security guard had been replaced by a younger man. The cop nodded at him as he stepped into the lobby. "Working hard?" he asked.

Steward gave him a weary grin. "Inventory," he said. He stepped to the clear plastic door and gave it a push. It wouldn't open. A warning tugged at his nerves.

He looked at the guard. The man was fumbling at his belt. "I'll need to unlock that," he said.

The warning faded away. The guard unlocked the door and Steward stepped out into the tunnel. He said good-night and repressed the urge to laugh out loud.

Later, near a waste receptacle, he took Angel's spike, put its needle tip on the alloy floor, and snapped it in half with his foot. He tossed the remains into the trash. Angel would miss it by the next day, and after that it would be far too dangerous for anyone to possess. Pulsar's software would be altered to look out for anyone using it.

The spikes would be hidden in one of the cargo holds that had already been filled with goods. He wasn't going to touch them till he'd left Vesta.

He wasn't going to leave the ship again. Not until it was docked someplace where Angel couldn't get him.

CHAPTER TEN

It was four days since Pulsar had let him go. Steward lay on his rack, watching a telecast of Kawaguchi's *Fourth Millennium*. This was a classic visionary Imagist drama from the previous century, set in a mannered future in which a genetically altered posthuman society was confronted by the return of violent human primitives from a forgotten space colony, a comedy of manners laced with acid and appalling violence. The NeoImagist Policorp Pink Blossom had recently produced an elaborate version of it, intended as political propaganda for their perception of the future, starring the free-fall kabuki actor Kataoka XXII. Brighter Suns, being a nonideological policorp, was broadcasting it on the feed link from Vesta. Steward was enjoying the show, but suspected the interpretation was slanted a bit toward the posthuman point of view, having been dictated by contemporary political realities. Pink Blossom was showing a decline in its rate of growth and might have concluded that their vision of tomorrow might need a little polishing in order to get the troops enthusiastic about their work.

Steward flexed his right hand as he watched the vid. Feeling was almost back to normal. No permanent damage, he thought.

There was a knock on Steward's door. "Come in," he said, setting his vid unit on record, and Reese entered.

There was an annoyed frown on her face. "Out of the rack, buck," she said. "We've been ordered to Vesta in an hour. We're going into the Power Legation."

Steward sat up. Alarms clattered in his mind. "Why?" he asked.

"There's a Starbright ship in dock," Reese said. "The cargo handlers got sick, and some of the autoloaders have broken down. It's a special cargo, and the Starbright people don't want anyone but our employees to deal with it. We're being ordered to help load the stuff by hand."

"Why us?"

"It's those blood tests we had to take. We tested out okay to work with the Powers."

Steward slapped off the vid. Anger was beginning to fill him. "It's a scheme

117

to get me onstation," he said. "They're going to provoke some kind of incident and toss me in a cell again. Or assassinate me."

Reese leaned against a padded bulkhead and crossed her arms. "Not likely," she said. "They let you go once. Why would they pick you up again?"

Steward hesitated for a moment. He had to think of something besides the fact he was suspected of stealing Angel's key spike. "Maybe they couldn't make up their minds till now," Steward said. He jumped out of his rack and began pacing. "Or maybe they just wanted me dead and it took a while to put a scheme together so that it doesn't look like their fault." His mind was whirling. "Look," he said. "I'll go to our pharmacy and give myself something to make myself sick. You just tell our bosses I'm ill."

Reese shook her head. "Take it easy," she said. "I've got an obligation to our superiors, here. If you don't show up, it could cost Starbright millions of its own dollars."

He looked at her. "If I *do* show up it could cost Starbright a promising young trainee."

Reese shook her head again. "I can handle this. I'm gonna get on the phone, see where this order came from. Talk to our consul—"

"Lal. That creep."

"Don't interrupt me, buck." Steward looked up in surprise at the venom in her voice. She was glaring at him. "I'm going to get some guarantees from the Vesta personnel. They're going to look out for you."

Steward laughed. Reese jabbed a finger in his face. "*I'm dealing with it*, Steward. If you get near the first-aid chest, I'll put you on report. I put myself on the line to get you out of the Pulsar Division and I'm not going to let you disappear again, but I'm not about to cost our nation a fortune, either. So pack yourself three days' worth of gear while I get on the telephone. I'll let you know how it all comes out."

He looked at her levelly. "They're going to kill me, Reese."

"I don't plan on letting them."

"I don't think you can stop it."

Her look was unreadable. "Then I'll be wrong, won't I?"

She closed the sliding door behind her. Steward could only stare at the door for a moment. There was something wrong here, something unbalanced in Reese's behavior. She'd *seen* the shape he was in when the Pulsar Division let him go. He wondered if Brighter Suns had paid her to get him killed.

He grabbed a ruck from his closet and packed in a fury for the first few minutes, then paced the cabin like a madman, patrolling back and forth in a room only three paces across, his fingers working as if clutching Angel's thick neck.

Then, slowly, he began to calm himself, forcing his mind to cope with what now seemed inevitable. He'd given away his plan to make himself sick, and although he could do it in spite of his announcement, the drugs would wear off sooner or later and then he'd be flung out into the Power Legation anyway.

He'd just have to be ready. He changed his belt to one with a heavier metal buckle in case he had to use it as a weapon. He clipped a knife inside the waistband of his jeans, where the top half inch of the hilt that protruded above his pants would be covered by his jacket. He had no other weapon—a rigger's knife wasn't unusual, and no one would look twice at his belt, but anything else would be cause for comment. He'd simply have to be ready for whatever Pulsar would use, the zap glove or dart gun or poison spray.

Steward changed his jacket to something heavier, to better resist attacks. He put on a pair of insulated gloves that he might be able to use to block a punch from a zap glove. He went to the crew locker and got a fire fighter's Kevlar hard hat with plates that fell from the rim to protect his neck and the sides of his head, as well as a detachable transparent shield to cover his face.

He sat on his rack and waited. Listened to himself breathe. Felt the blood course through his limbs. Trying to ready himself to face the moment of annihilation when it came. He was going to be following his Alpha a little sooner than he'd thought.

One arrow, he thought, one life. A short ride from bow to target.

Reese was gone half an hour. When she came back, she had a printout in her hand. She looked at his helmet and grinned. "Take a look at this, samurai," she said, and drifted it across the room toward him.

There were two documents. The first was a statement from the Starbright consul—Steward sneered at Lal's signature—that he had Brighter Suns' assurance that Steward was not a subject of inquiry. The other was a signed statement from Brighter Suns security stating they had no further interest in Steward, that there was no investigation concerning him, and that he was free to come and go as he wished.

He grimaced, folded the sheets, put them in his jacket pocket. "They'll make a great epitaph."

"Off the rack, Steward," Reese said. "I'm tired of your doubting me."

He stood and slung the ruck over his shoulder. "Lead on," he said. "I'll look out behind."

As Steward drifted down the access tube, Vesta's gravity tugged at his stomach and for a moment there was panic, the sense of falling head-downward. Bile surged into his throat. He swallowed it with savage anger and tried to resurrect his calm. Before he could, the whistles and sirens, the crashes and bustle of the loading dock, roared up around him. His head moved wildly, looking for things out of place, for big men in bulky jackets.

"I'll stick to the wall, okay?" he said, remembering the feeling of drifting helplessly in that vast space, but Reese shook her head and pointed to the Starbright logo on a long narrow tunnel shuttle stuck to the chamber's alloy wall by electromagnets. Eight seats were lined up behind the driver. It looked like an alpine bobsled.

"That's our transportation," Reese said.

Steward kicked off from the wall and shot the ten-yard distance to the shuttle. He absorbed the shock of impact with his arms and swung himself aboard, into the seat behind the driver. The driver looked back at him.

"You planning on putting out a fire or something?"

"I'm just safety-conscious, buck."

"Whatever you say."

Reese swung herself gracefully into the seat behind Steward. They buckled themselves in and the driver cast off from the wall. Blipping the air horn to let others know he was moving, he guided the craft across the loading dock and into a narrow one-way tunnel. There he programmed his destination into the shuttle, gave command of the transport to the Vesta traffic computer, put his foot on the deadman, and crossed his arms. Steward was punched back into his seat as the Vesta mass drivers began to sling the shuttle down the tube like a needle out of a gauss gun. Wind howled over Steward's helmet. Shining bits of mica and nickel in the tunnel walls flashed by in the shuttle's headlights. He could feel himself tensing, waiting for the crash. A simple accident, that was all it would take. Override the controls on the mass driver from the central security computer and plow this bobsled into the back of an ore carrier.

The shuttle began to decelerate in a hiss of air. Steward's straps dug into his lap and shoulders. The shuttle came to a stop. The driver took his foot off the deadman and piloted the shuttle across another large space—an empty one—and toward a small airlock.

"This is as far as I go," he said. "I'm not allowed into the Legation—I got bugs, I guess. Your job's to unload a Power cargo ship, get everything on pallets, then to the big cargo airlock. We can move it from there."

Sweat was trickling inside Steward's helmet. He was still looking for an enemy, but the room was empty. "Right," he said.

"You'll be decontaminated on the other side of the lock," the driver said. "No worry. It's to make certain you're not carrying anything on your skin or clothes."

There was a green light over the airlock. Inside the air had a tangy, antiseptic smell. Chrome nozzles protruded from the walls like automated weaponry, and batteries of UV lights waited behind screens. Reese and Steward were told by an automated voice to remove their clothing and place it in the lockers provided. Small personal articles were to go into a bin behind a small hinged lid.

Steward's sweat floated out in salt, reflective globes as he took his helmet off and tossed it tumbling into the locker. There was a thud as it hit the padded wall. He was trapped in this situation, inside a huge machine that, sooner or later, was going to try to kill him, and he had no choice but to go through the motions and wait for the moment that the machine would choose, and somehow be ready.

Reality was taking on a hard-edged, surrealistic quality, as in a nightmare. Everything he saw was filled with potential menace, the chemical smell, the row of shining nozzles, the small padded room with its battery of screened lights like those in his Pulsar Division cell. His heart was hammering, and he tried hard to control it. He and Reese stripped and put their gear in the places provided. He found it hard to put away the knife—he held it to the last and had to take several breaths before he could bear to put it in the bin. He could feel Reese's eyes on him as he gave up his weapon.

The automated voice returned, telling Steward and Reese to put on the UV goggles provided and float in midroom with their arms held high. When they were ready they were to say "Okay."

They obeyed and the UV lights came on, a short, high-intensity dose to kill bacteria on the skin. Then the chrome nozzles began to track them and fired a gentle mist of disinfectant over their bodies. Steward tried not to shiver at the silken touch of the spray. The spray ceased and powerful fans came on, sucking the disinfectant out of the air, blowing warm wind over his skin, drying him. He spun in the nearly nonexistent gravity, drying evenly, his arms held high like a figure skater doing a scratch spin.

The fans ceased and the doors on the lockers unlocked with a solid click. The automated voice told them to put on their clothes and leave via the door with the blinking light. Reese kicked off from the wall and floated across the lock to one of the doors, then opened it. She reached in and pulled out items of clothing. Steward noticed an old scar that tracked down her lower back.

The clothes were dry and warm and smelled of disinfectant. They'd been folded neatly. The pocket flaps were all open—some security personnel, or perhaps a robot, had gone through them for harmful items. There was nothing missing.

Steward, his mouth dry, reached for the personal items bin and pulled it open. His knife waited. A credit needle floated out. He clutched the knife and only then reached for his clothing. Reese looked at him, indicating some units set in the walls. "Those look like X-ray scanners to me," she said. "They were looking for implants."

"Those I don't have," Steward said.

"I've got a few pins holding my ankle together," Reese said. "I wonder if they're going to ask me about them."

Reese rotated clumsily as she struggled into her trousers. She reached out to one of the walls, stabilized her tumble, then Velcroed her fly. "Gut bacteria must be okay," she said. "They're not handing us suppositories."

"That might be the next room."

They finished dressing and Reese pressed the button that signaled the inner door to open. It slid neatly to one side, and an alien breeze entered the airlock door.

The air of the Power Legation was rich and thick, cooler than in the human section of Vesta but filled with organics, an airborne soup that made Steward's nape hairs tingle. There was a yeasty taste on his tongue. He had read of the Powers' using hormones for communication but hadn't realized that the air would be so filled with them, that it would make his movements seem like swimming through a fog.

Steward followed Reese into the next room. His heart lurched as he saw a man in the uniform of a Brighter Suns internal security cop standing on one of the walls, his feet planted onto Velcro strips, and Steward tensed, ready for combat, keenly and suddenly aware of the pressure of the knife along his side. The cop had a scanner in his hand. His skin was bright orange and Steward concluded the man had been overdoing carotene supplements.

"Reese?" the cop said. "I'd like to look at that ankle, please."

Steward warily moved into a corner, putting his back against one wall and his feet on the Velcro strips of another. Reese drifted up to the cop and hung onto the wall near his feet. He reached out, scanned her ankle for a few moments, looking for explosives or wetware or a reservoir of hostile biologies, then the cop smiled and lowered his scanner.

"You scan clear," he said. "Your ride's waiting on the other side of the door."

Steward kicked out hard for the door, hoping to catch the cop by surprise, then hit the button and tumbled out as soon as the door started to slide open. A sound arose like the whining of an untuned organ. The hairs on the back of his neck rose. The next room was big, and it was full of Powers.

Something squirmed in Steward's insides. There was an acid tang to the air here that had been muted in the airlock antechamber. The Powers ignored him, their centauroid bodies rocketing at high speed across the long chamber, propelled by thrusts from their powerful rear legs. Their forelegs and ropy arms were cocked forward to absorb the shock of impact, and their eyes were moving constantly in their flexible heads. The organ-pipe sounds came from their upper nostrils and echoed from the hard stone and alloy walls. Steward hadn't realized they'd be so big. Though they were shorter than he, their body mass exceeded his by at least a factor of two. Their size seemed threatening.

And they were *fast*. Their heads twitched, and their bodies, arms, and legs moved with inhuman fluidity as, nearing each other, they performed their rituals of obeisance and power.

Reese drifted gently up from the door. Her head moved as if on a stalk, scanning the echoing, shrilling room. "Jesus," she said.

"I thought you'd be used to them. Having been on Archangel."

She looked pale. "I don't like the Powers. Even if they did save our asses in the war."

The organ keening wailed in Steward's ears. He shuddered and thought of Griffith. "Some people love them."

"Not me."

The cop emerged from the door, his face set in a knowing smile. Steward imagined he saw this reaction often, on people first exposed to the Legation. The cop waved a sketchy salute, then jumped out across the room, swimming for an exit marked with a bright orange holographic numeral. There was the sound of an air horn, blatted twice. Reese looked down, then tugged Steward's sleeve. "Our transport," she said. He took his eyes away from the Powers and saw another shuttle waiting, a smaller four-seater, driven by an impatient man in Starbright coveralls.

"Sorry to rush you," he said, as they began buckling themselves in, "but we've got a situation here." The accent seemed faintly South American, but he could have been born anywhere in human space. "The Powers' automatic unloaders have broken down completely, and a lot of our people came down with dysentery from some bad food in the cafeteria."

"I don't mind," Reese said. "I wasn't doing anything." Steward gave her a look.

The driver turned around. His skin was blue-black, with diamonds set into his brows and cheekbones and a black plastic radio receiver implanted where his left ear had once been. "I'm Colorado, by the way," he said.

Steward looked into Colorado's eyes and wondered if he was the assassin. The man seemed too soft, but you never know. "Pleased to meet you," Steward said.

Colorado blatted the horn and fired his hydrogen maneuvering jets. He took them across the room, toward an exit marked by a flashing green holographic target symbol.

The next room was huge, a kilometers-long docking bay so vast that the far edge of it was obscured in a haze of the organic smog generated by the Powers. Aliens and robots were moving giant blocks of cargo about in the near-zero gravity. The shuttle entered a nonautomated traffic lane and whistled half the length of the dock before braking. Its electromagnets engaged a ferrous strip laid near a twenty-meter-square docking gate.

The smell was different here. More acrid.

Steward began to unbuckle. "The cargo's all consigned to Starbright,"

Colorado said. "The auto cargo movers in the Power ship are slagged out—I heard they're going to crucify their maintenance officer, or chief engineer, or whatever it's called. We've got to go into the holds, grapple the containers manually, and wrestle them out of the tube and onto the dock, then snug 'em down to pallets. The station equipment handlers can take it from there." He looked at Steward and grinned. "Good idea, bringing your own hard hat. The rest of us have to draw them from stores."

Steward worked one and a half shifts, sweating in his helmet and jacket, and no one tried to kill him. There was an ozone feel to the air, and he could almost feel the hair on his arms crackle when he moved. There were four Powers on the work gang in addition to nine humans, and the aliens worked like demons, moving in utter silence save for the keening organ calls that rose up in a strange minor-key chorus when one of their superiors arrived to check their progress.

The cargo, whatever it was, was in standardized alloy containers that allowed the contents to be flooded with disinfectant or radiation when they moved out of Legation territory. Ferrous strips along the side of the containers allowed them to be held by electromagnets to the surface of the cargo hold. Steward had to grapple peroxide maneuvering jets to the containers, turn off the magnets, then fly the cargo out of the hold and onto a pallet attached to the wall of the dock. It was tricky work; some of the containers held up to six tonnes. Gravity could be discounted but momentum could not, and a container that massive could do damage if it hit the interior of the Power ship's bay. Steward moved his containers very carefully.

At the end of the second shift there was a lot left to do. They had emptied one bay and started on a second. There was a third untouched cargo space yet to go.

After work, Colorado took Steward and Reese to a human habitat in the big Legation centrifuge. They were to share a small two-room guest apartment, and were given meal tickets for the cafeteria. Here the rich smell of the Powers faded into the background.

"I'd stay and show you around, and maybe have a drink," Colorado said, "but I'm dead tired. I've been working two and a half shifts. Sorry to be so unsociable."

"You won't join us in the cafeteria, at least?" Steward asked.

He shook his head. "I called my apartment from the dock and told it to cook me dinner. I'm going to eat and hit the rack."

"See you tomorrow."

The cafeteria was okay, Steward thought. It was completely automated, and he chose his food at random, planning to avoid poison. He sat with his back to a wall and ate warily.

Reese watched him, quietly amused. Her attitude irritated him. "Going to take your helmet off when you go to sleep?" she asked him.

"Maybe."

"If they wanted to," she said, "they could have gone on board the *Born* and killed you just as easily. You know that."

He thought about it for a moment, then nodded. Reese was right.

It didn't stop him from taking a chair and blocking the door when he went to sleep. He put the knife under his pillow.

The next day Steward was scheduled to work two shifts, with an hour-long meal break in between. During the break, Colorado and his friend Navasky joined them in the cafeteria. Navasky was a tall girl of about sixteen, blond and pale, with the perfect features and delicate appearance of the genetically altered. She had painted her face yellow, with a red chevron over the bridge of her nose.

The early Imagists had struck boldly into the realm of genetic engineering, hoping for vast leaps out of the human fleshly prison and into a grand, unseeable future, a period in which Imagist achievement curved upward into infinity, a "posthuman singularity" composed of "posthuman tropes." They'd created marvels of increased intelligence and heightened cognition, and they'd bred as well for adaptability to nonterran environments, for second-stage humans who would live forever outside of gravity, true inhabitants of space. They'd moved too fast and underestimated the fragility of the human DNA they were dealing with. Their superintelligent, superintuitive creations proved susceptible to schizophrenia, epilepsy, bursts of paranoia. Immune systems proved vulnerable to even the most common bacteria. The Imagists hadn't realized the limitations of the human genetic structure, that adding to one characteristic might detract from others. The second-stage humans lived well in their gravity-free environments and were useful in nongravity manufacturing, but their sturdier ancestors proved more durable during the high-g acceleration burns that powered human commerce, that moved the goods from the Belt to Earth to Saturn and beyond.

The NeoImagists were more modest. Navasky's delicacy showed that her mind had probably been altered in some minor way, but still she was sturdy enough to join Colorado and Steward in their task of unloading the Power ship. She had joined Starbright on scholarship, which meant she was in the top two percent of humanity and was starting at the bottom of the shipping business, but she planned on working her way up to starship captain.

Before she ate she startled Steward by bowing over her plate and offering a prayer. Steward didn't know to whom.

"They boosted the wiring on my linguistic centers," she said during the meal, discussing her genes as other people talked about their shoes, "and I've had special training in socialization theory. My genetics were intended to make me useful as a diplomat, but that's what starship captains often have to be. They're always months out of communication, and if they're on discovery missions, they often have to negotiate with other policorporate ships. Or even aliens, if there are any more like the Powers around."

"Can you understand Power speech?" Steward asked.

Navasky frowned, sipping at a bulb of tea while she considered her answer. "A lot of it," she said. "But not in all its senses or contexts. Simple things only. Power idiom is full of references and patterns that humans haven't been able to decipher yet, not even with Power cooperation." Her frown turned to a confident smile. "But I'm just starting—I'd be in class right now if we didn't have to unload all that cargo." She rotated her shoulder and grimaced. "I'm not used to hauling stuff."

"Wrong genes." Colorado grinned. Navasky laughed and put her arm around him.

Steward smiled. They were relaxed now, and maybe his questions wouldn't seem strange. "I remember," he said, "a few months ago, I read about some kind of biological alert on Vesta. A contamination."

Colorado made a face. Navasky put down her bulb of tea. Her eyes were disturbed. Since the Orbital Soviet fell in a blizzard of biologic strikes, space habitants in general tended to be paranoid about contamination, and Navasky's NeoImagist history, Steward thought, probably made her even more wary of bacteriological outbreaks. "I was on the other side at the time," she said, "hadn't got my clearance to come into the Legation." She looked at Colorado. "Colorado was here, though."

He looked at his plate. "Bad time," he said. "I wasn't around the worst of it."

"Any people get hurt?" Steward said.

Colorado shook his head. "Not many. The outbreak was mostly confined to the Power quarters. There are contamination drills here all the time—once the alarms went off, everyone knew to stay in their quarters or jump for the nearest hardened radiation shelter. The Power crews in the ships just sealed themselves inside once the alert was announced, but the rest, the ones living on Vesta, got hurt bad. They say the Power police were just shooting any Powers that were infected. There were a lot of dead ones anyway, someone told me. The whole Legation smelled like"—he shrugged—"like dead Powers, I guess. Bad. There must have been a lot of them."

"We're not supposed to talk about this," Navasky said. She gave a nervous glance over her shoulder.

"A few people got hurt. Trampled to death by stampeding Powers, I suppose. They say the Powers just went mad once they found out they were infected. They did a lot of damage to their own quarters. When we got back to work, the docks were a mess, too."

"It didn't last long, though," said Navasky.

"Just a few days. Apparently any Power infected got sick within hours, so the plague burned itself out. Now they don't let any human into the Power quarters, just in case he might be carrying something."

Steward regretted he couldn't record this. His brain was whirling, trying to remember it all. He wished he wasn't so tired.

"And then there's the new Samuel," said Navasky. There was the sense of an electric snap in Steward's mind, like a switch closing—somehow he knew this was important. Colorado looked at Navasky in surprise. She turned her dark eyes to Steward and explained.

"Samuel's the Power Head of Legation," she said. "See, Powers don't have names in their own language—all they have are titles, like Second-Cousin-in-Charge-of-Waste-Disposal." She laughed, and Steward laughed with her, trying to encourage her. "All the prominent Powers," she went on, "have been given human names, because they've got human public-relations people working for them who are trying to give them a kind of human media personality, so that people will feel easier dealing with them. Now that I've been around the Powers for a while, studying them, I can tell one from another. I've seen tapes of the Samuel before the plague, and I've seen the current Samuel up close, and it's not the same person—I mean Power."

Steward hunched toward her. "You think he died?" Navasky seemed startled by his intensity. He leaned back, took a breath and tried to relax, to ease the taut muscles in his shoulders and arms, act as if the answer didn't mean anything.

"It seems reasonable," she said, a bit subdued.

Navasky had all manner of training, as well as genetic adaptation, in reading people, in being able to persuade and manipulate them, and she'd seen something strange in Steward that had made her wonder. He had to get her to talk now, before she decided he was some kind of spy from her Starbright superiors who was trying to find out if she'd babble classified information. He grinned, trying to ease her suspicions. "I'd like to know," Steward said, "a little about Power social organization. What happens when the Head of Legation dies?"

"They're completely hierarchical." The expression in Navasky's eyes was wondering and a little suspicious. Her wording was precise, as if she were censoring herself, trying not to give anything away. Steward cursed himself for being so obvious. "Only Samuel was authorized to make certain kinds of decisions. If anything major came up now, the current Samuel would have to refer it to their superiors back in Power space for a ruling."

"And their bosses are months out of contact," Steward said.

Navasky nodded. Steward had the intuition that he'd got as much out of her as she was ever likely to offer. He drank from his squeeze bulb of water and considered. The Alpha's biological strike had decapitated the Power hierarchy, left them unable to deal with any major issue or crisis that might arise. It had also devastated the Power population, lowering the efficiency of the colony as a whole, slowing the rate of goods moving into the waiting ships. Replacement personnel were probably on the way, and in the interim they were very likely drafting as many crew out of their ships as they dared for use as replacements. Steward wondered what issue had arisen that had made Curzon and Consolidated Systems so eager to make such an attack, and at that moment. They'd stunned Starbright for at least a year. Why, he thought, was this year so crucial?

Colorado's voice was wondering. "Does this stuff *mean* anything to you? Why are you asking?"

Steward tried to shrug in an offhand way. "I know someone back on Earth who's been around the Powers, who really loves them. And he can't get into space because he's got the disease, whatever it is."

Navasky was still watching him, trying to read his body language, his tone. But Colorado seemed to relax. "Yeah. We have those kind of Power lovers here, too." He shook his head. "Strange people. It's not even love, I think. It's like the Powers are something they *need*."

Navasky quietly dropped her hand from the table and put it on Colorado's thigh. He looked at her in surprise. She pursed her lips, gave him a quiet shake of the head. Colorado seemed startled, and then it seemed as if a shutter drew across his eyes, closing Steward out. He bent to his plate.

Steward imitated Colorado. He was aware of another set of eyes on him: Reese who watched as he busied himself with his meal, who had been watching all along. And drawn, no doubt, her own conclusions.

There was a group of them, each in a uniform jacket cut like the standard Starbright collarless uniform but a dark purple instead of gray, and with a bright red bar sinister sewn across their chests and backs, like the ribbon of a knightly order. They were at the next loading dock down, clustered around one of the medium-sized alloy shipping containers. They had opened the container and some of them were clustered around it, scooping out packing foam, bringing out small plastic boxes.

Steward saw them as he guided a six-tonne canister past them, his head swiveling as he alternated little bursts of his jets, blipping his horn to make certain the path was clear and that others saw him. The people in their deep purple jackets, held to the roof of the docking bay by grip pumps, hardly noticed him. One of them, a small, dark barrel-chested man, had taken one of the plastic boxes to the fringes of the group and had opened it. He was frowning at its contents.

Suddenly Steward was awash in a flood of recognition, images flooding in his mind in swift repetition. Sereng. Icehawks. Outdoor training. Hanging on a rope ladder, twisting in a thirty-knot wind, with the crampon-equipped boots of the Nepalese planted on a flexible rung inches from his nose. Sereng almost buried beneath his pack, smiling, on his belt the big inward-curving knife that looked like the shoulder bone of some prehistoric animal sharpened and turned to steel. His eyes glittering as sharp as the knife.

Heat rose in Steward's skin. His weariness vanished. His glance flickering from Sereng to the alloy pallet; he halted the container's motion, spun it, dropped it gently into place. He signaled another crewman to turn on the electromagnets that would hold it to the pallet, feeling the solid impact beneath him as the container slammed down on its ferrous strips. Then Steward detached his maneuvering pack and kicked off straight for where the Nepalese was gazing into his box. He tumbled in space, reversing himself, and landed boots-first on the Velcro strip directly in front of Sereng.

The man looked up. His face was fuller than Steward remembered, his body softer. His eyes were distant, preoccupied, not at all surprised. He had grown a mustache. The voice was the same. "Captain," he said.

"Hello," Steward said. "It's been a long time. What are you doing way out here?"

Sereng quietly closed his box. There was something that gleamed in it, with coils and a space for a tiny fuel cell, a little refrigeration unit smaller than a pack of cigarettes.

"I'm a member of the Power Legation," Sereng said. "A Power citizen. Couldn't you tell by the uniform?"

Surprise flickered through Steward. Sereng had been a soldier, not a trader or diplomat. He couldn't see what use the Powers could have for the man.

"I don't know Brighter Suns uniforms yet. I'm Starbright. It's just an accident that I'm here at all."

Sereng nodded. He didn't seem to be surprised at all that Steward was here. "It's a good job," he said. "I'm with the Powers all the time. It's where I want to be."

There was something wrong with Sereng's eyes. They were clouded somehow, turned inward. They weren't the eyes Steward remembered.

A breathy voice sounded near Steward's elbow. He jumped. There was an alien there, its lower voice box speaking precise, educated English, like a video announcer.

"Violation," it said. Its arms moved in rapid patterns. Steward flinched from the sourness of the thing's smell. "You are not to speak to Legation personnel. This is a violation of your contract. Your policorp will be fined."

"My apologies. I know this man from years ago. I was not aware he was a Legation member."

"Were you not briefed on the significance of the uniform? This man is a quarantined Legation member. I will file a protest with the Starbright consul."

Wonderful, Steward thought. All he needed was to be the center of another incident crossing Lal's desk.

"I do apologize. A protest will not be necessary now that I have been warned." He looked over his shoulder. "Sorry to bother you, Sereng," he said, but the Nepalese had already turned away, heading back to the group around the container.

"Away, away," said the Power. Its long ropy arms were making scissoring motions at Steward's knees, as if offering to slice at his hamstrings. Steward saw Colorado moving toward him, gliding with deliberate haste along the Velcro strip.

"Yes, yes. My apologies," Steward said, and let the Power chivvy him away.

Colorado's big hand reached out and slammed down on his shoulder. "What's the matter with you?" he asked. He was almost dragging Steward away. "Don't you know about the goddamn redstripes?"

"No. I don't. What's the matter?"

Colorado was furious. "Somebody fucked up, that's the matter. You were supposed to get a lecture about not talking to Power personnel."

"One of them was an old friend. Are they really Power citizens?"

Colorado looked over his shoulder at the group, his fingers tightening on Steward's shoulder. "Damn right they are. They're the only humans allowed into the Power section of the centrifuge. They're the crazy ones."

"The ones who love them."

Colorado spat. The globe of saliva traveled out into the room and vanished into the distance. "The ones who have cheese for brains," he said.

Steward looked up as a shadow passed between him and the big bank of floodlights that illuminated this part of the dock. It was Reese, the straps of her maneuvering jets wrapped around her body, hovering over him with quick bursts of peroxide.

"Trouble, Steward?"

Steward looked up at her. "I knew one of those guys from before. I was in the Icehawks with him. But now they're taboo or something."

"The ones in the purple jackets with the stripe," Colorado said. "Stay the hell away." His eyes narrowed. "Icehawks?" he said.

"I'm older than I look."

Reese had tumbled slightly in space, was craned over looking at the Power citizens through her wide-spaced legs. "I know one of those people, too," she said in surprise. "The tall redhead. She was in a recce unit on Archangel." She was silent for a moment. When she looked at Steward her eyes were questioning. "Can they *all* be ex-military?" she wondered. "What do the Powers need them for?"

"They work for Samuel," Colorado said. "They build his media image, arrange for release of information from Power space, negotiate trade agreements."

"Why does he need former military?" Reese demanded.

"I dunno," Colorado said. "They never leave the Legation, so far as I know."

Steward said nothing. He was thinking about Sereng's eyes.

CHAPTER ELEVEN

Steward had something new in his cabin. Like SuTopo with his bonsai, Fischer with his mountain, and the former occupant of Steward's cabin with the labia of anonymous women, Steward had refined his aspirations to a single image. He'd cut it from a magazine the day *Born* left Vesta behind.

It was a picture of a video set in a blue plastic case. The picture was a jagged haze of interference lines. Behind the interference, a vague image could be seen, or perhaps imagined.

The object of Steward's desire.

The picture was in his mind, mingled with the patterns of the engine analogs that still pulsed in Steward's brain, the images that lingered even after a six-hour sleep. The high-g engine burn out of the Belt was over, and *Born* was on its fifty-two-day return trip to Charter Station—Earth and Vesta were farther apart than they had been during the outward leg, and the return journey would be longer. To give everyone a break after the long three days of one point five g, the flora's centrifuge was locked in place, and Steward floated weightlessly in webbing, his arms drifting out in front of him like the forelegs of a dead animal.

He was thirsty. His body was a collection of aches. The engine analogs wouldn't leave his mind.

But Steward was alive. The assassin hadn't come, and Steward rejoiced in the intensity of the aches, the thirst, the cold fire of the mental afterimage. He'd got in and out of Vesta, he had a dozen spikes of bootleg data, and he felt the touch of the Alpha on his shoulder, saw his image behind the interference pattern thrown in front of his eyes by the enemy, by their security. He was getting close to things.

Time to get closer. Time to see what was on the spikes.

He closed his cabin door and locked it, then disconnected his cabin comp from the ship's central computer just in case Taler had some kind of surveillance program running on the Starbright employees who lived on their ships. Then he'd put in the first spike and scanned it till he found

FILESECUR:STEW ARD.1 . He could feel the nerves in his fingers tingling. This was what he came to Vesta to find.

He took a deep breath and punched it up on the screen.

The first page was a warning of the penalties—imprisonment, behavior modification therapy, or execution—incurred by anyone of insufficient security grade who read the dossier. Some of the information contained in the file was accessible only to individuals of the highest security grade.

There was a rush of pleasure up Steward's spine. He smiled. This was going to be good.

The first part was pedestrian stuff, medical history, vital statistics, early biography. The text was filled with endnotes referring him to medical and psychological analyses elsewhere in the dossier, and then the post-Sheol biography scrolled onto the screen.

Steward couldn't read it fast enough.

The Alpha Steward had held a succession of jobs on Earth after returning from Sheol, none of them successful. He'd had trouble with the law, assault charges mostly. Just before the child was born, Natalie got a job in New Humanity and went into lunar orbit. A year later, still living in space, she had divorced him.

Memory moved through Steward like a long ocean roller: Natalie laughing, tumbling in a long arc across the gravity-free hold of a Ricot-bound freighter, her hair spilling about her face, her green eyes joyful and intent. New Humanity was a gravity-free world, Steward knew, an old second-stage Imagist habitat crawling in a slow orbit about Earth's moon.

He knew where she was now. It was worth it, if only for that.

He read on.

The Alpha had gone into the security business then, for an outfit called SonnenSystem Elite. They did bodyguard and surveillance work for a number of small corporations that hadn't achieved nation status and that didn't have an apparatus for handling their own security and intelligence. The Alpha had been assigned to develop penetration security on behalf of a small cutting-edge company, Sivi Source, a group specializing in implant wetware enabling people to translate from one human or machine language to another. Sivi was a paranoid company—competition on that particular frontier was serious, and not always polite. After a series of well-exploited breakthroughs, Sivi sold out to Consolidated Systems, and its personnel moved into orbit, with the intention of working on the problem of human-Power communication. The Alpha Steward was recruited by the Consolidated Systems security apparatus at that time—apparently he'd made himself invaluable to Sivi by repelling a number of penetration schemes launched by the opposition, and his efficiency in defense of Sivi had caught the eye of Consolidated. They'd bought out his contract with SonnenSystem and taken him to their headquarters on Ricot.

From that point on there had been a slow rise through the Consolidated security hierarchy as the Alpha performed, apparently well, a number of routine tasks. He devised a number of means for keeping the Powers biologically secure. He worked out ways for vetting the large number of foreign nationals that were on Ricot at any given time. He also married a woman named Wandis, who was an engineer specializing in Penrose-tiling crystal growth. She was a recent graduate of the Ricot College, ten years younger than the Alpha.

There was a photo in the dossier. Wandis was blond, short-haired, dark-eyed. There was a scatter of gemstones implanted in a starburst pattern around the left eye. She was smiling, and there was an air of fragility about her.

Steward looked at her, frowned. He had no reaction to the face at all. The Alpha had found someone as far away from Natalie's type as he could.

Within a few years the Alpha reached high enough in Consolidated Systems to attract the attention of the Brighter Suns hierarchy. De Prey, now a Colonel in the Pulsar Division, recognized his name and photograph in a dossier and set about a recruitment scheme. De Prey himself contributed to the dossier in an outline explaining his plan of recruitment.

Ice touched Steward's nerves as he saw de Prey's words. He could hear the Colonel's voice resonating in his mind as he scanned the page, absorbed every cold, reasoned sentence.

Icehawk recruitment policy was directed at a specific kind of recruit, intelligent enough to be able to think, act, and survive in the absence of his superiors, yet with a cultivated devotion to authority, specifically to the aims and goals of Coherent Light. The Icehawks were not to be mercenaries, soldiers, or assassins, but intelligent warrior fanatics, able to credit no objectives other than those of Coherent Light. Specific attempts were made to recruit rootless individuals, mainly citizens of noncorporate Earth nations, who had received no indoctrination from other policorps, or who had come from backgrounds in which chaos and violence were common, and who might therefore perceive Coherent Light, by contrast, as a force for stability and order. Icehawk indoctrination, rather than concentrating on formal ideological training, substituted instead the cultivation of a religious-military mystique. Zen mysticism, with its concentration on the perception of a vague "truth" at the core of all things, a truth divorced from concepts of moral order, was a useful tool in this indoctrination program.

Steward thought of Dr. Ashraf, remembering the psychologist's anger at the Zen emphasis in the Icehawks' training. Here were Ashraf's ideas, coldly and precisely paraphrased by Colonel de Prey.

The success of this indoctrination is evident on reading the history of the Sheol campaign, in which the Icehawks followed their training to the extent of conducting suicidal attacks on their CL-designated enemies, long after concerns of mere survival would dictate an alternate course of behavior. That the subject Steward broke his training before the others and became the focus of a rebellion against his superiors who were still loyal to CL is less a failure of indoctrination than evidence of another factor in his background. Subject Steward was a survivor of the civil chaos following the failure of Far Jewel's program in Europe and the deliberate gutting, by Far Jewel, of its own and Europe's capital and resources.

On Sheol, the subject Steward appears to have reverted to an earlier pattern of behavior, based on survival rather than loyalty. This may be taken as a failure of indoctrination, but under the extreme circumstances of the war on Sheol, indoctrination was bound to fail at one point or another.

Steward snarled. De Prey's excuses were too elaborate, and unnecessary. His indoctrination had sufficed to kill over ninety percent of his own men.

Though concentration on the ideology of survival served Steward well enough on Sheol, it seems to have been less successful on his return to Earth. It appears that, for Steward at least, a ruthless policy based on survival was inadequate to cope with the stress caused by his sudden lack of status, the demands of his family, the collapse of Coherent Light, the appearance of the Powers, and his own return to his planet of origin in a state of destitution not far removed from that in which he left it. His sense of frustration may well have turned inward, and blaming himself for his misfortunes, he may have destroyed his marriage and his new life in his frustration, and perhaps with the concealed motive of freeing himself from the burden of familial responsibilities.

Drops of sweat were forming on Steward's forehead. "Callous bastard," he said. De Prey's face rose in his mind. Ghost claws tore the image to pieces.

His job with SonnenSystem seems to have been something of a turning point. The subject appears, in the absence of other commitments, to have thrown himself into his work. His work with SonnenSystem was outstanding enough to have attracted the attention of Consolidated Systems security. In accepting their offer of recruitment, the subject Steward may have hoped that a sense of his old commitment and loyalty to Coherent Light would develop. But reports of his work at Consolidated Systems indicate, rather than the new frontier that he may have hoped, a series of uninspiring tasks performed with competence, if not enthusiasm.

Brighter Suns recruitment efforts should focus on the sense of purpose that the subject felt in working for Coherent Light. The recruiter should try to reawaken that commitment, or at least a nostalgia for it. Careful mention of the name of de Prey may serve to make the subject conscious of old allegiances and old friendships....

Steward laughed at de Prey's referring to himself in the third person. He thought of the man's cultivated image, the way he'd presented himself to the Icehawks as someone who was more teacher than commander, a leader devoted to finding ways for his soldiers to excel… and here was the real man revealed in all his chilling vanity, his persona a tool used to manipulate his underlings. There was a bad taste in Steward's mouth. He read on, and then straightened in surprise at what he read.

Efforts should also be made to determine whether the subject is a vee addict, and whether he resents Consolidated as the author of his addiction, or is grateful to them.

Vee addict. The words flickered along his mind, and he mouthed the words silently, trying their feel on his tongue. His pulse quickened. He paged back, then, to the long sections of medical history. Appendicitis, scarlet fever, malaria… ah. *Vee tag. Vee addict.* There was a Y next to each, a Yes. And an endnote just beneath, which led him to an appendix at the end of the file.

Knowledge of the existence and etiology of vee addiction is restricted to those with Grade XVI Clearance or Grade XII (Medical) Clearance, or higher. Violators may be subject to criminal penalty involving imprisonment, mental rehabilitation, execution, or worse. Anyone found disseminating knowledge of vee addiction is to be reported at once to the Pulsar Division or other Brighter Suns security personnel.

Execution or *worse?* Steward thought, and laughed. Thoughts were crackling through his mind like summer lightning. He jumped up and began to pace his cabin, needing movement now, a complement to the storm in his brain.

His first thoughts were that vee addiction was caused by a drug under development by Consolidated, something not yet on the market that had been tested on Consolidated personnel, perhaps without their knowledge, and that it had produced addiction, perhaps unintended. And then, since Consolidated and Brighter Suns both seemed to have it, that the drug had been imported by the Powers and was being kept secret, possibly because it gave the two policorps some unforeseen edge. Maybe the drug led to radically increased intelligence, enhanced intuitive or prigoginic leaps, or altered behavior in some useful way.

Vee tag, he thought, and then, *I'm not allowed into the Legation—I got bugs. I guess.* The words of the taxi driver on Vesta.

When the thought came, it came all at once, a waterspout that he could feel rushing up his spine and exploding in his head, a wave of leaps and hunches wrapped together with the few facts he knew, and Steward had to stand still for a moment and sort it out before he could tell whether or not it made sense.

The Powers had left Earth, allegedly on account of cross-contamination.

Everyone who entered Vesta was given a blood test. To find the vee tag?

Some people were forbidden, on unknown medical grounds, from entering the Power Legation.

Some people loved the Powers beyond reason. Some even had Power citizenship. And so far as people knew, they never left the Legation once they'd entered.

Sereng's eyes were funny.

The Powers, Steward realized, were addictive. They saturated the air around them with hormone aerosols, and some of these had unintended effects on humans. When the Powers first delivered the Icehawks to Earth, enough of the Icehawks had been exposed to them for periods long enough to result in addiction. Griffith had been an addict, and hadn't known it. His life had been a misery after his return, and he'd never understood why. Sereng was an addict, too, but he had skills the Powers wanted, and so he was taken into Vesta to live with them. Susceptibility to the addiction had to be transmitted genetically, hence the blood test, the vee tag, to spot the chromosome that led to addiction.

Vee tag. Y. *Vee addict.* Y.

Cold horror flooded Steward's mind. He could feel his skin contracting, turning to gooseflesh. He had the tag, and he'd been exposed to the Powers for three days.

That's why the Pulsar people weren't interested in him as a prisoner. Instead they'd exposed him to the Powers, then waited for the transformation, or the addiction, to take its effect. After that he'd do whatever they wanted, just to get back to the Powers.

Panic throbbed in his chest. Steward took a series of quick breaths and sat down in front of the monitor, the cold glowing spider-letters that spelled the penalty for knowing about vee addiction. *Or worse.* Steward was beginning to understand what that phrase meant.

Then, slowly, the fear ebbed, and his mind began to worry at the problem. He hadn't felt high in the Power Legation, or felt anything out of the ordinary. He'd done a lot of active physical labor and hadn't been slowed or hampered. Whatever the vee addict felt, it had to be very subtle.

Steward looked up at the monitor suddenly, seeing his own ghost reflection in its dark surface. He didn't feel any different. He didn't miss the Powers, or want to be around them.

He wasn't an addict. And that meant his theory was wrong.

Steward's head was swimming. He rested his head between his knees and took a long, shuddering breath. Sweat dripped on the Velcro padding beneath his seat. Steward didn't know whether or not to be grateful for this new realization. His thoughts had made perfect sense up to a point, and that point was his own experience, and experience contradicted everything and stopped his theory dead in its tracks.

He couldn't discount the evidence of his own body.

So vee addiction was something else. Steward thought about it for a long moment, the flawed construct of his earlier theory hanging before him in his mind, mocking…. Nothing else made as much sense.

Steward concluded that vee addiction probably had something to do with the Powers, related to something they were importing. Perhaps the Powers were tailor-making drugs, chemicals, or hormones for Consolidated and Brighter Suns, and that these were addictive, somehow, to those who worked with them. Maybe the Powers were experimenting with human subjects, dosing them, hoping to find out how humanity worked, how humanity could be controlled. Maybe Consolidated and Brighter Suns knew this but couldn't stop it without bringing a halt to trade with the Powers, their only reason for existence, and so the policorps were just trying to limit the number of people exposed.

Steward decided his speculations were growing increasingly pointless. He went back to his file.

After de Prey's report, the Colonel appended a plea to the Brighter Suns Commissaire of Corporate Safety asking for permission for the Pulsar Division to attempt the Alpha's recruitment. Though de Prey conceded that the recruitment of defectors was usually the task of Group Seven, he asked for a special exception to be made on the grounds that the recruit's previous relationship with him would aid in the recruitment. There followed a letter of protest from a director of Group Seven, and then the Commissaire's decision to allow de Prey to attempt the recruitment. The Pulsar Division, Steward thought, was gloating a little bit, letting the correspondence relating to de Prey's bureaucratic maneuvering remain in the file.

There followed a number of communications from Brighter Suns agents who had observed the Alpha in the Power Legation on Ricot. The Alpha Steward had seemed bored with the restricted life in the Legation, had been observed drinking heavily, seemed to be spending little time with Wandis. Cautious approaches were made and not rebuffed. The Brighter Suns agent grew bolder. The Alpha seemed pleased with the notion of working with Colonel de Prey again. The agent pointed out how the Alpha's addiction had been engineered by Consolidated for their own benefit, to make him dependent on them, and pointed out how Brighter Suns personnel had a much less restricted, a more active life. He even mentioned the possibility of detoxifying the Alpha, freeing him from his addiction, but the Alpha seemed indifferent to the idea.

Eventually he asked the Alpha to steal something for him, just to prove his sincerity. The Alpha obligingly copied some of the work his wife had brought home with her, a classified document on a new method of Penrose tiling, and Consolidated had responded with a payment of 4,000 Starbright dollars put into a numbered account in a bank in Antarctica. A receipt for the amount was given to Steward, and the number of the account. It was pointed out to him that although he could access the money at any time, his life was so monitored on the Ricot colony that he would have difficulty spending it.

Weeks of haggling followed. Eventually the Alpha agreed to defect to Brighter Suns for the sum of 10,000 Starbright placed in the numbered account, a promotion to a high rank in the Pulsar Division, and transportation to Vesta. In return he'd bring large numbers of classified documents from his own department, from Wandis's, plus his knowledge of the personalities and policies of most of Consolidated's high-ranking security personnel. The Alpha also mentioned that when he had designed the security system to Sivi Source's data banks, he'd also designed himself a way into it. Sivi was still the cutting edge in certain types of wetware, and Brighter Suns' wetware people were anxious to get their hands on the information. Some of the Pulsar Division's memoranda began to take on a gloating, congratulatory tone. Here was one in the eye for Group Seven.

The mechanics of the defection were arranged, and the Alpha transported to the Belt in a small cargo shuttle. An offer to move his wife with him was declined without fuss. Wandis would remain behind, marked for life as the wife of a defector.

A report from the agent who accompanied him indicated that his withdrawal from vee addiction caused him considerable discomfort on the journey, but that sedatives provided seemed to ease his trouble. Once the Alpha arrived, he was shown to lavish quarters in the Power Legation, his health and spirits revived, and he was debriefed, under drugs, by Brighter Suns specialists.

Debriefed under drugs. That, Steward realized, was why Colonel Angel had used the zap glove. The drugs hadn't worked the first time, and Angel had gone for more direct methods.

The rest of the file was an attempt to explain and cover up the subsequent disaster. The Alpha, as a new high-ranking security officer assigned to the Legation, had requested an interview with the Head of the Power Legation, the Prime....

Did the Prime know? Was it the Prime's idea? Two of Angel's questions, repeated over and over again.

...The Alpha got his meeting with the Prime, and there had released a spore that, a few hours later, caused the Prime to begin uncontrollably dispersing a hormone meant to warn the colony of an attack by outsiders. Others were infected as well, and when the hormone began to spread through the colony, the Powers grew uncontrollably agitated. The Prime and the others in the Legation headquarters, the center of the infection, attacked and killed one another. At this point, warning was given, and the human personnel were evacuated to their shelters. One-third of the Legation, over eight hundred Powers, were killed in the two days that it took for the outbreak to run its course. Before the outbreak grew chaotic, the Alpha visited de Prey in his office and shot him four times with a large-caliber silenced weapon. Resuscitation efforts failed. The Alpha then escaped Vesta by means unknown.

Damage to the Powers was limited by the fact that the Prime's deputy, Prime-on-the-Right, had left for Power space just a few days before the outbreak and had escaped the catastrophe. Damage to de Prey was not confined, however. His insurance company, LifeLight, a former division of Coherent Light located on Earth, had failed to implant his memories in a clone. The mindthread recording was somehow defective. De Prey was going to stay dead.

Good work, Curzon, Steward thought. The Alpha couldn't have arranged the de Prey clone's failure. That had to be the work of Consolidated agents on Earth.

He smiled. His own insurance company had been another branch of Coherent Light, but if he'd ended up with LifeLight, he might have been going through revival at the same time as de Prey. What would de Prey have thought, Steward laughed, to see his assassin going through physical rehabilitation at the same station?

He paged through the rest of the file. There were long records of his interrogation by Angel, internal Brighter Suns correspondence questioning the evidence of his being a clone without appropriate memories, then proof positive from the hospital in Arizona that the files had not been updated. The final order had been countersigned by Angel in a smudged, angry hand. Steward grinned.

He flipped out of his file and into de Prey's. *Vee tag.* N. Degrees in psychology and military science from St. Cyr, a school specializing in producing policorporate mercenaries. A picture of a young man with a lean face, cautious eyes, and a beret. Thesis: *Warrior Fanaticism: A Study in Combat without Morality.* The quality of the thesis work and a staff position during a short, highly successful Far Jewel campaign in Szechuan had caused Coherent Light to take an interest and to sponsor his defection from Far Jewel. That was among a series of Far Jewel defections that should have been taken as a warning sign of the failure of Far Jewel's Earthside program, that the horror of Petit Galop was about to engulf Europe.

Pilot studies in de Prey's indoctrination techniques, combined with combat experience in policorporate brawls on Earth triggered by Far Jewel's collapse, proved the value of de Prey's methods. De Prey was promoted to Lieutenant Colonel and given the authority to form two battalions of Icehawks. Another promotion came soon after, and so did four more battalions.

During the Artifact War, de Prey was high in the councils of Coherent Light. His policy was to convince the other warring policorps that CL was aiming at conquest of Sheol. Apparently the appalling escalation of the war was part of de Prey's policy, and he intended much of Sheol to be destroyed or rendered uninhabitable in order to deny its effective use to whatever policorp finally conquered the place. When Coherent Light collapsed, de Prey defected to Seven Moons, along with information that allowed Seven Moons to absorb a lot of CL's fragments.

Seven Moons was one of the policorps that helped set up Brighter Suns, and de Prey made a transfer to the Pulsar Division at that time. His work was in counterinsurgency, counterintelligence, and countersabotage, the reverse of what he'd done with the Icehawks, and some of the documents indicated he had some understanding with the Pulsar hierarchy to the effect that when Pulsar and the Renseignement General set up their own external affairs office in direct competition with Group Seven, de Prey would be able to resurrect the Icehawks as his, and Brighter Suns', tool in the policorporate struggle.

Steward found that interesting. So far as he understood the charters of Brighter Suns and Consolidated Systems, they forbade the policorps to create a military that could act as anything other than a small, highly restricted internal police unit, and they were also forbidden to own territory outside of Vesta and Ricot. Somehow, Brighter Suns expected to alter its charter to the extent of creating a military force. How could they expect the other policorps to allow that? Was that the plan that the Alpha's attack had been designed to forestall?

It occurred to Steward that the implications in this document might well be of vast interest to other policorps.

Steward looked at the picture of the vid screen, the totem he'd pasted above his bed. What was Curzon up to? he asked. What was Brighter Suns up to, that Consolidated had to stop it?

The de Prey file finished with yet another page on the LifeLight debacle, and Steward punched up the file on A. C. Curzon. She was a trade representative for a minor mining policorp in the Belt, and Steward flipped instead to Carlos Dancer Curzon, who turned out to be Brigadier-Director of the External Directorate of the Consolidated Police. Which meant, apparently, that he ran Consolidated's spies.

The file was disappointingly thin. Curzon had been born into the trade, his father and mother both highly placed in Outward Ventures' security apparatus. Both his parents had gone down with Outward Ventures and were presumed dead. At the collapse, Curzon had fled to Charter Station on a ship full of Earth-bound refugees, but he'd jumped ship on Charter and was known to have opened negotiations with several policorps for information he'd brought from Outward Ventures. He'd disappeared from Charter, and rumors were that Outward Ventures, which was growing savage in its search for defectors, had killed him to keep his stolen data a secret, but then three years later he'd turned up on Ricot as head of the External Directorate.

There were a few photographs in the file that showed a fleshy man with a square, high-browed face and thin brown hair. Curzon's precise age was unknown, but he was believed to be in his forties. Sexual orientation and marital status were unknown. Ideological and religious beliefs were unknown. The names of his close associates and sponsors in the Consolidated hierarchy were unknown. Any genetic modification or wetware implants were unknown, but if they existed, they were not obvious. The budget for his organization was unknown.

Steward massaged his aching temples. He was gaining information, but none of it seemed relevant. The rest of his files had been chosen at random and probably constituted tens of thousands of pages of information, all of it having a high probability of being less relevant than what he had here.

He got out of Curzon's file and constructed a search program that would wander through his data, logging the location of key words like "Curzon," "Prime," "Prime-on-the-Right." He implemented it, then leaned back in his chair and watched it run.

The next few days were going to be long.

The next day Steward went into the commo room while Fischer was running his exercises in the gym and used the number three antenna to send a coded message to Griffith telling him that he hadn't met Tsiolkovsky's Demon on Vesta, but he'd come across some classified files on his own. He coded the first fifty files, keeping his own, and sent them out, making certain to erase any records of the transmission from Fischer's instruments. It wasn't hard—the radio was a simple commercial job, intended for ordinary use, and hadn't been built with covert transmission in mind.

Steward had vetted all the files, and they'd furnished him with no more information than he already had. He told Griffith that on no account was he to sell them to Brighter Suns or Consolidated agents. He also pointed out that the file on de Prey might give Brighter Suns' client/owners some knowledge of the mindset on Vesta and what Brighter Suns' long-range intentions might be.

The next day Griffith sent a one-word reply: *Awesome.*

Two days later Steward looked at his bank account. It had increased by 8,000 Starbright dollars.

He went through the files, looking for references to himself, de Prey, the Powers. He learned a great deal about the Byzantine nature of internal Brighter Suns politics and the various schemes by which outsiders tried, and usually failed, to make money off the Powers. Some of the files concerned known or suspected spies. Steward fired the files to Antarctica in batches of fifty or a hundred and watched his bank account grow.

By the time the last file was auctioned, his cut of the action amounted to

56,000 Starbright and change. He was rich, set up for life. There was no point in keeping this job unless he just wanted to travel; he could buy himself out of his contract with ease. He moved the money to a series of accounts all over the planet and invested a lot of it in safe blue-chip policorporate stock.

He was getting connected with things. Stock, money, whatever was implied by his deal with Griffith.

It was a strange feeling, somehow unreal. He'd never been wealthy before.

He went up to the docking cockpit and looked out through the armored bubble canopy at the universe of stars. They seemed closer now. He peered ahead, finding Earth and Luna gleaming white and gray against the diamond backdrop, each surrounded by its constellation of industrial stars, and he thought for a moment of New Humanity, where Natalie lived, and how close it was to Charter, a hundred dollars by intraorbital shuttle.

Memories moved through him, laughter, distant song, supple skin. A body in a long controlled tumble across a tunnel of empty air. A phantom taste that he couldn't forget.

A question touched him as well as memory. He had knowledge now, knowledge bought with pain and cunning. It brought him closer to where he wanted to be. But he wondered if the knowledge implied action, if his coming closer to the Alpha also obliged him somehow, obliged him to finish the Alpha's business.

There was a knock on the airlock door behind him. A piece of politeness in case he was doing something strange here, floating in the velvet darkness and performing the act of Onan or something. He reached out from his couch and pressed the intercom button. "Come in."

It was Cairo, with a flask of pepper-flavored vodka. The door hissed shut behind her. She looked at him with her dark, direct eyes. "Are you troubled in spirit, Steward?"

He grinned. "Can't say I am."

The diamonds on her cheekbones winked soft starlight. "Too bad," she said. "I often find that when people are troubled in spirit, they come up here to look at the stars." She webbed herself onto the other couch and looked up. "I was born up here, Earthman," she said. She tilted her head back, sweeping her eyes over the silent, awesome starscape, the cold and steady points of light.

"What do you think of my home?" she asked.

Thoughts of Natalie trickled over his skin. This was her home now as well. "I think it's got possibilities," he said. "There are, however, problems of scale."

She offered him the vodka, and he declined. "It's a matter of perspective, Earthman," Cairo said. "You have to get used to the big picture if you want to get ahead in this life."

"D'accord." Steward thought his perspective was just fine. There was a memory singing in his ears. It was a memory that, later, he would have to make up his mind about—he would have to indulge it or exorcise it somehow. But now, it seemed to be what he needed.

In the silent darkness, the memory sang on.

CHAPTER TWELVE

Images glowed in Steward's mind. A bundle of cable brushed his cheek. He stuck it back in its clamp and it slid out again.

"Station power coupling engaged," Cairo reported. "The board is green."

"SHUT THE SHIP DOWN." SuTopo's voice came with overwhelming clarity over Steward's interface disk, his tones broadcast straight to the audio nerves, very loud, almost an invasion of privacy. Steward winced. The cable touched him again.

"Four-A and seven up," Steward said. He mentally took command of the audio and turned down the volume. "Shifting to station power."

Reese was already stripping off her harness. "Indian Ocean this time, buck," she said. "Kenya, the Seychelles, then Western Australia. Maybe the Barrier Reef for dessert. I'm gonna spend at least half my time underwater." She looked at him pointedly. "*You*," she said, "are not invited."

He pulled the plastic interface disk from his mastoid. "Fine, billie," he said. "I'm sick of you, too."

Reese was grinning at him. "No offense."

Steward grinned back. "None taken."

Reese floated free of her webbing, turned an awkward somersault that spoke of strained muscles and complaining bones. "God, I hate gravity," she said. She kept her eyes focused on Steward as she tumbled in slow motion. "Where you planning to spend your leave?"

They had six weeks' leave coming, and back pay to spend. Crews exploded off long haulers like shrapnel from a grenade.

"I'm going to get some sleep," Steward said, "then think about it."

"What else have you had to think about, the last fifty-two days?"

Steward floated out of his webbing, stretched his muscles, kicked for the exit port. "My investments," he said.

Steward didn't see Reese leave, but she left him a sardonic farewell on his message recorder, along with a stock market tip just in case the remark about investments had been serious. An old friend she'd met onstation had mentioned that Brighter Suns stock might take a fall. It had already lost a couple of points, and Reese's friend, who was a transportation executive, had told her about a charter shuttle of executives, originating in the policorps that actually owned Brighter Suns, heading for Vesta at a steady point nine g. Reese advised Steward to sell short.

Fast work, Steward thought. Those dossiers had probably raised all sorts of questions concerning just why Brighter Suns thought it needed a military. Steward concluded that Brighter Suns might just release all its surplus cash in a big dividend for its stockholders, just by way of showing they couldn't afford armed forces. Selling short might be the wrong thing to do.

Steward drifted to the lounge to drink a bulb of coffee and punch up a Charter scansheet to see what exciting attractions the station currently had to offer. They seemed much the same as six months ago.

His muscles were still aching from the deceleration burn, so he decided to find a quiet bar someplace and contemplate the stock market from over the rim of a trailing willow.

The sound of business rose around him as soon as he left the airlock, the purposeful bustle of life in Charter. The gravity was light here, and the air was filled with the liberated crews of commercial freighters, leaping from bar to hostel to bar in a continual, noisy celebration of their temporary freedom. Bridge and todo music bounced from metal walls. Laughter sounded brittle in the air.

This seemed too sudden for him—Steward wanted to adjust a little more slowly to station life. He stepped on a Velcro moveway that would take him down to the original Mitsubishi spindle. A brain supercharger whined as it passed on the next moveway. Holograms burned overhead, advertising the station's attractions. Gravity drifted slowly through him, growing until it stood at point nine g. The Vesta reflexes were still working; Steward found himself scanning ahead and behind, looking for faces, silhouettes. He came out of a tunnel to see a curved material sky over his head, the vast tent divided into squares and rectangles, reflecting day and somber night, bits of green shining here and there. Bright ultralight aircraft floated by the polished spinal mirrors in an aerial ballet. Habitats this open weren't built anymore. Steward stepped off the moveway and knew he wasn't alone.

He was being followed, and a cold humming built in Steward's nerves and blood, a hum like the sound of Charter, the noise of something happening. There was one tail at least, a middle-sized man in a dark blue jacket with zips. Zippers suggested Earth origin: People who lived in space usually preferred Velcro tabs, which couldn't jam or catch on things.

Steward smiled. The Vesta reflexes were still working, but this wasn't Vesta;

this wasn't enemy turf anymore.

He noticed a bar built on a corner, something called the Kafe Kola. It had a lot of exits. He entered and sat with his back to a wall. A woman two tables away was smoking, and the taste in the air made Steward want a cigarette. He suppressed the longing and ordered his trailing willow.

The man in the dark blue jacket came in, sat across the room, at an angle so Steward could see his profile. He seemed about forty, brown-haired, dark-skinned, clean-shaven, unremarkable. There was a delicacy to his hands that suggested genetic alteration, and his ears seemed too perfect to be real, but the hint was not reflected in his face, which didn't have the sculptured prettiness so common among the altered. He ordered a cup of coffee and a biscuit. When they came he took them, stood up, and walked over to Steward's table.

"You spotted me," he said.

"Yes."

He was altered, Steward saw now, but care had been taken with the face. He'd been created with the intention of looking ordinary, blending in with a nonaltered population. Born into the trade, Steward thought. Like Curzon.

"My name's Stoichko. I was going to talk to you anyway. If you weren't busy."

Steward sipped his drink. "About what?"

"Can I sit down?"

Steward put his trailing willow on the table. "About what, buck?" he asked again.

Stoichko gazed at him quietly, thoughtfully, without offense. "About those files you stole on Vesta," he said.

Steward grinned and thought of connections coming into being, springing into existence at the speed of light from the first moment he'd bounced a communiqué to Marie Byrd Land. "Sit down," he said, and nudged a chair away from the table with his foot.

Stoichko sat down, put his coffee and biscuit on the table. "First thing is," he said, "I don't particularly care that you took those files. In fact, the people I work for think it was a pretty good trick."

The trailing willow burned down Steward's throat, merged with the humming warmth that moved through his body. Business. Connections. All that was represented by Tsiolkovsky's Demon.

"Since you brought it up," Steward asked, "who is it you work for?"

The man shook his head and laughed. "Those files got incredible distribution, Steward. Your friends in Antarctica had one hell of an auction. One price for exclusive rights to the file, one price for nonexclusive rights. It went on for days. People in the Pulsar Division were having apoplexy. They kept trying to buy their stuff back."

"The Pulsar Division wasn't supposed to find out."

"The auction was too public. Of course they found out. After a while, the people I work for told them."

Evidence fell into place. "You work for Group Seven," Steward said.

Stoichko was still reminiscing, a happy smile on his face. "Pulsar got what they deserved. A bunch of dumb cowboys is what they were. To get taken by a drive rigger. You're smarter than all the cowboys put together." Tears of mirth were sparkling in his eyes. "You never saw such panic." He shook his head. "Vesta deserves people with more delicacy running things, not all those ex-military types. A policorp in Vesta's position requires individuals capable of subtlety."

Steward tried to repress his own smile. Stoichko was too jolly to be quite real. "Group Seven," he said again. "Right?"

Stoichko raised his biscuit as if in salute. "The *professional* Brighter Suns intelligence service."

"And you want to recruit me. To work for the people who tortured me."

Stoichko laughed. "*Pulsar* tortured you, buck. Not us." He bit into the biscuit. "You're really too good to stay in Starbright, you know. And as for your friends in Antarctica—well, they're amateurs. They'd never have come up with anything like this on their own." He leaned back in his chair, stretched his arms. "We wouldn't want you on staff. You're too independent, and your talents would be wasted. We'd just want to hire you for special contract work. You could always refuse."

"I could retire. I made a lot of money on those files."

Stoichko's expression remained benevolent, but Steward saw his pupils contract just the slightest bit. "You could," Stoichko said. "But you'd never see the Powers."

A warning chimed through Steward, resonating in his bones. This was important. He looked down to conceal the knowledge from Stoichko, then sipped his drink to gain time. "Yes," he said. "I'd like to see them again." Steward let his eyes drift away to a point above Stoichko's shoulder, remembering how Griffith looked when he talked about the Powers, how Sereng's eyes had seemed clouded, turned inward. He tried to will himself into that state, that dream.

"Look, Steward," Stoichko began. Steward snapped his eyes away, stared at Stoichko as if in surprise at being startled out of a reverie. The agent went on. "I don't know what your plans are while you're on leave. You probably want to do some partying. Here." He unzipped a pouch on his jacket sleeve and pulled out a gleaming rectangle of brushed aluminum bound in dark plastic insulation. He pushed it across the table toward Steward. Steward reached a hand toward it. The object was cold to the touch. A wave of recognition passed through him as if in response to the chill. He'd seen this before, in the box that Sereng had taken off the Power ship. It was a drug inhaler, the same sort Griffith carried, but it had a refrigeration unit built in it, with a small rechargeable power supply and a socket to take a power jack.

"Take it with you to your party," Stoichko said. "Have fun. I don't want to put any pressure on you. But if you want some work for a lot of cash, and maybe see the Powers again, give me a call." Steward took the inhaler and put it in an outside jacket pocket. His fingers were chilled even through the plastic insulation. He wondered how much it would cost to buy the use of a chemist.

"Thanks," he said. He tried again to pretend he was seeing the object of his desire over Stoichko's shoulder.

"Something else, Steward," Stoichko said. "We'd want to hire you first for ice work."

There was a bad taste in Steward's mouth. "I don't know if I'd want to do that."

"You might, if I told you the name of the target. It's Colonel de Prey."

Steward's heart lurched. He was suddenly aware of small details, all of them somehow important—Stoichko's level gaze, no longer quite so jovial, the pattern in which one of the fluorescent lights over the bar was flickering, the way the liquid surface of his trailing willow reflected a blue hologram advert gleaming from all the way across the room. Steward gazed at Stoichko and controlled his words carefully. "He's dead. They couldn't revive him."

Stoichko shook his head. "He's dead to Vesta. But three weeks before de Prey was shot, Consolidated Systems bought a hidden controlling interest in LifeLight as part of a friendly stock exchange. When de Prey died, he was revived successfully, but Consolidated took possession of the clone and brain recording. They told Pulsar the revival failed." He laughed. "Consolidated's been getting some of the best people out of Coherent Light's old operation that way. Sometimes, if their information is valuable enough, they just revive them without waiting for the Alpha to die. It's a good trick. Pulsar doesn't know about it yet."

Steward's mouth was dry. He tried to summon saliva. "I'll think about it," he said.

"Hey," Stoichko said, and smiled. "I didn't mean to dampen your party. Have fun. Use the stuff I gave you. No one else onstation has what's in that inhaler, so make the most of it." He reached out and touched Steward on the wrist. "We'll talk," he said. "I'm at the Hotel Xylophone. Just call when you want to talk."

Steward licked his lips. "I'll do that," he said. "Sure."

Stoichko grinned and finished his biscuit. He zipped up the pocket on his sleeve. "Be seeing you," he said, and ambled away.

Stoichko, Steward thought. A face and manner to set one at ease. His genes must have come from ten generations of salesmen. Friendly, jovial, complimentary, and inside nothing but liquid helium. There should have been a chill mist rising from his eyes.

De Prey, he thought. Still alive. Cold revulsion tugged at him. He felt sick. The inhaler was heavy in his pocket. He wondered if it was poison, if Vesta's revenge was supposed to be self-administered.

He left without finishing his drink, and then followed an elaborate escape and evasion procedure to make certain he wasn't being followed. He didn't think he was.

The Charter directory gave him the names of a number of chemists. He jacked a credit spike into a telephone and called the first.

"Interesting." Zhou gazed with clear plastic artificial eyes at a three-dimensional hologram of a complex molecule. The model of the molecule looked like a geometric abstract of a sperm cell, with an indole ring making up the bulky head and a hydrogen-carbon chain forming a long tail. Something deep in Zhou's eyes gleamed silver.

Zhou was twenty years old and a pharmacology student. One of the chemists Steward called had suggested he might be available for hire. He lived in a cubbyhole apartment crammed with apparatus, with computers and cryogenic units and chemical synthesizers. He wore bright stripes of fluorescent paint on his cheeks and forehead. The chemist looked at a comp printout, then back at the hologram model.

"It's a neurohormone of some sort," Zhou said. "The kind that's on the juncture between hormones and B vitamins. But it's not registered. I'd say you got hold of an experimental hormone that hasn't been trademarked yet. It's complex, and it would cost a lot to synthesize."

"Is this artificial or natural?" Steward asked.

Zhou shrugged. "Can't say. But I don't think something like this would appear in nature. I'll show you why later."

Steward had told Zhou that he'd got the chemical from a rigger friend of his who didn't know what it was. He suspected Zhou didn't believe him, but if Zhou was skeptical, it hadn't affected his work. It had taken Zhou only a few minutes to analyze the sample Steward brought with him. It had taken him two hours to decide what the analysis meant.

"Any guess as to its effects?" Steward asked.

Zhou gave a taut, self-satisfied smile. He bent over his computer deck and tapped the keys a few times. A slightly different molecule appeared. "There," he said. "That's Genesios Three, the new Pink Blossom neurohormone. B-44, or Black Thunder." Soft surprise whispered through Steward. He remembered the hum of a neurosword, his reflection in Spassky's teeth, a steel needle slippery with blood. Zhou took a credit spike from his pocket and gestured at the model. "The head of the stuff you brought is the same, with a carbolic functional group here replaced by a nitrite functional group. And the structure of the tail is slightly different, with the same aromatic groups, but in different locations in the chain"—the spike moved deftly among the illusory atoms—"and there's another very curious difference. Watch here. Let me show you." He touched a key on his comp deck and the hologram shifted to the earlier model, then back again. One structure disappeared, then appeared again.

"See?" Zhou asked. "That side branch of the molecule. It's present in your sample, and missing in Genesios Three. That's the major difference, I think."

"What would it do?"

"Genesios Three is stable. Degradation won't occur at normal temperatures. That's why it's a perfect street drug—you can carry it around in a plastic bag for months and it'll remain potent. But *this* stuff"—he flicked back to the first model—"that additional side branch makes the tail unstable. This whole tail wants to break off from the indole ring and float away. It's so unstable that it's going to do it within a short time, a matter of days. Especially if it's exposed to air, light, or heat. That's why your source refrigerated the drug, to keep it from breaking down. In a week, your neurohormone would be inert. Useless."

A pulse of distant music invaded the apartment from next door. Zhou's expression did not change. Steward watched the molecule as it rotated.

"What do you think it does?"

"My guess is that its effects would be similar to those of Genesios Three: enhancement of brain function, stimulation of neural connections. But it would be much easier to metabolize, so you'd need a lot more of it."

"Would it have the same depressive effect on the brain's own neurotransmitters?"

"Hard to say. I wouldn't be surprised." Zhou looked intently at the model. Something in the depths of his eyes reflected the bright neon colors of the hologram. He smiled and reached into his pocket for a nicotine stick. "I'd like to keep a small sample of it," he said. "Do some checking."

"That might not be wise," Steward said. "If this is an experimental hormone, that means someone put a lot of work into it. And if it's not trademarked, that means they'd have to defend it without recourse to the courts. Some of these groups kill people."

Zhou seemed offended. "I'm not a fool," he said. "There might be some reports in the literature. I'd be able to connect the reports with my knowledge of the drug and put two and two together." He sucked in a fine spray of liquid nicotine and smiled coldly. "A very interesting problem you've set for me."

"I'll call tomorrow," Steward said. "I don't have a place where I can be reached just now."

A slow smile crossed Zhou's face in answer to Steward's lie. Steward assumed he didn't care—the problem, or the dollars, were enough to buy his interest.

"As you wish," Zhou said.

Steward took the refrigerated inhaler from Zhou's tabletop, slipped it into his pocket. His fingers tingled with the chill. "I'll call," he said.

He stepped out into a narrow apartment corridor. The life of Charter hummed distantly in the walls. The inhaler hung heavily in his pocket. Stoichko had advised him to have a party, and probably he would. But first, Steward had to reach a decision about what was in his pocket.

He went to a restaurant first of all, a place that catered to Earth tastes and that didn't serve vegetable paste flash-fried in a high-pressure oil cooker. He figured he might as well get used to being rich, and ordered rôti de veau au céleri-rave. The veal was fresh, shot up from Earth in the luxury space of the daily shuttle. Before the waitress brought his wine, he went to the bathroom. He washed his hands, then took the inhaler from his pocket and looked at it.

Vee addict. Y.

This was the stuff, he assumed, that had addicted the Alpha, the neurohormone that the Powers had brought with them from their alien labs. Steward knew that he had the vee tag, whatever it was, and that the hormone was potent. Memories of the Powers flooded his mind, the long, oddly proportioned arms with their quick, unlikely movements, the scent of the heavy hormone-saturated air, the look in Sereng's eyes. If he took the drug, he'd know what Sereng had seen.

He had to know. Addiction couldn't result from just a single dose—addiction didn't work that way. And if the stuff was poison, there were a lot of simpler poisons, easier to manufacture, that Vesta could have chosen from. He watched himself in the bathroom mirror as he raised the inhaler to his nose. The touch of the chill metal on his upper lip made him shiver. He triggered the device once up each nostril.

Biting frost flooded his sinuses. The pain brought tears to his eyes, but through the cold he could smell the Powers, their heavy essence. Memories flooded him again: the uncanny way the aliens moved, spoke, flew bounding through the air wailing discordant cries from their organ nostrils. Steward shivered again. Blood roared through his veins as his heartbeat thudded in his ears.

His heartbeat slowed. Nothing was happening. He looked at himself in the mirror, and the face that looked back at him seemed surprised. Stimulation of brain function, enhancement of neural connections—he should *feel* that.

Adrenaline hit him then, the aftereffects of terror, and he could feel his knees turn watery. He controlled it, bending over the sink with his weight supported by his trembling arms. The neurohormone didn't do anything, at least nothing that he could detect.

He gave his mirror image a shaky grin, raised the inhaler, fired again. Nothing.

It was a good dinner.

Steward found his party later, after dinner, when he went to the light-grav bars near the docks. He wanted to laugh, to dance, and he found a partner in a Pink Blossom recruit named Darthamae, onstation during the last part of a thirty-six-hour leave. She was genetically shaped with ultraefficient heart and lungs for adaptation to a low-pressure environment, and through bio-feedback techniques she had gained conscious control of her dive response. Her legs and arms were long and delicate, her dark-skinned face unnaturally placid, Madonna-like. She was surprised when he didn't want to take a room in one of the inexpensive dockside hotels, but moved instead deeper into the old spindle, to the King George V, and got a low-gravity penthouse room with a transparent roof that gave a view of the arched habitat above them. The other side of the spindle was in night, and streetlights glowed above like new constellations.

Darthamae moved with the fluid grace of the altered, and when she spoke, she talked as well with her hands, a language she used among her peers in airless environments, her arms and fingers moving like flickering tactile signposts in the air. She hardly seemed to breathe at all. When she spoke, she often had to inhale first, to get enough air in her lungs to say what she wanted. Her hands often got it said before her lips.

She wasn't at all like Natalie. Steward preferred it that way—he wanted Darthamae's placidity, her calm. She was his exorcism. He wasn't certain it was successful.

The landscape overhead grew light, grew new patterns of green and brown rectangles. Steward ordered champagne with breakfast, jumped out of bed, stretched. There was a persistent soreness in his ligaments. The light gravity here was a mercy. Darthamae was watching him from the bed.

"How did someone with your money end up as a rigger?" she asked.

"I just got lucky. Got a good stock market tip."

Her hands floated in the air, gracefully encompassing the penthouse, the glass ceiling, the distant habitats in the sky. She breathed in. "Must have been a hell of a tip."

He smiled. There was a knock on the door. "Ever had champagne?" he asked.

"Not out of a glass."

"It's better that way. Gives it what we call nose."

A slow smile appeared on her placid face, then burst into a laugh. "I'll have to remember to breathe it in, then," she said.

After Darthamae returned to her ship, Steward left the George V and went to a public phone. Identifying himself as Captain Schlager of the Security Directorate, he called passport control and found out that Stoichko had come to Charter on a trans-lunar shuttle originating in Tangier. Stoichko was a citizen of Uzbekistan. His tickets showed he had appeared in Tangier on a flight originating in a town called Mao, in central Africa.

No one at passport control questioned the existence of Captain Schlager. Charter Station was living up to its reputation.

Steward called the library and referenced Mao. It was a small place, its major advantage the remoteness that permitted research to take place in Saharan isolation. Its only industry was Express Biolabs, a wholly owned subsidiary of Policorp Brighter Suns. Brighter Suns was forbidden to own territory, and Express didn't have policorporate nationality or customs, and at least officially was run under local law—Express was just a very private investment.

Steward punched out of the phone network and frowned at the terminal as it flicked on a directory of the hotel's attractions. Stoichko's story seemed to be holding together. Maybe it was time to visit him and find out what he was after.

The Hotel Xylophone was a medium-priced hotel of the sort that catered to ships' officers and traveling businessmen. The lobby was full of holograms of miniature ultralight aircraft darting overhead, recordings of real pilots who flew their ultralights in the low gravity of the central spindle. Steward looked up in surprise as one of the hologram pilots raised a hand to wave to him.

There was a brisk touch on his right shoulder. His nerves flickered as he turned to the right, then heard a laugh from his left side.

"Hi, buck." Reese was grinning at him, holding a traveling ruck on one shoulder by a strap. She was wearing a photojacket that ran pictures of distant beaches, white sand, blue sky, Heineken greenies. He wondered if she'd bought it from the waitress at the Spindrift Hotel.

"Take my stock tip?"

"Not yet." He looked at her with mild surprise. "I figured you'd be on the shuttle by now."

"I'm shacking up. I ran into an old friend and decided to postpone my departure."

"Well. If he gives you any more stock tips, let me know."

Her eyes were bright, reflecting the blue ocean that patterned across her chest. "Getting any yourself, mystery man?"

"I found someone nice."

"Good. I called you last night at the *Born*. My friend had a friend I thought you might want to meet. But she took off for Spain this morning."

"That was a nice thought. Thanks."

Reese poked him in the ribs. "Gotta go. I'm having lunch with my financial adviser."

"See you later, billie."

Steward watched as Reese walked toward the door with her assured long-legged stride. The photojacket beaches passed through the door, across the alloy street outside. Steward looked for a phone and called Zhou.

The chemist told him that he'd been searching the literature but hadn't seen anything even resembling a description of what Steward had found. Steward told him that the hormone may have originated at Express Biolabs.

"That's a hard one," Zhou said. "Nothing gets out of there. They've negotiated a deal with the government giving them control of thousands of square miles of desert around them. It's like a little piece of Vesta, right there in the middle of Africa, even though the land doesn't officially belong to Brighter Suns. It's a way of getting around Brighter Suns' restrictions about having national territory outside Vesta. They're also the sort of outfit you mentioned yesterday. Who don't like competition."

"I'm not surprised."

Steward recognized the sound of Zhou sucking on a nicotine stick. "I'll find out what I can. But I don't think there's going to be much to find out, buck."

"See what you can do. I'll call tomorrow."

He called Stoichko, then took the stairs to the second floor, brightly colored holograms pursuing him as his feet padded on the carpet. Once out of the lobby, the corridor was silent save for the hum of a cleaning robot moving from one room to another. He found Stoichko's door and knocked.

Stoichko was dressed in white canvas pants and a shirt with lots of buttoned pockets. The buttons alone told Steward the man had come from Earth.

Stoichko grinned. Steward found himself grinning back. Salesman genes.

"Come in. Sit down. Cognac? Coffee?"

"Coffee, thanks. Black, no sugar."

There was a room-service automated tray with a heavy pot of coffee on the warmer. "Bulb or cup?"

"Cup. Thank you."

"You drink Earth-style. Good."

"I'm Earth-born. As you know."

Steward took the coffee cup and sat on a chair with plastic cushions and a battered chrome frame. Stoichko poured himself cognac. "You may not believe this," he said, pulling another chair close, "but I actually enjoy staying in hotel rooms. Just sitting away from everything in a quiet little place, watching the vid, listening to music, drinking good cognac." He shook his head. "A nice change of pace."

"Away from the hurly-burly of the latest ice mission."

Stoichko laughed lightly. His finger circled the rim of his glass. "Something like that." He nodded. "I'm not a specialist in ice work, though. That's why I wanted to talk to you."

"To get me to kill de Prey for you."

"Not really. Whatever damage de Prey was going to do to Brighter Suns has already been done. We don't care about him. He was just"—he raised an eyebrow—"an added inducement. Something to catch your attention." He looked at Steward quizzically. "I wasn't sure whether you'd have the same feelings toward de Prey that your Alpha did. Apparently you do."

Steward laughed. "Curzon offered my Alpha a shot at de Prey in order to get him to spread contamination among Vesta's Powers. Now you're willing to give me a shot at him if I'll do something for you." He sipped his coffee. "If de Prey ever stays dead, what are you people going to use to get me to work with you?"

Stoichko leaned closer and winked. "Will money do?" he asked, and then he laughed. His laugh was hearty and smelled of cognac. It was the kind of laugh that wanted company, that set whole rooms of people to laughing without quite knowing why. This boy was good.

Steward restrained his impulse to mirth. "Depends on the job. Suppose you tell me what you want done."

Stoichko frowned, then rose from his chair with a graceful movement that reminded Steward of Darthamae. Altered inner ear structure, maybe, for better balance, or jacked-up coordination. Stoichko paced the length of his room, then gazed out the window. Outside, Steward could see the tops of trees. There weren't any green spaces in the new habitats.

Stoichko turned. He had a short cigar in his hand. "Mind if I smoke?"

"Go ahead."

He lit it with a match—more evidence of his Earth citizenship, there—and puffed for a minute. "Lit a cigar on the Marcus colony, once," he said, "and set off every fire alarm in the place. Got a face full of chemical foam from the automated system." He peered carefully at Steward.

"How do you feel," Stoichko asked slowly, "about the Powers?"

Steward waited a long moment before he answered. "I think they're...better...than we are, somehow. I think"—he feigned an embarrassed laugh—"I think they may be our salvation."

Stoichko nodded. "You may be right," he said. He breathed in smoke, then exhaled. "Consolidated launched an attack on the Vesta Legation," he said.

"None of us know why. But the Powers there died horribly—you read the files, and you know."

Steward nodded. "I know."

"Vesta is afraid that this may be the first shot in a very unpleasant war," Stoichko said. "We have to show Consolidated that this kind of cowboy behavior can't be tolerated." He sat on the bed across from Steward's chair and leaned toward him, creating an intimacy. "It will mean a sacrifice. But the sacrifice will stabilize the situation. It will save lives in the long run, human lives and Power lives."

There was a coldness in Steward's chest. "A counterstrike," he said.

Stoichko looked at him quizzically from under his eyebrows. "Does the idea horrify you? It does me."

Steward swallowed. He had a good idea what he was supposed to say. "The Powers...they'll die."

Stoichko shook his head sadly. "Yes." His fingers toyed with the rim of his coffee cup. "But it will be a sacrifice that may prevent an all-out war from developing. Better that a few should die now than there should be total war. We have to show Consolidated that their biologic defense isn't perfect, that they can't escape the consequences of their acts."

Steward shook his head. "I'll have to think about this."

The other man put a friendly hand on Steward's shoulder. "Take all the time you need. But I want you to know that the weapon that we'll use is far more merciful than the one Consolidated used on us. Our Powers died in agony. They went mad and tore each other to pieces. Our weapon just makes them go to sleep. And it won't hurt humans at all."

Steward tried to look impatient. "That doesn't matter as much."

Stoichko shrugged. "And if you put the ice on de Prey, that's another warning to their hierarchy. That we're on to some of their tricks."

Steward stood up and began to pace around the room. He wanted to get out from under Stoichko's gaze, the sincerity that seemed so convincing and that yet was watching him so carefully. He took a breath, made fists of his hands, stuck them in his pockets. He didn't know how to play this anymore. He wondered if, in the case he turned this down, he would leave the room alive.

He went to the window and gazed at the green space outside. Faintly, the shriek of children passed through the window. The old Mitsubishi spindle had been built for people who were born on Earth, who wanted trees and grass. Nowadays such things were considered a waste of station resources.

"We should talk about money," he said, playing for time while he thought about how to react.

"Ten thousand Starbright in advance," Stoichko said calmly. "Thirty on completion."

"Twenty-five in advance," Steward said.

"Twenty."

"I'll think about it."

Stoichko's cigar stench filled the room. Steward sniffed. "We'll also arrange access," Stoichko said. "We'll route a priority cargo to Ricot through Charter and make sure Taler puts it on the *Born*. We'll let Taler make the insert. It'll look much better that way."

"Support? Backup?"

"We can get you plans of Ricot, of their security setup. We can give you weapons. But do you need anything else? If you handle things right, you'll get clean away. They'd have no reason to suspect you."

No way off the station, then, but the *Born*. "And a lone operator can be disavowed."

"Of course."

A young woman with dark hair was walking on the green below. She was bent over a small child, helping him take his first steps. There was a pain in Steward's throat. He turned to Stoichko. "I can't make up my mind about this now," he said.

Stoichko nodded. Steward looked hard for a warning in his eyes, for some twitch, a narrowing of the eyes or dilation of the pupil that might mean Steward's swift death, right here in the hotel. Steward tried to stand in a balanced way without seeming obvious, his arms and legs ready to lash out in the event of attack. Probably, he thought, his body was screaming readiness to Stoichko's trained eyes. He tried to relax. Stoichko was stubbing out his cigar, his gaze fixed on the ashtray. He looked up. "It's a lot to think about," Stoichko said. "Could I see you tomorrow? Here, for dinner?"

"Yes. But maybe I won't have an answer just yet."

"That will be understandable," he said. "If you think of more details, and need to know the answers, that will be all right. But there is something that won't be okay with Vesta, and that's if you tell anybody."

Steward shrugged. "I'm not stupid," he said.

Stoichko's eyes were hard. Steward was looking at the real man now, he knew, not the salesman with the infectious laugh. "Don't think your friends in Antarctica can peddle the information that we're going to strike at Ricot without our finding out. And if we find out, that you'll ever be safe."

"Give me some credit, buck," Steward said.

"I just thought it needed to be said."

"It's fair." Steward ran his hand across his forehead, wiping away imaginary sweat.. He wasn't going to die, not right now.

"Just so you know." Stoichko smiled, and Steward felt the answering urge to laugh. Salesman genes.

"Did you find a good party?" Stoichko said. "Have fun with the inhaler?"

Steward grinned. "I used all of it," he said. "You wouldn't happen to have any more?"

Stoichko laughed and walked to his suitcase. "Try and make this one last, okay?" he said. "It's the last I've got."

Steward accepted the chill flask in his hand. "Thanks." He put it in his pocket, then began moving toward the door. He feigned hesitation, then looked at Stoichko. "You know," he said, "I used some with a—a friend. And it didn't work for her at all. Do you know why that's so?"

Stoichko made a dismissive gesture. "Maybe she had a high resistance," he said. "Chemistry isn't my strong point."

"Yeah. I guess." Steward moved toward the door. "I'll be back tomorrow. Eighteen hundred?"

"I'll be here. Have yourself a party." He put a hand on Steward's arm as he opened the door. "Don't worry about this thing. If you have any problems, we can work them out."

All the way down the corridor and out of the hotel Steward felt an awareness like a cold draft touching his nape, his spine. Wondering if there was someone following, if he'd made himself a target. Wondering who else was tapped into the network in Marie Byrd Land, who else might be in search of Steward's services.

Steward checked out of the King George V and went back to the *Born*. He decided that he'd feel safer there. He stretched on his rack, and took the inhaler out of his pocket. Metal chilled his fingertips. He held it to the light and wondered what the hormone meant, how it fit into the picture. High resistance? He should have felt *something* even so. He touched the cold metal to his upper lip, wondering if he should try the stuff again, and then the coldness seemed to move by conduction through his bones. A thought had chilled him to the marrow.

The flask might be filled with poison. Stoichko might have given it to him when he didn't jump at the chance to massacre the Power population of Ricot. Steward restrained a sudden impulse to throw the inhaler across the cabin and put it respectfully on a shelf instead, snugging it out of habit with Velcro straps.

Run a mission into Ricot, Steward thought. Find de Prey. Find Curzon.

And while doing so, kill a lot of aliens who had nothing to do with him, with anything that happened to him. He didn't want that.

He looked up at his totem, at the picture of the video with its blurry pattern of interference lines. The Alpha had taken a similar mission, taken the bait of de Prey and massacred the Powers of Vesta. He must have had reasons for doing that job—Steward hoped he had anyway—but Steward himself had no feeling for the aliens, neither the love that Griffith bore them nor any hate that would make him want to kill them.

Steward didn't like Stoichko's offer. But he wanted to know what was behind it, how much Stoichko knew about Consolidated, the relationship between Curzon and de Prey.

He'd try to talk to Stoichko, he decided. Fly with the Zen of it, accept or turn the mission down as the moment seemed to urge him.

He went to his comp terminal and punched up the departing shuttle schedules. There was an Earth-bound shuttle leaving at nineteen-thirty.

If he turned Stoichko down, he'd run for the shuttle. And hope he didn't die en route.

That morning Steward phoned his robobroker and told the 'broker to sell Brighter Suns short, then buy if it dropped more than ten points. Steward ate lunch on the ship and then visited Zhou. The contents of the second inhaler proved to be identical to the first: Stoichko hadn't given Steward a pistol in chemical form. The chemist hadn't found any information on the hormone or what it was intended for.

He looked up at Steward, his pale face striped with paint, and gave a cold smile. "We could pass some of this around at a party," he said, "and see what happens."

Steward shook his head.

Zhou's smile twitched. "I didn't think so," he said.

Steward took both the inhalers and put them in his traveling bag. Then he went to the Hotel Xylophone and walked through the hushed lobby. Hologram ultralights flickered overhead as he walked to the stairs. None of them waved to him.

He moved quietly down the corridor. Stoichko's door was slightly ajar, as if in invitation. A babble of vid came from the room. Steward smelled cigar smoke, warmth, wrongness. Heat flickered through his nerves.

He stood for a brief second in the corridor, then reached out a hand and carefully pushed the door in. Something told him not to walk into the room.

Stoichko was sitting on one of the chrome-and-plastic chairs, plainly visible from where Steward stood in the door. He had been shot in the heart and lungs. His head was bent on his chest, his eyes slitted with an air of cunning. Bright arterial blood was pooled in his lap. A cigar still burned in an ashtray near his hand.

Mission canceled, Steward thought.

Video colors ran over Stoichko's face, shone dully in the dead yellow eyes. The impulse to run plucked at Steward's arms and legs. The killer might still be in the room.

He thought of connections, of communication links running to Vesta, to Antarctica, here to Charter Station, of Tsiolkovsky's Demon sitting in public-use computers throughout the solar system. Links that were in being now, that he could not touch, could not access, without information. He might be able to find things he needed to know here, in Stoichko's room. Steward looked at the bag in his hand, then hefted it, ready to throw it in the face of anyone waiting.

Silently, he stepped inside.

CHAPTER THIRTEEN

Every so often, Steward thought, it's possible to forget that all of this is real.

This was not one of those times.

He and Stoichko were alone in the room. On the video a woman dressed in leather was using a hand-flamer on a swarthy man in black leotards. Shrieks and flames echoed off the hotel walls. Steward lowered his bag and nudged the door gently shut with his foot. Excitement bubbled lightly in his veins. Reality, at last. The mind a void, he thought. Quoting Musashi.

He tried to remember what he'd touched the previous day. The door, the coffee cup, the chair, maybe the window. The coffee cups had been changed by the hotel service—two cups sat by the coffee machine, each still wrapped in paper. He took off his jacket and used it to wipe the window and its frame, then swabbed down the door and its knob. With his hand in the jacket he pressed the switch near the door that lit the red DO NOT DISTURB light on the doorframe.

The room was beginning to smell like death. Congealing blood dropped from the chair to the carpet. Title music throbbed from the vid. Steward tried to empty himself, to make an airless space in his interior, allowing Stoichko and the influences here to fill him with meaning. He began working through Stoichko's belongings, erasing his fingerprints with his jacket as he went.

The Group Seven agent traveled light. He had a single bag—it was made of real leather, with a steel spine—and Steward found it open in the closet. He dumped the contents onto the bed. There was an assortment of dirty clothes, a small plastic pouch of tools—screwdrivers, adjustable wrenches, and so on—and a small bag with four slots in it, intended to carry small flasks of liquor but which in this case held only a single flask of cognac. Probably Stoichko had carried the inhalers in two of the other slots. They were the right size.

The closets held only clothing. Steward appropriated a handkerchief to wipe prints with. There was nothing hidden behind the drawers in the small bureau or in the desk. The bathroom featured standard toilet articles. Steward put a tube of toothpaste and a container of stick deodorant in his pockets to go through later, in case there might be something hidden there.

The bedside table held a paperback thriller and a pair of data spikes neatly labeled, in what Steward assumed was Stoichko's hand, as music. Steward put the spikes in his pocket.

Steward's eyes moved over the room again. Stoichko slumped in his chair. His cigar had burned out. On the video an olive-skinned woman with bright eye makeup like butterfly wings was kissing a small Oriental man in a black silk gi.

Group Seven is going to think I killed him, Steward thought. I'd better run fast, when I run.

The hotel staff wouldn't discover the body till tomorrow at the earliest. Maybe later, if they paid serious attention to the red DO NOT DISTURB light glowing outside the room.

There probably wouldn't be any other Group Seven people on Charter— they'd have to come up from Earth. There would be no immediate pursuit. Unless whoever killed Stoichko was calling the Charter cops and letting them know. A chill ran up Steward's neck at the thought.

Certain chances, he concluded, ought to be taken. The mind a void.

He tried to let the room talk to him.

Steward wondered what the tools were for. And he wondered if there had been a fourth flask in the small case.

He looked at Stoichko again, and felt a coppery taste on his tongue. He knew what happened next.

The body was still warm, the blood still wet, and the reality of it moved through Steward in a wave of nausea. The whirlwind seemed to beat in Steward's ears. He patted Stoichko down, found which pockets were full, emptied the ones he could reach. A credit spike, a waferlike hotel key, a ring of other, anonymous keys. Steward tossed them on the floor. The back pockets next. Steward stood up, then reached for the man's belt and pulled, trying to move the heavy corpse. It was a dead weight, seemingly boneless, and was harder to manage than Steward expected. A belt loop tore with a startling, ripping sound. Pools of blood poured across Stoichko's tilted chest. Steward stepped back quickly to keep the stuff off his pumps, then walked around to the other side of the chair and went through Stoichko's back pockets. Nothing there.

Void, Steward thought. Let the meaning enter him.

What were the tools for? Steward wondered.

He looked around the room again. From the vid came the sound of cartilage breaking. The man in the black gi had just spun and planted a foot in the face of a blond man.

Steward turned the vid off and unplugged it. He took the tools and removed the back with one of Stoichko's screwdrivers.

There was a small black metal flask taped to the inside of the narrow chassis. Steward reached in, pulled on the tape. It came free with a sucking sound. The flask was light and fit in Steward's palm. It had a small paper sticker on it with the biohazard symbol: WARNING, it said, BIOLOGIC SEAL. OPEN ONLY IN STERILE ENVIRONMENT.

Steward put the flask down and wiped anything he may have touched. He reattached the back of the vid set and wiped it, then put the flask in his back pocket.

Stoichko's blood oozed slowly through the carpet. Steward stepped carefully around it.

The hollowness in him had become an ache.

Time to go.

Zhou wasn't home. Steward stopped by a delivery service, wrapped the flask in a package along with instructions and a spike with advance payment, then mailed it to him. He walked for the shuttle docks, scanning behind him regularly, trying not to run. Gravity slowly relinquished its hold. Holo adverts hammered at him. There seemed to be continual movement at the periphery of his senses, but when he looked, he could see nothing. He still felt the emptiness inside, and it was beginning to hurt. He wanted to fill it with something.

The Starbright shuttle to Earth had gone. He looked at the winking video DEPARTED notice and wondered if Reese was aboard.

He scanned the bright glowing columns of the shuttle schedule and saw one yellow column that represented a shuttle that moved from one habitat in lunar orbit to another, carrying salesmen from one hotel to the next. From SOLON, PORT ARTHUR. To PRINCE, NEW HMTY, KEYSTONE, SOLON, PORT ARTHUR.

New Humanity, where Natalie lived with the Alpha's child in gravity-free seclusion. The price of a ticket was absurdly small.

It was weak of him, he knew. He might be bringing trouble to her. But he needed to fill himself with something real, something besides violent death in a small hotel room, a slumped and ultimately sad man cooling slowly while the video nattered on. And he didn't expect to have to deal with Group Seven for a while yet.

And if they caught up with him after a few days, this might be his last chance.

He decided that New Humanity was what he wanted.

CHAPTER FOURTEEN

To confuse anyone following he bought a ticket all the way to Port Arthur. Most of the people on the shuttle seemed to know one another, and they smiled, greeted, and chatted as they came aboard. They watched Steward with genial curiosity. Steward declined the attendant's offer of food, and tried to rest.

Thoughts roared through his brain like a fire blown before the autumn mistral, touching his mind with burning. When he closed his eyes, he saw patterns like bright splashes of blood that printed themselves in laser color on his retinas. Coherence eluded him. He knew nothing other than the fact that Tsiolkovsky's Demon was breathing down his neck. He gave it up and ordered a scotch.

When it came, he could tell from the taste that the whiskey was Japanese. He grimaced and drank it.

The need was growing inside him. He knew there was a madness in this, and he fought it with logic, with the words of Ashraf: "Nothing to do with you now." The words seemed as dead as Ashraf, and spun meaninglessly in the chaos of Steward's mind.

Six hours and three slow drinks later Steward watched New Humanity grow through the shuttle window. It was a silver shining structure, several kilometers across, without the toroidal or spindlelike shape of a habitat with artificial gravity, a maze of modular tubes and tunnels and bright, boxlike zero-g factories, studded with antennas, receiver dishes, and solar power collectors. Steward was the only passenger to disembark.

Eighty years ago four Imagist concerns had built New Humanity as a showplace for their ideology, a habitat for the second stage of humankind, populated solely by individuals bred to live in space, free of gravity.

When Steward got off the shuttle, it became obvious how the dream had failed. The air tasted sour, as if the purifiers were contaminated by some manner of fungus or bacteria. The apathetic six-armed frog woman drifting before her video terminal at the customs desk seemed faintly surprised to see him, and the tunnels and corridors seemed empty even of the altered humanity who lived here. Graffiti covered the tube walls. There was still manufacturing going on here, but competition was stiff in metals and pharmaceuticals, and more modern plants, better supported by their policorps, were making things hard. The original four sponsors were long gone. New Humanity was a policorporate national state now, and on its own.

There was no visible security onstation. Steward assumed there was nothing here worth stealing.

Darwin Days had come to New Humanity. The colony was losing its niche.

Free-fall sleeping bag, lav, shower, and comp terminal, all in institutional gray—that was Steward's state-sponsored hotel room. There was a 3-D poster of happy frog children at play in a bright, clean habitat. WE BUILD THE FUTURE, it said. He stuck his bag to the wall with Velcro straps. Local time indicated a shift change coming up in the next hour. He stuck his feet into restraining straps in front of the terminal and punched up the station directory.

Natalie's address burned in front of him. He felt a dryness on his tongue, an awareness flickering like static on the surface of his skin. Hunger. He was very close to something he wanted.

He asked the terminal how to get from his hotel to Natalie's habitat. She proved to live in a housing unit on the far end of the station, near the bio plant where Steward assumed she worked. He memorized the connections he'd have to take to get there, then left the hotel and kicked off from the wall, heading for an access tube.

The shortest route proved not to be the most well traveled. After Steward took one branch, he noticed the passage was dark. Only one light in three was functioning, the others having been removed. The tunnel emptied into a darkened housing unit. There was a broad pathway along the interior of the unit, hexagonal in shape, with six banks of apartments opening off the six sides. The air was musty, and Steward realized the air circulation here had been shut down. The housing unit had been abandoned. New Humanity's population was draining away.

A few lights still gleamed along the main route through the unit. Steward kicked off, aiming for the distant green light that meant the access tunnel to Natalie's living module.

Steward's path drifted slightly, nearing some of the housing units. Some of the apartment doors, he saw, had been forced in, some had been removed. In the dim light he could see that the interior of the apartments were gutted, the fixtures pulled out, pipes and wires thrusting in clumps from the walls. Graffiti coated every flat surface. Rubbish hung motionlessly in the interior. Steward brushed one of the unit's internal struts, seized it, spun around, and kicked out, correcting his trajectory.

Something ahead eclipsed the green light that was his destination. Steward looked closer and saw a pale face moving in his direction. There was something wrong with the silhouette, and as Steward came nearer, he saw the bulging brain case sparsely covered with pale hair, the six limbs, four of them growing from modified hips and terminating in hands. A high-pitched giggle sounded in the still air, echoed from the many walls. Steward felt his nape hair rising at the sound. As Steward came closer he saw eyes bright with madness returning his gaze.

Two of the hind limbs seized one of the padded cross-members of the habitat, then the body swung around, redirecting its motion toward one of the apartment doors. The limbs were sticks only, the elbows standing out like knobs. The huge brain was absorbing nutrition and oxygen, starving the body. The frog man was no taller than a ten-year-old child.

Another titter broke the silence. Limbs reached out, snatched a rung near the apartment door, and then the frog man opened the door and crawled inside, moving with fast, unnatural movements, like an insect diving down a drain. Blue light glowed through the door, casting azure highlights on the frog man's naked skin, on the computer equipment floating in the apartment amid a bright collection of rubbish, empty drink containers, fast-food trays, old-fashioned ROM cartridges, on the slogan painted on the door, COVALENCE RULE. One of the slogans of the New Rejuve Movement.

The frog man stuck his head out the door and looked at Steward with a nervous grin. "Germs, you know," he said in a high voice, and then the door slammed shut. Steward drifted on in the growing darkness.

Building the future, he thought. Darwin Days.

The next tube accessed Natalie's apartment cluster, identical to the other but inhabited, brightly lit. There was life in this place after all. Steward was relieved by the sensation of circulating air on his skin, by the laughter of children playing some kind of complicated brachiating game on a jungle gym attached to one of the cross-members. It was shift change, and people were floating to and from their apartments. Most of them were frogs, a few were unmodified humanity. Floating directional holograms told him which of the six banks of apartments he wanted. He kicked out and soared toward Natalie's door.

His veins seemed afire. Sweat was prickling his eye sockets. He planted his feet on the Velcro strip by the door and bent to ring the buzzer. The scent of fresh coffee drifted from the closed door. Memories fluttered in his belly.

Natalie opened the door. She floated in the apartment with her head toward him, and looked up at him with eyes he knew. A slow pulse of shock moved through him. He hadn't known what to expect, what blend of old and new, but whatever he'd anticipated, it wasn't this.

Her hair was short now, the black shot lightly with gray. She was wearing gray canvas pants and a reinforced short-sleeved shirt with metal harness rings attached, enabling her to anchor herself to a desk with straps. Her feet were bare. She held a bulb of coffee in one hand.

Her skin was white and slack, blotched red in places, the sign of a life lived indoors. Her face was rounder than he'd expected. She had been long without the gravity that gave tension to the skin and character to the face.

She looked up in shock, took a breath, let it out. Her fingers tightened on the doorframe.

"I should have known you'd come," she said.

The voice hadn't changed, and at the sound Steward felt fire burn him to the marrow. "Can I come in?" he asked.

Her eyes looked him up and down. "You look so damned young."

Steward shrugged. "It's the way I look."

"A hard boy. Nothing soft. I remember that."

"You liked me that way," Steward said. "As I remember."

She was looking at him, saying nothing. It bothered Steward that he couldn't read the look, that his memories provided no clue to what was passing through her mind.

"I'd like to come in," he said.

"I have to go to work in just a few minutes."

"I'd like to come in. For just a few minutes."

The shadow of a decision crossed her face. With a push of her arms she moved back from the door. She touched the far wall, absorbed the momentum, and waited, hanging there, looking up at him. Steward pulled his feet from the Velcro strip and hooked one shoe under the doorframe, then pulled himself in till he could grip the edge of the door with his hands and control his motion. He closed the door behind him and pushed off to the wall where Natalie waited.

The room was small and neat. No floor in zero g, no ceiling, just six walls. Small tables and a desk were folded against the wall. There was a small kitchen, a computer console with straps and hooks to hold someone to the keyboard. Books, magazines, and labeled data spikes were strapped into shelves. A door led to a darkened bedroom. A small robot clung to the wall, doing the cleaning. There was no sign of the boy. Steward wondered where he was. Boarding school, perhaps, offstation.

Steward's mouth was dry. "Could I have some coffee?" he asked.

"Help yourself." She was watching him with a thoughtful expression. He found himself surprised by it—it was uninvolved, objective. As if this didn't matter to her.

He took coffee, rotated in place near the kitchen to face her, hung in space, and tasted the coffee. It wasn't bad.

"You've been drinking," she said. "I can smell it."

"Yes. Japanese scotch, on the shuttle. It wasn't good."

"Do you drink in the morning, these days?"

"It's a little past midnight, my time. I think."

She opened her arms, making a gesture that indicated herself, the apartment, New Humanity. The movement was graceful, assured, as he remembered. "I hope it's worth staying up late for," she said.

He watched her, looked for clues, something he could touch, could hang on to. He wasn't finding anything. "Me, too," he said.

Natalie cocked her head at him. "I had forgotten about the intensity. It mellowed a little, with the first one. But he could always call it up when he wanted it."

"The Alpha."

"That makes you a Beta, I suppose?" A smile twitched at her lips. "The terminology doesn't do much for your self-esteem, I suppose."

"I try to work at it a little harder."

Her green eyes gazed at him. "Work at what? Being the Alpha?"

Steward felt a spasm inside him. He looked for an answer, found nothing. He shrugged instead. "At being what I am, I guess."

"And your coming here? Is that a part of your work?"

He looked at Natalie, held her gaze. "A part of my hope. I think."

Her eyes slid away from his, nervous. She bit her lower lip. "That's not a real description of me, Beta," she said. "I don't exist in that way."

"You can't know that."

She turned from him, began to drift toward the bedroom. "I'm going to have to make myself up for work." She waved an arm toward the door, dismissing him.

"You can't know that," Steward insisted. "What my hopes may be."

Natalie's voice was muffled as it came from the next room. "I know what's possible between us."

Steward rotated in place, kicked off, shot across the small room, checked himself at the door. Natalie hung next to a mirror. She flicked a switch, and bright light illuminated her face. It was merciless. Even halfway across the room Steward could see the slack skin, the blemishes. Steward remembered sand, ocean, distant song. He swallowed coffee. "Can't you tell your people at work that you'll be late?"

She peered at her mirror image expressionlessly and shook her head. "I don't think so." She closed her eyes and sprayed her face with something that darkened her complexion and gave her features a kind of relief instead of being a blob of white. She waited for the spray to dry and then began rubbing her cheeks with something that brought color to them. She took another bottle and sprayed her cheekbones with faint stripes of green.

"Don't dismiss me so lightly," Steward said. "I'm rich. Set up for life."

Natalie turned to him. Artificial color bloomed on her sallow skin. "I don't want money." Her voice was matter-of-fact. "I don't want to know how you came by it. You don't owe it to me. You have no responsibility in this. Any obligations died with"—a shadow crossed her face—"with someone else."

Steward searched for words. "I feel…differently."

Her look was direct. "I'm sorry for that. I'm sorry that Etienne…your Alpha…didn't give you the memories that would help you understand what I'm saying. But the memories—they weren't good ones." She turned back to the mirror.

Surprise whispered through him. "You know about my memories."

Natalie was busy at the mirror. Her voice was distracted, spoken to her reflection. "Yes. I had a few calls from your doctor. Ashley, or whatever his name was."

"Ashraf."

"Right. He didn't want me to talk to you. I agreed with him."

Anger twisted Steward's nerves. He felt his teeth trying to clench. "Ashraf took a lot on himself," he said. "Somebody killed him, finally."

Natalie's eyes turned to him for a moment, then turned back to the mirror.

"I didn't do it," Steward said. "It had nothing to do with me."

"I never said it did."

He bit on his anger, forced it down. It didn't belong here. He touched the doorframe and moved toward Natalie, took hold of the sleeping bag and harness that she'd rolled up to the wall, and stopped himself behind her, so that he could see her in the mirror. She was painting verdant wings above her eyes.

"Why don't you call work?" he said. "Tell them you have company from offstation."

She spun in the air to face him. The painted olive face, distorted by emotion, seemed a painful caricature of Steward's memories. It contrasted with the white neck and hands. He tried not to flinch.

"I have other things to do with my spare time," she said. Anger crackled in her voice. "I'll show you." She moved hand-over-hand to the door, then pushed off for the comp terminal in the front room. Steward followed. "Here," she said. She snapped at buttons. Synthesized chords moaned from hidden speakers. The screen flickered on. Steward followed toward it.

There was a child on the screen. He was hanging weightless in a room, a keyboard strapped to his chest. Stubby fingers made expert movements across the keys. The sounds scraped across Steward's nerves. His heart lurched at the sight of wrongness.

The face was smooth, round, placid, smiling. Perhaps it had never held any other expression. The head seemed strangely proportioned, the eyes were rolled up, largely hidden by the lids. The legs were dwarfed, half the size they should have been.

"My son," Natalie said. "Spinal bifida, severe retardation of the speech centers, borderline autism. A lot of his chromosomes got broken on Sheol. His name is Andrew."

The music was discordant, slow, deliberate. Expert somehow. Steward watched the face, the inverted expression, and felt coldness touch his insides, a mixture of horror and pain. He wondered if he could love this child.

"Gravity would kill him. He'll only survive if he stays in space," Natalie said. "He needs special care twenty-four hours per day. This picture comes from the station hospital."

Steward looked at Natalie, found his voice. "He'll be all right?"

She shrugged. "He'll never learn to talk, but the rest of his mind is un-damaged. He learns fast if I can interest him in something, but getting his attention is hard. If he can find a job he can perform by remotes from his hospital room, he'll even be able to earn part of his keep."

"Does he know we're looking at him?"

"There's a red light on the camera, so he knows when he's being observed. But he's doing his music now and isn't paying attention." She turned her face to the screen. "He'll do that for hours. He's more interested in music than anything else." The boy's fingers pounced on a chord and the chord cried through the speakers. Natalie's eyes softened. "He's why I'm here, in New Humanity. No one else would take me, not if I came with Andrew. But New Humanity was desperate for biologists, a project to tailor a new lichen form they wanted to use for breaking down asteroid material, absorbing oxygen and water for harvesting later. The team came close." She bit her lip. "But New Humanity couldn't capitalize the idea. We didn't have the resources to do it ourselves. So I have a new job now, a dead end. But Andrew still has a home. New Humanity hasn't reneged on that. A lot of the old-style altered go wrong sooner or later—the hospital here is very good."

Steward thought of the frog man he'd seen in the deserted complex, the strangeness, the eerie voice: *Germs, you know.* There was a pain deep in his sinus. He looked at Andrew again and tried not to shiver. His chromosomes, broken. His love, shattered. "I want to help," Steward said.

Natalie shook her head. "It's not your problem. Is it?"

"They're my genes, too."

"Wrong. Your genes and half of Andrew's come from the same source.

He's not your son, he's your half-brother. That's all."

"It's not that simple."

Her look was cold. "I don't want to be your new crusade, Steward," she said. "I'm not interested in being the object of your current war for justice. The…Alpha—he joined one crusade after another. Always trying to find lightness somewhere or other. Evening scores that were dead for everyone but him. And all along"—she nodded at the monitor—"it was *that* he couldn't handle. He blamed himself for coming back from Sheol with his broken chromosomes. He found out being fast and hard wasn't enough, that there were kinds of Zen he couldn't run with. He thought maybe he should have died. And so he chased after every cause he could find, so that he didn't have to live with what he thought he'd done to Andrew."

She reached to the monitor and flicked it off. The music terminated in midchord. Steward looked at the empty screen and felt bits of himself—his hope, his life—dying. He remembered the voice on the video recording, the clatter of glass on glass. The raw shriek bottled up in the voice.

Natalie drank the last of her coffee, moved across the room, put the bulb in its rack. She turned to Steward. "I've made my peace with it all, years ago. I don't have any emotion, any energy left to deal with him, with what he was. I don't have any…*feeling* about it anymore. He doesn't *mean* anything. And you don't, either. Not to me."

"I'm not him," Steward said. Wondering if it was true.

Natalie gazed at him. "Then what are you doing here?"

"I can help."

Natalie shook her head. "We don't need it, either of us. We're doing okay here. When the Alpha got himself killed, we found out he had some insurance. And when he was working, he sent us money. So we've always done all right."

"You can do better than all right."

She didn't answer. Steward thought of lines of mirrored buildings reflecting people lined up in rows, each desperate for a place in the Darwinian lottery. Makeup washing away in rain, revealing faces that were new. A bottle cracking against a glass, shattering it. Chords cried in his mind like children.

"I have to go to work." Gently.

The coffee bulb was cooling in Steward's hands. He drifted to the kitchen, put it in its place. Drifted to the door, and out.

The great open central space was full of people changing shift. Their chatter filled the air like birdsong. Steward pushed off and moved slowly toward the hologram that marked the tube that would take him through the old housing unit and then to his hotel.

He reached out, seized a padded strut, swung around, hesitated. He remembered the dark scarred unit, the glow of blue light on white skin, a distant titter of laughter. He could feel his skin contracting as with cold.

Steward swung around, put his foot on the strut, kicked again, heading the other way.

He would take the long way home.

CHAPTER FIFTEEN

Steward floated into his bare hotel room. On the wall, smiling children were still soaring into a bright future. Steward's tempered tungsten need had been dulled by shock and he could feel himself fragmenting, the reaction to his few moments with Natalie urging him in a hundred different directions.

Steward hung in the room, the circulating air slowly giving impulse to his stillness, pushing him in a slow, pointless circle. He tried to calm his wailing mind. He wanted his instincts to be pure, to be right.

He closed his eyes and thought of his video totem, the invisible voice harsh with rage, the image a brilliant rainbow splintering, a flickering incarnation of chaos. He felt closer to it now, separated only by a few paces, a distance he could easily cross.

Nothing, he knew now, stood between him and the Alpha. Not even his most cherished memory.

There was nothing left to keep him alive.

Steward knew he couldn't sleep and so he worked away the length of his night while New Humanity went through its bustling first shift. He was fueled by a pot of coffee he stole from the hotel restaurant after they'd told him they wouldn't deliver to his room.

Knowledge, he thought, implied action. He wasn't certain what action as yet, but he knew he was moving.

He went through everything he'd taken from Stoichko's hotel room. The toothpaste and deodorant stick proved to hold nothing but toothpaste and deodorant, which was disappointing but expected. The data spikes had music, but on one spike the music seemed to be taking up more space than really necessary, and Steward spent three hours cracking the code and bringing the hidden data to light.

When the first charts flashed onto the screen he recognized them instantly. They were detailed plans of Ricot, with information on station security marked where known.

A warm sense of familiarity settled into Steward and he smiled at the plans on the screen. He knew Ricot well—he'd spent eight months on the Coherent Light planetoid, doing penetration and sabotage training. He looked at the plans as they came up on the screen, the IR and heat sensors, schematics of the Wolf Model 18 extermination cyberdrones that patrolled its forbidden corridors, and his sense of lightness increased, his sense of a pattern.

Ricot. It would be like coming home.

Zhou's voice whispered coolly over the phone. Charter was on the other side of the moon, and there was a second's delay as the signal was bounced off Prince Station.

"Yeah," he said. "I looked at it. The stuff in the flask looks like a fine brown dust. What it is, buck, is a live virus contained in an inert freeze-dried medium. If the medium encounters moisture, say like a mucous membrane, the virus wakes up and starts to do its job."

"Any idea what the job is?" Steward was in a public phone in one of New Humanity's shopping areas. Hologram hype burned on all sides of him. Music slid like syrup through the air. Caffeine was still afire in his nerves.

"No notion, buck," Zhou said. "I don't have the equipment to check that kind of thing in any detail. These viruses are about two hundred millimicrons in size, and that's small even for a virus. And the internal structure is very strange—the nucleoprotein that carries the genetic material is like nothing I've seen. Not that I'm an expert—a virologist might be able to tell you more."

"Is it contagious?"

"I doubt it. The virus has a limited tolerance for oxygen environments—it's got to get into a host in a few hours at the most or it dies. But I don't know what the host would be. I put the virus into a couple of rats and it died. Maybe the pH wasn't right, or something. I can do more specific tests."

"Anything happen to the rats?"

Zhou chuckled. "They're thriving. Having a nice time, here in their sterile boxes. I'll destroy them after I check for long-term effects."

Bright holograms urged Steward to buy. He was floating at the limit of the phone cord. Frogs swam by in the air.

"Don't bother with more tests," he said. "But I want you to take very good care of that flask. I'd like to impress something on you—that stuff's very hot. If you tell anyone about it—*anyone*—you'll die. Probably in a very unpleasant way. That's a certainty."

Zhou's voice was quiet. "Are you threatening me, buck?"

"Not me. If you talk, I'll die right along with you."

"Ah." Steward heard the sound of a nicotine stick being inhaled. Zhou's voice, when it returned, was philosophical. "Then I won't talk."

"It's best all around, believe me. Now, I'm going to be gone for some weeks. I want you to put the flask in a safety deposit box and send me the key. My mailing address is on Moscow."

"You're going to give me your real name and address? I can't believe it."

"It's not going to make much difference, is it? If either of us talks, we die, no matter what name we use. Right?"

Zhou gave a chill laugh. "You know," he said, "I think my rates for doing these little jobs have just gone up."

Steward grinned. "I can't blame you in the least," he said.

"I want to talk to somebody about trust funds," Steward said.

He'd shuttled from New Humanity to Solon. Solon was a quiet place, a twilit torus full of soft conversation, flickering communications screens, and the soft digital hum of accumulating dollars. Solon was a banking center and a disproportionate amount of the wealth belonging to the habitats in Earth and lunar orbits passed along its coded threads.

From here Steward could get a shuttle to Earth. He'd checked the latest news from Charter and his luck was still holding—there was no news of a dead man being found at the Xylophone. As far as he knew, he was unpursued.

This place was called the Stone Bank, and from Steward's researches it seemed the kind Steward wanted. There were no teller windows, no vid screens connecting the customer to an AI. There was dark wool carpet imported from Earth, solid mahogany desks, and quiet, cool cubicles where officers could meet with their clients and enjoy a drink or smoke while doing business. Steward had visited banks like this all through his Canard period. He had always been mildly surprised how well they treated him.

The woman at the front desk was dressed in a dark silk shirt and a carefully cut blue blazer with white piping. An interface stud was inserted at the base of her skull to connect her mind with the financial information flow. She looked Steward up and down, noting the battered jacket, the worn jeans. "I'm not sure—" she began.

Steward held up a needle. It glowed in the subdued lighting like old, polished silver. "Thirty K Starbright," he said. Just by way of establishing common ground.

The woman took it in stride, without a change of expression, just another piece of data in the long string being fed to her mind. Steward smiled in admiration.

"I think Janice Weatherman is the person you want," she said.

Weatherman was about twenty-five. She had delicate features and dark blond hair, and Steward admired her cashmere rollneck and gold jewelry.

She treated Steward very nicely indeed and helped him set up a trust fund in the name of Andrew Steward, current address New Humanity Hospital. Natalie would have nothing to do with the administration of the trust—she could neither profit by it nor refuse the money, and none of the money would ever be in her name. The trust officer would spend such monies for Andrew's benefit as he saw fit and would consult with New Humanity's doctors in any treatment Andrew might need. Stone Bank's person on New Humanity would be required, however, to submit an accounting of his expenditure to Natalie, so that if there was something wrong with the accounting, Natalie might be able to inform the bank. Steward himself, once he'd put his thumbprint on the desk scanner, couldn't free the principal. It was so divided among various investments that even the collapse of the Stone Bank and half the policorps would not inflict mortal damage.

Steward and Weatherman shared a piece of cream pastry in celebration, and then Steward walked for the shuttle gate. He booked onto the Earth shuttle that would bring him to a water landing off the port of Trincomalee.

From there, he was going to Uzbekistan. They had hospitals that would do what he needed, and legally.

His instinct, he thought, had been pure. His action had been correct.

No one needed him now. He was free of responsibility, and free to act.

And suddenly, as if the knowledge of his rightness had somehow released the necessary synthesis, an idea appeared, cold and perfect, gemlike, in his mind. He examined the blue diamond brilliance of it and could find no flaw.

Neither he nor the Alpha had the vee tag. He was not susceptible to the Powers or to their addictive aerosols. *The Alpha had lied!* He'd told his re-cruiter he was a Power junkie in order to get access to the Prime, the better to do his penetration mission into the heart of the Legation, but it had not been true, and the Pulsar Division had not checked it—hadn't thought they needed to check it. It wasn't the kind of thing a defector would lie about. And when he—the Beta—had gone through the blood test on Vesta, they hadn't checked the results—their security comps were setting off so many alarms they'd just picked him up, and not coordinated their data. It had *said* on his file he had the tag—once again, they hadn't thought to check it.

Steward closed his eyes and smiled. Beneath his lids he saw the shadow of a dream, the pulsing redness on the horizon, the way the ground rushed past under the slate sky. He was coming closer. He remembered Hagakure:

When one thinks he has gone too far,
he will not have erred.

Words to live by.

Gravity pressed on his chest as the shuttle brought him to Earth, fire trailing from its polymerized wings.

CHAPTER SIXTEEN

Steward walked onto Charter Station from the Moscow shuttle with every nerve alert, moving in the middle of a knot of Taler employees returning from leave. Two large, soft traveling bags weighed down his shoulders by their straps. Holo adverts blossomed into life around him. He walked lightly, scanning the people waiting for the shuttle. Food smells came out of the fast eateries across from the gate. The air hummed with the noise of business.

Steward moved out of the old spindle toward the cargo docks. Gravity decreased and his strides lengthened. He bounded up the moveway, jumping over intervening pedestrians, holo images passing over his skin. The load on his shoulders lightened. He didn't think anyone was following.

Born was taking on cargo as he arrived. The dock was bright with the sodium glow of floodlights. Cairo stood with her back to Steward, casting half a dozen distinct shadows, supervising the autoloaders. Noise racketed brightly off the metal walls. Small standardized containers moved up an endless belt. Steward narrowed his eyes, looking over the long dock, and saw no one else. He came up behind Cairo.

"Hey there, engineer," Steward said.

She turned around and gave him a grin. Spotlight glare sparkled in the jewels on her cheeks. "Hi, Earthman," she said. She put an arm around his waist and gave him a brisk hug.

"I brought something for you," Steward said.

He opened one of his cases and brought up a magnum of champagne. "One of the better products of my planet," he said. "Be sure to drink it in a glass, now. One that isn't made of plastic."

She held up the bottle to the light and smiled. "We'll synthesize this stuff right one of these days, and then we won't have to haul it out of the gravity well."

"Yeah. Right. Any day now."

She handed it back to him. "Could you put this in my cabin?"

"Sure."

Cairo looked at him sidelong. "There's a lot of stuff waiting for you in your rack. All your mail. A bagful."

"All my friends on Earth sending me presents, I guess."

"Do most of your friends live in Uzbekistan? I couldn't help but notice the postmarks."

Steward shrugged. "The Uzbeks are a generous people." He began following the cargo into the ship's hold.

Cairo looked after him and shouted over the noise of the loaders. "Get your body ready for a long boost. We're going trans-Belt."

Steward stopped moving, a cold touch on his nerves. "Where?"

"Jupiter space. Ricot. Last-minute priority drug shipment."

A feeling of rightness passed through Steward, a knowledge of patterning. Somehow he'd known this was inevitable. He wondered if it was Vesta's work, if they somehow still assumed he was going through with Stoichko's plan. It didn't matter. Even if this was not strictly coincidental, *Born* was still going to Ricot. He was going home.

While on Earth, Steward had watched the news from Charter with care— Stoichko had been discovered on the second day following his death, but the Charter police had made no announcements of any suspects and had commented that Stoichko's origins were uncertain. The implication was that Stoichko's death was the consummation of some business whose genesis had nothing to do with Charter, an assumption in which the Charter cops were perfectly correct. Steward was inclined to think that another implication of their statement was that the Charter police had no leads. Steward concluded that he and the Charter cops had this, at least, in common.

Steward had been moving carefully on Earth, jumping fast from place to place, doing all his business in cash on the needle head and visiting all the necessary hospitals and supply houses under false names. He hadn't contacted Griffith or his people, not knowing how many ties Tsiolkovsky's Demon had to Vesta. Group Seven, for all Steward knew, might be interested in avenging their dead agent, and Steward's body was all that they might find to avenge him on.

There was a message light burning on Steward's comp as he entered his cabin. There were four messages from Natalie. Steward felt a knife of memory jab his heart. He punched the messages up and discovered that all complained about the arrangements Steward made for Andrew's welfare. Steward read the phosphor messages carefully as they ran by on his screen, and decided there was no point in answering. He had acted. The action had taken a life of itself, independent from Steward. It didn't have anything to do with him anymore.

The packages he'd sent himself were secured in his rack webbing. He opened them carefully, checking the wrapping first to make certain they had not been tampered with. There was nothing unexpected. Most of the packages carried data spikes that represented keys to things—keys to boxes, to information, to money, to the way things moved. Other mail contained various souvenirs—Indian religious statues, Russian art, Tibetan prayer cloths, things that could be taken as the private ventures his company allowed. These were mixed with parts that, when assembled, transformed themselves into a custom-made long-barreled pistol, made entirely of an advanced plastic that would pass most detectors and which fired recoilless, near-silent cartridges with self-consuming casings, He'd brought the ammunition himself on the Earth shuttle. Also in the packages was chemical equipment that would allow him to put together plastic explosive and detonators out of chemicals the *Born* had in stock to clean its toilets, maintain fuel cells, and strip old paint. In one of Steward's bags was a hooded one-piece environment suit that would reduce Steward's body heat to background levels, lowering his profile to IR detectors. One of the needles held a schematic for an ultrasonic sound suppressor that would reduce the sound of his movements, breath, and heartbeat and that he could build on his way to Ricot. He'd also bought a new-model pair of night specs, with image enhancement and image enlargement abilities, IR and UV detectors built in, and with interface pickups built in the bows, so that he could control them with a push of his mind. They looked like a heavy pair of mirrored sunglasses. On Earth, they had been a part of Urban Surgery, a fashion. Here, they were something real.

Steward spent a half hour stowing it all away. His cabin was going to be crowded on his way to Ricot, and he regretted that he had no clear idea how much of this gear he was actually going to need.

He was acquiring equipment at the same time that he was paring himself down, becoming leaner, faster, harder. He tried to expunge the parts of his personality not strictly functional, not relevant to the task at hand. He could look at himself now, in the reflective canyons of Earth condecos or the mirrored lenses of his night specs, and understand what he was looking at.

Day by day, he was turning himself into the instrument of his desire.

Reese arrived the next day, her hair turned bright copper by the sun, just in time to begin the four days of engine checks necessary before undocking. Following the first engine check, sparring with Reese in *Born*'s little gym, Steward tagged her on the ear with a reverse heel hook and she stepped back in surprise, grinning at him warily through her mouthpiece.

"You didn't used to be able to do that," she said, her words slurred by plastic.

Steward spat his mouthpiece into his glove. "Sublimity. Constancy. Perseverance," he said. "Modes of living for the successful martial artist."

"Fuck sublimity," Reese said. "You got your nerves jacked up. Nobody's that fast in the real world."

"I got tired of you beating me up," Steward said. "Now we're more even."

He inserted his mouthpiece and slid into a five-strike combination suggested by his new data threads. He drove through Reese's defense on his fourth punch before her counterattack developed and he had to back off to avoid being beheaded by a spinning back-knuckle punch. Through his mouthpiece, he laughed. Six weeks ago, he would have had to take that punch just to get his attack through.

The threads running through his brain and tagged to his nerves held coded artificial reflexes, knowledge of martial-arts techniques and patterns, weapons, small unit tactics, all courtesy of labs in Uzbekistan. Better, more varied and advanced than the standardized implant knowledge the Alpha had carried as an Icehawk and that Reese carried now, reflexes Steward had longed for, and if the implant threads proved inadequate, he could access more through the interface socket set in the base of his skull. It was like carrying a small army in his head, ready for use when he needed it.

He decided to let Reese discover the army on her own, soldier by invisible soldier.

Ricot's vast silver flank reflected the glowing ocher sphere of Jupiter with a slight distortion, like a heat shimmer over alloy. *Born* drifted by the station's side, waiting its turn at the polar docks. Steward had to restrain an impulse to reach out of the docking cockpit and touch the alloy planetoid with his hands. Need was pulsing through his veins like blood. He was close.

Ricot was the ultimate, obsessive artifact of Coherent Light's hubris, the relic of an attempt to physically relocate humanity's future beyond the Belt by building a structure so vast, so elaborate, that sheer awe would draw future generations into its pattern. Humanity would take Ricot as its template, Coherent Light as its messiah, and wealth and technology would shift from the Belt and inner economies to areas dominated by the Outward Policorps.

Huge as it was, there was a practical dimension to the place. Jupiter space was rich: Enormous dronescoops skimmed the surface of its atmosphere for the raw materials of the new plastics, and the upper reaches of the planet were rich in other materials, ranging from hydrogen to polypeptides. Minerals were plentiful in Jupiter's major and minor moons.

But the place was dangerous. Jupiter's size made every inch of its grasping gravity well a battleground, radiation was a continuous hazard, and tidal quakes rocked its moons, threatening instant decompression to any human environment. The smart money had long been in the Belt—development was considered easier there.

Ricot was conceived as an answer, a grand human outpost on the border of Jupiter's devouring gravity. The artificial moon orbited beyond any of Jupiter's satellites, on the rim of the Jovian gravity well, beyond the dangerous reach of major tidal stresses and armored with enough stone and alloy to prevent the penetration of gene-warping radiation. It was big enough not simply to repair and maintain the Jovian dronescoops, but to build them. It was intended that eventually all Jovian commerce was to pass through Ricot's docks.

The planetoid was built to handle it. It was shaped like an American football, twelve kilometers long and three across, its blunt polar caps stationary and gravity-free while the rest of its cylindrical bulk was set in a slow rotation. Three to five million people were seen as eventually inhabiting its alloy corridors. The design featured enough redundancy in its systems and structure to minimize any disaster, from plague to collision. From its armored command centers, the fastest and brightest AIs were to assist Coherent Light executives in charting the future of humanity.

But Coherent Light had to mortgage much of its future in order to build Ricot, and no matter how well the policorp strained the vast wealth of Jupiter passing through its docks, it was difficult to justify Ricot in economic terms. The housing blocks held 150,000 people at their greatest extent: Most of the housing remained in potential only, and the hollow interior remained a webwork of skeletal girders ready for the modular housing that never came. The Artifact War drove all belligerents to the brink of bankruptcy; with Ricot and the war, Coherent Light had a double monkey on its back. Toward the end of the war, CL citizens were rioting in their stainless alloy corridors and sabotage tested the redundancy of safety systems. Executives defected by the hundreds to other policorps that were, themselves, soon caught in the panic. At the end of the war, Ricot was home for a skeletal population composed of Jovian miners working out their contracts with other firms, off-center visionaries and political ideologues unwelcome elsewhere, the lost, the looney, and a few remaining true believers. Only the appearance of the Powers and the astonishing wealth they represented, combined with the Jovian mining, had finally made Ricot profitable. Consolidated Systems was paying unprecedented dividends.

Steward looked at the planetoid's long, brilliant expanse, the shimmering kilometers-long reflective wall that stood alone and featureless against the darkness. Memories of humming corridors filled his mind, the chorus of whispering vents, the crackle of hydraulic joints constantly readjusting themselves to the stresses of rotation and gravity, voices that spoke to him in terms of yearning, of yielding.

Readiness filled him. His action would be correct.

Born would unload, then spend two weeks floating at the end of a tether in Ricot's improbably huge gravity-free interior. Steward concluded this was time enough to do what he needed to do.

For a few days he just moved around Ricot, trying to find the rhythm of the place, the way things worked. Warm familiarity touched his mind and he fought it, wanting to see everything with new eyes, clear, untouched by memory.

Security was tight and omnipresent. There were cameras above a lot of doors, and armed men guarding critical installations. Consolidated could afford the best. Sometimes there were spot checks, men with guns and body armor moving into an area and running every ID through security comps. Living in Ricot, he decided, was a lot like living in the army. After a while the uniforms and security became invisible, just part of the background hum. Steward's ID and passport were in order, so he never had trouble.

He began moving his equipment onstation, piece by piece, storing it in out-of-the-way places, vent shafts, maintenance storage spaces, the girders of unfinished structures. Up near the north pole, far away from the Powers, where security was lighter.

Wondering, he looked up Wandis. She lived in a small apartment in an old housing unit that a lot of Icehawks had once lived in. Steward hung out in the unit's recreation space for an hour before the first shift, picked her up when she left her apartment, and followed her to work. Wandis was a tall blond woman in her thirties, broad-shouldered, wide-hipped. Jewel implants winked from around her left eye. About as far away from Natalie as she could get, and Steward wondered if the Alpha had been attracted to her for that reason. She worked in some kind of metal-processing plant in the zero-g north pole, and Steward turned away from the heavy security at the plant entrance. It didn't seem to be a high-prestige job, and her housing unit wasn't anything special. He wondered if Consolidated was penalizing her for leaving her secrets around the apartment, even though Steward had been following their instructions when he sold them. He wondered also if Wandis had known what the Alpha had been planning, or whether it had all been a surprise.

Still curious, he picked her up at shift change and followed her home. She didn't talk to anyone. After she went into her apartment, Steward hung outside for a while, but she didn't leave again.

Steward didn't feel anything at all for her, a matter of some surprise. He had expected some kind of resonance, some glint of the Alpha, and he found nothing. A moderately attractive older woman, living alone, whose life seemed so spare, so restrained, that he could not help but wonder if she had deliberately crafted it that way out of preference.

His lack of reaction disturbed him somehow, and he followed Wandis for two days. Her behavior was much the same. He stopped following. He had other plans.

Most of Ricot's security was concentrated on defending the Powers from intrusion and, presumably, infection. Steward wasn't interested in the Powers—he had left Stoichko's virus sitting in its safety deposit box on Charter—and much of the rest of station security was gathered around air recyclers, power mains, dock autoloaders—traditional targets of sabotage. Steward wasn't interested in them, either.

He was interested in Consolidated's insurance company.

The company was called Iapetus, and the part Steward was interested in was built into a new structure, a module recently added to the skeleton of potential housing in Ricot's giant interior space. Steward donned a vac suit and examined it from the outside, seeing the vast compressors and huge webwork of coolant pipes that kept genetic material in cryogenic stasis. He noted the places where he could put explosives even as he rejected the idea as inelegant and unnecessarily... noisy, he decided, noisy in the way that noise has of attracting attention.

Steward wandered by the place during each shift and found Iapetus open for business only during the first. During other two shifts a pair of armed guards patrolled the lobby, their jackets stuffed full of armor, helmets jammed with scanners. There were only a dozen or so people working in the place—any revivification would be done outside, in a hospital—and the guards would probably know each employee by name.

So much for the front door. It didn't bother him. Sublimity, he told himself. Constancy. Perseverance.

He had a lot of tricks left.

Through his fingertips, his toes, he could hear the planetoid's metal joints as they crackled around him. The sound of his breath was loud in his ears. He was moving up an air main, swathed in the loose all-body combat cloak that masked his infrared emanations. Moving air tugged at the cloak's polymer skin. Insulation swathed his limbs.

Stoichko's plans didn't cover this part of Ricot in any detail—he'd been interested in the south pole, the Power Legation. But Ricot's designers had been faithful to their modular concept—throughout the gleaming cylinder, patterns repeated, the major power, air, and hydraulic mains and their access tunnels rang changes on one another, repeated throughout the structure until they came up against the bulkhead that had been built to seal humanity from the contamination of the Power Legation.

It was hot in Steward's cloak. Perspiration trickled down his nose. He moved deliberately in point nine g, scanning through his enhanced senses for alarms or sensors planted in the main. There were cyberdrones moving through here, he knew, and they were programmed to kill any unauthorized personnel. Odds were he wouldn't run into one—most would be guarding the Legation, and the dwellings of Consolidated's major figures. A few would be scattered through the utility mains, but there were a lot of mains. There were also a lot of unusual structures in the tunnels, put there for one good reason or other—interfaces with power or communication mains, strange bulges to accommodate equipment installed on the other side, bulkheads, connections to nonmodular buildings that had been added to Ricot since the mains had been put in place. If the drones didn't perceive Steward as alive, he could be mistaken for something that belonged there.

A cockroach scuttled across Steward's path, and he grinned. That had been a problem during his time, as well.

He came to a smaller access shaft that led, he calculated, to LifeLight's air vents, and he scanned his detectors. No radar pulses were coming from the tunnel, no sonar probes. He gently worked his way into the narrow shaft, then began climbing it. Sweat spattered on the inside of his mask. He couldn't avoid an extermination drone here. The shaft simply wasn't big enough, and even the drone's imbecile mind would realize he was something out of place. Claustrophobia began to touch him with lamb's-wool fingers. His respiration increased.

Cramped though it was for Steward, the shaft was a lot wider than it needed to be in order to serve Iapetus—Ricot's designers had anticipated the possibility of more than one module being connected to the same air supply. Cool air whistled about Steward's suit. He climbed steadily.

A tunnel branched to Steward's left. Above him he could see that his own shaft ended, and he worked his way into the branch, moving along on his back with careful shrugs of his shoulders. Barred light gleamed through a vent ahead. He moved to it. The ventilator louvers were nearly shut. The air moved through them with a faint, almost ultrasonic whine. Steward opened the slats with his fingers and peered through: the Iapetus front office. Below was the head of a guard, his helmet bobbing to soundless music fed to the audio centers of the brain. The other guard was gazing out through the glass windows of the front door. Steward closed the slats and moved on.

A red light winked in his mind. Through his interface stud, Steward's cloak was telling him that it had stored all the body heat it could and would have to vent it soon. In another few minutes the suit would start to randomize

Steward's body heat rather than blend it in with the background. It would give him a nonhuman IR profile, but he would still be conspicuous.

There were subtunnels moving off deeper into the building, but they were too small for Steward to crawl through. Staying in the main tunnel, Steward crawled to the next room vent, opened the louvers, peered in: an office of some kind, dark. Steward went on to the next vent: a toilet. He moved back to the second vent. He looked carefully for alarms and found none.

Tools were held in padded pockets in the front of the heat-masking cloak. Steward had removed the Velcro pocket strips because they made too much noise when opened—instead he'd shut them with transparent tape. He opened them, took out his tools, and pried off the flat metal unit containing the louvers. Reaching outside, he removed the vent grille, his fingers holding the louvers throughout the operation so the grille wouldn't fall. He took the grille inside the tunnel with him and placed it carefully above his head.

He wondered if there were alarms inside the room. He turned on his UV light and switched his specs to UV. There was one sensor in a high corner of the room. Infrared, he decided, probably for detecting fire—there was a sprinkler system in the roof—but possibly for detecting people. He moved up in the tunnel and told his cloak to vent his body heat. He thought of the movement of heat in the tunnel and the possibility of an extermination drone downwind from him, and coldness that had nothing to do with his cloak tingled in his nerves. Steward moved back down the tunnel and contemplated the size of the ventilator. It seemed far too small for him. He decided to try it feet-first.

During the first attempt Steward jammed at the waist, squeezed through thanks to the slick surface of his cloak, then stuck again just below the armpits. He emptied his pockets silently, hoisted himself out, and tried again. He was caught again beneath the arms. His cloaked boot touched the corner of a desk and then flailed in the air. He tried squeezing out by holding one arm down and working one shoulder out first, but failed. He put both hands over his head and tried once more, facedown this time. Pain flickered at the touch of the metal ventilator frame. The skin of his back and chest was turning raw. He was jammed thoroughly.

Sweat poured like quicksilver down his face, smudged the backs of his scanner shades. The air in the face mask tasted of acid. He remembered the guard's head bobbing to music and wondered how the guard's head would bob in laughter when he saw an intruder's ass hanging out a ventilator.

He rested for a moment, caught his breath. Tried to perceive the Zen. Steward began to breathe carefully, feeling how gravity tugged at his legs, the way the ventilator held him. Becoming a part of it. Each exhalation seemed to make his body looser, more relaxed. He poured air from his throat, feeling the humid warmth of his lungs filling the face mask as tried to make himself empty, a thing of limp slick boneless plastic, a nerveless creature who couldn't feel the flaming agony of torn skin as he began to drop through the ventilator, as the metal edges tore his flesh even through the cloak that covered him....

Relax, he thought. Breathe out. Blackness touched his vision. His head spun.

Steward dropped to the floor and staggered as his muscles tried to adjust from a relaxed mode to a supportive one. A desk caught the back of his legs and he almost pitched over backward. Stars flashed in his eyes.

Gratefully he breathed in. Within the space of a dozen heartbeats, the world came back.

He took his tools out of the ventilator and turned to inspect the sensor in the corner. It seemed set up to detect IR, but he couldn't tell how sensitive it was, whether it would register a person or not. He took a sheet of plastic insulation material from a pocket, taped it into a box shape, and then taped it over the sensor.

Steward peeled the cloak off his body and breathed happily in the cool air. His T-shirt and shorts were soaked with sweat. He told the cloak to dump all heat and checked the office for other alarms, finding none.

According to the holographic nameplate on the desk, it belonged to a man named Morrison Falaye. His desk had holo cubes of two children and a pair of elderly parents or grandparents. He was also careful with his passwords, and didn't leave them lying in his drawers on pieces of paper.

Well. That's what the black labs in Uzbekistan were for.

In Vesta, Steward had Angel's key to the Pulsar Division's data files. Here he had nothing except the mercenary talent of renegade computer jockeys living on the bitter shores of the Aral Sea. He'd tested their programs before he left Earth and found them satisfactory. They'd custom-tailored the latest intruder software to his specific needs, and promised him no legitimate policorp was going to be able to counter these intrusion programs for at least another year.

"Brute force," he'd been told, "combined with a certain elegance. Force to break in, elegance to make sure nobody finds out about it."

Steward sat down in Falaye's desk and put three needles into the terminal and an interface stud into the socket at the base of his skull. He switched on the terminal with a push of his mind. Programs flashed on the screen too fast for Steward's eye to follow, their phosphor afterimages glowing faintly on the crowded screen after the programs did their job and went. The same long strings of data formed in his mind, projected by the interface stud, and he rode along with the intrusion program, watching the magic do its work, ready to intervene if necessary.

It wasn't necessary.

Within a period of twenty seconds, the programs had found the Iapetus data banks, broken into the high-security file, scanned for Curzon and de Prey, found the backup files, and randomized them all. The long strings of data representing the specific configurations of the two minds, their memories and reflexes and knowledge, were instantly rendered useless.

Biographical information representing Curzon and de Prey were encoded on Steward's needles. He needed to know the name de Prey was using now.

READY, the screen told him.

He was going to make a thorough job of this. Through the interface stud he guided the program as it sought the codes of the genetic material representing potential Curzons and de Preys, waiting their time in cold baths of liquid nitrogen. In the deep misty cold of the cryovaults, robot manipulators began to whine. The little Curzons and de Preys were moved into the file marked WASTE and dumped into the outflow like so much organic garbage. Genetic material was borrowed from other vials and put in its place. The records of the transactions were removed.

Interface of mind and body was a complex thing. Consciousness—memories, abilities, possibilities—was too integrated with the specific configuration of the brain to be reconstituted reliably independent of the body that once held it. Even if Curzon and de Prey updated their memory files, as they were bound to do eventually, and erased over the randomization that Steward had introduced, the memory implant would very likely fail when it went into the wrong body.

A coldness hissed through Steward's mind like a touch of the cryovaults.

He had just committed murder.

Steward tasted the feeling. He had assured the eventual permanent death of two people, one of whom had killed the Alpha, the other of whom had killed the things that made the Alpha's life meaningful. There was no sense of wrongness in it.

Conflicts with right and wrong are a sickness of the mind, he thought. Funny that the old Zen poem de Prey had taught him was used in booting de Prey off the wheel of incarnation.

Savoring the thought, Steward gave the last command through his interface stud: LOGOUT.

The afterimage of the command flickered in his mind, then died.

Steward put on his IR cloak, removed the plastic mask from around the detector, and put his tools back in his pockets and taped them down. He had to stand on Falaye's chair to ram himself back through the vent—brute force, he thought, as opposed to elegance. It cost him a lot of skin, and he could feel blood running down his flanks, soaking his T-shirt as he replaced the vent and used an adhesive to cement the louvered vents back on.

He hoped Falaye wouldn't wonder why his chair had been moved.

He paused in the tunnel before he began to move, listened to himself breathe, hardened his mind. Extrication following a successful mission was a dangerous time: The tendency was to grow overconfident, to think of withdrawal as a happy epilogue rather than something requiring as much skill as the penetration itself. Steward pictured the return trip in his mind, regulated his breath, calmed his heart. Remembered the guards he would pass, a helmet nodding to music he would never hear.

Steward began crawling down the tunnel. Blood felt warm on his flesh. He could feel sweat beginning to bead on his scalp. Bars of yellow light patterned his body as he moved past the lobby/guardroom. He began to breathe easier.

Red warning lights flashed in his mind. Adrenaline slammed into his system.

Radar trace, dead ahead, from the access shaft that led to the main. There was a cyberdrone in the tunnel.

It was suddenly very hot in his cloak. Steward's heart flailed within its cage. He tried to control panic as he rolled to one side and snatched at one of his pockets. The adhesive tape stuck to his fingertips and he fought it. He thought of the Wolf Model 18, the sensors that could hear a victim's heartbeat or taste his sweat, the armored spiderlike body with its flexible legs that could wind around the victim, holding it helpless for the thrust of the long steel poison needle. At longer range there was a fléchette gun that would fill the tunnel with a cloud of a hundred poison darts that would shred flesh and strip bone.

And it was fast, faster than any human. Sophisticated programming, in which the drone was required to compare target shapes or internal maps or configurations, could slow a machine down. Instead the Wolf 18 was told to kill anything that looked or smelled wrong, and then jack into a communications main to inform authority what it had done. Keeping the programming simple kept the extermination drone deadly. The Wolf Company on Ceres suggested its use only for guarding critical areas, where mistakes would be minimized.

Consolidated Systems considered all of Ricot's subsystems a critical area. If repairs were made in a given stretch of tunnel, coded commands were pulsed down the tunnel for the drones to patrol elsewhere. Consolidated didn't care about mistakes. Mistakes shouldn't have been in the tunnels anyway.

Steward didn't have access to the codes that would tell this drone to go away. They changed hourly, and the communication systems in the tunnels were protected by far more safeguards than the internal comp in an insurance company.

The red light grew stronger, the pulses more regular. The drone was getting closer.

Holding a blade in his gloved, insulated hand, trying to move without a sound, Steward crawled down the tunnel on elbows and knees. His breath was loud in his mask. Schematics of the Wolf 18 flickered in his mind, in the threads tagged to his memory. Cold wind poured past him like a tide.

He was down a side tunnel from the shaft in which the drone was moving. The drone couldn't detect him around the turn with its radar. He might have a chance if he could ambush the drone here, if the drone tried to go straight along the tunnel to the top instead of crawling into the tunnel with Steward.

The drone's shaft ended just above Steward's branch. Did the drone's programming include that knowledge, or would it just have to bump into the top of the shaft?

Steward's mouth was dry. He came to the tunnel branch, waited for the moment, aware of the scrabbling sounds of the drone moving up the shaft, the monotonous, mental red throb of the radar signal scattering down his tunnel, most of all the sound and heat of his own pulse.

One chance. At least death would be quick. Fuck that thought.

One life, he thought, one arrow.

The antennas came first, taste sensors on the end of whipping stalks. Lucky the thing was upwind. Then one of the thing's feet, a flexible metal tentacle, flopped into Steward's tunnel and slid over one arm. He had to restrain himself from jumping back.

Concentrate, he thought. Everything ready for the one strike with the right hand. The body a spring, coiled, ready to project the hand, the arrow, with all Steward's weight, with all his assurance. The pulse beat in his ears like a shrieking wind.

Eyes next, peering lenses set in a flat armored head that featured the stainless poison needle, retracted save for the tip. Stubby radio antennas set beside the eyes. The Wolf was moving fast, upward, full of death and inhuman purpose.

The arrow struck, one hand shooting out to ram a thin ferrous alloy blade between the Wolf's head and cylindrical body. There was a flash, an arc of light as electrical connections were made. Steward's mind quailed as he realized that he'd lost his vision, that he'd been dazzled. Something struck him in the face, and he recoiled. The red beating light was gone from his mind.

His vision cleared. The Wolf was dying, its poison needle thrust from the bullet face, firing a diminishing spray of poison high into the tunnel. Steward could hear it spatter like rain on his arm.

He pulled his arm back and the Wolf fell down the shaft. Distantly Steward heard the crash. The capacitors of his suit signaled him that they were drained.

He stuck his blade back in his pocket and crawled into the shaft.

Steward's nerves were keening with adrenaline and he needed it all as he dropped down the shaft, seized the drone, dragged it behind him as he ran along the main. He didn't want this dead thing found anywhere near his target. Its radio signal was gone now, and when it failed to report in on schedule, other drones and their human masters would be moving in toward its last location.

A colony of roaches bolted from under his feet. He ran down the main, beneath one vertical shaft, then another. A grating echoed under his feet. He lifted it and dropped the drone there, down another shaft. He opened a pocket and took out a small screwdriver, then dropped it after the drone. Maybe it would look like someone had left a tool in the shaft and the drone had some strange accident with it. If nothing else was amiss in the shaft, the security people might actually choose to believe this theory rather than have to fill out a half-hundred reports explaining how they didn't know why their drone was lost.

There was an access door nearby. It wasn't the one Steward had entered, but he wanted to get out fast. He cracked open the door, saw through darkness a roomful of stored maintenance equipment. He jumped out and closed the access behind him, then pulled off the heat-suppressing cloak. The air was cool and welcome. He rolled the cloak into a bundle, taped it shut with Velcro straps, and left the room.

Blood was drying on his T-shirt under his arms. Nobody seemed to notice.

The next day he drifted again, moving up and down Ricot's corridors, trying to find the rhythm. It hadn't changed. There was no hint of Consolidated's reaction to finding one of its cybernetic sharks with a melted brain at the bottom of an air shaft.

De Prey's name was St. Cyr now, or so Steward's penetration programs told him. He'd named himself after his old college. Lucky for him, Steward thought, he hadn't gone to West Point.

Steward was fairly certain he couldn't get into the executive housing unit where Curzon and de Prey almost certainly lived. Security was ferocious, and even if Steward jacked himself in through a utility main he'd probably be picked by a street patrol within minutes. He decided he'd have to find them at work.

The Consolidated Security Directorate was in the same detached modular office block that had housed Coherent Light's intelligence effort. This was near the north pole. The place had only two tunnels entering it and was otherwise surrounded by a wide area filled only with scaffolding and single-mindedly homicidal robot guards. The tunnel entrances were heavily guarded. One tunnel led to the gravity-free polar industrial area that included the plant where Wandis worked. The other led into broad metal Methane Street—a lot of the streets here were named after Ricot's products—which featured clothing stores, specialty food stores, restaurants, and bars at which the tables were separated from one another by ultrasonic privacy screens. The executive housing unit was a short distance away by moveramp.

To absorb some of the local style, Steward bought clothes in Methane Street. He also bought a briefcase and a comp deck and began frequenting the local bars, sipping his drinks and playing with the comp as if it were part of his job. Mostly he played computer games and watched the windows. When the shift change came, he went out into the street, looking for faces he knew. After the first two days he knew the rhythm of the street fairly well. Security patrolled up and down Methane but never rousted the execs in their watering holes. He started keeping his pistol in the briefcase, under the deck.

Looking for faces. Gathering power. Waiting for the moment.

Information implied action. Action was latent in him, in his briefcase.

One life, one arrow.

When the moment finally came he was in motion instantly, and when the susurrus of surprise whispered in his mind, it was only an afterthought. Suddenly, on a street bustling with quiet well-dressed people going off shift, there were two faces he'd seen only in pictures—Curzon's square and heavy-lidded, the shadow of a dark beard on his cheeks and chin, moving next to the young de Prey, the face Steward had seen in the man's St. Cyr dossier, a dark diffident face moving a half-step behind his superior. Steward saw them in three-quarter profile, moving past, and he didn't need to look again.... Instead, he was scanning for bodyguards, knowing they had to be present around a Brigadier-Director of security.

He found two at least—young males in big jackets—one medium-sized man moving behind, a big man stepping ahead, each marked by the purposeful robotlike movement of the head that indicated sophisticated threadware impelling their regular visual scans. Their hands were stuffed in their jacket pockets. Steward heard a whisper of triumph in his mind as he saw them. There was a third man with them, flanking Curzon, a gray-haired older man, smoking a short cigar, who had the look of an exec rather than an ice expert.

Steward couldn't see anyone else. The crowd was too big, too varied. A few were looking alert, most weren't. He decided it didn't matter. This kind of chance—de Prey and Curzon in the same place—would never happen again.

He drifted after them, tucked the briefcase under his arm, opened the latch. Awareness tingled in his body, his limbs. His enhanced neural connections seemed to branch out, extend beyond his body to touch the crowd, the two execs, the metal street. He had never consciously chosen a purpose, had moved instead through a kind of instinct, a half-certain sense of what the Alpha had wanted done, moving as a Zen arrow aware of its target only at the end of the journey. Now a conscious decision needed to be made, and he was only faintly surprised to find that he had made it long ago and that the sight of the two men, walking side by side, had only confirmed the judgment. He, the arrow, now perceived the end of his journey. Readiness filled him like fire.

A few days before he had lain in the tunnel, gathering power, making of himself a spring with its focus at the blade, becoming in the end the blade itself moving, a rushing and a light. Now he felt himself gathering in another way, toward another end. Though he could not touch it, felt it only as a weight under his arm, he was becoming the pistol, the cocked mechanism, the bullets… potential violence in self-consuming casings.

De Prey and Curzon split at the second intersection, de Prey and the gray man going right, Curzon and the two guards left. Steward hadn't expected that, but he didn't quicken his pace. He could work with this. Head lowered, he scanned left and right for movement that seemed out of place, for any wrongness…. He found none. From the middle of the street he cut on a diagonal, closing the distance to de Prey. The cross street was called Molybdenum Way. He lowered the briefcase from under his arm to his left hand, and its own weight opened it. He seemed to feel the touch of wind on his face.

Threadware calculated trajectories, distances. Ricot was so big that Molybdenum Way was, for all intents and purposes, flat, the curve imperceptible. De Prey was probably wearing armor, and that meant a head shot. Steward, with the support of the threads in his nerves, was confident of hitting anything he needed at sixty meters provided the target image was sufficiently uncomplicated.

People bustled around Steward, intent on their own business. He could feel the whirlwind building in him. There was certainty in his mind. This would be good Zen.

He reached into the case, took out the gun, raised it to aiming height almost casually, and fired a single shot from behind at a distance of thirty-odd meters. The self-consuming casing made a mild nonthreatening hiss along its course, like a whisper of wind. The gun's mechanism made a gentle click as it jacked the next bullet into the chamber. When de Prey's head burst open in a spray of red, Steward was already poised to return the gun to its case, turn on his heel, move in the other direction.

The gun thunked into the case. He was already turning, moving after Curzon. The individuals in the thinning crowd continued on their courses.

Pure Zen, he thought. The movement had been so natural that even in the midst of the crowd it hadn't seemed out of place. The gun had made no sound that would awaken people from their postshift dreams. It would take a few seconds for the afterimage of the movement to register, and then for the crowd to react…. By that time, Steward intended to be on his way. Be another person, another silhouette, another bullet.

"Hey." Anger hummed in Steward's nerves at the disruption. This was too soon. Someone must have been looking right at him.

"Hey. Hey, you." A young voice, still filled with surprise. Behind him there was a growing disturbance.

"Hey, *I saw that!*" Insistently, but with a touch of wonder in the words. As if he were asking Steward to confirm what he had just seen.

Steward still felt the lightness in his soul. He spun in his tracks and raised a finger to his lips. He saw a young dark-skinned man with a scatter of jewels implanted as a starburst on his forehead. *"Hush!"* Steward told him, saw the confusion in the man's eyes as he turned back into the crowd, and felt the long hesitation behind him as he took one step, then another, then a third… and by then he was invisible, moving in the crowd that trailed after Curzon.

A half-second later, when he heard the cry of, "Hey, wait a minute. *He just shot somebody!*" the man and he were absolute strangers, whatever moment that had once connected them now long gone.

Steward put on his shades, opened his blue jacket to reveal the yellow T-shirt underneath. Changing the profile just a bit. Moved fast through the crowd, almost flying, carried by the wind that howled inside him.

Ahead there was a disturbance in the pattern. One of the guards was looking back, standing on tiptoes to peer over heads. Curzon's ponderous head, glimpsed briefly through the confusion of bodies, was seen in the act of lifting, as if in surprise. The peering guard had one hand pressed over his temple, perhaps to hear an inner voice more clearly.

More bad luck. The cigar smoker, de Prey's companion, must have had a radio, and the guards receivers planted in their skulls.

Curzon turned and peered back himself, an ideal, hesitant target. Steward's hand began its move to the briefcase. And then the guards grabbed Curzon and began moving with him toward one of the shops. Steward felt the moment ebbing away, the wind dying in his brain. Frustration began to bubble in his veins as he pulled his hand back. If he hadn't had to stop and quiet the stranger, the second bullet would have found its target.

Steward continued his movement, purposeful, still on his old course toward where Curzon had been. The guards would have perceived any altered movement as suspicious—their wetware worked that way. He decided to try a snap shot as he passed the shop.

In the window of the shop a holographic bottle of beer rose from an ice planet in a rush of chill ammonia vapor. Curzon was standing in the doorway, looking a little ruffled, brushing his hair back with a wide palm. His guards were holding their hands in their pockets, turning to scan the street one last time. Steward slowed slightly, maneuvering one passerby between him and the guards, and chose his targets as he reached for the pistol. First guard, second guard, Curzon, he decided. Inelegant, less surgical than his original plan, but if he gave the guards any leeway, they'd kill him. And the guards could be revived as clones, assuming they'd bought any insurance....

The whirlwind wailed in his ears. He lifted the gun and turned, a move simultaneous with the concealing pedestrian's movement out of the line of fire, and anger boiled in him at the change in target image, the last glimpse of Curzon's balding head moving into the dark interior, behind the hologram that concealed his form, the cold eyes of the two guards whose level gaze returned his own. He lifted the pistol slightly, the merest tensing of the upper arm, to put the first bullet between the eyes of the taller guard, and then, as the nerve impulse to squeeze the trigger was already on its way to his hand, Steward's upper arm was shattered by a bullet that came from his right.

Steward's shot went somewhere into the bar. He tried to tell his hand to retain the pistol.

Without hesitation he turned left and ran, trying to disappear into the crowd, hoping to let the wind carry him. The briefcase tumbled onto the metal street behind. The pistol was still clutched in his hand.

The third guard, the one he hadn't seen who had fired the shot, caught him before he'd moved three steps. He stumbled to his knees as a flying heel slammed into his left kidney and pain shrieked along his nerves. On his knees he twisted left, tried to use his good hand, but another kick smashed into his ribs and his parry went nowhere. He could feel something break deep inside him. The third guard was a woman, he saw, a small black woman in inconspicuous clothes, her upper lip drawn back in a bright, intent parody of a smile. Moving air screamed in Steward's mind. He swept out with one foot, caught her by the ankle, and brought her down, but before he could stagger to his feet, Curzon's two guards were closing on him. Steward recognized zap gloves on their left hands.

He ducked beneath the first punch, hit Molybdenum, and rolled, pain from his broken arm driving bright needles into his skull, and then he came up again, one foot lashing out, catching a guard in the midsection. The breath went out of the man, but he snatched at Steward's pants cuff and held on, delaying him for the fraction of a second it took Steward to snap his leg back. It unbalanced him and spoiled the next kick, which was aimed at the second guard and parried by the guard's left hand—the glove contacts failed to touch Steward's flesh, luckily, and he staggered back, saw the woman jumping up to join the fight again, and suddenly the big guard was flying at him, trying to knock him down bodily—he caught a blow on the face before he could move aside, and then the woman's foot slammed against the side of his knee, buckling it.

One life, one arrow.

Shit.

After the impact with the alloy street he could hear only the wind, see nothing but the zap glove coming down, landing right on his chest, pinning him onto Molybdenum Way like a butterfly transfixed by a shining electric needle.

CHAPTER SEVENTEEN

Steward felt a needle—another needle—jab his thigh. A tidal wave of broken glass rushed through his body. Nerves awakened and sang in pain. His mouth was dry, his lips cracked. From somewhere was the hum of a ventilator. He opened his eyes.

From out of a tunnel of blackness a calm female face gazed down at him from beneath cropped blond hair. There was a sunburst of jewels implanted around her left eye. His mind fumbled at recognition.

"Wandis," he said. It hurt to speak the word.

Her mouth twitched in the beginnings of a smile. "Steward," she said. "Better have something to drink."

A bulb mouthpiece touched his lips. He drank gratefully. Spots of warmth leaped on his skin like jumping spiders. He tried to scratch and found he couldn't move.

As he sipped at the bulb, vision seemed, in a Coriolis swirl of dim color, to drain slowly into his head. He was wrapped in a kind of sheet and strapped to a table of brushed alloy. At least, he thought, the table didn't have blood gutters. He could feel electrodes pasted to his head, and his interface socket had something in it that wouldn't answer when he tried to give it orders. Human figures moved in dim light behind Wandis. Steward recognized Curzon's blocky silhouette standing between a slim frowning woman in a uniform and a man in a white coat with a stethoscope around his neck. Steward's clothes were in a pile by his table.

Pain throbbed in his arm, his side, his kidneys.

He looked at Wandis. "Sorry I got you into this," he said.

She took the bulb away and shrugged. "I'm just here to help in the debriefing. Because I know you."

Steward saw now that she was wearing a tailored blue jacket with an ID holobadge clipped to the collar. SECDIV, it said.

"You work for Curzon," he said thickly.

Her look was matter-of-fact. "Have all along," she said. "I'm plant security now."

Steward tried to grin but a pulse of pain ran up his side and he gasped instead. There was a flash of concern in Wandis's eyes. "Debriefing," he said. "Isn't 'interrogation' the word you're looking for?"

"Whatever you like," she said. Wandis stood up, and behind her, a battery of floodlights turned on. She dissolved to a fractured silhouette. Pain stabbed Steward's eyes and he turned his head away. He heard footsteps, then another voice.

"Steward." The voice was mild, unconcerned. The English was lightly accented, and Steward assumed it belonged to Curzon. "We're here to learn the truth."

"Écrasez l'infâme," Steward said. "Will that do?"

A pause. "We're going to find the truth, Steward. We have drugs, we have power over you. Most of all, we have time. All the time necessary to find out what we need to know." He cleared his throat, a cold sound. "You've already been condemned, you know. Three of the people in this room are empowered to constitute an emergency security tribunal. We've passed sentence on you. All that remains to be done is the paperwork." Another throat clearing, even colder. "A lot of paperwork, unfortunately. Irregular procedures, however legal, must always be justified by expenditure of paper."

"You have my sympathy," Steward said. Things were still crawling over his skin.

"The sentence was death."

Steward turned to him and gave him a grin. "Is that supposed to terrify me?" Through slitted eyes he saw that the voice was Curzon's. He was standing nearer, under the lights, while the others were behind him, seated at a desk. Probably watching the monitors that were supposed to monitor Steward's state of mind.

Curzon's arm was wrapped in bandages and hanging in a sling. That last wild shot into the bar had actually hit him. Steward squinted at him, saw his paleness, the little hint of pain in his eyes. He'd probably had a broken arm and lost a certain amount of blood.

"The law requires I tell you the sentence," Curzon was saying. "Now it's on the record of the proceedings. I don't care whether you're terrified or not. You've ceased to become a problem other than a bureaucratic one." Pause. "I suppose I should also tell you that we can rescind the sentence, provided you cooperate with us, et cetera. Understand, Mr. Steward?"

"A ray of hope. How nice."

The bright lights were making Steward's eyes water. He looked away. Insect legs dug into his skin. He tried to shift his position, failed.

"Are you uncomfortable, Mr. Steward?" Another voice. Steward squinted at it, found it belonged to the man in the white coat.

"Yes," Steward said.

"The drug we used to bring you to consciousness may cause some discomfort. It will be momentary."

"Thanks."

"We haven't given you any painkillers. They would make you drowsy. So there may be pain as well."

"I'll be on the alert for it. Thanks again." He closed his eyes.

Curzon's voice came back. "Shall we begin, then?"

Steward didn't answer. He wished the sheet he was wrapped in would permit him to shrug.

"Who are your contacts on Ricot?"

A smile, the sort made when you know the truth won't be believed. "I don't have any."

"Who are you working for?"

"Myself."

"Does that mean you are a mercenary?"

"That means I am working on my own behalf."

"No one hired you to kill St. Cyr."

"No one."

There was a pause. "These are the answers we expected, Mr. Steward."

Steward grimaced through a spasm of pain. "Then you are not disappointed," he said.

"They are the answers any agent would give—that he acted alone, under no one's instructions."

Steward again suppressed his urge to shrug.

"Untrue answers will drag out these proceedings," Curzon said. "We will find out the truth regardless. You can only delay matters."

Steward looked at him. "Take all the time you need. I've got nothing else planned for today." Pain throbbed in his forehead at the intensity of the light.

"Why did you kill St. Cyr?" The question came quickly, a riposte.

Steward closed his eyes against the floods. There was a bright yellow glow on the backs of his lids. His skin crawled and he tried to ignore it. "Because St. Cyr tried to kill me. Back when his name was de Prey. He sold out my unit, and a lot of friends died."

"Icehawks."

"That's right, buck."

"Why did you try to kill me?"

Steward looked into the lights. "Because you killed me, Curzon. Brought me out of Vesta just to put an ice jacket on me."

There was an intake of breath from somewhere behind the lights. Steward tried to find Wandis behind the floods. "Is that a surprise, Wandis? You didn't know Curzon had your husband killed?"

"That," said Curzon, "is untrue."

Steward laughed. The drug and pain put a nasty edge to the laugh. "Now who's not telling the truth?"

Curzon's voice was calm. "Steward died on Vesta. The extraction went wrong. We only got the body back."

"Rien n'est beau que le vrai," Steward said, a proverb. For Wandis's benefit he repeated in English. "Nothing is beautiful but the truth. Your lies reek, Curzon."

"I want to find out about this." A flat declarative from Wandis.

"Someone's programmed him," Curzon said. His voice showed no excitement, nothing that proclaimed Steward's allegation was worth his consideration. "Someone who wanted me to die." He cleared his throat. "Wandis, I'll show you the reports. You can talk to the pilot if you like."

"I'd like that."

"Wandis," Steward said. "Pilots lie. Reports lie."

Curzon cleared his throat again. Steward wondered if he had a head cold. "Our information shows you were implanted with memories fifteen years out of date. You can't have experienced anything since before the war. Is that correct?"

"Yes."

"So where did you get your information, Mr. Steward?"

Steward laughed. "From me. My former personality. He sent me a message, saying you were going to kill him."

"You believed him."

"Wandis." Steward peered urgently into the darkness behind the lights. "He sent the message after he got out of Vesta." A lie, but Steward reckoned that even if their monitors showed the lie for what it was, it wouldn't matter much—it wouldn't put him in a worse position.

"The point is, they wanted de Prey," Steward said. "I killed him on Vesta, and then Consolidated stole his clone and memory threads when they took over LifeLight Insurance. He was more valuable to Consolidated than I was, and if I returned from Vesta to find de Prey here, that might make me...I don't know. Rebellious...difficult. So Curzon had me killed. The reward for doing a good job for him."

Wandis didn't answer. Instead the next voice was Curzon's. "You received a communication from your—former personality..."

"My Alpha."

"From your Alpha. Informing you that de Prey had betrayed him and that I had killed him. And that's the sole reason you have for trying to assassinate us?"

"I suppose I could have sought a murder indictment in Flagstaff. But I don't think that would have done much good."

Steward had the impression the people behind the desk were consulting. Running the conversation back through their monitors, trying to certify the truth of Steward's statements.

He smelled tobacco. Someone in the room was smoking. The scent made Steward's mouth water. He was grateful for the returning moisture.

Curzon cleared his throat. "I think," he said, "that Wandis and Dr. Nubar can leave. Mr. Steward and I are about to begin discussion of things for which they do not possess the proper clearance."

Steward laughed. "Right. Grownup talk now. The boys and girls may leave."

Curzon continued unruffled. "Thank you both. Wandis, I think you can go home. Dr. Nubar, I'd like you to wait at your station in case I need you."

There were the sounds of feet, a door opening, more feet, a door closing. Pain filled Steward's eyes, his brain. He wondered if he'd just wrecked Wandis's career. If Curzon thought she believed him, it was possible she'd be under suspicion in case she tried to avenge the Alpha, or spread a scandal about his death.

That was stupid of him, if that was what he'd just done. He was going to have to attempt better control. With the pain and the lights and the speed they'd just shot into him, control was going to be difficult to achieve. He began breathing, trying to use his training, establish control of himself.

I have no tactics, he thought. *I make existence and the void my tactics.*

The floodlights died, and Steward breathed his relief. Their brightness still burned behind his lids. The pain in his head receded slightly. He heard Curzon moving, sitting in the chair Wandis had used, clearing his throat again.

I have no talent. I make a quick mind my talent.

The blaze slowly faded from Steward's vision. He opened his eyes, saw Curzon frowning down at him. There was a plastic headset on his balding skull, electrodes pressed against the skin, allowing him, Steward assumed, to monitor the readouts connected to Steward's body and brain.

I have no castle. The immutable spirit is my castle.

"You are correct in one thing," Curzon said. "I had your Alpha killed."

Steward's mind flooded with surprise, followed instantly by suspicion. If Curzon was this open, there was a reason.

"I hope it didn't cost you too much paperwork," Steward said.

"There were overriding reasons," Curzon said, "which you cannot appreciate."

I have no sword, Steward thought, and the thought was triumphant. *From the state which is above and beyond, from thought I make my sword.*

Steward barked a laugh. "I can appreciate bacteriological attacks on an alien race. I can appreciate a Brigadier-Director having a colleague assassinated after successfully completing a dangerous mission. I can appreciate the value of a man as cynical and evil as de Prey." He glared at Curzon. "I am not lacking appreciation for the details of your business. So tell me your reasons. Maybe I can appreciate them, too."

Curzon reached with his good hand into his pocket for a tissue and blew his nose, then leaned back in his chair and looked at Steward. He still wore a fairly abstracted frown, looking like a middle-aged exec working at a difficult acrostic, a purely intellectual problem.

"Your Alpha," Curzon said, "went to his death with a certain grace. Death was what he wanted, Steward—he never convinced himself he should have survived Sheol. But he wanted an honorable death, and he wanted to accomplish certain tasks beforehand. The de Prey mission, mainly. I think he was happy when he died."

"Nice of you to help him along. When you kill me, I suppose you'll be doing me a favor as well."

"Perhaps I will not kill you. Perhaps not." Spoken as if the possibility was somehow intriguing. Salesman genes, Steward thought. Lies built right into the DNA.

"If I cooperate," he said.

Curzon shrugged. "Your cooperation is irrelevant. We have our methods, we have all the time we need. The answers we want are assured one way or the other. No"—a brisk shake of the head—"I think I may recruit you instead."

Steward laughed. A spear of pain entered his side and he gasped for air.

Curzon showed no surprise at the laughter, no resentment. His voice continued in the same quiet fashion. Steward began breathing again, striving for control. Speed ran down his flesh like nails on a slate.

"I think your Alpha wanted to give himself to our purpose, but he was too scarred by his personal trauma to appreciate what we were trying to build here. He affected cynical, mercenary attitudes for which I have little patience or respect—people whose loyalty can be bought have never impressed me. De Prey, for example. He would work for me, for Vesta, for the Powers if they gave him what he wanted. He was of limited value—we could not trust him. He could indoctrinate ideals into others but he had none himself." His voice turned meditative. "I wonder if your Alpha realized how much his attitudes made him like the man he wanted to kill."

Steward shook his head. "You're a gem, Carlos Dancer Curzon. A real original."

Curzon looked at him. "No. Not at all. I am simply a man superbly adapted for his work. As are you." He looked at the woman in uniform. "As is Colonel

Godunov, sitting behind her desk." His eyes turned to Steward. "As is our Prime, Mr. Steward. The undisputed king of his people."

Steward said nothing. Curzon tilted his head to one side, looking at his problem from another angle. The gesture was spoiled when he went into a brief spasm of coughing. He cleared his throat and dabbed his tissue to his lips. "Bronchitis," he said. "Just getting over it." He stuffed the tissue into his breast pocket, then frowned down at Steward once again. There was something merry in his eyes. Like Father Christmas.

"What do you know, Mr. Steward, about the Powers?"

"They're hierarchical. Alien. Complicated. Not like us. I know you sent my Alpha to kill Vesta's Prime and a lot of his people, but Prime-of-the-Right escaped. I know that Powers are addictive to people with the vee tag, that their aerosol hormones make the addicts think the Powers are God."

Curzon stiffened in surprise, and shot a quick glance at Godunov. Steward rejoiced at getting a reaction out of the man at last.

When Curzon spoke, his voice was meditative. "It is going to be more difficult to keep you alive than I expected, Mr. Steward. Most people who find these things out simply disappear."

"Can you loosen this sheet around my shoulders? I'd like to be able to shrug." Steward bit back on his words. The speed was making him talkative, and every word he spoke was monitored, compared against every other word, forming a pool of data against which to test his future reactions. He had always been told that during interrogation he should keep his answers short and simple, and never elaborate or launch into long-winded explanations. Interrogators wanted their prisoners to get boastful and talkative—it gave them so much more rope with which to lasso their victims. Steward started his regular breathing again, tried to concentrate on something else. Conflations, as he had on Vesta. Make the universe in his skull. M44, he thought. Where the hell was it?

"I wonder if I can ask you the source of your information?" Curzon's voice was conversational.

Cancer, Steward thought. Merde. He couldn't think. No reason Curzon shouldn't know this. "The *Born* put into Vesta last year," he said. "The Pulsar Division thought I was the Alpha and picked me up. Their interrogator gave away a lot more information than he got. And then I worked in the Legation as part of a backup crew. There were some old Icehawks working there. Power citizens. I got a look at them."

"And you put it together from that."

"I'm superbly adapted for my job. Or so people tell me." Steward looked up at Curzon. "The Pulsar people weren't nice. Brutal, in fact. They don't like you killing their Prime for them."

Curzon pursed his lips. "I didn't like it, either. The operation was put together very quickly and for reasons I don't entirely understand. It wasn't my idea. Our own Prime insisted, I'm afraid. We undertook the operation as a courtesy to him."

Steward was trying to build Orion in his mind and the picture vanished under a wave of surprise that jangled like sleigh bells along Steward's cranked nerves. "The Powers go around poisoning each other?" he asked. "I thought they were all so disciplined and perfect." Orion, he thought once more. Rigel here, Betelgeuse here. Curzon's voice came from far away.

"That is a story we find advantageous to spread. We wish to encourage people to believe they can be like the Powers. Stable, intelligent, cooperative."

Obedient, Steward added mentally.

"The truth is that there are…nations within the Power community. They are as divided as we are."

The picture of Orion disappeared again. Ideas flickered like gunflashes through Steward's mind and it took a moment to assemble them into a coherent whole. If the Powers were as fragmented as humanity, if the Artifact War had been fought on territory divided between two Power nations…that would explain the necessity of two ports of entry, Vesta and Ricot. And explain as well the way the humans of Vesta and Ricot were suspicious of each other—their success depended on their own Power nation's success. And it explained as well the fact of one Prime launching an attack on the other.

Steward thought of that huge cone-shaped part of the sky where humanity was barred. Where there were other Power nations that might pose a danger to, or at least prove competitive with, the two nations already contacted. No wonder the Primes have forbidden human exploration of that area.

"Come now." Curzon was talking to Godunov. "Mr. Steward already knows enough information to justify our having him killed three times over. I'm just giving him a little more to reason with. Maybe he can tell us about our friends on Vesta."

It occurred to Steward that Curzon might be high on painkillers and that this was making him talkative. No wonder he seemed so jolly. Curzon turned to Steward. "Yes?" he said. "I can tell you've been thinking."

"I—I'm not sure," Steward said. The picture of Orion was firming. "The feeling I got from Vesta was that things were divided there. Pulsar and their other group—"

"Group Seven."

"Yes. They were taking different positions over things. Over me. Pulsar was interested in what I knew about Ricot. So maybe they were interested in retaliation."

A muscle in Curzon's cheek twitched. "Yes. I warned the Prime of that. But he said that Vesta's Powers had to be stopped. That his sources told him they were about to conduct some kind of major operation, and they had to be warned not to go through with it."

Orion gleamed in Steward's mind, the hunter with his studded belt. Hunting not the Powers, like Steward, but the Pleiades.

"Worse," Curzon said, "the operation missed its target. It was Prime-of-the-Right we particularly wanted. Not the Prime. We were told that, but not why." He frowned at the floor. "A damned bad op. Lucky we accomplished as much as we did." He reached for a tissue and coughed into it. Frowned again, but there was a twitching grin in the frown. The man was full of painkillers, and they were warring with his salesman genes. *From thought I make my sword*, Steward repeated, and watched carefully.

"It won't matter in the long run which of these little factions triumphs. One of us will command the future."

Goad him, Steward thought. Orion was glittering in his skull like diamonds. Diamonds that could cut. "I've heard that before," he said. "From Coherent Light. Derrotero. Gorky. Far Ranger."

Curzon looked at him in mild surprise. "Ah," he said, "I recognize that warrior cynicism of yours." He cleared his throat. "I used to agree with you, you know. That the policorps were nothing but squabbling factories for conformity, each motivated by nothing but scorn for weakness and greed for power. Each looking for an *edge*, hoping their ideology or system would prove what they needed. I was…brought up in a particular craft. Destined for it by my genes. I did it very well. But I lacked a certain…inspiration."

"You've got it now, I gather."

Curzon seemed amused. "I sympathize with your point of view, I truly do. During the time of the Orbital Soviet, there was an ultimate authority that ruled on policorporate conduct. But the Soviet fell in a haze of nerve gas and tailored viruses, and since then it has been—"

"Darwin Days," said Steward. It was getting hot in his sheet. His mouth was turning dry.

Curzon smiled. "Yes. Nothing but policorps struggling for their edge. A war of all against all. And in the absence of any other responsible authority, in the presence of a corrupt ethic in high places, you, Mr. Steward, have set above all else your own sense of personal morality. You have ruled on de Prey's conduct, and mine, and found it inexcusable. But it is a very…*lonely*…mode of existence, is it not? Perhaps even sociopathic. You can find no others worthy of your company, saving only yourself."

"I have plenty of friends," Steward said. "And apropos sociopathy, one thing I don't do is have them killed."

"Your Alpha did," Curzon said. Steward felt himself stiffen. "On Sheol he killed his superior officer." Curzon pointed a finger at Steward like a gun.

"*Bang!*" Curzon's eyes twinkled merrily. "Shot him dead. And he gave orders, in battle, that resulted in many of his friends being killed. He was in a position of responsibility, and responsible people sometimes are compelled to decide these things." Curzon looked at him. "You feel free to be virtuous because you are also free from any degree of authority. Your Alpha was never as lucky. He had responsibility over human life, and the responsibility scarred him for life. That is part of his tragedy."

"It didn't have to be a tragedy," Steward said. Sweat was beading on his scalp.

"Listen," Curzon said. "When the Powers came, I knew instantly I wanted to work with them. I knew the interface between humanity and the Powers was the place to be, where our consanguineous destinies were to be forged."

Consanguineous destinies, Steward thought. Orion was laughing his britches off.

"The Powers are divided," Curzon said. "So are we. Consolidated and Brighter Suns are kept deliberately weak, and that is out of fear. The other policorps know what we are creating here, and hope to control it. They will fail." He shook his head. "The synthesis of Power and human will prove greater than either. The Powers recognized that right away. That was why the Primes relocated to human space. They were searching for the *edge* as well. And they knew they could find it in us."

"It doesn't make them better," Steward said. Sweat coursed down his face. "Or you."

"Perhaps not," Curzon said. He was flushed. His pupils were dilated black obsidian. "Not in the sense you mean. Not more moral, or ethical, or better behaved. But it makes us better in another sense, an evolutionary one. Because we are the future, and all else is obsolescent."

Orion blazed in the night sky, the towering, threatening hunter. The sweat that poured down Steward's face tasted like blood. He bared his teeth. "Your victory is inevitable, so that makes you right," he said. "I've heard that before, too. That was de Prey's line."

"The vee tag and the vee addiction—that was an accident," Curzon said. "But it gave us a key. The Powers are as intelligent as we, as imaginative. But why are they so disciplined, so...cooperative? It's the aerosols, Steward. The ultimate socializing tool. There is no dissent in Power society, no disruption. And mark this, Steward—their intelligence is not hampered. They are as smart as they would have been otherwise, smarter because some of the aerosols enhance intelligence. But the intelligence is harnessed for the social good. The pursuit of happiness is not a problem—they have found it. Working for their own betterment and that of their species."

"Sounds good. Why are their bosses poisoning each other?"

Curzon was glaring at Godunov. "I know, Colonel," he said. "We're going to kill him anyway, so what does it matter?"

"Some things are best not said aloud."

Steward was mildly surprised at her voice. It was breathy, surprisingly child-like. Not the sort of voice you normally expected from a torturer.

"Pah." Curzon began to cough, barking into a wadded tissue. He waved a hand, gulped air. "I'll conduct this interrogation in my own way. By the book, or not. I wrote the book anyway, so what does it matter? We have all the time in the world. And Mr. Steward may prove an apt recruit." Godunov started to speak, but Curzon cut her off: "Yes, we *can* ascertain whether his conversion is sincere. We have the drugs, don't we? Fuck this nonsense." He turned back to Steward. "Colonel Godunov is a specialist. So am I. Her training leads her to different conclusions from those suggested by my experience."

"I will note my protest in the log," Godunov said.

"Note it. What the hell do I care?"

Steward wondered if this exchange was genuine or some strange, implausibly baroque variation on the good-cop, bad-cop theme. Curzon was loaded with drugs, but still there was something here—some hint of falseness—that suggested the second alternative was a possibility.

"The Powers," Steward prompted, as perhaps he was intended to. He shook sweat from his forehead. "Killing each other."

Curzon frowned. "Yes. From our point of view their species evolution is...unfortunate. The aerosols are intended to assist their nations—tribes, perhaps a better word—their tribes in building internal solidarity. They are still competitive with one another. That is something we can help them with."

"Jesus," Steward said. "You're going to start using aerosols on us, aren't you? Make us all bright, happy junkies."

Godunov was making throat-clearing sounds. Curzon ignored her. "We will make of humanity what it has always wanted to be. Cooperative. Peaceful. Forward-looking. A more perfect union. Workers' paradise. Equality, fraternity. From each according to his abilities, et cetera. All the old slogans, coming true." He waved his good hand. "After that, we can give the Powers a hand with their tribal problems. Our Primes will have their *edge* in the human-Power synthesis. Darwin Days will be over. In the end it won't matter who wins, Vesta or Ricot, their Prime or ours, humanity or the Powers. It will be a synthesis." He knotted the fingers of his good hand with the fingers of the other. "One commonwealth. One future."

"You can't keep this kind of thing secret. Not much longer. Hundreds of people must know."

Curzon seemed pleased. "We don't need secrecy much longer. And fewer people know than you would suspect. A few hundred know about vee addiction, but that is only a small part of the true story. Only a dozen people between Ricot and Vesta know our real business.

"We have appalling reserves of capital. The best biochemical researchers in human space, each compartmentalized, working on only one part of the picture. We have the Power social model to follow. Ten years, perhaps fifteen, and then we'll have what we need. We will have to work at it very subtly at first. But after the others see it succeed—well, the other policorps will each want a piece of our *edge*. And all we'll want in return is for them to join us."

"And you want me to join, too."

Curzon smiled down at him. "Yes. Perhaps for some very specialized work."

"You never give up, do you?"

"You might be interested to learn how the Powers train one of their spies, someone who is intended to infiltrate a rival tribe and learn what they're up to. They have to resort to biologic surgery. They disassociate certain sense receptors, sever a few nerve junctions. Make their spy immune to the aerosol hormones dispersed by the other side. The shock is too much for a lot of their people. They go mad. The alteration makes their agent...an individual. More than that, a maverick. A sociopath. A renegade." Curzon peered down at him. "Someone like you, Mr. Steward."

Amusement skated along Steward's nerves. "That's how you want me to work for you. A renegade in the workers' paradise."

"A renegade *for* the workers' paradise."

Steward grinned. "I'll think about it."

Curzon stood up. He gestured with a fist. "I don't want you to think about anything," he said. "I want you to *feel*. Feel the rightness of this. The correctness of this vision. The necessity of it." Steward could see patches of sweat under Curzon's arms. "I want you to sense, Steward, that this is something worth having."

"I can't sense much of anything wrapped in this sheet, Brigadier-Director."

Curzon gave a harsh laugh and stepped away. He paced the length of the room, and sweat poured down Steward's brow as he turned his head to follow Curzon's movements. Curzon stopped by Godunov's desk, took the headset off, and held it in his hand. His voice was muted by the soundproofing. "I don't need the headset to see your resistance. A little too much maverick pride in your case, I think. Perhaps I'll just clone some cells and put your mind on thread. Keep you in storage till we need someone like you. Once you see the future in action, maybe you'll be convinced by it. And after we take the cells, you won't be necessary at all. Colonel Godunov can do...what she's so good at. Find out if you've been spinning me a story all along."

Fear trickled up Steward's spine. They could do it. His vision of Orion dimmed. He spat salt from his mouth.

There was a buzz at the door, a red light blinking behind Curzon. He stepped to the door and pressed the intercom. "Yes?" A woman's voice, American, grated from the speaker.

"Security breach, sir. In the Power Legation. I need to talk to you."

Curzon gave a quick glance over his shoulder at Steward. Steward knew Curzon was wondering what knowledge Steward had of this, if he should have conducted the interrogation along other lines.

Curzon opened the door and admitted a tall Security Division officer in full equipment—armored jacket, helmet, heavy gloves, transparent plate lowered over the face. The voice came from a speaker clipped to her belt. Steward thought of Orion striding across the sky. Anything to conceal his surprise.

"We think we've got a biological contamination in the Legation. Maybe a weapon."

Curzon turned to Godunov. "The telephone," he said. "Sound the alarms."

"Already done," the woman said, and then a purring sound filled the room. The sound of Darwin Days.

Curzon fell heavily, his good hand still reaching for the phone as a line of red splashed up his chest. Godunov's head exploded in red froth and she fell back against her chair.

The woman walked to Godunov's desk and tapped on the Colonel's console for a moment. "I'm erasing the interrogation," she said. "Wouldn't want to give them any more data than necessary."

Steward grinned at her weakly. "Hi, Reese," he said. "I didn't expect to see you."

"I thought maybe I owed you something."

Her long-legged stride, even in the heavy combat suit, was completely familiar. She walked to Steward's table and began pulling electrodes off his head.

"I've got a broken arm in here somewhere. Don't just roll me out."

Reese began undoing straps. "You've got a catheter, I see. I'll let you take that out yourself."

"Thanks."

They'd put his arm in plastic before they put him in the sheet, and taped his ribs. After he was unwrapped, he stood up, swaying a bit. Sweat chilled on his naked skin. He reached for his clothes and with Reese's help managed to put them on. There was a sling in a medical cabinet that made it unnecessary to take Curzon's from his body. Reese put something heavy in the sling next to Steward's arm.

"It's a fragmentation grenade," she said. "If we're caught, pull the pin and fall on it. It wouldn't be smart to get captured again."

He looked at her through the transparent blast shield over her face. "You're the boss," he said.

Her eyes were painted like butterfly wings.

CHAPTER EIGHTEEN

"You're Group Seven, aren't you?" Steward said. Gravity pressed on his throat. There was bitterness on his tongue.

Reese looked at him, her face shadowed by webbing. "I can't say."

"You're Group Seven. And I've been working for you all along."

The freighter increased acceleration as it cleared Ricot's safety zone. Steward had to fight for breath as gravity climbed to six g. They were falling toward an independent mining colony sunk into the surface of Regio Galileo on Ganymede, from which, Reese explained, they would in a week or so hitch a ride on a supply ship headed directly for the Belt.

Pain seized Steward's ribs. He clenched his teeth and fought it. Tears welled in his eyes.

Reese had led them out of the Ricot Security Division without incident, showing the proper ID at every station. No alarms had gone off anywhere. In five minutes Steward had been back on Methane Street, walking in silence along the alloy floor. Reese led him to an interior airlock, where he'd stepped into the boarding tube of the small Jove system freighter. The freighter's pilot, a small, well-muscled man of sixty or so, let them through the hatch without a word. The freighter was old, its bulkheads scarred, access panels long vanished, the wiring they revealed hanging in clumps restrained by duct tape. Reese took her grenade back. She and Steward were shown to a small passenger cabin, and they webbed themselves in. Within the hour they were moving toward Regio

The engine cut off, and Steward floated in his webbing. Reese began pulling off straps. He looked at her. "That alarm in the Power Legation," he said. "That's real, isn't it?"

"It will be," Reese said. "We wanted to get the Powers on their ships as well as in Ricot. The virus takes a while to work. There'll be a lot of alarms in another twenty-four hours." She smiled grimly. "Much good it will do them."

Speed was still wiring his system. He couldn't stop thinking, no matter how much he wanted to. "You used me as cover," he said. "You let me develop my own mission, and when the security people were stirred up over me and covering their execs from nonexistent assassination attempts, you were able to run your own op into the Legation with less chance of trouble."

Reese plucked at straps. "Something like that."

"That's why you said you owed me. That's why you got me out. I made things easier for you."

She drifted free. Her hair floated in a halo around her face. She looked at him. "Our employers aren't always honorable, buck. They don't always pay their debts. I figure people like us can behave better." She shrugged. "And I had the documents, the uniform, and so on. I could get in and out. I had better support than you."

"You're a mercenary, then. Working for Group Seven."

She tossed her head. "A mercenary anyway."

"Griffith was part of it, too. Tsiolkovsky's Demon was just a gimmick you cooked up so that I could seem to earn some money, then use it to develop my mission. And that business in Los Angeles—was that a plan that went wrong, or did you just want to see my moves?"

"We had to see whether you still had what it takes. You did. Your conduct was exemplary."

"I killed somebody." Pain jetted up his ribs. "You set it up that way." He remembered the way the wire tugged at his hand, the screams amid the billowing smoke. He shook his head. "I wondered why people were storing secrets on a place like Charter, with plenty of transmitters for hire. There weren't any secrets, ever. You were putting Tsiolkovsky's Demon into the station comps when we arrived. When I broke into the Vesta computers and started sending real secrets back, it must have caused some comment."

She grinned. She drifted to the padded bulkhead above her and she put out a hand to stop herself. "Yep. You should have seen the query I got."

"And the two high-priority last-minute shipments: first to Vesta, then Ricot. That was Group Seven again, making sure we got where we needed to go. I was so eager that I never stopped to wonder how I got there. And you put the information about station security into *Born*'s computer." Speed jittered up his spine and turned into a laugh. "I wondered why you kept insisting I go into the Power Legation when we were on Vesta. That was something your bosses arranged. The food poisoning, the autoloader breakdown."

"I had orders to expose you to the Powers as much as possible. Even if that put you in some danger."

"So that I'd put things together. I'm surprised your employers would want me to."

"Maybe they didn't want you to figure out as much as you have. People have a way of underestimating you."

"Why send me to Vesta in the first place? Why not send me to Ricot right off?"

"The weapon—the virus—it wasn't going to be ready for months. Why not use the time?" She looked at him indulgently. "Do you want out of the web?"

He laughed again. "No. I've been in a web the whole damn time. Carried from place to place so that I could be an accomplice to poisoning a whole community."

Reese shrugged. "They started it. Or so I'm told."

Hot rage tore at him. He punched the air with his good arm. "Fucking mercenary. Fucking mercenary bitch."

She looked up at him, held his eyes. "I've been called worse."

"Let's find out. I'm just starting."

Reese kicked off from the wall and flew to the door. She slammed open the partition into the corridor outside, then turned. "Being a bitch is better than being a sheep," she said. "That's the choice, the way I've always seen it."

"Shit." He was fumbling with his webbing, not knowing precisely what he was going to do once he got loose. By the time Steward was through unwebbing, Reese was long gone, and he was long out of ideas.

Reese came back in for the deceleration burn and landing, webbing herself in without a word.

"Sorry," he said.

"I just do the job," Reese said. Her voice was stubborn. "I work for all sorts of people. Policorps, outlaws, gangs, police. I don't see a lot of difference between them."

"I don't either. That's why I don't want to work for any of them." Bile rose in his throat. "*Didn't*, I should say. Because I helped you kill thousands today."

She looked at him. She was still wearing the uniform shirt and trousers. He couldn't read her expression. "I probably could have got in without you. For what it's worth."

Steward looked at the scarred bulkhead. It wasn't worth much.

"We didn't start out like this." Reese blurted it out, as if she wanted to justify herself somehow. "We started as a bunch of veterans trying to help each other out. We all knew each other. It was friendly. And then things happened and it all…evolved. It got heavy."

"Heavy," Steward repeated. The word meant nothing to him.

He thought of the Powers, the sounds they made. He wondered how they sounded when they were dying in agony.

Fire exploded from the engines. Gravity returned and took Steward by the throat.

Ganymede was a cold black piece of stone. Jupiter burned high in the radiant sky and offered no heat. Reese gave Steward a new passport with a new name. He was now a citizen of Uzbekistan. With the passport came a credit needle with 5,000 Pink Blossom dollars on it. "I insisted they make provisions for getting you out," she said.

"Thanks." He looked at the passport and thought again about how he'd earned it.

Reese put her hands in her jacket pockets. She was out of uniform now, in clothes borrowed from the miners' store. Some of the people here seemed to know her.

"Want to work out?" she said. "The light gravity here will make it interesting. I'll go easy on your arm."

Steward shook his head. "No. Thanks. I think I'll get some sleep."

"It's been a long day."

"Yes. It has."

He wanted sleep to come. It was the better part of a day before it did.

Steward spent most of his time on Ganymede in his room, reading whatever he could find in the library, or watching the vid. On the long trip back to the Belt he did much the same.

He missed the *Born*, the informal friendships, the structured life, the sense of purpose. He wondered if SuTopo had tried to find them, had assumed that Steward and Reese had been disappeared by the authorities. It would be in SuTopo's character to think that.

Reese tried to be friendly, but although Steward was polite, he didn't really respond. She learned to leave him alone. Once they landed in the Belt, she shook his hand—he was out of the cast, hormone infusions having knitted the bone in a matter of days—and walked away with her trademark long-legged stride. She didn't look back.

He heard a lot about the plague on Ricot. Thousands of Powers had died. The destruction was so appalling that there was no hope of Consolidated being able to cover it up.

In another three months he was on Earth. He took a small apartment with a view of the Aral Sea and spent hours watching the steppe wind as it scudded across the water. He was trying to decide what to do with his life. He wondered what occupation would allow him to be the most anonymous.

One day it just came to him, a realization that dropped into his mind from nowhere. A gift from the void. He knew he had been wrong about everything.

He began to make preparations. Knowledge implied action.

CHAPTER NINETEEN

LA. Night.

One of the condecologies on the Orange County horizon was topped by a revolving searchlight, a masterpiece of arrogance, and blazing white fire lanced into the room every few seconds, turning the bed, the table, the lamp into flashing monochrome images, all shadow and silver. Steward sat silently in the secure blackness of a long deep shadow, breathing slowly, listening to the humming of his nerves, his mind. There was no sound but that of circulating air. It sounded like far-off applause.

Steward waited, building power. He had all the patience in the world.

His mind hummed. An endless ovation came from the air vent. On his neck he felt the touch of the whirlwind.

At last a new sound came, the solid thunk of an electro-magnetic bolt slamming back. Then footsteps. A compressed-air hiss, a sniff. Footsteps again. Then the click of a light switch. The flash from the distant condeco was drowned in light.

Griffith's ravaged face gazed into the barrel of Steward's gun. He froze. The inhaler, in its insulating plastic jacket, was still in his hand. A light touch of frost was visible on the metal parts.

"Giving yourself a fix, buck?" Steward asked. He rose from his crouch and started walking toward Griffith.

Only Griffith's eyes moved, flicking from Steward's hand to his feet, his body, his other hand. Measuring things. "I've got wired nerves, buck," Steward told him. "I can kill you before you can try anything. So don't try anything, right? D'accord."

With all his power Steward drove the ball of his right foot into Griffith's solar plexus. The breath went out of the smaller man and he folded. He hit the floor hard, with his shoulder and the side of his face. His fingers were white on the inhaler.

Steward searched him for weapons, found none, and stepped back. Griffith was still trying to breathe.

"Hey," he said. "This is mild, compared to what you did to Dr. Ashraf. Right?"

Griffith tried to speak. Tears rolled down his face. Steward watched him. "No hurry," he said. "We've got all night." He stepped back and sat on the bed.

Griffith clawed for the doorframe, pulled himself upright, leaned back against the frame. His arms folded around his stomach, pressing hard against the pain. "How," he said.

"I had it almost right, friend," Steward said. "I was being used as cover to run a mission into the Power Legation at Ricot. I thought Reese was working for Group Seven—that would make sense. But then I realized there was no truth to that scenario at all." Griffith was wheezing for breath. Steward looked at him. "You want a cigarette or something? Go ahead."

Griffith closed his eyes. "Jesus."

"Are you paying attention, buck? See, a real Group Seven agent approached me on Charter, trying to recruit me for a similar mission. His name was Stoichko, and somebody shot him dead just as he started getting close to me. I never worked out why he died until just now.

"Reese killed him. She was staying in the same hotel as Stoichko. She told me that she'd changed her plans after she met some old friend of hers, but I never saw that friend. So I decided that what must have happened is that Reese saw Stoichko following me and that she recognized him. She knew he was trying to recruit me for something, but didn't know what. She reported to her superiors, and they told her to put an ice jacket on him." Steward laughed. "You must have had to pay her a bonus for that one, right?"

Griffith swallowed. "You're wrong, man. You've got...the wrong angle."

A chill hurricane of anger rose in Steward. "Don't insult my fucking intelligence," he said. Griffith froze again, hearing the edge in Steward's voice.

"I remembered some things," Steward said. His voice fired syllables like bullets. "I remember meeting with you in Flagstaff, how your health got worse the longer you stayed there. You said you had the flu. But it wasn't influenza, right? It was withdrawal. You had the shakes, the running nose, all the symptoms. You've got the vee tag, and you're a vee addict."

Griffith's face drained of color. His terror was palpable. He shook his head. "I . . ." he began.

"You had your inhalers with you—I remember the way you kept going to the bathroom and running the water to cover the sounds of the compressed air—but the Power hormones broke down fast, the way they do. Your inhalers weren't the new type, with the refrigeration unit, and you were out of luck. You must have been glad to see the last of me."

Griffith pressed the heels of his hands into his eyes. "Jesus," he said. His voice was a sob. "This can't be happening."

"You were behind the whole damn thing," Steward said. Bitterness rose in his throat. "You knew me well. You knew my attitudes about loyalty, about trust. You know the way we were trained, and you had access to de Prey's program, the keys to the way he manipulated us. You cut up Dr. Ashraf to make him talk about me, tell you where my loyalties were. He told you I had an unhealthy interest in my Alpha, that I could be manipulated through my image of the Alpha. So you concocted that recording, that audio. You weren't sure you could pull the video off, not with me, so you just did the voice. And it worked just like you thought it would."

Griffith's head rolled back against the doorframe. He had caught his breath, and now his eyes were bright with calculation. "But why the hell would I do it? I don't have any"—he swallowed—"any reason to kill a bunch of Powers. And how would I find out that the Captain was dead in the first place? We hadn't been in touch for years."

Steward barked a single, angry laugh. "You found out from your source, Griffith. From the same place you've been getting your vee hormones, and your money." Griffith's eyes were showing stark, yellow terror.

"I've been following you for a week, buck," Steward said. "I know the building down on the waterfront where you go every night. I know your source is there." He smiled, feeling the carnivore in him baring teeth. "Prime-on-the-Right, Griffith," he said. "He's here on Earth. Building his organization, his troops. Making his plans for what he's going to do with the largest population of humans in existence. That's the plan that Ricot was trying to forestall with its attack. And that's why he doesn't care if Ricot retaliates with another attack on Vesta. Because he's here already, right where he wants to be."

Griffith closed his eyes. Tears ran down his cheeks.

Steward laughed again. "I've got it, don't I?" he said. "And I've got *you*, buck. Fellow veteran."

Griffith fumbled for his inhaler. "What do you want, man?" he asked. He fired hormone up his nose. "If you'd wanted me dead you would have killed me. So just what the fuck do you want?"

A smile blossomed on Steward's face. He could feel the power in him. "I want to join the team, old friend," he said. "I want to meet Prime-on-the-Right. And then I want to go to work for him. Just like my old friends. Just like you and Reese."

CHAPTER TWENTY

Griffith looked at him for a long moment. "You want to join us," he said. He looked as if he were saying the words for the first time, exploring the way they sounded.

"I want to work for a winner, and Prime-on-the-Right is going to win," Steward said. "He's smart, he's got the right moves. I've seen his opposition up close and they haven't got a chance."

Griffith brushed a hand over his eyes. "This is weird," he said.

"Prime-on-the-Right uses people who don't have the vee tag," Steward said. "Reese doesn't. He needs people who aren't addicted to him for use in long-distance errands."

There was color in Griffith's face again. He took a cigarette from his pocket and lit it. "The people without the tag don't know about the Prime. We can only trust tagged people not to tell."

Steward grinned at him. "You can trust me. I found out and I haven't told anyone. And I won't—so long as I get a piece of the action."

Griffith's look was sharp. "What do you mean?"

Steward barked another laugh. "You sure you can't figure it out? Let's say that I've got a friend in an orbital habitat who will release certain information to the scansheets unless I make contact every few hours and give the proper code. The code changes every time, and only I know how it changes. You won't be able to get to my friend in time to prevent it—it's many hours to where he lives. And he won't release the stuff to anyone but me, in person. That means that even if you, ah, do an Ashraf on me and get the codes, you still won't get the information my friend is holding, just delay its release. And eventually it'll be released, because there's a time limit on the codes, and if I don't appear in person within a certain time, they get released anyway."

Satisfaction welled in Steward's mind. The best part of this was that it was true. Only the pronoun "he" was a blind—Steward had gone through Janice Weatherman in the trust office of the Stone Bank on Solon. They'd shared a piece of cream pastry while setting up the deal and calculating her commission. Weatherman acted as if she performed similar tasks every day.

Possibly she did.

There was a muscle working in Griffith's cheek. His gaze was stone. "You're dangerous, buck," he said quietly.

"That's why you wanted me to run your mission for you," Steward said. He laughed. "Hey, I've already done a good job for your boss. Why should he mind if I want to do a few more? I just want to get better wages next time."

"I have to think."

"Let Prime-on-the-Right do your thinking for you. He's better at it." Steward reached into his pocket and took out a piece of paper, tossed it in Griffith's direction. "There's a map that will take you to a phone booth down the street. Be there at nineteen hundred tomorrow night. I'll call and then you can tell me what your source has to say."

Griffith looked at the white slip of paper that had fluttered to the floor near his legs. He reached out with nicotine-stained fingers and took it.

Steward stood up. "I'll be going now. Talk to your boss."

Griffith was still looking at the paper as Steward stepped over him, keeping the pistol trained at Griffith's head. "I don't know how I'm going to explain this."

"That's easy, comrade," Steward said, moving for the door. "Just tell him you fucked up."

The revolving searchlight was visible from Steward's hotel room on the waterfront, flashing in mute time to the rhythm of his thoughts. He listened to the telephone purr. Griffith answered on the second ring.

"Steward?"

"That's right, comrade."

The sound of a cigarette being inhaled. "You've got your meet."

"When?"

"Right now, if you want it."

Steward smiled. The searchlight strobed at the edge of his vision. "D'accord," he said. "I know where it is. I'll meet you there."

He hung up before Griffith could object, then reached for the freeze-dry canister on the table, the one he'd picked up from the safe-deposit vault on Charter the same trip he'd arranged things with Weatherman.

WARNING, it said, BIOLOGIC SEAL. OPEN ONLY IN STERILE ENVIRONMENT.

Steward peeled back the foil that protected the seal, then twisted the cap off. The seal broke with a hissing sound. He raised the flask and poured the brown dust over himself, brushing it into his clothing. He put some in his pockets, then rubbed powder on a pair of handkerchiefs and wadded them into his pants pockets. He checked the pistol in his shoulder holster, then put on his jacket and took his car keys from where they waited on the hotel dresser.

He left the room to the silence and the flare of the searchlight.

Entire moth nations danced in the halogen glow above Lightsource, Limited. The building was prefabricated, two stories, built next to a warehouse on a piece of landfill sealed from the Pacific by a seawall. As Steward walked toward the entrance, he saw Griffith standing by the entrance with a cigarette in his hand. The tattooed boy, Spassky, waited with him, smiling from behind his video shades. Spassky's tall goon waited like a malevolent lamppost in the shadows behind.

Steward had left his rented car on another street, with a hand-drawn map on the seat showing the way to get to Lightsource. A clue for the local police in case he disappeared.

He walked toward Griffith, his skin tingling, alert, waiting for the breath of violence on the back of his neck. It didn't come.

He stopped in front of Griffith and smiled. Griffith was expressionless. "Hi, comrade." Steward looked at Spassky. "Where's your girlfriend, buck?"

Spassky's video shades stared back. "She died," he said.

"Easy come, easy go."

Spassky grinned with his metal teeth. "You said it."

Griffith ground his cigarette underfoot. "Let's go."

The office tasted lightly of the organic smell of the Powers, a maintenance dose filtered up through vents. The hair on the back of his neck prickled.

Steward followed Griffith through armored doors studded with sensors and security cameras, down a long hallway patrolled by armored guards. The guards all were in their mid to late thirties, Artifact War veterans. Spassky and his goon walked in step behind, moving a little too close for Steward's comfort. The corridors featured deep carpeting and closed paneled office doors. Their footsteps were muffled on the carpet. Griffith came to a door with his name on a brass plate, then opened it with his thumbprint. Steward and the others followed him inside to a large office. There was a desk, plush chairs, a computer, a one meter inflated world globe. Griffith went to the desk and picked up a portable detector.

"Take off your clothes," he said. "We're checking them and you for weapons."

Steward shrugged. "Whatever you say." He took the pistol by two fingers and handed it to Spassky. "This is all I have."

While Steward was being searched, Griffith told him the rules. "You'll be staying in a dorm downstairs while we check you out. You will be allowed out to make your phone calls to your friend. You will have an escort during that time, but you can choose any phone you want."

"Just so long as this doesn't go on too long," Steward said.

"The Prime's a good judge of character. It shouldn't last…beyond what's necessary."

"The Prime. So his highness got a promotion, when the other Prime was killed on Vesta, right?"

"*She* got promoted. The Prime is currently female. Biologically inactive right now, though." Griffith seemed stubbornly insistent, as if Steward had invaded his sense of rightness. "And it wasn't a promotion, it was a succession. The Powers have worked it all out decades in advance. The Prime is the descendent of a ten-thousand-year genetic manipulation program. She could be nothing other than what she is." He looked up at Steward, and there was resentment in his eyes. "And she's not a highness. Just a Prime. That's how you address her. *Prime* says everything that needs to be said."

Steward shrugged. "D'accord." He began putting his clothes back on.

"They live for *centuries*, Steward. The Power elite. So can we—and not through cloning, either. We can have life in our natural bodies indefinitely prolonged."

"Sounds good."

Griffith gazed at him. Steward wanted to flinch from the intensity in his eyes.

"It's better than good," Griffith said. "It's like being God."

Steward leaned toward him, showing teeth. "Being God sounds good," he said. "I want it."

I have no strategy. A flicker of thought from nowhere. *Freedom to kill and freedom to give back life—there is my strategy.*

Uncertainty flickered into Griffith's expression. He turned away. "You don't know how good it is." He took a spike from his pocket and put it in his computer console. He tapped in a code and a piece of the wall paneling slid back to reveal a private elevator.

"Down we go," Spassky said. There was a smirk on his face as he tossed Steward's gun from hand to hand.

Steward moved into the elevator and the others followed. "The Powers," Griffith was saying. "You know why they left Sheol and the other planets?"

The elevator's descent was silent. Steward looked at Spassky's leer, the goon's stolid lack of expression, Griffith's eagerness. "Tell me," he said.

"They were picking their leader," Griffith said. "Not the Prime, but the head Prime. The head Primes rule for thousands of years, and when they die, all the Primes come to the center of the empire to choose the next, and they bring all the people with them they can spare."

"A war of succession," Steward said.

Griffith shook his head. "That's another place they've got us beat," he said.

The elevator door opened. Beyond was a tunnel painted a pale green and lit by fluorescents. It dipped downward, out of sight. They began walking toward the end.

"Not a war, buck," Griffith said. "It was a political and economic struggle. There are rules for it. Sometimes it goes on for centuries. And when the head Prime is finally chosen, he can redistribute much of the wealth of the other Primes. Our Prime was on the losing side, and so was Ricot's. But they're enemies of each other, see? So the new head Prime gave them territory side by side, so they wouldn't cooperate. And that's where they met us."

"And," Steward said, "a thousand years from now . . ."

"A thousand years from now"—Griffith's eyes were shining—"our Prime will have the edge. She'll have humanity behind her, as well as her own people. She'll win the succession. And that'll put us right in the center of power." His fingers clamped down on Steward's shoulder. "Gods, buck," he said. "We'll be gods."

"Gods," Steward repeated. Tasting the word. They passed a heavy freight elevator that apparently connected with the warehouse above.

Ready, Steward thought. He was ready for this. So in sync with the Zen of it that all he had to do was move with it, follow the series of events as they wound toward their conclusion.

The tunnel leveled off. Steward sensed he was under the Pacific. He saw an airlock door ahead.

"We put the Prime in a sunken caisson," Griffith said. "At first we had to launder a lot of money and Power goods to pay for it. But now the Powers have a base out beyond Pluto, just a big piece of rock they found out there, and they're sending goods to us in quantity. If they have the right markings, no one knows they don't go through Vesta or Ricot first. Now we've got our own companies Earthside, and they're starting to make a big profit. We can finance this ourselves now. Soon we'll be too big for any Earth government to move against. A few decades at the most. And that's nothing on the kind of time scales we're talking about."

The airlock door was a big one, capable of handling cargo. Griffith pressed the code into its lock and the party stepped in. The thick smell of the Powers flooded into the chamber, stronger than on the outside. There was a blissful expression on Griffith's face as he breathed it in.

The inside of the caisson echoed to the organ-pipe sounds of the Powers. The unpainted supports of the roof curved above Steward like the ribs of a metal beast. Fluorescent lights hung from the ceiling, the wires taped to the beams. Shipping crates were piled on pallets, obscuring vision. The place was as attractive as the interior of the warehouse next door.

Hell of a place for a god to live, Steward thought.

He tried to avoid shrinking back as a Power came rushing out from among the boxes. He had forgotten how fast they were. The Power raised its head, inflating it, the two eyes focused forward. "This is Steward," it hissed.

"Yes, cousin," Griffith said.

The spines on the Power's back arched. Its hands scissored near the floor. "You will come," it said.

Steward followed the Power, moving fast to keep up with the Power's four scurrying feet. They came to a cleared space. The floor was spread with dark plastic sheets. Portable heaters and computer consoles were plugged into snaking cables. Three Powers waited there. One of them stepped toward Steward. The others made ducking, shrugging movements. The smell of Power was particularly strong.

"I am the Prime," the Power said. The muscles on its back twitched in rhythm.

Steward looked down at it and thought of Vesta and Ricot and Sheol and places beyond, places where the Prime's word was law, where its schemes and plans had set millions of its species dancing to the music of its organ pipes. He thought of the thousands of years of struggle for power, the hordes of ranked Powers marshaled in their chorus, disciplined by chemistry. The gleam in Griffith's eyes as he spoke of godhood, his bliss as he breathed in his hormones. He thought of Ashraf lying dead in his office, Stoichko bleeding in his armchair while the vid glowed, the Alpha turning toward the bullet that perhaps he welcomed...

"Pleased to meet you," Steward said. And he took out his handkerchief and sneezed into it.

The organ sounds had changed. There was a strange keening in them, something that set Steward's teeth on edge, and Steward knew the second the airlock opened what it was.

He had been out on the second of his trips to the outside to make his call to Janice Weatherman. Spassky and the goon had driven him at his instruction to a public phone, then stood ten feet away while he transmitted the codes.

Steward had been interviewed twice by the Prime. He talked to the Prime about his qualifications, about how he had penetrated both Vesta and Ricot and could improve the Prime's own security here and, as the Prime's base expanded, elsewhere. He talked about the shape of the future, about the Power-human synthesis that was bound to dominate in both spheres. He remembered Curzon's discourse on the same subject, the way he flushed and gestured and paced, and he tried to imitate Curzon in the way he talked and moved. The Prime had let Steward talk, and watched Steward from its strange goggling armored eyes, its back muscles twitching. Other Powers moved in the background. Steward thought there were perhaps a dozen of them. Groups of humans appeared from time to time, standing diffidently in clumps, breathing their fix from the air. Some of them seemed to live here, in crude barracks in the back.

During the interviews the Zen seemed to do the talking, not Steward. He was latched into it now. He had become the whirlwind, a force larger than himself, moving in self-contained perfection.

Now, as the airlock opened, he heard the high grating overtones in the piping of the Powers, and it sounded like the wail of the whirlwind.

Griffith waited behind the airlock door, panic in his eyes. "Something's happening," he said. He wiped sweat from his forehead. "The Powers are getting sick." He looked at Steward and his eyes widened. His mouth opened.

Steward stepped back with his right foot and drove his right elbow into Spassky's solar plexus. The little Russian, he thought, should never have followed so close. Steward grabbed Spassky's nape and swung him around to the left, between him and the tall goon who was only beginning to react as Steward grabbed for the pistol he knew Spassky carried in a belt holster.

The goon's fist lashed out. Steward swayed back out of reach, and he felt the comforting checkered grips of the pistol against his hand. He closed his fingers, raised the pistol, thumbed the safety. Griffith was moving on the edges of Steward's vision. Steward drove Spassky toward the goon with a kick, as if the boy were a football.

Steward fired twice: once into the goon's chest, a second time into Spassky's neck. The unsilenced pistol boomed loudly in the airlock. An ejected casing bounced off the airlock door. Steward swung the pistol toward Griffith and saw the other man raising a pistol, his wired combat reflexes bringing the weapon into line with unnatural speed....

Steward flung himself backward, his pistol crashing twice. There was a blow in his side, another against the back of his head. Then Steward was sitting on the floor of the airlock, his back to the wall, and Griffith was dropping, his gun clattering on the ground. Griffith sat down with surprise in his watery eyes. Powers were screaming somewhere in the caisson. Steward looked at Griffith and raised his pistol again. He could feel blood pouring like a hot wave down his left side. There was a sad smile on Griffith's riven face.

"Sheol, Captain," Griffith said. "Sheol."

"I didn't need you to tell me that, asshole," Steward said. Before he could fire again, Griffith was dead.

The Powers moaned like the whirlwind in Steward's ears. He reached up to the airlock controls, pressed the button that would seal the door and cycle in the clean outside air. He could hear running feet. The closing door cut them off.

Steward felt cycling air ruffling his hair. He opened his jacket and looked down. Griffith's bullet had gone into his left side, smashing at least one of the lower ribs. There seemed to be no exit wound, so probably the bullet had bounced around inside him before it came to rest. Blood was soaking his shirt and pants. The signs weren't good.

Sheol, he thought, is a thing that does not end. It is a process. It is a choice between betrayal and death.

He pressed his handkerchief to the wound and stood up. There was no pain as yet. He took a full clip from Spassky's body, reloaded, and waited for the airlock door to open, and when it did, he pulled one of Spassky's shoes off and jammed it in the open outer door. Whoever was sealed in the caisson was going to stay there.

During the long walk down the green tunnel, the pain came, a hot jab so sudden that it took Steward's breath away. Tears dazzled his eyes. He began breathing carefully, regularly, filling his lungs and then exhaling thoroughly. He could feel broken ribs grinding together in his side, but he tried to keep his mind entirely on breathing, on walking, on rhythm. The pain faded. Blood trickled down his leg.

He could sense the Alpha's nearness. His breath, his voice. He wanted to smile.

Griffith's office was deserted. He could hear movement and shouting in the corridor outside. Steward looked through the closets and found one of Griffith's tailored jackets, a dark one that wouldn't show blood. Wincing at the sharpness of the pain, he dropped his own jacket on the floor and pulled on Griffith's. He put one of Griffith's handkerchiefs over the wound, put the pistol in his belt, and stepped out into the corridor.

The building was full of panic. Guards were moving up and down the corridors with weapons drawn, but didn't seem to know where to point them. The head had been cut off and the body seemed not to know what to do. He wondered if Power panic was coming up the air vents, affecting the vee tag somehow.

Steward set himself to walking. It was difficult now, and he had developed a limp. He tried to build a rhythm, breathing and movement, making the limp a part of it. This, he thought, was good Zen. Spittle in the eye of the void.

I have no purpose, he thought. *Opportunity is my purpose.*

He could taste blood in his mouth. Shit. Nicked a lung.

I have no miracle. Just law is my miracle.

He was forgetting the rest of the poem except for the end. The Alpha filled his soul.

Bright light dazzled his vision. The glass doors were right ahead. He limped past three secretaries and into the street. LA was hot enough to take his breath, again. The sun was so bright he could barely see. He reached for his shades and came up with the pistol instead. He looked at it for a moment.

Merde, he thought. He moved down the street. One foot in front of the other. He heard people shouting.

There was a pay phone on the corner. He reached into his jeans with his free hand, trying to find a credit spike. Blood rattled in his throat and he wanted to retch. He sat down.

There were sirens in the distance. Steward hawked up blood and spat. Another in the eye of the void.

He became aware of people standing around him. Staring. He gave them the finger.

"Écrasez l'infâme," he said.

There was a guard on his door, and outside, Steward could hear police arguing with doctors. "The Powers," someone was saying. "In a bunker." He couldn't hear more because there was something wrong with his IV drip, and the monitor kept making bleating noises that sent nurses scurrying. Finally they replaced it.

He sensed the doctors winning the argument. He smiled and went to sleep.

Steward woke to the sound of a footstep. Somehow he knew the sound was wrong.

He opened his eyes, saw burnished copper hair, tanned skin, a lab coat, a gun. Reese. Covering her tracks, and probably having no choice.

"Sorry," she said, and raised the gun.

Hey, he wanted to say, *I owe you one.* But he couldn't make his throat work right, so he just tried to smile.

The Alpha rushed into him with the force of a whirlwind. He perceived the wail of the Powers. Griffith's smile. The sound of gunfire on a sunny day. Sheol as the blizzards came. The voice of the Alpha whispering in his ear. Blood on the spinning horizon, growing closer, burning in night....

What he had wanted, all along.

CHAPTER TWENTY-ONE

Steward felt the regular rush of the air into his lungs, a tube lax and warm in his nose. Coldness receded as they filled him with warm fluids. He heard the hiss of the machine that was breathing for him.

He knew, from the rush of life into his lungs, that he was dead. He wondered how it had happened, how the end had come. Dead in LA, he thought. The terminus of a very long trajectory.

One life, he thought. One arrow.

He hoped the Beta's action was right.

The first nonmedical he saw was Janice Weatherman. She brought a package of pastry and a packet of very good coffee with a machine to make it in. She was dressed in a soft tawny beige jacket. Silver gleamed around her wrists, her neck. "I wanted to bring the bank's regards," she said. "We're hoping to keep your business."

"In the afterlife," Steward said. He had to whisper. The machine was breathing through a tracheotomy and he couldn't use his vocal cords.

Weatherman leaned closer. "I couldn't hear you," she said.

Steward didn't have much money left, not that he knew of. Almost the last of it had gone into the clone insurance. No point in telling her that.

"D'accord," he said.

She smiled. She was wearing, he saw, platinum earrings. She took his hand. "The trust's going well," Weatherman said. "Andrew is responding to Genesios therapy. His spine has grown and fused. He may have partial use of his legs one of these days. They're using biofeedback techniques to retrain his optical centers to handle speech as well as the visuals, and he's learning to use a speech synthesizer. That part's coming along real well. The music helps."

He nodded. Something decent had come out of this at least. Satisfaction welled up in him.

"I released the information when your code didn't come," she said. "The Los Angeles cops had already found a secret hideout for some Powers on Earth, with a lot of dead aliens in it. All the Earth governments are going crazy.

228

Demanding answers."

Steward tried to laugh. It hurt, so he just grinned up at Weatherman and squeezed her hand. She was smiling back at him.

"There are a lot of people wanting to see you," Weatherman said. "Diplomats, cops. They seem to think you'll be able to explain things to them. But they'll have to take their turn. Bank hath its privileges, at least on Solon."

"That's why I like this place," Steward whispered. "Everyone knows what's important." And why the Beta had bought insurance here, just before he'd gone down the gravity well for a meeting with Griffith. The whole place was security-mad, full of paranoid millionaire criminals hiding their funds, banks ever alert for breaches of security, brokers on the lookout for swindles. No one was going to see Steward whom Steward didn't want to see.

"There are media people, too. I imagine you'll make some money from the rights, if you want to talk to them. I can handle that for you."

"Later."

Weatherman's eyes cut to one side of the room, as if there was someone there giving her a signal. She straightened. "They tell me I have to go," she said. "I'll see you later."

"Bye."

She smiled, squeezed his hand, left.

Capital, Steward thought. And laughed.

Steward found out later what the LA police thought had happened, and he more or less agreed with them. "Why didn't you—your Beta—just *tell us?*" their representative wanted to know. "We could have searched the damn place."

"He wasn't certain," Steward said. By now he was used to talking about the Beta in the third person. "And some things were…personal. Between Icehawks. People who had been through Sheol."

"The Beta," the police captain said, "wasn't on Sheol."

"Sheol," Steward said, "was the whirlwind."

The police captain didn't understand. Afterward, Steward avoided speaking to him.

The scansheets were telling him about "Power panic" on Earth. Ricot and Vesta were busy issuing denials that no one believed. Their stock had thundered into the basement. Steward told the diplomats and such that he was only interested in clarifying his Beta's statement, not amplifying it, that he wanted questions in writing ahead of time. He had temporary Solon citizenship and he didn't have to give any answers he didn't want to.

They protested, but they played by his rules. He answered the questions he wanted to.

Janice Weatherman was going to conduct a media rights auction and collect ten percent of what promised to be a ridiculous amount of money. Steward didn't want to think, right now, about how rich he was going to be.

He thought about Ashraf: *Nothing to do with you.* He'd been right all along. He'd just been talking about the wrong clone.

Weatherman was spending a lot of time with him, more than she really needed to. That was something else Steward didn't want to think about, not yet anyway. He needed to get his bearings first.

Surrounded by guards, he took a trip to Solon's hub. He went alone into a room where he could float before a perfect clear pane and look out of the metal humming world of the station. Earth dazzled his eyes, cold amid the emptiness.

His predecessor, the Beta, had twinned his brain and donated a scrap of flesh, and then he'd gone in pursuit of the Alpha. Found him, Steward thought, in the underwater Sheol that had been built in California. Finished what the Alpha had started to do. Become the whirlwind together. And then ended, blew apart.

Whatever the Alpha and Beta had done, it was finished now. Steward had lost them both. He felt the pulse of hollowness, where they had been, deep in his throat.

The Beta, Steward thought, had been created in order to finish the Alpha's work, pay off his karmic debt. Conclude all business with de Prey, Curzon, Sheol, Andrew. He, the Gamma, was someone else. On a different wheel altogether.

He was, he thought with a laugh, a Zen saint. No karma left, no consequence, no desire. A clean slate. The Beta had done a good job.

Steward floated amid cold Earthlight that shone whitely on his skin. The vast bulk of the station revolved around and behind him.

New life, he thought. New arrow.

He wondered where he was aimed.

Night Shade Books Is an Independent Publisher of Quality SF, Fantasy and Horror

Walter Jon Williams is an author, traveler, scuba diver, and a fourth degree black belt in kenpo. He lives with his wife Kathleen Hedges on an old Spanish land grant in the high desert of New Mexico, and is the author of twenty-five novels and two collections of shorter works. After an early career as a historical novelist, he switched to science fiction. He has won two Nebula Awards for short fiction.

Walter's subject matter has an unusually wide range, and include the glittering surfaces of *Hardwired*, the opulent tapestries of *Aristoi*, the bleak science-tinged roman policier *Days of Atonement*, and the pensive young Mary Shelley of the novella "Wall, Stone, Craft," which was nominated for a Hugo, Nebula, and a World Fantasy Award.

His next novel will be *Implied Spaces*, appearing soon from Night Shade Books.